CHARTING the COURSE

Launching Patient-Centric Healthcare

John J. Nance, JD

Kathleen M. Bartholomew, RN, MN

SECOND RIVER
HEALTHCARE PRESS

CHARTING THE COURSE:
Launching Patient-Centric Healthcare

Second River Healthcare Press
26 Shawnee Way, Suite C
Bozeman, MT 59715
Phone (406) 586-8775 | FAX (406) 586-5672

Editor: Tiffany L. Young
Cover Design: Lan Weisberger — Design Solutions
Cover Art: Roger Schillerstrom
Authors' Photographs: Tami Ewing
Typesetting/Composition: Neuhaus/Tyrrell Graphic Design

Nance, John; Bartholomew, Kathleen
CHARTING THE COURSE: Launching Patient-Centric Healthcare
John J. Nance, JD & Kathleen M. Bartholomew, RN, MN

ISBN-13: 978-1-936406-11-1 (hard cover)
ISBN-13: 978-1-936406-12-8 (soft cover)
ISBN-13: 978-1-936406-13-5 (e-Book)

1. Patient safety   2. Quality care   3. Health services administration

Library of Congress Control Number: 2012936237

First Printing   June 2012

Disclaimer: While every precaution has been taken in preparation of this book, the publisher and author assume no responsibility for errors or omissions. Neither is any liability assumed for damages resulting, or alleged to result, directly or indirectly from the use of the information contained herein. If you do not wish to be bound by the above, you may return this book with receipt to the publisher for a full refund.

This book is a work of fiction. All participants in the story line are fictional. Names, characters, businesses, organizations, places, events and incidents either are the product of the author's imagination or are used fictitiously. Any resemblance to actual persons, living or dead, events or locales is entirely coincidental. References to real people are either noted or are individuals who are known professionals in the healthcare community.

Second River Healthcare Press books are available at special quantity discounts. Please call for information at: (406) 586-8775 or order from the websites:

www.SecondRiverHealthcare.com or **www.WhyHospitalsShouldFly.com**

TABLE OF CONTENTS

DEDICATION

To the nameless,
who have been harmed or died
in our care:
To the blameless
who were devoted
to their care
in a flawed system
And to a future,
where we all
are truly safe.

AUTHOR'S NOTE

How do you completely redesign and rebuild a ship including its hull while at sea in a storm? That, in a metaphorical capsule, is the challenge facing every American healthcare organization—from hospital to hospice.

As a recent article from the Wharton School stated, "*While the U.S. healthcare system is not yet on life support, it remains a fragmented and unwieldy structure whose rising costs bear little relation to improvements in access or quality.*" Indeed, as of today, we're spending 2.8 trillion dollars on healthcare services affecting only 10 percent of American health with half the quality of other industrialized nations while wasting 50 percent of every dollar spent and killing 30 people per hour (on average) with preventable medical errors and infections. The stark realities are terrifying: If unchanged, by 2030, 35 percent of our GNP will go for healthcare, leaving no money for schools, fire departments, basic human services, energy independence or defense.

From the C-suite's point of view, collapsing reimbursement, end of fee-for-service, advent of ACO's and the looming hegemony of HCAHPS and value-based pressures seem the nexus of the problem.

In reality, however, what's driving the crisis is a collective ignorance of reality—and denial.

A week before the date of this note, the two of us stood before a board of hospital CEO's representing an entire state <u>who did not feel the situation was urgent enough to involve their boards, or themselves!</u> In essence, they perceived no need for change beyond their current technical maneuvers—most of them financially-based. With the rogue wave looming on the horizon, they're satisfied with moving around deck chairs (in the old Titanic analogy), rather than throwing over the wheel.

In **WHY HOSPITALS SHOULD FLY** we advanced a paradigm—a model of what a good, successful, safe and efficient hospital looks like. In Naval terms, the name of that fictional hospital could be stated as a Class—a "St. Michael's-Class" hospital (like a Nimitz-Class carrier). In **CHARTING THE COURSE**, we're addressing head-on the challenge of actually *becoming* a St. Michael's-Class institution by illuminating leadership's role in changing the culture—and we do so by continuing the personal and professional journey of Dr. Will Jenkins. His battle, and emerging wisdom born of tragedy, illuminates the norms of the current culture and illustrates why each member of every medical facility *regardless of rank* must be a leader and owner of the cultural revolution needed to keep our system viable and our patients safe.

John J. Nance
Kathleen M. Bartholomew
15 May 2012
San Juan Island, Washington

FOREWORD

By
Donald M. Berwick, MD, MPP

My younger daughter is studying to become a middle school teacher. She has had to choose a specialty for licensure: natural science, humanities, or social sciences. I understand why that is convenient, but somehow it seems wrong—a misleading choice. We operate in a world of intersection. Ask yourself how we can solve the important problems of our time—sustaining our ecosystems, educating our children, providing clean water everywhere, or making healthcare safe. Will it take science or humanism or large-system savvy?

It will take all three, of course. To stop runaway global warming, we must understand and master the sources and effects of atmospheric carbon. (That requires science.) We must care enough to control it. (To that aim we will be called, if at all, by our hearts and our vision and our poets.) And we must muster the organizational forms and the political will to engage effectively. (For that, we need managers, political leaders and the formal and information processes of law and social action.) In the Institute for Healthcare Improvement, we label these essential factors for success in large scale change: "Will, Ideas and Execution." For those, read: "Heart, Science and Socio-Political Skills."

Do not read this book if you want the pursuit of patient safety to seem simple—if you want to preserve the hope that one of those alone will do. John Nance and Kathleen Bartholomew know far too much about science, humanism and politics to gloss over the difficulties of making healthcare safer. Indeed, as a team of two, they themselves embody the intersections that lead to real and new insight. John is a modern polymath—attorney, commercial airline pilot, award-winning novelist, nationally-known journalist and charismatic public speaker with more than two decades dedicated to healthcare. Kathleen—as a veteran nurse-manager, speaker, author and consultant, combines the scientific and professional disciplines of a master nurse and the passion and eloquence of a clarion agent for cultural change in driving for a Renaissance in the way we deliver care. It is little wonder that, in this compelling book, they can bring alive the several domains of knowledge that the improvement of safety requires. They help us see what is required even better by using the form of a novel; they illuminate the complexity through the powerful medium of storytelling.

The central character in their drama is Dr. Will Jenkins. A deeply caring and courageous physician-executive, he has made a long, psychological, developmental journey from relative ignorance and complacency about the safety of the hospitals in which he has worked to deep, relentless and soulful dissatisfaction and a commitment to patient safety as a driving, centralizing imperative. He now realizes that safety is not a condition of excellence in the healthcare he leads, but (in Paul O'Neill's wonderful phrase) a "precondition" to excellence. He has come to realize that a hospital that concedes willingly to any level of patient injury at all—no matter how inevitable injury seems—concedes thereby to the forces of randomness and entropy it's very reason-for-being. He has come to see that the (re)assertion of the moral foundations for healthcare, itself, requires, without compromise, that the interests of patients comes first, and the first interest of patients is not to be harmed by the care that is supposed to help them. He has come to see that the buck stops for that commitment on the desk of the executive and in the chambers of the board, and that that is not an empty duty: they will be tested. As the new CEO of a troubled hospital, he knows as much as anyone else—including his own CFO—about the necessity of financial stewardship. But he has come to see clearly that the oft-quoted maxim, "No Margin, no Mission," has it exactly backward. It is, rather, the relentless focus on sound and valued social purpose (especially purpose as easy to understand as "Do No Harm") that is the front door to being valued, and, by being valued, to securing resources in the long run. "No Mission, No Margin" is closer to correct; because, in the long run, society pays for what helps it, and rejects what does not.

John and Kathleen are tough-minded about the ground-rules for safety, and, in their fictionalized account, they draw starkly the choices that leaders face in an intransigent professional: "Dr. Adams," it is in this parable—whose disruptive behavior threatens the community of effort. The reader squirms as Will Jenkins forces the issue to a decisive leadership choice. It is, unfortunately, a choice that, in some measure, every would-be leader of system safety will encounter. But, they are equally, and accurately, generous in their understanding of the healthcare workforce as a whole; good people who, even when trapped in systems that set them up for failure with undoable jobs, broken supports and unreliable processes, yearn deeply to find the meaning in their work—to help people. I have, myself, found the Dr. Adams's very few, and the willing workers many in healthcare. The potential of the latter—the great masses of noble, committed healthcare workers are ready and willing to engage perfection as a goal if they are properly led, authentically respected and correctly supported.

The patient safety movement in the US and worldwide, has, give thanks, begun. But it has not yet done its job. We know tons about what to do—the science is ready. We know how urgent it is to do it—the stories tear at our hearts. And we know a good deal about how to execute change (and you will know even more if you read this book). What we do not have yet are momentum and mass effect. It is time for the total pursuit of patient safety—the charismatic healthcare quality dimension of our time—to become non-negotiable, pervasive and successful everywhere. This book will not make leaders comfortable; it is too honest for that. But it will show them the way, if they will choose it.

And, one last word, if you think this book is just about patient safety, think again. It is not. It is about excellence. For, in the complex, technological, interdependent world in which we now live our lives, to achieve what we want for ourselves, our loved ones and our posterity—whether in healthcare or in any other worthy domain that requires us to work together—the same challenges arise. Will we look honestly at the gaps between what we achieve and what we wish to achieve? Will we have the courage and vision to reach beyond our current grasp, and to announce that we are doing so? Will we trust, build, and learn the scientific foundations for design and redesign? Will we put our faith in each other, and call upon common spirit and mutual support? And, will we ask our leaders to accept—will we *demand* that they accept—the full burden of stewardship for remembering with us what adds meaning to our work and assuring that we have the tools and support to seek it? These are the questions that Will Jenkins—the hero of this book—will not give up on, and they are universal beacons for organizational excellence.

Donald M. Berwick, MD, MPP

Former President and CEO
Institute for Healthcare Improvement

Former Administrator
The Centers for Medicare & Medicaid Services (CMS)

INTRODUCTION

By
David B, Nash, MD, MBA

"What Happens in Vegas Stays in Vegas!" Everyone, by now, knows this widely regarded piece of advertising wisdom. Perhaps some of our readers have even practiced this in person. At Las Vegas Memorial Medical Center, certainly "What Happens in Vegas should stay in Vegas."

Once again John Nance and his accomplished wife, Kathleen Bartholomew have woven a story of such compelling nature that I was transported to Las Vegas and found myself cheering on the new hospital president, Dr. Will Jenkins, as he battled the forces of entrenched evil present in too many of America's community hospitals. Drawing on the lessons he learned at St. Michael's Memorial in John's previous bestseller, *"Why Hospitals Should Fly,"* Jenkins approaches Las Vegas Memorial warily, recognizing the many cultural battles that lie ahead.

We learn that Will, himself, has stared down a fatal hospital mistake that cost him dearly, both professionally and personally. He carries this baggage from one posting in Portland, Oregon to his new role at Las Vegas Memorial. It lingers in his consciousness; he's almost obsessed with the death of his godson, Ronnie Noland. Ronnie's death propels him subconsciously to take on the impossible. That is, to change the culture of typical American community hospitals, from the top down and the bottom up, with one singular goal—*Do No Harm!*

By a laser-like focus on this singular goal of doing no harm, Will transforms Las Vegas Memorial into a hospital that truly can fly! A hospital that is committed to clear communication without any punitive implications. A hospital that has a board ready to remove any attending physician who cannot participate in the new culture. A hospital that stands behind its employees at all levels in the organization and makes sure that they are a part of the cultural transformation.

Personally, I was transfixed by some of the characters. I have seen Claudia Ryan, the chief nursing officer and Richard Holbrook, the chief financial officer in person, many times, in my own consulting work. The board chair, Gary Mason and others, leapt out of the pages at me and I could picture them clearly in my minds' eye. I felt badly for the previous CEO, Joan Winston, and could viscerally appreciate the pain she had in her leadership journey.

What are the take home messages of *Charting the Course?* There are many. Clearly the central message is cultural change must occur for America's community hospitals to tackle our biggest problem, *Do No Harm*. Through the transformative work of *Doing No Harm*, we actually will improve all outcomes and lower costs and improve our operating margins. That is the "secret sauce."

Added to the "secret sauce" are additional ingredients, including a strong board with support from the CEO. Other ingredients include physician leadership training and a commitment to making our work truly patient-centric and not physician-centric. This will be a difficult lesson for many persons to integrate.

Additional take home messages include the possibility that one needs to hire a chief research officer, ready at a moments' notice to provide the evidentiary basis for cultural change. Finally, a take home lesson for me was, we cannot let the loudest negative voice prevail. We must be focused on our core mission—every day, and every moment of every day.

I'd like to go back to Las Vegas Memorial Medical Center sometime in the near future and see how Dr. Will Jenkins is doing. I'd love to meet Ivy, his long-time assistant, and peak in on them unobtrusively, as they go about their daily work together. I think it would be fun to meet Sanjay Ghalia, the newly appointed chief research officer, and compare notes with him about our own reading of the *New England Journal of Medicine and Health Affairs*.

I'm sure he would be an agile sparring partner.

But in all seriousness, *Charting the Course* took my breath away! I felt transported to Las Vegas. I know that "What Happens in Vegas" now will not "Stay in Vegas." Rather, Las Vegas Memorial could become a new benchmark just like St. Michael's. The story will leap out at you. My only question is, are you ready to accept its' powerful message, or will it stay in your consciousness like everything else in Las Vegas does today?

David B. Nash, MD, MBA
Founding Dean
The Jefferson School of Population Health
Thomas Jefferson University
Philadelphia, Pennsylvania

Chapter One

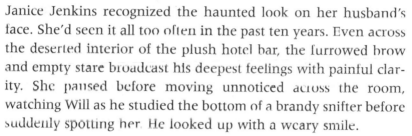

Janice Jenkins recognized the haunted look on her husband's face. She'd seen it all too often in the past ten years. Even across the deserted interior of the plush hotel bar, the furrowed brow and empty stare broadcast his deepest feelings with painful clarity. She paused before moving unnoticed across the room, watching Will as he studied the bottom of a brandy snifter before suddenly spotting her. He looked up with a weary smile.

"Honey!"

"I can see you're not alone," she began, noting a shadow of confusion cross his face like a small cloud. He looked to his left in defense, as if a dangerously alluring female had slipped onto the stool beside him, but the seat was empty.

She nodded toward the void. "It's the same crowd, Will. The ghosts. The ones you drink with all too often."

He started to get up and she motioned him back down as she slid onto the adjacent stool.

"Why are you so worried?" she asked.

"I'm *worried?*" he chuckled, his reply was unconvincing.

"I know that second-scotch look, Dr. Jenkins. Was our trip a waste of time? Is this such a bad hospital?"

He shook his head, relieved that the 'ghosts,' as she'd put it, needed no further discussion. "No, no! Well...yes and no. This hospital certainly has its problems, which is why they jumped at the chance to have me come down and interview. In fact, it's flattering, being told that I'm now number one on their selection list for chief executive officer and they're going to make a decision within a few days."

"That fast? And the pay package?"

Will looked a bit sheepish as he glanced down at the almost empty glass. "More than we were going to ask—and they'll pay for the move from Boise."

"Sounds like you're walking into a major challenge. Why did the previous CEO leave?"

"I'm not sure, but I intend to call her. I have her number."

"Tell me the problems, Sweetheart...in a nutshell."

Will sighed and rubbed his forehead in troubled thought, a gesture she knew well. His stylish gray suit was as sharp and unwrinkled as when he'd left their hotel room hours ago, but he'd loosened his tie just enough to betray the fatigue he'd been denying for many months.

Psychological fatigue, she knew, far more than physical. The Boise clinic and the memories of his failures at the Portland, Oregon, hospital he'd run until 2004 were leeching her husband away before her very eyes. Almost any challenge he could face would be better than the gradual atrophy of spirit she'd been witnessing. It was the same erosion that wore down so many.

"I'm just getting the merest glimpse of the whole story, of course," Will was saying. "The members of the selection committee who met with me were the board chair, who's a local business owner, and one of his board members, a retired surgeon. Like most hospitals, Las Vegas Memorial's leadership is in a deep panic and deep denial at the same time."

"About what?" Janice asked.

"About almost everything. I feel sorry for them, not that I have all the answers. For one thing, they're terrified about this new ACO model. They couldn't even call it by the correct name, accountable care organization. It's scaring them because they haven't a clue how to guide Las Vegas Memorial into becoming one, or whether they should even consider trying. But worse, the unspoken monster in the dark is what they consider the perplexing federal hostility to our traditional fee-for-service model. Those two fellows—and presumably the entire board—can't conceive of how they're going to pay the bills and keep the doors open without charging for as many services as they can provide, the way they've always done it."

She was nodding. "Frankly, Will, I don't think anyone knows

how to pay for improving the health of the community, especially if it means reducing the need for all those services with billing codes attached. How are they regarding best practices, standardization and patient safety?"

"Equally perplexed. They told me the medical staff is unhappy and still resentful of the previous administration's efforts to improve safety with some of the physicians still refusing to adopt even the most boiler plate best practices and standardized procedures, like checklists. Most of the physicians want to be involved, but it's the few outliers that are destroying it for the group. One physician even refused to support the IHI (Institute of Healthcare) bundles in their ICUs. There's the usual angry fight over physicians being on call for less money than they want, and they're down to fifteen OB/GYNs, one of them a big time disruptive doc. The chief medical officer, an anesthesiologist, quit last year after his practice was essentially sabotaged by surgeons angry at something he did to address a major patient safety threat. I'm told he may yet have to file bankruptcy. Also, the outside hospitalist group they hired to save money has been garnering a lot of internal complaints, clashing constantly with the staff and generating patient complaints. Patient satisfaction numbers are too low and staff satisfaction hasn't even been gauged lately. The nurses, I'm told, are complaining about the staffing grid and are simply burnt out on the floors where there's the usual hiring freeze."

"But, Honey, those are things you know how to fix, right?"

"Well," Will began, "I do, mostly. I know what tactical programs to install, but the challenge is to make this into a version of St. Michael's in Denver, and all those techniques are very new to me. For instance, what I never understood before was how vital it is to create a single-minded team who will adopt all the right methods simply because they dearly want to do the right thing. That's what Jack Silverman and St. Michael's has taught me. When we were in Portland, I thought patient safety was a top-down driven initiative that I had to instill forcefully. I never saw it as a core value. But it is. The biggest challenge, in fact, will be winning hearts and minds, not issuing directives."

"The gospel according to Jack Silverman?"

"Wait till you meet him, Honey. The man is a force of nature, and successful."

"I'm looking forward to meeting him. In fact, I'm strongly considering making St. Michael's the centerpiece of my PhD thesis next year. It sounds like Silverman had quite a challenge."

"The challenge may be even bigger here."

"Tell me."

Will looked around, suddenly aware of the gentle piano music coming from an adjacent part of the bar—whether by a human or machine he couldn't tell—a rendition of Sinatra's *My Way*, he noted, returning his attention to Janice.

"For one thing, they have no hope of reforming their care of this community if they can't get the basics right. But aside from the major financial terrors, this hospital's board may be far too worried about just catering to the physicians to clearly see the systemic deficiencies in safety and quality of the old model, the 'Farmer's Market' approach. It's a traditional physician-centric institution."

"Where the hospital is run for the physicians and the patients get the trickle-down theory, right?"

"Exactly. In part, it's a panicked reaction to the Affordable Care Act and healthcare reform in general because they know they now have to work more closely with the physicians. But both physicians and board members are grossly misinterpreting what that means. For one thing, too many members of this board are wanting to wait it out, thinking that Congress may significantly change the law again following the Supreme Court decision on healthcare reform, and then maybe they can resume their prior business-as-usual, fee-for-service, physician-centric ways and avoid uncomfortable changes. That attitude I'll have to address from the start as I could feel the pushback from these guys the moment I started talking about substantial change. But we simply cannot put off major reform and survive, regardless of the politics, because the traditional ways of providing healthcare are clearly unsustainable no matter what happens with the Affordable Care Act. On top of that, they're smarting from having to cancel a capital building campaign for lack of donations and public support. Much of the community here in Las Vegas lost faith in them after a major wrong-site surgical disaster last year, and although no one said it, I get the impression that the board is, at the very least, confused, and probably completely impotent to face these problems. They're flailing around in search of an omnibus solution and expecting their new CEO to *be* the solution. Las Vegas Memorial, stated another way, is about as close to the opposite of St. Michael's as I could get."

"Really?"

"In Vegas terms, Honey, this could be a real crap shoot."

"You mean there's no teamwork? No collegiality?"

He laughed. "I'm sure there's some, but I haven't seen it yet. I'll put a call into St. Michael's to talk with Jack Silverman before we decide."

"And, we have a dinner to attend, you said?"

He nodded. "Tomorrow evening with the same two guys, board chairman Gary Mason and Dr. Brent Roget, plus their wives and maybe one other."

"The ritual examination of the prospective CEO's wife, correct?"

He smiled. "Don't worry. I think you'll pass."

"You *think?* Big vote of confidence, that!" She laughed.

"Seriously, they're good people, but as I say, I think I'm only seeing the tip of the iceberg."

"Of course you are." Janice turned toward the far end of the bar and motioned for the bartender to refill Will's glass and bring her one of the same.

"I'm drinking Oban," he said.

"I know. Me, too," she added. "Especially since you look like a guy about to put all his chips on one number."

He hesitated, a look of uncertainty crossing his face. "You think this would be a bad move?"

She shook her head, perhaps too energetically, and then smiled. "No! Are *you* nervous?"

Surprised at himself, Will Jenkins grinned at his wife. "No. Not really. Like the majority of the hospitals in America, Las Vegas Memorial is ideally and typically dysfunctional. Success here would truly be a seismic change, not a fine-tuning. If I could pull that off..."

"You realize it means giving up a private practice that's just beginning to pay off as well as the assistant professorship I was just awarded for my leadership work at the business school?"

"Yes. And I'm not going to do this if you'd rather stay."

"Honey, I can commute to Boise to teach my classes for the remainder of the semester. And I'm sure there are grad schools here that need business school professors. Those aren't problems. My biggest worry is what it will do to you if you fail."

Will nodded soberly, "I already have, once." The haunted look returned as his gaze focused far beyond the bottles on the bar. "But at least this time, I'd know why."

She glanced at her husband, a proprietary flash of pride flickering through her consciousness that even at the age of fifty-two he could pass for a much younger man. Athletic build, sandy hair with an occasional fleck of gray, the few lines on his face were no match for his easy smile and bright blue eyes. Patients and peers alike had always found first-impression reason to trust him on appearance alone—as had she.

Janice shook off the retrospective. "Tell me what's different this time, Will? Other than meeting Silverman and being impressed to distraction with St. Michael's, what tools do you now have that you didn't possess before?"

Will looked at her for the longest time. "Well, at least three things," he began. "First, the top-down problem. In Portland, I ordered and cajoled people into compliance with procedures and objective measures. I didn't know I needed to win them over first, instill a completely different philosophy; essentially drive the message simultaneously from the top down and the bottom up, leading, not ordering. I made no provisions for listening to what our front line folks thought regarding what we were trying to accomplish, or letting them drive it. In fact, I had no understanding of how doomed a hospital is without a truly shared philosophy, a common vision. That's also the key to serving an identified community, which is the core element of the ACO concept—making people healthier so they need us less. Of course, I also realize *that* won't happen until we find a way to profit from investing in community health."

"You mean making money from a diminishing need for medical services?"

"Yes. One of the biggest hidden elephants in the so-called healthcare debate is how in the world we are going to re-channel the money investors' invest from responding to illness with critical care, to investing in community wellness instead? How do we provide a reasonable rate of return as people stay healthier and hospitals close entire floors? Whether we're dealing with a not-for-profit investment organization or a for-profit, it's the same dilemma. How does a free market reward with a profit community wellness and a lower need for critical care? If we don't figure it out, the future holds an imposed governmental solution that no one will like."

"Understood. But you had three points. The first was the top-down mistake. What's the second?"

"The second is that I now know what I never saw before, that human organizations can't achieve high reliability performance without minimizing variables, using evidence-based best practices, standardizing things that work and constantly reinventing every process."

"You're talking cars and manufacturing, not medicine," she added.

"Which is exactly my point. What *they* do works. What *we* do in medicine doesn't! It is the same point Dr. Atul Gwande made so effectively in his book *The Checklist Manifesto*. Medicine has to change. To use the old Titanic metaphor, I was trying to change things by moving deck chairs around rather than changing the course of the ship to avoid the icebergs altogether. When you look at other high-risk industries that have achieved high reliability, the methods are very well established: the Toyota production method, Lean, Six Sigma and a whole infrastructure of building systemic reliability. But it requires a major systemic overhaul that we've been unwilling to undertake."

"And the third?"

"The third is the biggest challenge of all, and I never even saw it. I never sensed its awesome power to thwart any initiative. It's culture. Hundreds of years of cultural momentum controlling everything. No one is aware of it, or talks about it because we're perpetually immersed in it. It's like suddenly discovering the dark matter physicists tell us makes up over 90 percent of the universe. We can't see it, yet it permeates virtually everything.

Culture was the black hole that kept swallowing all my patient safety initiatives, the massive inertia against change that hamstrings everyone. I just couldn't see it from the top. And you know what's good about figuring this out? Just knowing the nature of my adversary changes everything. If we take this, I'm committing to changing a culture."

"What about the buzz word problems? The categories keeping all CEOs and CFOs (chief financial officers) awake these days?"

"You mean, 'patient satisfaction,' 'reduced reimbursement,' 'never events,' 'mission versus margin,' 'HCAHPS (Hospital Consumer Assessment of Healthcare Providers and Systems)'and 'value-based purchasing,' right?"

"Yes."

"All of them fall under those three things. How can we have patient satisfaction if patients are in grave physical danger in our hospital, and if the people providing the care aren't unified in their dedication to doing the best for the patient? Without a shared philosophy, patient satisfaction is an impossible quest. For that matter, chasing patient satisfaction scores without real patient safety reform is a fool's errand. Same thing for dealing with drastically reduced reimbursement and never events and margins. Without unifying the organization on a very basic level, the rest of the problems are essentially unsolvable."

They sat in silence for several moments as Janice sipped her drink, studying her husband's reflection in the bar mirror. His eyes turned smoky blue, like they always did when the past played louder than the present.

"Will, you can't bring Ronnie back. You know that. If that's what this is about..."

A cascade of painful memories of Wayne and Cindy Nolan and the little boy named Ronnie who hadn't survived his encounter with Will Jenkins' hospital pressed in on him again as if it had happened ten minutes ago, not ten years. Ronnie had been his godson. Wayne had been his best friend. Could everything he was thinking of doing—uprooting Janice, selling his Boise practice, moving from the mountains to the desert—come from something as mindless as a need for personal forgiveness?

"It's not, and I know. Believe me, I know."

She reached over and squeezed his hand, more aware than he of the real answer.

"Okay," Janice said, turning part way toward him on the stool and supporting her right elbow on the bar. "So, if they make the offer and we take it, you have to do *more* than make Las Vegas Memorial into St. Michael's. You'll be blazing a trail. People still look at Silverman and St. Michael's and think it's a fluke, an anomalous dream. You know that's right. You said so yourself."

"Absolutely," he nodded. "They're out there saying: 'Wow, how nice! Wish that were possible here, but it isn't.'"

"And they conclude that it can't be done, *why*?"

"Because, so far, at least, St. Michael's seems to be the only example of St. Michael's."

"Yes," she nodded enthusiastically, "because the cultural resistance of the American hospital refuses to be swayed by just one, or even just a handful of good examples, no matter how powerful. They're always perceived as the exception rather than the rule. St. Michael's is the ultimate example of what can happen. What's missing is an example of how a St. Michael's is *created*, and that will require mud wrestling with each objection."

"In other words," he added, "the naysayers and their flat rejections about how we can't afford it, or the physicians won't follow, or the nurses are too stressed to redesign the work flow, or the board isn't willing to risk losing important physicians who bring in big dollars?"

"Yep. Why checklists will never work in medicine. All of it. That's what I see this being, Will, a chance to show *how* it's done. To reorganize everyone's thinking to clearly see it in a very different light. If you take this job, it's really about something much bigger than yourself."

He looked at her for the longest time, struggling to understand and then smiled, kissing her softly. "Thank you, Beautiful."

"You're welcome."

"I'm not sure I'd want to tackle this if I didn't have your expertise to fall back on."

"What do you mean?"

"You're in a unique position, Honey. An experienced nurse who's made a name for herself as a business school professor with specific expertise in healthcare management. It amazes me that you have more management experience than I do, and you're still willing to put up with me being the top dog!"

"Oh, I just let you *think* you are," she sat back, smiling. "What time is it?"

"Eight thirty-two," he replied after a cursory glance at his watch.

"So, superdoc, how, exactly, *are* you going to accomplish this?"

"I have a few ideas."

His smile, she noted, was getting bigger.

JANICE'S NOTES:

FROM: JANICE.JENKINS@Northnet.com
TO: JACK.SILVERMAN@STM.org
SUBJ: Hello and Request from Will's wife

Dr. Silverman,

I'm looking forward to meeting you in person, and visiting St. Michael's next month. As you can imagine, Will has been greatly impacted and motivated by what you've accomplished there—as am I. You may or may not know that in addition to being a nurse, I am also a professor preparing a new syllabus for a course in healthcare leadership from a sociological perspective (B.S. major in Sociology). As such, I would like to follow Will's journey closely, for reasons that are personal and professional. The reason I am writing to you is to ask if you'd be willing to, more or less, look over my shoulder as I chronicle the next months (or years), and provide any insight that could help me better understand the cultural elements—which I'm sure will help Will as well. I understand there is no detailed map to follow—yet! Chronicling Will's journey into this new CEO position will help produce a baseline record that I can use later as a formal management case study, and perhaps even my thesis.

Thank you for your time and consideration on this matter,

Janice Jenkins

FROM: JACK.SILVERMAN@STM.org
TO: JANICE.JENKINS@Northnet.com
SUBJ: Re: Hello and Request from Will's wife

Dear Janice,

Of course! I'm looking forward to meeting you in person as well—
perhaps only to apologize for getting Will into this challenge!
Seriously, though, I would be more than delighted to assist you
since I'm forever on a learning curve myself, and constantly asked
by others how to duplicate our success. Please send me your
commentary and I'll respond periodically as necessary.

Fondly,

Jack Silverman

FROM: JANICE.JENKINS@Northnet.com
TO: JACK.SILVERMAN@STM.org
SUBJ: First Installment

Jack,

I think I understand why Will, as he puts it, failed at the Portland
hospital he ran. You know the story, but in a discussion last
evening, several elements stood out:

1. Will (and in turn his senior team) never understood the vital
   nature of creating a single-minded focus on something—in
   this case patient safety as a common goal—in order to lead a
   team to figure out the ways of achieving that common goal.

2. The prevailing attitude Will and his team had in the
   Portland hospital was that patient safety was a top-down
   initiative that had to be instilled forcefully. In reality, it
   must be a core value; and as such, it must be voluntarily
   embraced by everyone. Will, as CEO, ordered and cajoled
   people into compliance with procedures and objective
   measures. The thought of winning them over was never
   on the table, nor was the idea of instilling a different
   philosophy and strategy based on shared values.

3. It appears to be axiomatic (and frankly I've long agreed with this) that human organizations cannot achieve consistent high-reliability performance without minimizing variables, embracing evidence-based best practices, standardizing processes and procedures where clinically possible, and being ready and willing to change any process when new knowledge becomes available (organizational flexibility). The new element for me was that while I've long understood this to be necessary in certain industries such as manufacturing and even aviation, I never realized that its point of applicability is to ANY human organization.

4. Culture is the most formidable challenge to patient safety or service quality improvement, in other words, cultural resistance to change is the greatest challenge to virtually any deviation from the cottage industry model of physician-centric care that is still our national norm.

Chapter Two

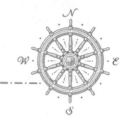

Karen Kinsey hesitated for a moment before she gently closed the eyelids of the dead patient.

This just didn't have to happen.

She turned to her preceptee, Maura Manning, her voice matter-of-fact. "Time of death, eight thirty-two. Please get me a body bag from the supply room."

The ashen look on Maura's face confirmed she was more than happy for any excuse to leave the room, and clearly, Karen needed a few minutes to pull her own thoughts together.

Karen's mind raced to the dead patient's husband, Doug, who had phoned before leaving his office to make sure his wife didn't need anything. He should be arriving on the floor any minute now.

Quickly Karen grabbed the patient's bedside phone and dialed the operator. "May I speak to whoever is on-call for spiritual care?"

"That will be Hector Padilla. Which room please?"

"Have him call Karen, the charge nurse on Nine East. Thank you."

"Will do."

Oh, God, Karen thought, *another suck-the-life-out-of-you-no-lunch-break-day.* Maybe she should take her husband's advice and retire early—before he divorced her for chronic grumpiness. Nursing just seemed to be getting harder, instead of easier, despite her years of experience. It wasn't the clinical part that dragged her down; it was the pace, the stress and emotional days like this one.

Maura appeared at the doorway, holding the body bag by the corner as if it was infectious.

"Just put it on the windowsill," Karen said, much too sharply, ignoring the look on Maura's face that begged for consolation. No time for hand holding tonight.

Karen's pager wouldn't stop beeping. From the messages she could tell that the patient in nine forty-two needed help to the bathroom and the staffing office was aggravated because she still hadn't staffed for day shift. That would have to wait—one less patient now. *That should help their staffing problems.* She paged the supervisor to alert her to the unexpected death, instructed Maura to help the patient in nine forty-two, and asked the secretary to intercept the patient's husband. Then she asked another nurse to do staffing and ducked back into the patient's room to call the physician privately.

"Dr. Adams," she began when he finally came on the line. *Maybe if she blurted it all out in one breath, she could get through everything.* "This is Karen. I'm so sorry. Mrs. Markowitz coded and died. I don't know what happened. We notified you yesterday afternoon and twice during night shift about her unusual swelling, and I know you came to see her on rounds this morning. Her vital signs were fine when I arrived on the floor. I was coming in to take her nine a.m. vitals when I found her and called a code, but it was no use."

Karen could hear the doctor shifting the receiver in his hand. "She was fine when I saw her just four hours ago. What did you do to her?"

What did I do? Karen thought, but the unit secretary's voice on the room speaker cut through her consciousness before she could give voice to it.

"Karen?"

"Yes, Laurinda?"

"Mr. Markowitz is here." She said struggling to maintain composure.

Dr. Adams's voice was still booming over the phone. "Karen? Karen! What the hell happened?"

Karen knew the question was rhetorical, and that the physician was just as shocked as the rest of the team. "Please come in now, doctor. Mr. Markowitz just arrived."

Click.

As soon as Maura opened the door, she could tell the woman in nine forty-two was furious.

"Where have you been? I'm going to have an accident if I don't get to the bathroom right now! I've been calling for over forty minutes and no one has come!" Mrs. Peters was throwing off the covers and pointing forcefully to the compression devices that kept her tethered to the bed.

"I'm sorry," Maura replied as she headed to the sink to wash her hands. "There was an emergency in another room."

"Well, this is an emergency, too! I can't remove these damn things, I can't reach my walker and no one comes when I call. Do you know what that it feels like to be tied down and ignored?"

There was no use explaining. What was she supposed to say after all: *I'm sorry, but dying is a slightly higher priority than peeing?* Better to just apologize and help the upset woman as fast as she could.

But just as they reached the bathroom door, Mrs. Peters had an accident.

"I'm sorry," the old lady moaned, a few tears rolling down her cheek.

"No, we're sorry, Mrs. Peters. This is *our* fault. Don't you worry about a thing."

Maura threw a towel down on the floor, noting that she would need to clean or change her shoes as she settled Mrs. Peters on the toilet. The patient rested her forehead on the walker, clearly depressed.

"Just leave me alone for a minute. Go on. Leave," she said.

"I'm going to run and get a clean gown and towels, and then I'll be right back."

The moaning reply was agonizing. "Agh! And what about the pain pill I asked for an hour ago? I need it!"

"I'm...sorry, but there was a problem with my getting into the medication machine, so I can't get that for you myself, but I'll remind Karen before I get the linens."

"That's all I've heard since I've been here is why people *can't* help me."

Maura let the last comment drop. She didn't know how to

respond anyway. Maybe if she stayed with Mrs. Peters, she wouldn't have to do the post-mortem care on Mrs. Markowitz, or deal with the devastated husband. Why hadn't someone told her in nursing school that being a nurse would be so intensely emotional? Maybe she'd been absent that day. School had been mostly about procedures and care plans and technical knowledge, and very little about how to deal with human reactions and the real experience of pain, psychological or emotional.

I don't remember even once practicing this in school, Maura thought, wiping the urine off her shoes with a Sani-wipe. Too many days lately felt like a game show where you had to juggle competing tasks in a brief window of time while charting, smiling and critically thinking as everyone judged how good you were, or not. Last week when she'd asked a question, the disgusted look on the other nurses' faces made her feel stupid, so she'd simply stopped asking.

Mrs. Peters was somewhat calmer when Maura returned to the room, and as she helped her into a clean gown and back into bed, it seemed a good idea to try to engage her in conversation. Maura noted that after a four day hospital stay, there were no tokens of affection; no cards or flowers, in the room.

"Could I ask where you're from, Ma'am? Were you born in Las Vegas?" But after several one word answers, Maura gave up. She re-filled the water pitcher and placed the call button next to Mrs. Peters' hand. "Just call me if you need anything."

Mrs. Peters rolled her eyes, turned toward the window and moaned. "My pain pill. Where's the pain pill I called for over an hour ago?"

"I'm going to find Karen right now so she can get it for you."

"Right. Same words someone else said over an hour ago."

There was a moment of pained silence between them before Maura closed the door feeling helpless, an incongruous phrase running through her mind: *All the king's horses and all the king's men...*

Chapter Three

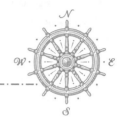

There was no question where the C-suite of Las Vegas Memorial began and the rest of the hospital ended. The glass double doors at the end of the ordinary linoleum corridor opened to plush carpeting with meticulously positioned studio photos of the past leaders.

Will had always wondered who'd been the first to coin the term C-suite, referring to the section of a hospital where all the "chiefs" hung out. But it had become endemic, and this version was very typical.

A well-groomed young woman got to her feet from behind the receptionist's desk, and greeted Will Jenkins warmly as she gestured to the two people who had obviously been waiting for him. Claudia Ryan, a conservatively dressed woman with steel gray hair and the title of CNO, smiled as she stepped forward with the caution of a soldier in a minefield. *Obviously,* Will thought, *their previous meeting had broken no ice.*

"Hello again, Dr. Jenkins."

"Claudia, good to see you," Will replied, shaking her hand as she turned to pass him off to an impeccably groomed younger man standing next to her. "And you remember Richard Holbrook, our chief financial officer?"

"Of course. Good to see you, too, Richard."

"Likewise, doctor."

Holbrook leaned forward and engaged him with a steely grip, his demeanor one of confidence and control—an alpha male making it clear where his territorial limits could be found. Will remembered Holbrook's cautious performance in their first meeting.

"Again, both of you please call me Will."

"Thanks, Will," Claudia replied, apparently for both of them as she turned to head down the hall.

"Give me a second." Will requested then walked back to the receptionist to introduce himself before turning to follow the CFO and CNO to the boardroom. The private phone conversation with Dr. Jack Silverman a half-hour before was still echoing in his head, and triggered a smile.

"Is the ink dry on your contract?" Jack had asked with a chuckle.

"Yes. As of yesterday. But I don't formally take the helm of the place for another month. Janice and I are still looking for a house."

"That was a good idea, demanding a board meeting a month prior." Will had laughed. *"I didn't demand, Jack. I merely requested."*

"Of course you did. So what's your flight plan?"

"Let them reveal themselves. I want to take their measure."

"Watch for the eyes-glazed-over board members who don't even speak the language and the nervous officers who're already plotting against you. I don't mean to urge paranoia on you, but these are the same kind of good folks I had to get off my board and out of my C-suite because they either had no idea what the challenges were, or were determined to just defend their turf."

"I had a long, revealing chat with the previous CEO, Jack. Obviously, she has her own opinions, and I'll only trust my own evaluations, but I'm sure I'm inheriting some problem children, and at least one bomb thrower. We'll see. I intend to be very direct, and they may want me out of here by the end of the meeting. You've had a great influence on me in terms of no-B.S. directness."

"Glad to hear it. Break a leg, and call me later. This journey of yours is already fascinating me."

"Why?" Will had asked.

"Because I know how we did it. I can't wait to see how you do it!"

The warm reception of the board members when Will walked in was a welcome contrast to the guarded demeanor of the CFO and CNO. He thoroughly understood their caution, however. Too often a new CEO swept the C-suite clean, replacing them with trusted outsiders.

Will waded into the smiles and handshakes concentrating

hard to merge each of the fourteen names he'd studied with their owners, but it was a struggle. He sat with a welcome cup of coffee as Gary Mason, the board chair, opened the meeting, introducing their CEO-designate with words that not so vaguely implied messianic expectations. It took a few minutes of pleasantries and acknowledgments before Will got to his feet, paused and locked eyes with each board member one by one.

"First, may I have your permission to be absolutely frank and direct? I don't mean to imply a desire to suspend civility, but you're hiring me to do a serious job and a rather high degree of brutal frankness is, I think, required."

There were nods and supportive comments around the room, and a slightly startled look on Gary Mason's face.

"Okay. Thank you. Now, I've seen the dashboards, read the numbers, reviewed the sentinel events, the finances and everything else Gary has sent me, and my take on the state of the hospital can be summed up like this: Las Vegas Memorial is full of wonderful people working their hearts out to provide the best medical care by using all the traditional methods, which include paying strict attention to the hospital-doctor relationship. This is, in other words, a fine, traditional American hospital. But, the prime question in pop culture terms would be just this: Is it working for you? And the answer reflected as each of you can clearly see by your own dashboards and by your concerns over public reputation—is 'No.' First, we're in a revolution, and the traditional methods don't work financially, or in terms of morale and teamwork. And certainly they don't work in lowering the number of preventable patient impacts to zero. The Center for Medicare and Medicaid Services (CMS) is increasingly calling the shots and change is virtually unavoidable. All of you know the statistics, and realize that regardless of what Congress or the courts do or don't do, we have to move now on safety and quality and value-driven outcomes, which is why you've hired me. Fence-sitting in today's environment will close a lot of hospitals across the nation, and I'm determined that we will not be one of them. What I'm going to ask you to do today is going to be essential to my own understanding and effectiveness. I'd like to ignite a no-punches-pulled roundtable discussion for the next hour as to where you see the problems, and what you think we need to do first, second and third. I need a solid sense of how this board thinks and looks at the challenges facing this institution."

Gary Mason was looking slightly dyspeptic. Dr. Brent Roget looked confused. Yes, Will had asked for the meeting, but they were used to having a set agenda neatly printed and bound in a leather binder sitting before each director. Today's meeting had no printed agenda, and the assumption had been it was going to be fluff stuff: a round of introductions and congratulations to the new CEO-designate.

Mason looked around the table, gauging the expected level of upset and wondering if his choice for CEO was suddenly going to be challenged behind the scenes. This was not the normal, deferential way for a new CEO to approach his board. No one was glaring daggers in his direction, but Mason decided Dr. Jenkins could conduct this discussion by himself. If the hour ended up a waste, it wasn't going to be his fault, and there were substantial business people in the room who suffered neither fools nor wasted time in silence.

The discussion and solutions came quickly, however, if defensively echoing the collective impression of the board's perception of reality. Las Vegas Memorial was, they assured him, a high quality institution that had made significant progress in leading the charge against patient safety disasters, and the dashboards actually showed that—if you looked closely enough. Handwashing compliance had hit nearly 74 percent, up from 61 percent a year earlier, and the hospital had received several awards for excellence from various sources. In addition, staff satisfaction—the last time they had surveyed it—had been reported in the seventies, and nursing turnover had dropped from 16 to 12 percent, a sure sign that they should seek Magnet recognition from the American Nurses Credentialing Center (ANCC) for their nurses, one member added.

Will kept his mouth shut and took notes, absorbing the initial surge of energy that seemed to be asking why their new CEO could not clearly see all the excellence and quality in the dashboard figures he'd just said he'd studied. Red—Yellow—Green, maybe he should've claimed to be partially colorblind. He let the statistic offerings peter out before looking up from his legal pad.

"So, clearly, you're telling me that Las Vegas Memorial is an institution of high quality. Other than the dashboard numbers, though, how do you know?"

Gary Mason jumped in to remind Will that the staff sampled such measures constantly.

"No, I understand what the numbers *say*, Gary. But in your hearts and souls, how do you *know* they're telling us the correct story? How do you *know* your interpretation of those numbers as 'excellence' is valid? Have any of you been a patient at Las Vegas Memorial lately, or had a family member here during a serious crisis?"

There were no takers, and Will nodded.

"Then let me quote true experts on this question, Dennis Pointer and Jaime Orlikoff, whose work with hospital boards is world class. They say we all want to believe we're quality health-care providers, but when you ask a group of great, dedicated people like all of you here *why* your hospital is so excellent, what it boils down to, all too often, is the *illusion* of knowledge that's prompted the delusion of excellence, not the fact of it. See, what boards believe to be true becomes a shared illusion. This is espe-cially true when safety and quality are considered. Why? Because boards actually know a lot more about finance than they do about safety and quality, but they are typically—if not universally—mesmerized into thinking they are equally informed regarding safety and quality. I would submit to you that this board is really no different."

Will waited for a few seconds before continuing, watching their reactions.

"Here's why I decided to let a skunk loose in here. We don't have time to tip-toe around these issues, and you aren't hiring me to blow sunshine at you. Let's talk about reality. We are not a quality insti-tution as long as there is at least one person out there suffering for the rest of his or her life because we couldn't get it right, or as long as one life ended prematurely. So, let's pull all the tarps off of all the hidden elephants and help me understand where you see the problem—safety, quality, financial, personnel, what-ever. I know there are great people here. Show me the warts."

The conversation began slowly, but heated up quickly, with only two of the members essentially sitting back and taking silent measure of Will and the subject matter. The topics whirled from greedy doctors and confrontational nurses' unions to the difficulty of getting Las Vegas Memorial's staff to accept their responsibility for cost-containment. Physicians were seen as a generic problem for demanding outrageous amounts for emergency room on-call coverage, and for pushing back on best practices as a concept. An hour went by with Will energetically taking notes and asking questions before standing again.

"Okay, in the interest of your time, I think this is a great start and has been very helpful, but I want to engage you in something I consider profoundly important. I've been ranking the amount of time and passion you folks have spent on each topic, and from that—this is not an exact science, but—from that I'd like to give you a graphic look at where your concerns lie."

He turned to a blank pad on an easel behind the table and picked up a marker.

"The number one concern is money: Keeping the doors open, reimbursement worries, making sure 'meaningful use' status is realized in your new electronic medical records system, dealing with 'never events' as a cost item when they cancel reimbursement for infections and other CMS mandated items, and the cost of recruiting physicians with an in-house recruiter as well as the cost of losing some of the most productive surgeons, which has been threatened. You're very worried about the financial impact of the HCAHPS if we can't substantially raise the scores by the time reimbursement linkage kicks in. Worse, none of us knows precisely what an accountable care organization should look like, and even fewer have any faith that it can be successfully funded or embraced by organizations like ours built on fee-for-service. And, of course the question of Las Vegas Memorial ever actually deciding to pursue ACO status is keeping you up at night, because of the funding challenge. What's the billing code for *not* needing our services? What's the billing code for safety? Does anyone disagree that money is the top worry category?"

Nods and agreement rippled around the room, though Will could see several members looking markedly uncomfortable.

"Okay, number two is physician retention. You're clearly quite concerned about losing any of the big admitters and their revenue. Number three is the failed capital campaign and the reputation of the hospital as a bar to raising funds to build a new wing. Number four is the challenge of raising the community's perception of quality here. The *perception* of quality. Number five is patient satisfaction—just the end result of the scores and the metrics, yet we need to focus on what goes into creating a highly satisfied patient—the means as well as the ends. Number six, by my estimation, is nurse staffing, dealing with nurse union demands, and trying to keep the CNO within budget, all of those problems previously articulated by Richard Holbrook, our CFO, in the board meeting several weeks back."

Each category was written on the sheet, one under the other.

"Priority number seven, in terms of the amount of time we spent discussing it, was the cost of liability insurance, and whether to take this institution to a self-insured status. As a component of that, you were also worrying out loud about the costs of medical malpractice lawsuits, both in terms of reputation and continuing to financially mount an aggressive defense each time we're challenged, regardless of the circumstance.

And, finally, your eighth priority is patient safety, primarily in terms of preventing repeats of sentinel events and incidents like the wrong-site surgeries of the past few years, which are primary concerns in keeping this hospital financially viable. Anyone disagree with my ranking?"

A hand shot up. The owner was a man who had introduced himself as Sal Bertelli, head of a major accounting firm. Bertelli had made dire predictions about the future if Las Vegas Memorial's finances were continuously impacted by never-event infections and curtailed reimbursement.

"Will, if you're implying that we should be less concerned about the money, I can tell you the doors *will* be in danger of closing if we don't pay primary attention to it. I understand we have to focus on safety, but without money, there won't be anything to be safe about because there won't be a hospital."

"Without question, we can't drop that ball," Will said, "and I have no intention of doing so. But, I would urge you to consider this. The capital campaign—and probably at least some revenue—lost ground due to the decline in reputation resulting from that highly-publicized wrong-site surgery several years back. It was damaged even further when it happened again just this past year, but less catastrophically. Am I correct?"

"Yes."

"Well, the very things that generate that sort of patient safety failure then become, by definition, a prime financial consideration, because of their potential catastrophic impact. That's true whether we're self-insured or commercially insured. Therefore, I think, since money is vital, we need to reconsider what's the cause and what's the effect. Get safety in line by attacking and changing the things that create the human and systemic mistakes that hurt our patients. Achieve zero preventable patient impacts, which includes ending never-events and hospital-acquired infections, and the money stream is not impeded. It's the difference between treating the symptoms and eliminating the disease."

A murmur of discussion rippled around the table as Bertelli nodded in thought and scratched his chin. "Okay, I'm listening, Will."

"Good. Here's my point. You folks started talking to me about the CEO position because Jack Silverman was good enough to recommend me. What I told you in repeated interviews was how determined I am that a patient-centric hospital—a hospital created by rebuilding the hospital for the patients with the physicians as vital partners, but not the physicians as the clients—is the only path to success. We can't achieve patient-centric reality unless we truly are patient oriented in word and deed and even bylaws, and that means being 100 percent intolerant of anything but 100 percent safety."

"Could you," Gary Mason interjected, "expand on your definition of 'patient-centric,' Will?"

"Okay. It's very simple, yet powerful. In a patient-centric hospital, everything—and I do mean everyone, everything and every interest—is subordinate to the best interests of the patient. Even the *physician's* best interests must be subordinate to the patient's, and that's not the way we've traditionally done it.

Now, by saying that, I do *not* mean patient-centric is a system that discounts the power or importance of a physician's, or a nurse's, professional impact on patient healing. The healing relationship is multi-faceted, and as Dr. John Burroughs describes it, the relationship combines three critical components: A patient who wants to be healed, practitioners who desire to provide healing services and a healthy organization to create the optimal environment for healing. But a patient-centric hospital can neither be a care-provider's democracy nor a loose confederation of aligned interests. Medicine now is far too complex for cottage industry methods. In fact, the ideal healing environment is one of harmonious synergy in which the hospital is the focal point of coordination and responsibility for standards, continuity and competence—as well as the means of forming and supporting the care team. The patient's best interests, however, must be the primary and overriding center of everything the team does."

There was an exchange of glances around the table and the scratch of pens as detailed notes were taken. Will paused before continuing, waiting until everyone had looked back up at him.

"Now let me ask you that provocative question again. Is Las Vegas Memorial a quality institution? If we accept anything less than perfect safety—zero preventable patient impacts—how can we be? And, remember, patient safety was way down on your list of priorities."

A beefy hand went up and Will recognized the board member as Jason Baldridge, a major building contractor in the Las Vegas community. "What are you saying, Will, that we're *not* a quality hospital? You, yourself, saw the numbers."

"May I call you Jason?"

"You bet."

"Jason, is 74 percent hand washing compliance de facto quality?"

"Well, it says we're on the way."

"Yes, of course. But with hospital-acquired infections so rampant and dangerous, not to mention being costly never-events from CMS's perspective, we can't afford to see these things in gradations of gray. Do you realize that nationally on average we're killing eleven patients per hour from nothing but hospital-acquired infections, most of them aided if not caused by contaminated hands? Seventy-four percent means we have *some* hand washing compliance, which also means we have *some* infection control, which means we have *some* safety. For the poor sick patient who catches an infection like MRSA from us and has to be told to put her affairs in order because, thanks to the infection, she's not going to make it, that 74 percent compliance figure is a scathing indictment and unnecessary since hand washing can voluntarily hit 100 percent when everyone is properly engaged and concerned."

"I think you're splitting hairs. We know this is a journey but you don't just mandate 100 percent compliance and get it."

"Jason, I understand that half the major casinos and hotels in this town were built by your company."

He laughed. "I wish! But we have built quite a few of them."

"Would you be able to tolerate just 74 percent compliance with your most important safety rules, such as hard hat wearing, or electrical double-checking before powering something up?"

Jason took a deep breath. "Well, no, but we're in a strict compliance industry."

"Shouldn't healthcare be a strict compliance industry? Seventy-four percent may show progress, but it does not show quality by any reasonable definition. I'm not trying to be assaultive or confrontational here, but I promised to pull no punches, and here's what I'm getting at: If we're anything less than 100 percent safe, we're simply *not* safe and therefore not trustworthy, and we are by definition not providing quality care. I'm trying to frame my thinking for you, too, and my overriding point is that we have to seriously change the focal point of Las Vegas Memorial from graduated improvement to a soul-invested quest for zero preventable patient impacts. Please notice, by the way, that I did *not* say zero errors. No matter how good we get, we'll never achieve zero human errors, but we *can* anticipate errors, and by catching those that we can't eliminate, achieve zero preventable impacts. We can do it provided we have unwavering support from this entire board. All the other challenges we face, including financial, in my view, start and end with how safe and trustworthy we are. And if one person is harmed because we failed to put safe systems and methods of teamwork in place, we are at fault. This, by the way, is saying that we must embrace safety and quality as core values, not statistically-measurable variants."

"So, what do we do then, close the doors if we have a sentinel event?" Jason sneered. "I don't see Hopkins or Mayo doing that?"

"And I wouldn't sign on with you if that was my recommendation," Will answered evenly. "What I'm saying to you is that, traditionally, losing a patient every now and then to a medical mistake or an infection was considered regrettable but just the cost of doing business, and I'm saying we cannot and must not continue that attitude. You've never aimed for zero before, and that's where I intend to take you."

"Will," Jeff Wallace, one of the other male members of the board interjected, "we're no different than the vast majority of American hospitals in that regard. We try to get to zero, as you put it, but it's not that easy."

"Jeff, I would answer you this way: Dedicating the institution to zero preventable impacts is that easy, while actually achieving it is *not*. But if you don't adopt that focal point, you have absolutely no hope of getting close." Will looked down at the table for a few seconds in thought before reengaging them, his eyes traveling from member to member. "So, given the previous discussion, and answering as if it were your loved one being brought in here for serious care, are we a *safe* institution?"

No one answered, as Will had expected and he waited a few pregnant seconds before filling the awkward silence. "Four months ago a gentleman named Richard Simonson came in our doors under his own power, walked in on his own for a routine back surgery. But this quality institution—and I'm not mocking that determination—made a terrible mistake and did not use the appropriate procedures post-op to ensure that no hematoma was growing at the site of the otherwise successful surgery that was performed. As a result, a week later he was rolled out of here in a wheelchair, a newly condemned, lifelong paraplegic, his nerves dead from the hips down because of our mistake. Was that quality care? Mr. Simonson will never walk again, never play tennis again—which was his favorite sport—because we made a series of simple human errors in a system that was not adequately designed to catch those errors in time, at a hospital that had yet to consider less than 100 percent a crisis."

Many of the board members shifted uncomfortably in their plush chairs and Will took the opportunity to lock eyes with each of them again.

"I think," he continued, lowering his voice slightly and studying the one-page recitation of the Simonson disaster on the table before him. "I think we would be hard-pressed to get Mr. Simonson's wife and family, let alone him, to say that the care he received from Las Vegas Memorial was quality. And Mr. Simonson will remember us, and not in a good way, for a very long time."

"Will," Jason began, shifting forward in his chair, clearly offended that his stewardship of the hospital was being judged indirectly as flawed, "we know we're not perfect, and we never claimed to be and no hospital is, but that sort of tragedy is a very, very rare occurrence here."

"Jason, I apologize for pressing, but what if that were your son?"

"Yeah, yeah, I get that point! But we have to have tough skins to run a hospital and keep the funds flowing, and a few tragedies can't be reason to give up and get so misty-eyed that we can't keep our focus in the right place."

"But what is the right focus, Jason? That's my challenge to you. Traditionally, it's to keep the doors open, keep the docs happy and try to minimize the number of mistakes and patient impacts, as I call them. I'm saying we have to reconnect with the human values here in order to be guided to what really matters. Zero preventable patient impacts really matter, and whatever it takes to get there must be a core value. And, yes, we *do* need to get misty-eyed and very uncomfortable when someone gets hurt. Simonson wasn't a statistic; he is a father and a husband and his life has been deeply impacted, maybe even shattered. We could've prevented that from happening by better methods, better systems and a changed dedication."

The slight chill in the room had not hardened to rejection, but Will knew he was shoving them hard.

"Our basic statistics underscore what I'm saying very clearly.

We admitted more than fifteen thousand patients last year, and two of our patients lost their lives to medical mistakes. There were three wrong-site surgeries, a long list of prescription errors resulting in an additional twenty-six days of hospitalization and one lady left in a vegetative state because of a CT contrast mix-up in which detergent was substituted for contrast. So, yes, they're statistically rare. But they are the most devastating disasters on earth for those directly affected, and as any one such patient goes, so goes the reputation of Las Vegas Memorial. That's why I'm hammering this point. Because one of the marching orders you've given me is to restore the public's faith in this great institution, am I right?"

"Of course," Jason replied, looking around at other nodding members.

"Very well, and the way to do that is not with buying billboards and crowing about awards, but with an unshakable dedication to safety and quality that aims at zero errors."

"I think," another member began, "we need to know a little more about what changes you're contemplating, Will."

"And how much they'll cost, right?" He replied, smiling. "At least one order of magnitude less than what *not changing* will cost. In fact, I don't think it's an exaggeration to say we're fighting to keep this hospital open, and without substantial improvement, it will be far more than building campaigns that will be in trouble here. No, I'm not going to break the budget. In fact, much of what needs to be done has to do with attitudes, leadership, communication and changing a hidebound cottage industry culture into a true unified organization of like-minded professionals, and happy ones at that. You all know what Jack Silverman has accomplished at St. Michael's in Denver. My understanding is you want to follow that same path. Am I correct?"

"Absolutely! Look at his bottom line," Jason Baldridge said, coming partly out of his chair. "That's *exactly* what we want, Will! Smooth running, no sentinel events, unimpeded money flow and everyone happy."

The one member Will had been unable to engage shifted in her seat. A trim, elegant woman in her seventies with piercing green eyes, she had been quietly taking notes, and on occasion, almost nodding. But he'd been unable to get a word from her. Will pushed at his memory for her name. *Aggie...Agnes...Angela. That's it, Angela Siegel.* He looked at her now, and decided to take a chance that he knew her thoughts.

"Ms. Siegel? Do you agree that those are my marching orders? Is that the way I should view things?"

A shadow of a smile crossed her face and she leaned forward ever so slowly before answering. "If you mean, Dr. Jenkins, do I agree that virtually everything, including patient safety, should be measured in terms of economics, then I must say I most decidedly do not. I'm sure it's merely a matter of semantics and that neither Jason nor Sal ever meant to imply that dollars trump human service, but I am immovable in my belief that a hospital—whether a for-profit or a non-profit like us—is a massive public trust, the purpose of which is quite simply stated and quite simply lived: To do the best for the patient and enjoy this great profession in the process. I like your definition of patient-centric. We must make money only to maintain that mission, as I'm sure Jason and Sal meant."

Jason Baldridge had already shot Angela Siegel a mildly disgusted look. "Of *course* that's what I meant, Angela. But those who fail to watch the money lose their mission. No margin, no mission."

"Agreed. But we have a duty to never, ever, stop talking about that mission as if it alone was the most important element of the equation, which it is. After all, money is like gasoline. Anyone here want to own gasoline just to own gasoline? Of course not. We own it as a means to an end, propulsion. That's how this and all hospitals should regard money, as a fluid means of propelling the mission, nothing more."

"Thank you," Will began, but Angela Siegel wasn't done.

"That ranking you wrote, doctor...I should call you Will, and I'm Angela, of course...that chart is disturbingly revealing." She wagged a finger in the direction of the easel. "You asked, in effect, what we value, and what did we say? We said money. We value doctors bringing money. We value big new buildings raising public trust, in order to bring in more money. We value improving our reputation to facilitate bringing in money, and we are not happy with how much of our money nursing takes. We worry about how much of our money is leaking away insuring ourselves against having to pay our money for things we shouldn't have done wrong in the first place. That's money times six! And patient safety is ranked by us at number *eight?* Remember our discussion last month? What did we say? We said that keeping patients safe is a worry *not* because it's the right thing to do, or the publicly expected thing to do, or our responsibility to this community, or even because it's the only moral and ethical thing to do; we're sitting here concerned about keeping our patient's safe so we can minimize the impact of mistakes on our *money!*"

There was a long pause before she added a postscript. "Shame on us!"

An embarrassed silence settled over the group for a few seconds, and Will broke it at last.

"I have to tell you that when Angela says that we should approach the goal of making money only for the purpose of supporting our mission, I am in wholehearted agreement. If that does not fit what this board wants, then you may want to reconsider bringing me on. My contract may be signed, but I'll let you out of it with no penalty and no parachute if you feel you've made a mistake. But my task, as your incoming CEO, is not to just *remake* this institution to follow the lead of St. Michael's in focusing on the patient in word, deed and philosophy. My challenge is to align our philosophies in a way that will eventually have thousands of hospital leaders visiting us the same way they now flock to St. Michael's."

"So what is *your* number one goal, Will?" Sal Bertelli asked, fully expecting to hear the words safety and quality.

"Leadership."

"*Leadership?*" Bertelli challenged. "We hired *you* to lead, and given everything you've said here today, I'd have thought your first priority was patient safety?"

Will smiled. "Patient safety can't be a goal or a priority, Sal, as I said, or implied earlier. It can't be, because goals and priorities change. Patient safety has to be a core value so thoroughly ingrained in the DNA of this institution that it can never be shown a backseat to any other value, including finance. My task is to guide us with the greatest urgency possible to that status, and my number one priority in doing so is instilling true leadership throughout the organization. We can't accomplish safety and quality, or keep the doors open in a complex adaptive system without strong leadership. Not dictatorship, not perpetual consensus, but leadership. Concepts don't change a culture, *people do. leaders do.*

First, the leader has to use some form of top-down leadership to create a new norm, align and ignite the passion of his or her people, while simultaneously dismantling the parts of the old structure that perpetuate patient endangerment or low quality performance and outcomes. Only when the people who are Las Vegas Memorial are ready and able to shoulder these changes and own them will the cycle be complete. This is a seismic alteration in the landscape, and neither tactics nor strategies can take the place of leadership. Even the meekest person in the organization must possess the courage and support to stop the line in the most intimidating situations. Leadership is more than a role. It's our ethical responsibility—that is, if you really mean your mission statement. Does anyone think I have this wrong? Let's not waste each other's precious time, or spend our energy playing political games. I need to know I have your unwavering support, and you need to know that I understand with crystal clarity and unshakeable determination the philosophy we're going to use and the goals we're determined to accomplish. And I must have the assurance that any disagreements, upsets, or worries by this board will be brought to me immediately, openly and fully. I need us to succeed. If we're not in alignment, then you have chosen the wrong man."

"You have my full support," Sal Bertelli replied.

"I think we're very satisfied, Will. And impressed," Brent Roget said, looking around the room to the nodding heads of the other directors.

"And encouraged," Angela Siegel added.

"And terrified," another voice added meekly, "uncharted territory you know." Many of the group suddenly found the need to readjust in their seats.

"Okay. Thank you most sincerely. One more thing. One very

serious concern for any leader is whether or not he or she really knows what's going on in the ranks. It's very common for new leaders to feel like they've been issued blinders. No one wants to tell you the truth. I can't start like that; we simply don't have the luxury of time. From a strategic standpoint, what I need most is information, information that you can't provide. Only the folks on the front lines can tell me what I need to know, which is why I'm making an atypical, formal request. I asked Gary and Brent that no formal announcement be made for three more weeks that I'm coming aboard as your CEO. No picture of me, no rumors, no biography, no use of my name, nothing. In the meantime, even though I will not be a formal employee, I need board authorization to put on a formal ID badge falsely listing my position at Las Vegas Memorial as one of several different slots, as I see fit. I want to spend time going through employee orientation like a front line worker, sitting around on the units, spending time in the pharmacy, housekeeping, sterilization, the ORs, the ER and anywhere else I need to be to become intimately familiar with the beating heart of this great place. All I'm asking, basically, is that as captain of this ship, I have the opportunity to look below deck and assess the situation for myself. It won't cost you a dime; it's all on my own time. And it will *not* lead to anyone being dismissed the moment I take office, regardless of what I hear. May I have your approval on that?"

There was general nodding around the room but Gary Mason pushed it to a unanimous vote before Will continued. "Thank you. I also need to add to your educational workload as a board. First, I'm going to ask you to institute a formal and intensive program of board rounds, not just walk-throughs, but a program of having you individually come in and spend an entire eight or even ten hour shift somewhere in the hospital. I'll have recommendations for you in detail on how to set up the protocols, but this is a very important request. I also want to plan a formal off-site board retreat within the next few months, and I'd appreciate all of you planning to spend several days in Boston later this year in intensive board training with IHI and their Boards on Board program, in accordance with CMS recommendations because we will be seeking board certification in the future. I have to tell you, I expect to push each of you very hard, and I intend to ask you for the help only a board can provide."

The meeting adjourned with handshakes and positive comments as everyone dispersed. Angela Siegel was waiting for him at the end of the corridor, her large, silver purse reflecting a beam of sunlight.

"I want to talk to you, Will, sometime in the next week at your convenience?"

"I'd be delighted," Will accepted.

"It's important. Are you already in town?"

"Yes, we've rented a condo temporarily," Will replied, a bit off balance as he fumbled for a business card. "This card's from my Boise practice."

She nodded, turned and was gone, leaving Will searching for the one comment the previous CEO had made about Ms. Siegel. It hadn't been particularly complimentary, but the details escaped him.

The board chair, Gary Mason, was waiting politely several feet away as Angela Siegel pushed through the doors into the main hospital. He smiled and extended his hand to Will. "Well, Will, I'd say you really know what it takes to rally the troops! I had no idea this was going to be a working agenda."

"I'm sorry if I blindsided you, Gary."

"No, no! That's fine. You won them over, most of them anyway, and that's what counts. Sometimes overstating the case and making things sound worse than they are is a really useful tool. But I do have to warn you that no one will go along with that three day thing in Boston. I'm sure one of us will be willing to go to represent the rest, but, you know, these are really busy folks."

"Gary, let me ask you something very pointed. May I?"

"Of course."

"What part of my case was overstated?"

Chapter Four

"Maura," Karen said as she eyed her preceptee from behind one of the computers at the main nurse's station. "How are you doing?"

"Alright, I guess."

Karen sighed. It was 10:30 p.m. There was still so much work to get done before the end of the day that her head was spinning. She needed Maura. Besides, wasn't this Maura's third month of orientation? If she was going to be up and running independently in less than two weeks, she would have to complete the post-mortem competency.

"How about if I respond right now to the '*alright*' part, and you and I sit down and talk after the shift about the '*I guess?*'"

"OK." Maura replied, and then asked tentatively. "Is Mr. Markowitz still here?"

"Yes. He's been with spiritual care in the quiet room around the corner calling relatives. And here comes a real difficult part of our job. We have to go in there and ask him about donating his wife's organs."

Maura's eyes opened wide in an *Are you kidding me?* glance, but she said nothing.

"I have the forms right here and I thought you could look them over before we went into the room. We can't leave this for the next shift, and Mr. Markowitz will be leaving soon, so we have to hurry. Do you have your competency checklist on your clipboard?"

"Uh-huh."

"Great, I'm going to fill out an incident report while you are reviewing the protocol, procedures and form."

Just then Laurinda interrupted, "Karen, nine forty-eight needs something for nausea. She says she's going to throw up."

"Darn," Karen mumbled under her breath. "Laurinda, I paged the house float an hour ago. Did they ever call back?"

"Yeah, said they would be here, but I heard the rapid response team paged overhead a while ago and I bet they got sidetracked."

"Can you page them again? There should be two on today."

Karen jumped up to get the nausea medicine. "Maura, let me know if you have any questions about the form when I get back."

The form? Maura thought. *Questions about THE FORM? Hell, that's the least of my questions. How about, how do you talk to a grief-stricken man about something as sensitive as giving away his wife's body parts? How do you take a justifiably angry patient and make them happy or restore lost dignity? And most of all, when in the world does anybody eat around here?*

Maura forced her attention back to reviewing the organ donation guidelines and form. Five minutes later, Karen returned. "Ready?"

Just as Maura started to answer, the door to the quiet room opened and a teary eyed Mr. Markowitz emerged.

"Never mind, hurry. Just watch me this time," Karen shot out quickly.

This time!?!

Karen moved to Mr. Markowitz and put her hand on his shoulder, absorbing his words as he said almost under his breath, "I don't understand. She was fine this morning. I was talking to her on the phone on the way to my office. She wanted her…"

He looked down at his wife's glasses in his hand, now broken from his clenched fist, and collapsed in grief again. Hector, the spiritual care advisor, helped him make a u-turn back to the quiet room with Karen following.

"Why? Why?" he cried. "What happened?"

Karen knew Dr. Adams had already spent a half hour with the distraught husband on this topic. Not that Adams ever spoke to her, not one word.

"Mr. Markowitz, we don't know. But I promise you, we will find out. The autopsy you authorized will help tremendously, and as soon as we know something, Dr. Adams will call you. But right now, there are other people waiting for you and I need ten more minutes of your time."

"Other people?" he replied, confused.

"Yes, Mr. Markowitz, other people who are in hospitals right now waiting for hope; for organ donors. Do you know what your wife would've wanted you to do in this situation?"

"Yes, it's on her driver's license. We talked about it."

"I realize that this is a horrible time to have you deal with details when you are barely handling your own grief, but would it be alright if I asked a few questions so that we can follow your wife's wishes?"

Maura stood at the doorway as if a guard was suddenly required; she watched Karen's every move. She noticed how confident and professional Karen was under all the emotional strain, and was momentarily thankful that she didn't get stuck with Julie as her preceptor. Unhurried and sympathetic, Karen finished and extricated herself from the distraught man's presence, gathering Maura as she left the room. Laurinda's voice reached them in the hallway as they emerged.

"They're waiting for report on the new surgery."

Karen and Maura filed into the report room and Maura started, "Nine forty-two, Mrs. Peters. Oh my gosh, Karen! I forgot to tell you she needed a pain pill hours ago. My password wouldn't work in the computer." Karen jumped up in response, motioning for Maura to continue the report. Julie waited until the door shut before raising her eyebrows and then shooting a glance to another co-worker. Maura felt awful. *Two weeks. How was she ever going to be up and running and competent and confident in only two weeks?*

After report, Karen reviewed Maura's charting. They talked about a plan for remembering key information, as well as dealing with distractions, and how to handle computer glitches, and then clocked out with only thirty minutes of over-time.

"Don't forget to put in for the missed meals and breaks today," she reminded Maura, stopping to drop off the incident report in the manager's inbox.

"I think you'd have to remind me to actually *not* charge for missed meals, since that seems a lot more common around here."

Karen ignored the last remark. She didn't have the energy. Ever since the staffing grid changed last year because of Las Vegas Memorial's financial problems, it had been harder for all of them. Many staff had spouses who had lost their jobs, or college kids that couldn't find jobs, so the grumbling had for the most part gone underground. *And now, yet another CEO*, she thought as she passed the elegant etched glass doors to the C-suite. *Well, I'll survive this one just like I did the others. CEOs come and go, and I'll still be here when the next one leaves.* She chuckled; *I couldn't identify the last one in a police lineup even if I tried.*

Darn, Karen thought, getting into her car. *I forgot to talk to Maura about the 'I guess' comment she'd made.*

But hadn't she felt that way herself? *I guess* I did everything I could for Mrs. Markowitz. *I guess* Dr. Adams was mistaken. Who could feel certain about anything these days? Better to just keep hunkered down and focused on her own world.

Chapter Five

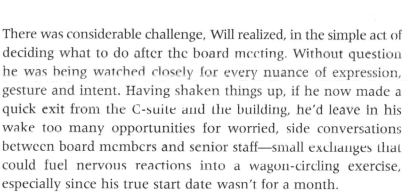

There was considerable challenge, Will realized, in the simple act of deciding what to do after the board meeting. Without question he was being watched closely for every nuance of expression, gesture and intent. Having shaken things up, if he now made a quick exit from the C-suite and the building, he'd leave in his wake too many opportunities for worried, side conversations between board members and senior staff—small exchanges that could fuel nervous reactions into a wagon-circling exercise, especially since his true start date wasn't for a month.

No, Will thought, *better to hang around for a bit,* although exactly where was the problem. The solution, he decided, would be a quick visit to the recently departed CEO's office—the one he expected to inherit—and with that decision he swung, turned and headed that way.

Seeing him approach, the attractive woman seated behind the secretary's desk stood up—and up!

Good grief! Will thought, *she must be at least six foot four!*

She looked down at him and smiled.

"Doctor Jenkins, I presume?"

"Yes," he said, returning her smile and shaking her hand. "And you must be Ivy Kessler. Good to meet you in person. I appreciate all the telephone coordination last week."

"That's what I'm here for. I appreciate your decision to have me continue on as your administrative assistant. Before I take you on a guided tour of your office, may I ask how you like to be addressed?"

"Addressed?"

"You know, every leader who is also a physician has his or

her preference, so I thought I'd ask. 'doctor?'"

He chuckled. "I think Will is sufficient."

"But, when others are present?"

"Then, 'doctor' is fine. Well, actually..." Will hesitated, mentally acknowledging the caution that had suddenly thrown his corporately-correct statement into doubt, "let me think about that one for a few days. But when it's the two of us, then Will, please."

"Thank you, Will."

"How about you? You prefer 'Ms. Kessler', or..."

"Ivy is great."

"Is that Ivy as in 'IV,' or Ivy as in the vine?"

"Well, now that you mention it, I *have* been dripping life into this institution for eighteen years, but the reality of my birth certificate is 'Ivy,' like a fine vine."

"So you like puns, I see. Then we'll get along just fine. It's important to have a sense of humor."

"I'll remember that," she said with a sly smile. "May I ask if there is a moving van in our future?"

"More like a U-Haul with a few personal items. There is a desk in my new office, right?"

"That's..." she paused, opening the inner office wide as she ushered him in, "the central feature."

"That's a huge desk." Will glanced around his office-to-be noting all the details.

"I know. You can actually hide under it until someone you don't want to see goes away."

He chuckled. "I'm not going to ask how you know that."

Will finished perusing and led Ivy back out to her office. She closed the ornate doors, turned and waited for his next move.

"Can we sit and talk for a minute?" Will asked.

"Should I get a notebook?" She inquired sitting in one of the chairs in front of her desk as he took the other one.

"No, no, just a few things I want to talk about early on; things about which I'm going to need your immediate help." Will outlined his anonymity request to the board and the need for various ID tags and clearances around the hospital. He was surprised when she nodded.

"Already taken care of, Will."

"Really?" He looked startled. "Has word already leaked?"

"No, no, no!" She replied, shaking her head to reassure. "Gary Mason swore me to silence and filled me in."

"Good. But here's the tough part. I have about a month to learn everything a CEO would normally not know about his hospital. How are you at being a clandestine tour director?"

"Well-l-l, I'm a bit too tall to be clandestine. Kind of like a giraffe in a preschool."

"No, I meant..."

"But I do have a higher perspective, so to speak!"

"I meant just getting me information and helping me understand the institution."

She nodded, smiling. "Understood."

"You understand I'm not interested in rolling heads?"

"Yes. But you need to know our history; who's effective and which silos are at war with each other, and which doctors can't be trusted to bandage a boil, right?"

Will smiled. "We're going to get along really well, Ivy."

"I thought so," she said reaching for a fat file folder held together by a thick rubber band he hadn't noticed sitting on the edge of the desk. "That's why I took the liberty of preparing a few things for you about the staff, the docs and the departments." He took the folder and thumbed through the hundred or more pages.

"A *few* things?" Will laughed.

"Oh, just a minute," Ivy said, jumping up and retrieving a single piece of paper. She gestured for him to return the folder momentarily, "I want to make sure this is completely up-to-date."

She stuffed a piece of paper into the "patient safety" section and changed a number on another form, before continuing. "For starters, I've prepared a suggested calendar for moving around the hospital, starting with an orientation class next week. A temporary laptop has been assigned, and it's ready along with the directions to security for your ID badge. And, I thought you might want a bit of private office time before you go today."

"I do. For one thing I need to talk to your old boss."

Joan Winston, the previous CEO, had been very helpful when Will had called prior to making his decision to accept Las

Vegas Memorial's offer. She'd briefed him extensively on each of the board members, and warned him that the board as a whole was at once well intentioned and largely ignorant of the depth of the challenge they faced.

"I could never get Mason past a certain point," she reiterated, as Will sat at his empty desk with a legal pad at the ready. "They're the old style board, Will, and they still believe that patient-centered and physician-centered are synonymous."

"Most definitely they're not," he interjected.

"Well, maybe as a physician yourself, you can get that across somehow. But, as I mentioned, your main challenge for patient safety, standardization and best practices will be the docs. I have to tell you that's ultimately why I decided to leave."

"The doctors were against you?"

"No, nothing that dramatic. They just…wore me down, I guess. Look, this may sound a bit sexist, but it's a boy's club there. The doctors, the board, all of them. Yes, we have some fine female physicians, and they work hard to be accepted by the boys, but ultimately, I just couldn't gain the boys' confidence enough to even convince them to take hand washing protocols seriously. You can imagine how futile it was to try for universal time-outs, central line bundles, or anything else that flew in the face of unlimited physician autonomy when they can't reach consensus on hand washing. Everything has to be a bloody vote, and if it's not 100 percent, they refuse to close ranks."

"I imagine you had your share of docs wagging their finger in your face and threatening to take their business elsewhere?"

She laughed, ruefully. "Only a few. But, see, that's all it takes to ruin everything—a few maximum resistors. I'm sure you've experienced that. Most of the docs are just wonderful, but they follow the leaders, and the leaders are the problem. And even when I told one particularly obnoxious surgeon not to let the door hit him in the ass when he threatened to leave, the board yanked the rug out from under me with Mason and Roget and two others bleeding all over my office that we couldn't insult such a great guy or afford to lose his revenue. I just grew weary of the never-ending battle, Will. And I respect you for trying to do what I couldn't, but I'm taking a year or more off with my family before even thinking about getting back in the game. It would try the patience of Job. No, actually, I think it would make Job homicidal."

"Can I call you from time to time for advice?"

"You certainly may. And I'll treat our conversations as privileged, if you'll do the same."

FROM: WILL.JENKINS@Northnet.com
TO: JACK.SILVERMAN@STM.org

Jack,

Just a quick note in lieu of an interrupting phone call. I toured the 'bridge' of this ship today—maybe I should call it a 'cockpit'—and I'm not forgetting for a minute your advice about constructive paranoia. I'll try not to lean on you too much for advice, but if you'll permit a periodic e-mail, it would help greatly. Any initial thoughts before I try to describe what the South Park class looks like up close when they're shocked and silent?

Will

FROM: JACK.SILVERMAN@STM.org
TO: WILL.JENKINS@Northnet.com

Call or e-mail me anytime, day or night, but (and I know you know this, but as a reminder) be careful not to accidentally reveal privileged information to me. I can always sign a confidentiality agreement for you as if I were an outside consultant. Happy to coach or mentor in any way.

Initial thoughts? Remember this quote and use it with impunity:
"The first accountability of a leader, is to know reality" ~Max Dupree

'South Park class,' huh? I can't wait to hear the details.

Jack
(Sent from my BlackBerry®)

Chapter Six

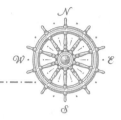

Karen Kinsey paused at her manager's door, hesitating a few seconds before knocking as a courtesy.

"What's up, Diane? I see I have a 'paper day' today."

Diane Martin smiled, forcibly ungluing her eyes from the long list of e-mails on the screen before her. Being a unit manager was more challenging than she had imagined. When they offered her the job a year ago, she had actually thought that she could make a big difference. But now, she didn't know what to think.

"I sent you an e-mail yesterday. Sorry for the late notice, but I had to wait until Dr. Adams could give me a time when he was available. We've scheduled the root cause analysis (RCA) into Mrs. Markowitz's death for noon today. The autopsy report finally came back last week. She apparently died from an internal bleed. The swelling was actually pockets filling up with blood."

"I tried to tell him that was abnormal. We *all* tried over twenty-four hours! The calls are all documented. We even insisted that he come and see the patient for himself."

"I know," said Diane, shaking her head. "I've read the entire chart three times now. So I'm prepared for the meeting, but wanted to give you the opportunity to do the same. The chart is over there on my table. Why don't you stay here in my office so you have some privacy or in case you have any comments or questions. I want to make sure we're on the same page. I was just about to head down for a latte. May I get you something?"

"Only if they have the valium-flavored kind," Karen replied, keenly aware of her sarcasm as she opened the chart.

The office door closed as Karen's mind engaged in a full blown review of the timeline leading to Mrs. Markowitz's death. The vast majority of patients did really, really well. So what the heck happened here? Complaints were rare and staff satisfaction was higher on this unit than others; after all, she had transferred here from the float pool specifically because the staff and the manager were so great. But she had to admit that part of her was resigned to the fact that stuff like this would happen once in a while. Why? Because it did.

Meticulously, she re-read her notes; recalling all too vividly the frantic call to the rapid response team. By then, of course, it had been too late. She'd even used the S-B-A-R tool for the third call to the physician and had explained it in the chart:

S—Situation: Mrs. Markowitz in room nine forty-four is experiencing abnormal swelling. This is our third call today.

B—Background: Thirty-five year-old female. Post-op day one from a tonsillectomy.

A—Assessment: She can only swallow liquids eighteen hours post-surgery. Vital signs are normal. Retro-pharyngeal swelling has increased steadily from this morning and we are concerned.

R—Recommendation: I recommend that you come in yourself and assess this patient immediately.

Response from MD, "Who? Marka-what? I've never seen this patient. I'm the on-call physician and the attending told me he just saw her himself four hours ago. Doesn't sound like there are any clinical symptoms. I'll be there when I get through in the ER."

In retrospect, Karen realized, she'd let herself be falsely reassured. *Still, hadn't she instructed Maura to keep a closer eye on the patient and asked for hourly vitals and pulse oximetry? Not that it made a difference. Mrs. Markowitz was still dead.*

Diane returned with two coffees in hand. "They had a special, so I got you a triple shot of steroids," she said smiling.

"So, can you beef me up before I come face-to-face with Adams?" Karen asked, trying to smile her nervousness away.

"I know he's not an easy doctor to deal with at times," Diane replied, "but he's a good physician. His patients love him, and he's very upset about this."

"We're ALL upset!"

For a moment, Diane couldn't read the expression on Karen's face. She seemed almost angry, yet...

"What's the matter, Karen?"

Karen sighed as she took measure of her boss and decided to roll the dice and bet on frankness.

"You don't have any idea what goes on out there. You're almost never on the floor anymore. Everyday feels like that Whac-a-Mole™ game at Chuck E. Cheese's™ where I took my granddaughter last week. I get to hammer a problem down every minute, only to have another one pop up somewhere else. I'm getting tired! If you don't believe me, follow me for a day and you'll see for yourself."

"I know. I wish I could," Diane said softly, pulling out her chair and sitting down to face Karen. "But you know what? *My* performance evaluation depends on my filling out a certain set of metrics, you know, like the thank you cards and rounding statistics. And I haven't gotten around to those all month because I've been doing other things, like the root cause analysis we're having today, performance evaluations, meeting with the union and then meeting with Maura at the end of her orientation. I already work twelve hours a day. I'd love to spend a day with you, but honestly, I just don't have the time."

Karen said nothing. Everyone knew the hours Diane put in and how hard she worked, and she was already feeling guilty for blurting out how she truly felt.

"I...I'm sorry. I didn't mean..."

"By the way," continued Diane, "I have a few incident reports filed by the night nurses on Maura. I thought you said she was doing a great job, but they paint a different picture. Any idea why she would have patient complaints about poor pain management and call light response and messy rooms? Or would you know why another nurse complained about almost tripping because the floor was so sticky? She *does* know how to page housekeeping at night, right?"

Chapter Seven

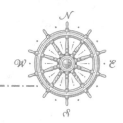

The immense size of the McCarran Airport terminal was always a bit overwhelming. It was the main artery pumping people and money into Las Vegas twenty-four hours a day—a constant pipeline of noise and urgency and human expectation. Will could feel his pulse accelerate as he once again walked from the parking structure into the terminal, looking for the portal from security that would shortly disgorge Janice on her latest return from packing and closing their Boise household.

She was already waiting—her flight ten minutes early—and she held him until he broke the embrace to guide her out to their car.

"How's the Undercover Boss thing going, Sweetie?"

"Lord, the stories I've heard so far. Had breakfast?"

"On a *plane?*" She laughed.

"Oh. Right."

They drove a few miles to a quieter section of town blessedly removed from the "Strip" and settled into a quiet booth at a restaurant Will had been frequenting too often at night with a legal pad. She looked at her husband as if handing him a microphone.

"Your turn."

"For effect, Honey, I'm tempted to just say, 'It's a mess!' But the startling thing is how little I apparently know of what life is like on the front lines these days."

"That deficiency is always common at the top, on the command bridge, so to speak."

Will looked at Janice and stifled the almost automatic urge to defend his management prowess. His respect for his wife's professional expertise in leadership had long pre-dated her foray into academics, but her assistant professorship over the last few years at Boise State had enabled her to provide deep insights based on research he would have never bothered to read. Will worked to suppress the otherwise incongruous smile that threatened to spread across his face at the realization that the majority of those revelations had come late at night.

"You remember that I attended rounds regularly as CEO in Portland?"

"Of course."

"I can see now it was ineffective in terms of reality. Every time I dropped by, they knew I was coming. I always thought it was a courtesy to let them know, but what those 'heads-up' notices apparently did—now that I look back—was ensure that I'd never hear the real story or see the real angst. I wasn't rounding for outcomes, as I now understand the concept. I was just looking around and showing the command flag, so to speak, and I rarely rounded alone back then either; I always had an assistant by my side. It wasn't a conscious shield, just the way we always did it."

"What, in particular, are you talking about, Will?"

"I'm talking about the difficulty of seeing the pressures these folks are under if you're not searching for problems and willing to make rapid improvements. Pharmacists, social workers, nurses, housekeeping, sterilization, dietary—the stories I get when they think I'm just a grad student trying to learn their realities, or an interested vendor selling a new product, or a visitor. They're massive eye openers!"

"Remember, Will, you married a management-savvy nurse. I tried to tell you back in Portland that your people were giving you overly rosy assessments and that there was no way you were seeing the real picture. But you bought their happy talk routine."

"I did. Because I thought we were different. I figured you were just remembering the dysfunctional nature of the places you'd worked before. I've always heard that old adage that if you've seen one hospital, you've seen *one* hospital."

"Completely false, Honey," Janice said. "They all have certain forms of dysfunctionality in common, from the C-suite to the front line."

"So here I am at Las Vegas Memorial, weeks into my own orientation, worrying about the strategic things I need to do in order to infuse a new view of patient safety and human failure and communication and collegiality—and the staff of this hospital are just hunkered down. I'm focused on strategy, and they're focused on surviving. I'm determined to change things profoundly and too many of them are equally determined to wait until anything new I introduce blows over."

"Like a Washington bureaucrat waiting for the political appointee to be replaced."

"Exactly. At times these past few weeks, I've actually felt terminally naïve, like I've been caught donating caviar to a soup kitchen. I've overheard so many conversations about hostile, unresponsive bosses, absent leadership, horizontal hostility; radiology at war with the hospitalists who are at war with the emergency room's leader over admission authority; sterilization's attitude that nobody gives a damn about their mission and on top of that their staff keeps being cut back; bed placement and throughput problems; stories about no one on duty in the pharmacy to watch an intern; the HR department patrolling the place like Nazis; I'm filling a couple of legal pads every day, and, of course, I can't come roaring back and throw people out when I takeover. But if this is a typical American hospital, we're in deep trouble nationwide. This is dangerous chaos."

"And, if that's what our Portland hospital was like..."Janice prompted as Will shook his head ruefully.

"It's amazing how much I've learned since then."

"Me, too," she added. "My focus on leadership in my MBA program was a direct result of watching your anguish."

His eyes were suddenly unfocused, "It's no wonder Ronnie died. This is far worse than herding cats, and that's before I even get to the doctors."

"So, good people are hunkered down in their own silos trying to survive the incoming artillery fire from financial pressures, job uncertainty, healthcare reform and now the threat of even more change with a new CEO."

He nodded. "How true. I already heard an earful, with exactly that phrase: 'So we're getting a new CEO. Big deal! They all bring in their own flavor-of-the-month. Every one of us has been leaned and meaned, tutored in smiles and 'sorries,' but in the end, nothing ever really changes. So whoever the new one is, we'll survive him, too!' That came from a very experienced nurse kvetching through lunch at an adjacent booth."

"So you're eavesdropping now?"

He smiled. "In the airline industry, they call it a situational awareness. Learning to just clam up and listen, even to adjacent conversations. I sat around the emergency room one evening just talking with the folks in the waiting room, and that alone was an upsetting eye-opener. The place is run specifically for the staff, not the patients, and clearly we have the wrong people and the wrong attitudes guarding the gate. But you were asking if I'd become an eavesdropper, I asked several of the techs where the staff goes for lunch and zeroed in on a small cafe a block away filled with scrubs day and night. If you quietly nurse a cup of coffee for an hour in one of the booths, you pick up all sorts of raw conversations. I promise you almost all of it is unknown at the C-suite level."

"So, how does all this new insight alter your plan of attack?"

"It makes me think I have to start out administering a large shock of reality and be a bit of a disciplinarian to get this house in order. After all, to be a transformational leader I have to blow up the old structure before building the new, helping *them* to build the new. And I won't have time as CEO to babysit dysfunctional attitudes. I mean, I can deeply sympathize, but I was sitting right here last night thinking, I'll squander everything if I start off micromanaging and handholding a hospital full of bad attitudes. On the other hand, if I don't respond to what's actually driving their discontent, then anything I do will eventually be sabotaged."

"They're crybabies, in other words?"

"Well...you're baiting me, aren't you?"

She chuckled. "That's what a good wife is for. Helping you see the obvious."

"What? What's obvious?"

"Honey, I know you know this, but let me put it back in perspective and in somewhat academic terms, from where I come from. There are two critical, primary concepts that have been virtually ignored here—concepts critical to creating a St. Michael's. The 'higher-ups' throughout medicine think of this as 'soft stuff,' so it falls off their organizational radar screen, but it's exponentially more powerful than anything else. Remember Maslow's hierarchy of needs? You can't ask for engagement and ownership—which are qualities of self-actualization—when the group is still wrestling with fear and survival. As you said, it's like sending caviar to a soup kitchen that's just trying to keep people alive, or sending a fine art exhibit to the front lines of an army that's critically short of ammunition. It's a dilettante's response, and a waste of energy—and it *will* fail. You have to deal with the basics, and that includes their ubiquitous fear. The first task for senior leadership is to know the true cultural reality no matter how scary, and then forcefully address it head-on."

"OK, so I know the cultural reality, and it sucks!" he said, mildly irritated.

"The second," she continued, leaning across the table, "is to create trust by eliminating fear. It's simply impossible to create the collegial teamwork you saw at St. Michael's at any level—the board, the physicians, or the hospital staff—until people know they're safe."

"Let me play devil's advocate here, Honey," he said. "We're talking about adults and professionals. I saw a lot of process messes and frustrations, but I'll counter your use of the word 'fear.' I can't say I saw that."

"You *wouldn't* see it because it travels as a powerful undercurrent, like an undertow that takes your organization way off course. My research confirms this syndrome. All the stuff you saw, those were the waves—some of them taller than others—like the tsunami physician on-call debate. You can plan for what you can see. It's what you don't see that drowns you."

"I guess I'm not really following you," he said, hailing the waitress for a coffee refill.

"Let me tell you a story, Will."

"You mean there's one I haven't heard?" he asked with a smile. "I mean, we've been married so long..."

She tried to suppress a smile as she swatted him. "Yes, there are few things I haven't told you."

"Really? A woman of mystery!"

"You have no idea! No, seriously, this concerns one of those big aha! moments CEOs sometimes get. A true incident from some research my team did last year."

"I'm listening."

"At a recent meeting of eight hundred fifty managers from seven different hospitals, I was talking about professional communication. I asked the participants: 'If I could guarantee you, *in writing*, that the conversation would turn out just the way you wanted, is there someone you would approach to have a conversation with; a crucial conversation that would create a healthier work environment for you, or your team?' Everyone in the room nodded. Then I threw them a curve ball. I pretended to rip up a piece of imaginary paper and asked, 'What if I didn't give you the guarantee? Imagine that person sitting across from you right now. How would you rate this conversation on a pain scale from zero to ten?' Everyone laughed as I described the pain numbers from one to ten. Of course, most CEOs don't attend manager level meetings, but this time, there was one CEO in the front row who'd brought his senior team. I then asked which of those contemplated difficult conversations, if they were held, would rate an eight, nine, or ten on the pain scale. At least 80 percent of the audience raised their hands, and when the CEO could see that the vast majority had their hands in the air, his jaw dropped. 'I had no idea,' he said afterwards, 'no wonder I can't make any great strides. No wonder I get to a certain plateau, and can never seem to rise above it.'"

Janice paused, searching his eyes to make sure he was listening carefully.

"You see, Will, he got a great gift that day—a dose of reality—first-hand knowledge that he was leading a fear based culture. But it's my studied contention that it's not just his hospital, it's the culture of all hospitals. That's why communication, or the lack of it, is the number one cause of error."

"So, what did he do about it?"

"He stood up and gave them a number to write down. He reiterated their mission, their philosophy and their goals and then guaranteed them safety because the phone number was his cell phone number."

"Did it work?"

"I don't know," she answered. "The paper is still in progress and we have yet to follow up with him. But I can tell you one thing for sure. The very first time someone does call him on his cell and is supported, that story will go viral in the organization—with rumors, e-mails or tweets, everyone will know it. His leadership gesture was a game opener, like singing the 'Star Spangled Banner' before the kick-off. And if he continues to sing it loud and clear, believe me, the team will all play their hearts out to follow, and they'll all be winners."

"I don't know how Jack did it," Will said somberly. "Seems like such a tremendous challenge. In some ways, I've marked it off to his being kind of a Knute Rockne or Tom Landry."

"Jack made sure he had the right people *and* the right number of seats *and* the right bus. He wouldn't even begin the journey without full board support, and he walked the talk in EVERY encounter."

"So did I," Will said, defensively.

There was a long pause. "No, you didn't Honey. You just believed you did. You saw what you wanted to see and chalked human emotions up to an HR problem or diplomatically handled referee call. Remember Dr. Epstein? Don't tell me you weren't aware of his demeaning behavior. Do you really think the OR staff felt safe to speak up to him after you had done little more than spank his hand?"

"Well, that was different."

"No, it wasn't. I remember your angst over him all too well. And remember what you told me Jack said? True success in creating a real team out of an entire hospital is measured from the point when there is no one left with the hospital's ID badge who would hesitate to speak up or take action when something critical needs to be done. I know that sounds like a fantasy, but it is achievable."

"Got it."

"And you're right. The word you're searching for is 'culture.' That's the name of the ship you have to turn."

"Lord, Janice. I know intellectually you're right but I still feel the need to fight it." He chuckled. "Maybe *you* should take this job and *I'll* stay home! I don't even know where to start."

"Yes, you do. You've been doing the right thing. You just need a little reassurance that it's the right course, and fortunately, you're living with a business professor who can reinforce everything you've been saying to these folks."

"You *know* about her?" He asked in mock horror.

"Yes, and I have to admit she's brilliant...and beautiful..." she swatted him again with a laugh, "and very long-suffering!"

"Poor girl."

"Seriously, Honey, you know what to do. Just continue the prime focus on leadership. You can't do it all by yourself, but you can, and you must, hold your leaders and directors and nurse managers, fully accountable for addressing every aspect of those feelings that have startled you so; that undertow that you felt pulling you when you finally stepped into the cultural ocean. For instance, the list you wrote out several weeks back?"

"Which one?"

"The codes of conduct to address disruptive behavior, peer evaluations for accountability, meaningful meetings that are multi-level and multi-disciplinary."

"Oh, yeah."

"You can't be everywhere, but your leadership structure can. And you are absolutely on target saying that they must be held fully accountable for enforcing a single standard and for eliminating the people who can't rise to the level of understanding and attitude required. This is the balance point between systemic structure and individual responsibility. Your greatest progress will be in making every member of this hospital a leader, and eliminating those who can't shoulder that burden."

"I had lots of those things at the Portland hospital. Or at least I thought I had."

Janice looked at her husband closely, noting the fatigue he was cheerfully hiding. Her week had been long as well, and the conversation was heading into deep water.

"Shall we go?"

"Sure," Will agreed, digging in his pocket for the tip.

"Class dismissed until tonight after dinner."

FROM: JANICE.JENKINS@Northnet.com
TO: JACK.SILVERMAN@STM.org
SUBJ: Second Installment of the Vegas Saga

Jack,

Will is three weeks into his "Undercover Boss" exercise and it's educating him brilliantly on the true scope of the problems at LVM, as you would expect. We had a detailed talk last evening and I told him something that I know is boiler-plate correct in any management/leadership context, but I want to elicit your insight as to the task at hand here of recreating St. Michael's. Will spoke of the fear and the disconnection he had found among the front lines, and I told him that there were two basic concepts that have obviously been ignored here:

One: You can't ask for engagement and ownership when people are wrestling with fear and survival. Senior leadership has to know and acknowledge the true cultural reality and forcefully and honestly address it head-on before ownership or even engagement can be created. Here, leadership has been unaware of the visceral fear.

Two: You cannot create the trust necessary to focus everyone on owning a common goal unless you address and dissipate the fear.

Am I correct that St. Michael's would not be what it is today if you'd left any fear in the ranks?

Also, we discussed the fact that in Portland, Will rounded constantly with an assistant and never realized that it was a form of "drive-by" rounding that did little or nothing to build relationships. He's seeing that with great clarity now in this undercover role, and by a form I describe as "management by sitting around" and spending real time with the people, even anonymously he's building trust.

Thanks ahead of time for your feedback.

Janice

Janice,

You are absolutely right. Without trust, all the changes we needed to make would have been DOA, and there was no way to get trust without a uniform standard of conduct, and a straightforward willingness by me and every leader in the hospital to honestly (and without defensiveness) address any concern or upset with one idea in mind: How do we change things systemically so as to achieve our common goal. Even the process of clearly agreeing on a common goal depended on creating trust. And it is also correct that you can't order people to trust you, nor order them to shed their fear. You have to earn it as a leader, not a commander.

Great to hear about your conversations.

Keep me informed.

Jack

Chapter Eight

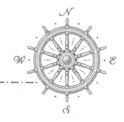

"I guess I should've listened," Dr. Adams said without a trace of emotion. The root cause analysis meeting was coming to a close and he was just as anxious to leave as he had been reluctant to come. Diane Martin, the unit's nurse manager, cleared her throat and locked gazes with Dr. Adams. *Come on,* her eyes shouted, *you know as well as I do that that isn't enough!*

"OK," he said, responding out loud to her non-verbal cue. He began slowly, "I should've listened to the intensity and obvious concern of the nurse for the patient, but I brushed it off as being a reactionary response. After all, they usually are."

The non-verbal racquetball game continued as Risk Manager Sandy Keaton rolled her eyes at Diane signaling, *He's hopeless! It's useless!* Quickly, Sandy re-gained her composure, solemnly announcing that it was time for them to wrap up the recommendations so that *this* would never happen again.

Abruptly, Dr. Adams stood up, and turned to leave. "I have surgery in twenty minutes and I have to scrub in. I think we're done with my part here."

But just as he reached the door, a small voice replied. "No, Dr. Adams, I don't think so."

Every head in the room turned to see who the voice belonged to, the petite woman who had said absolutely nothing for the entire meeting. Maura Manning.

"Pardon me, missy?" Dr. Adams said, surprised that anyone would challenge him.

"I said, I don't think so. I am a new nurse here, and I worked with Karen that terrible shift. I saw everything: the phone calls, the code and for the rest of my life I will never forget the first time I zipped a human being into a body bag. And to tell you the truth, if I am ever in a similar situation in the future, I don't have any confidence or reassurance—especially based on this meeting—that you won't react exactly the same way you did then, and are now. Intimidating."

Well! Little Maura! Karen thought, proudly. *My Maura found and shot the elephant in the room!*

Dr. Adams walked over to Maura and, towering over her, boomed in the most intimidating baritone he could produce: "Just who do you think you're talking to? Do you have ten years of medical training? Well? Do you? *DO YOU?*"

When she said nothing in the two seconds he gave her to respond, he glared and roared, *"Well then, just shut the hell up!"*

Diane jumped up, signaling for the doctor to sit down again, but Dr. Adams all but knocked her back into her chair as he stormed out of the room.

No one spoke for several uncomfortable seconds.

"Maura, you said what we all wanted to say. That was an excellent demonstration of leadership," Diane said.

"That took great courage." Karen added.

"What courage?" asked Maura, confused. "It doesn't take much insight to see that my next patient may very well end up in the same predicament and that he never listens to you, and that your concerns about the patient were completely ignored."

"I should've called the rapid response team sooner," said Karen soberly. "But the last time I called, he acted like I was a hysterical female."

"He's just as upset at this as we are," Diane explained.

"But that's not an excuse for his behavior, is it? I thought people were supposed to treat each other with respect at Las Vegas Memorial, at least that's what they said in orientation; that you have a code of conduct, and that your mission and values statement said something about respect?"

"Maura," interjected Karen, "being new has its advantages. You don't know the personalities and you're not encumbered by the history. You can see us more clearly than we can ourselves; but it also has its disadvantages in that you can get into trouble if you don't watch it. Dr. Adams can, well, make your life miserable."

"He makes *my* life miserable," said the pharmacist from the sidelines. Everyone was relieved that someone new had jumped in and they waited for more of an explanation. Mark Jacoby had been the head pharmacist at Las Vegas Memorial for more than a decade. He was a quietly assertive man, always publicly advocating for patient safety and following up on unit problems, but privately depressed that after three years of lobbying, he still could not obtain the funding for something as primary as barcoding and an additional pharmacy tech. "Adams is still giving me a hard time for even suggesting that we have pharmacists and doctors rounding together."

But before the conversation could veer off any further, Sandy Keaton pulled the meeting back to order, "OK, let's stay on track now." She reviewed the recommendations, acknowledged the difficulty of the situation, and thanked everyone for their participation.

Karen left the room aching with guilt about not calling the rapid response team sooner—or escalating her concerns to the CMO. Diane literally ran to a budget meeting because she was twenty minutes late, while Mark looked around for someone who would listen to the rest of his story. Maura just sat for a moment and did a quick reality check. Everyone was acting like the scene with Dr. Adams never even happened—or like it happened all the time.

Meanwhile, Sandy was jotting down final notes on the root cause analysis, pleased that the meeting had gone so very well (except for that minor glitch), and that she was finished before three p.m.

Chapter Nine

The small, family-run Italian restaurant Brent Roget had suggested in the Las Vegas suburb of Summerlin was less than five minutes from the two bedroom condo Will and Janice had leased. Will thought back through Ivy's briefing on Dr. Roget—his two decades at Las Vegas Memorial, his time as chief medical officer and chief of surgery, his election to the board, his grandchildren, likes, dislikes, country club memberships—her thoroughness had been startling and he'd complimented her.

"Thank you. I fancy myself somewhere between Abby on *NCIS*, and Brenda Leigh Johnson of *The Closer*."

"You would've done the CIA proud."

"Oh, I didn't tell you about that affiliation, huh?" Ivy had raised an eyebrow then winked. "Dr. Roget, by the way, was an Army doc in Vietnam. He's a purple heart, wounded twice, and he's still fighting the war, just so you know. He hates hippies, the so-called peace symbol and Jane Fonda—in that order."

"Got it."

"And loves Jack Daniel's Black Label®."

"Okay, Ivy! Enough! I'm dreading your report on *me* and I haven't even started working with you yet."

Brent Roget was waiting for him as Will emerged from his Land Rover precisely on schedule.

"So this is what they drive in Boise?" he said with a smile. "I think the kids would call it your 'sweet ride.' I've always wanted one of these to ramble around the desert, but I'll probably never get there."

"You're retired now, Brent! Go for it."

He shook Will's hand with a firm grip, "Yeah, well, we have this new young whipper-snapper of a CEO at the hospital, you see, and he says he's gonna work my tail off as a board member. No time to play in my future."

"I need to meet that guy!" Will said, jokingly.

"Yeah," Brent added, picking up the ruse. "Invite the kid to dinner sometime and see if he likes whiskey and fine cigars."

"I will, I have and he does."

They pushed into the restaurant, Will noting the immediate appearance of the owner and his deferential treatment of Brent as he escorted them to a booth where a bottle of fine Chianti was already waiting.

The first fifteen minutes of conversation, Will surmised, was much like two friends sparring in a boxing ring—probing, punching lightly, weaving and dodging with no concerns about real battle—then digging in by mutual agreement to learn more substantial lessons about each other.

And suddenly Dr. Roget was ready to focus.

"I like you, Will. But you didn't suggest a dinner to discuss baseball teams and my war service. You have the helm of Las Vegas Memorial as of next week, we're deep in the woods and we're expecting you to lead us back to the sunshine, so to speak. You took no hostages in our first formal meeting," he paused and chuckled, "and, actually, I rather enjoyed watching you scare the crap out of old Mason. He can't handle unpredictability. But the most important thing is that you need every one of us on the board completely aligned with you, and for my part, that means I want to know straight up what you need from me."

"Information, to start with. You know the physicians, and I have to know as much about the key doctors as possible. Who are my saboteurs, who are my early adopters and innovators and who are the maximum resistors?"

"Oh, well, that's pretty easy. It's the usual lineup of talent, and, yes, we have a few old curmudgeons who bark a little, but even they want to do the right thing."

"You were medical director, CMO, for what, eight years?"

"Yes."

"Did they treat you like most medical directors when you

took the job, like you'd crossed over to the dark side?"

He chuckled. "Oh, that old saw. Sure, some kidded me, but I could always jawbone or arm-twist them back into some form of harmony."

"One hundred percent hand washing, for instance?"

"Ouch!" Brent replied, sitting back slightly as he swirled and sipped his wine. "In truth, Will, that initiative came up a few years after I retired."

"But, if you *were* still CMO, how would you handle it today?"

"Fair enough. I'd certainly be more proactive than Kirk Nelson, our interim CMO, not that Kirk isn't doing a good job, mind you. I'd get out my Rolodex and start calling the guys and gals in for a little heart-to-heart in my office."

"Starting with those who refused to comply?"

"Well, the main ones: the surgeons first, then the general physicians that the rest of the group respect the most, and then the heads of the different physician groups."

"So what would you do then, Brent? Ask them to comply, or lay down the law and order them to comply or be thrown out?"

"You never get anywhere using a stick on doctors, Will. You know that. You're a doctor and you were a CEO before."

"Brent, I don't want you to get the idea that I think the only thing I have to address are our physicians and their compliance. I'm acutely aware of the myriad of other non-physician issues we face. But physician leadership is paramount in so many aspects of patient care that I decided that coming to you for guidance and insight on these points was vitally important."

"Understood. I mean, of course we have a few doctor issues, but for the most part, we have reimbursement issues, government and regulatory issues, infrastructure issues, nursing issues and pharmacy and housekeeping problems We're facing Nevada legislative issues, money leaking out in all directions and gross failures of staff to adhere to the procedures already in place. And, we have this cockamamie new federal push for accountable care organizations, whatever they're supposed to be."

"Back to what you said, though," Will prompted, "about not using the stick on doctors. As CEO, and not CMO, I had to draw lines in the sand on several points in my Portland hospital, including hand washing and abusive behavior. And I had to summarily dismiss a few guys when they arrogantly crossed that line, and essentially challenged me on who was going to make those overall best-practice calls. Those suspensions worked very predictably, although it didn't make me too popular, to say the least. But it's the stampede principle. When a herd is stampeding in the wrong direction, you shoot a few of the leaders to stop or turn the stampede. A hundred and fifty years ago they figured that out in the Wild West."

"Well, we're actually sitting here in the old west, but that principle concerned cows, not doctors."

"That concerned cows *and* bulls, Brent, and we physicians will follow a stampeding leader just as faithfully as a herd of cows. Right?"

"Hmm. Okay, it does seem like that at times, but I still think you get more compliance with reason and cajoling."

"Brent, a very direct question: If you were CMO today, would you be able to get 100 percent hand washing compliance, acceptance of indisputable best practice bundles and zero disruptive incidents primarily using cajoling and reason?"

"You are direct, aren't you?" he said, his chuckle a bit forced as he examined his plate a few seconds before answering. "You can never get 100 percent alignment from doctors, Will. And that's not what a hospital is here for. We provide the tools a doctor needs, and we have to be compliant with their needs. Oh, sure, we can ask really forcefully that they comply with important stuff, like those IHI bundles to prevent central line infections, for instance. I believe in those, too. But the doctors are our primary *customers*. Forcing doctors to waste their time aligning with aviation's view of the world by using checklists, or...or forcing them to go to charm school so they never upset some whining, overly-sensitive nurse, I think that distracts them from their primary mission of taking care of the patients."

"But leaving our fellow physicians to do what they want has been the standard, and we're still killing twenty-two patients per hour, on average, twelve years after the Institutes of Medicine (IOM) report. How can we justify that?"

Brent Roget smiled and leaned back slightly, as if regarding a slower-than-average resident. "Will, come on. There are inherent risks and a lot of sick people in hospitals. We've all had to walk over dead bodies in this career, and that won't change anytime soon."

"The numbers don't incite you to change?"

"Oh, to improve quality, certainly. But that twenty-two per hour stuff is the kind of scare tactic pushed by the same doomsday politicos who want us to think the atmosphere is heating up and the sky is falling. You really shouldn't parrot unscientific figures like that."

"Brent, that figure equals 192,720 deaths per year, and several very authoritative papers in the past year place the figure significantly higher."

"Well, I think it's all overstated and misses the point."

"Do you agree with the studies that say that serious disruptive behavior by a physician or nurse directly imperils patient safety?"

"Again, it's probably a bit overstated, but I do agree it distracts and disrupts people and can cause them to not pay attention to what they're doing."

"If you were CMO again, how would you handle a disruptive doc who yelled obscenities at a nurse?"

"Oh! I got a call from a very upset senior physician just this week, one of our best, who was enraged about a tiny little incident and some upset nurse who was raising hell—something that got blown way out of proportion. I called Kirk Nelson and he took care of it just like that. Just took a little talking to the doc and he's just fine again, and he promised to behave in the future. See? No need to take draconian action. If they'd handed it to the HR department, there would've been all sorts of unnecessary hullabaloo. When I was CMO, one of my best contributions was to keep our guys and gals away from HR. I sometimes wish for the good old days before we started employing physicians and all physician dealings were through the department of medical affairs that reported to the CMO"

"You're speaking of Dr. Adams, I presume?"

"Well, obviously you know the story. Yes."

"Would you define how you see a 'patient-centric hospital,' Brent?"

"Well, I'd say it's one in which, as you said, everything is subordinate to the best interests of the patient."

"And who determines, ultimately, what those best interests are?"

"The only way it can be done in medicine, Will. The physician makes that decision. It can't work any other way."

"The hospital, as an institution, has no say?"

"Well, of course, the hospital provides guidelines and education, but ultimately nothing can be allowed to intercede between the doctor and the patient, which means the doc's decision has to be determinative."

"You are aware that there are a growing number of physicians who disagree with you?"

"I know. Some of them are women entering the profession, and they have a different point of view. Some of them are just docs who've been beaten down by the system. But the heart of medicine is, and will always be, the physician."

"Brent, as a member of the board, are you willing to support me without hesitation in using a different approach? One that involves nurturing the early adopters who understand that compliance with known best practices aligns with what the experts and researchers—and the lawyers we love to hate—tell us is the only safe and ethical way for a hospital to proceed? Will you support me in a major realignment of Las Vegas Memorial's attitudes, so that *we*, as a team and a family, make the final decisions about the things that can't be negotiable, including indisputable best practices like the National Quality Forum's Centers for Medicare and Medicaid Services (CMS)-adopted list; zero tolerance for bad conduct from anyone, docs included, with specific consequences for violation; and commitment to the idea that when an MD walks into our building, he or she becomes Las Vegas Memorial, not a separate practitioner using a farmer's market stall?"

Brent sat back against the plush upholstery of the booth and regarded Will as if seeing him for the first time. He nodded and glanced away for a second, twirling his wine glass before locking eyes with Will again.

"On the doctor bad conduct thing, I will never agree with the idea of sanctioning a good doctor because someone got their little feelings hurt, okay? You can forget my supporting that kind of affrontive nonsense, because it will lead to bankruptcy. We have other hospitals in this big town, and they'll suck up the docs we insult in an instant, and take the thoracic, the orthopedic and the neurosurgical revenue with them. I don't know if you've studied the spreadsheets enough, Will, but you drop about twenty million worth of doctor driven revenue from Las Vegas Memorial and we're on the edge of bankruptcy."

"I've studied them incessantly for the past few weeks, but I also know what one bad result can bring legal costs and reputation loss equal to or greater than twenty million."

"Misbehaving docs are a tiny fraction of your challenge, Will. I'd advise you to not get too focused on that. It's a side issue."

"But to engage you on just that issue, Brent, ancillary though it may seem, if I could show you the irrefutable research that one single, solitary rogue physician has a direct, measurable and exponential negative impact on patient safety, staff retention, quality of service and the bottom line, all at the same time—not to mention losing nurses at a cost of approximately seventy to eighty five-thousand dollars per departure—would you be willing to reconsider the idea of being lenient versus a zero-tolerance policy? I know it's not the way that we've always done it, but we're talking hard figures and hard consequences for our patients now as a scientific certainty."

"Well..."

"I agree with you that the physician's decision should be the most respected and honored in medicine, but the decisional base for physicians has to rest on what the science tells us are the correct ways of doing things, and what the law will require of us. The science confirms that allowing one disruptive physician to continue undisciplined, without serious consequences, hurts our patients exponentially and out of proportion to the event, and it also shows that a mere talking to seldom, if ever, changes conduct. Would you make any other decision if you knew that science?"

"For every study, Will, there's an opposite study."

Will smiled, his eyes locked on Brent's. "I had a doctoral friend of mine named Al Diehl hang a sign on his wall that said

'For every PhD, there's an equal and opposite PhD.' But you see, in this case, there is no equal and opposite study. This is hard fact. I'll send you the papers this afternoon, but let's shift gears for a second. I've been trying to win you over by logic and reason and in doing so opposing everything you held to be true as a CMO and a physician in terms of tactics, and you're being very gracious and tolerant of me. But let's start with our points of agreement. We're in absolute agreement, aren't we, that our most important job is producing the best outcome for our patients?"

"Damn right! Absolute agreement."

"Okay, so any disagreements here are over the means by which we deliver that goal. Physician conduct, acceptance of best practices, feeling of ownership when a doc walks in the building, all those are questions of how we get there."

"That's fair."

"And when we shift to talking about ethics and morality, that aspect of wanting the best outcome for our patients doesn't change a bit."

"Of course not. But where are you going with this, Will?"

"Do you have kids, Brent?"

"Yes. Four. They range in age now from twenty-five to thirty-six, two boys and two girls."

"What's the name of your youngest?"

"Katherine. Why?"

"Okay, bear with me, please. God forbid, but your BlackBerry corks off right now. Katherine is in town and is suddenly very ill and needs to be rushed by ambulance to a hospital. Her condition is very serious, and she may well need immediate surgery. Let's not specify what for."

"Well, I'd be scrambling out of this chair, I can tell you that!"

"Of course."

"I gotta tell you I don't much care for personal hypotheticals."

"Understood, but I'm using your daughter for exactly that reason, because it's uncomfortable. May I continue?"

"Yes."

"Here's the hypothetical question, Brent, and I would truly

appreciate a completely candid answer. Let me set this up carefully. Knowing what you know about the unacceptable state of infection control at Las Vegas Memorial; knowing what you know about the few curmudgeons on staff but accepting, for the sake of this example, that their toxic effect on the people they work with and everyone around them when they get ticked off is dangerous; knowing the data on our sentinel events; knowing what you know about our failure to adhere to best practices in those areas that are well established, knowing what you know so well that few of our doctors talk to each other and coordinate their care even when they share the same patient; let's say you're given a serious choice. If you tell the ambulance driver to bring Katherine to Las Vegas Memorial, there is a special requirement only for Brent Roget. At any other hospital in town, you can be the good father and the wise doctor and monitor every aspect of whatever care she needs. But, if you have her taken to Las Vegas Memorial, you cannot interfere or influence her care in any way, and, therefore, any surgeon, any hospitalist and any doctor on staff may be involved in taking care of her, triaging her, opening her up in an operating room and trying to fix whatever's wrong and monitoring her recovery, if she makes it. If any doctor could take care of her at Las Vegas Memorial with zero input from you...and absolutely no one could be told that she was Brent Roget's daughter, would you still send her to Las Vegas Memorial?"

TO: Brent.Roget@LVM.com
FROM: Will.Jenkins@Northnet.com

Good to spend a few hours with you this evening, and I very much appreciate your time and candor. If every conversation with a board member is as substantive and honest as ours was tonight, I have no doubt that we can start turning this ship.

Here are the references I mentioned:

1) From a segment on the NPR radio show, "This American Life."

Dr. Will Felps, a professor in the Department of Organisation and Personnel Management at Rotterdam School of Management, speaks of conducting a sociological experiment demonstrating the surprisingly powerful effect of bad apples on other people's behavior. A written summary of the experiment can be found at:

http://www.illuminaregroup.com/one-bad-apple-does-spoil-the-whole-darn-bunch/

And the audio track of the interview is available at:

http://www.thisamericanlife.org/radio-archives/episode/370/ruining-it-for-the-rest-of-us?act=0

2) Dr. Gerald Hickson & Joseph Ross published a paper entitled: "Strategies for Reducing Unnecessary Litigation: Tort Reform and Professional Accountability."

3) Christine Pearson and Christine Porath co-authored the book *The Cost of Bad Behavior.*

And for insights on our own MD culture, my vote for THE definitive work is: *Inside the Physician Mind,* by Joseph Bujak

And to get an excellent overview of what fee-for-service has done to us in promoting greed, check out *Overtreated,* by Shannon Brownlee.

I hope you enjoy them.

Sincerely,

Will

Chapter Ten

Sandy Keaton was pleased with how smoothly the day was running. With the RCA meetings finished she would have just enough time to run up to Nine East and visit her mother before giving her monthly report to her boss. Currently, she reported to the CMO, but there were rumors that the entire organizational structure would change when the new CEO came aboard. Then, she would probably be reporting to the new VP of quality, whoever that might be. Her performance evaluation last month had reflected her own feelings about her work. Risk management was a perfect fit for her meticulous nature and inquisitive mind, and after five years, she felt confident in her role.

She re-applied some mauve lipstick and swept her unruly blond hair up into a barrette using the mirror behind her office door, surprised that she didn't look worse after the emergency phone calls from her father in the middle of the night and the missed shower this morning. But just as she was heading out the door, the phone rang.

"Sandy? Hi, it's Jose from Customer Service. I have a lady on the phone who is very upset about her hospital experience here a month ago. I can usually handle these calls, but she's, well, angrier than most. Do you have a few minutes to talk to her?"

This was the part she hated the most. These calls *never* took a few minutes and always left her feeling hopelessly out of control.

"Look, Jose, my mom was admitted early this morning and I'm just heading up to see her now. Can you just give me her name and number and I'll call her back in the morning?"

"Well, sure, I guess. It's Mrs. Madeline Peters," he said, passing her the number. "But you really need to call her in the morning because that's one of her complaints, people not following through."

"Sure, I understand."

"Look, Sandy, I can tell you have a lot on your mind today, so I'll send you a reminder e-mail in the morning as well."

"That would be great, Jose. I really appreciate it. Thank you."

She rushed to catch the closing elevator door but Terri Morales, the manager of the OR, stuck her hand out to keep it open. "Oh, Sandy! I've been hoping to run into you. I'm glad you came by when you did. Did you make any progress on getting leadership aligned with the physicians for time-outs? We literally have 90 percent of the surgeons doing time-outs correctly, but you know as well as I that it's the other 10 percent that are the next potential sentinel event. I've done as much as I possibly can without back-up from administration."

"I brought this up to my boss last month, Terri, and I'm meeting with him again today, so I promise you, we'll get you some answers."

"I don't need answers," said Terri in frustration. "I need support. I need to know that they have my back when I stop a surgery. And the preference card situation is getting out of control."

The elevator doors opened to the ninth floor. "Got it," Sandy said convincingly, although she was just a hair shy of 'losing it' when it came to battles with the surgeons. If her father wasn't a physician, she wouldn't understand them as well as she did. Only after the elevator doors had shut did Sandy realize that Terri's main purpose for the elevator ride was to talk to her.

Diane was apparently still in the budget meeting and Karen was now at the shared governance meeting. She looked around for a familiar face.

Good. Charles.

Charles was the charge nurse for the evening shift and was heading to the copier machine to make copies of the assignment when Sandy intercepted him.

"Well hi, Sandy. What's up?"

"My mom is in room nine fifty-four, Charles, and I want to make sure she has an experienced nurse tonight. She won't be going to surgery until after five p.m."

Charles looked down at the assignment sheet, glanced at his

watch and winced internally. There was no way he was going to re-do the assignments after all the energy he'd already put into making it fair and balanced! He'd just finished five minutes ago when Eleanor started complaining that she had to walk too far, and it was her fourth night on in a row and whah…whah…whah. No way.

"She has Laura tonight. Laura is really nice, and I'll tell you what, Sandy, I'll watch over your mother myself. I'll check in on her frequently and besides, she is going to be gone for more than half the shift. So when she comes back, I'll recover her." That was decidedly not what Sandy had wanted to hear, but Charles was tall and strong and using his, 'For you only. Today only!' voice.

"OK," she replied reluctantly, "but I'm still going to leave a note for Diane."

Sandy headed down the hall, literally following the nursing assistant into her mother's private room.

"Hi, Mom!" she said cheerfully, giving her mother a big hug as the assistant calmly waited to wrap the blood pressure cuff around Mrs. Keaton's left arm. Sandy saw her mother every week at Sunday dinner, and called her every single morning. As an only child, they were each other's world. Sandy smiled at the huge bouquet of flowers that she had ordered from the gift shop earlier. The long stem coral roses were beautiful, and her mother's favorite.

"You shouldn't have," her mother was saying, "but thank, you honey."

Abruptly recalling the hand washing stats for Las Vegas Memorial, Sandy turned to the nursing assistant. "My name is Sandy. And yours?"

"Megan."

"Nice to meet you, Megan. Could you please wash your hands?"

Megan looked surprised, then defensive. "I already did."

"OK, then. Would you mind washing them again, or using the alcohol gel, since we didn't see you wash your hands?" Megan was not happy. Instead of responding, she flounced to the gel station, her overly dramatic gestures communicating her retort loud and clear: *FINE! So I'll do this all over again just to waste my time and make YOU happy!*

Mrs. Keaton was sleepy from the pain medicine, so Sandy took her cue.

"How about if I come back after my meeting, Mom?"

"That's fine dar…ling," she answered, eyes already closed.

Quickly, Sandy scribbled a note to Diane and taped it to her door before leaving.

The CMO's office was on the administrative wing with the CFO, CEO and COO's offices—the C-suite as they were collectively called with little affection. Wanda, the secretary, waved Sandy right into Dr. Nelson's office. He always had a way of making her feel so welcome, standing up when she entered just like her father who was the consummate gentleman. She pulled the leather-bound side chair closer to the desk as was their custom.

"Hello, Sandy, how are you today?"

"Fine," she said, "but my mom's here in the hospital and she's going to have surgery today. She fell and broke her right hip last night."

"Oh, I'm sorry to hear that. Then we'll make this brief. I can see you have all the stats for the month compiled; I'll look those over later. Anything else I should know?"

"We just had another sentinel event and I finished the RCA today. The information is in your file. As you already know, there have been two deaths this year—and this latest one makes it three—but that's better than last year. I'm hoping all the initiatives we have going around here will make a significant impact in the near future. Anyway, the autopsy on this one showed a bleed. The nurses saw abnormal swelling. Dr. Adams did not respond to the nurses' concerns and the nurse was intimidated into believing her concern was trivial so she didn't escalate it." A part of Sandy was amazed that the more than two hour RCA meeting could be boiled down to only four sentences.

"Let's talk about that next month after I review the chart and RCA summary. What else is on your front burner today?"

"I need your support in mandating 100 percent compliance with time-outs and decreasing the number of preference cards. As of now, the nurses have three preference cards for colonoscopies alone: one physician wants the gel on the tube, another on the chuck pad and the third wants his gel on a four by four."

"Sandy, that topic's much bigger than me; why don't we wait until the next CEO takes the helm and see what happens there, ok?" Dr. Nelson shifted in his chair uncomfortably. "Anything else?"

"Yes, actually," Sandy wondered if she should even bother opening this door again. She felt like she was stuck in the movie, "Groundhog Day," with the same scene playing over and over again with absolutely no hope of the movie ever ending. No matter how many clever variations of this topic she tried, nothing ever changed. Six months ago Adams had acted up in the operating room and Dr. Nelson's resolution was that he 'had a really good heart-to-heart with him' and the result was 'he'll never do it again.'

"I need to give you a head's up that you will be receiving an incident report about Dr. Adams again. He screamed and cursed at a nurse today in the RCA. I was there, so I'll be signing it too."

Dr. Nelson's shoulders slumped and he looked down for a moment before capping and uncapping his Montblanc pen. *Here's where the paternal stuff didn't work so well,* she thought. His subtle body responses indicating that he was disappointed in her for participating in the perceived mutiny. She could see he was containing himself, because as a child she had watched the same type of constraint in her father. He raised both eyebrows, searching for the most politically correct response, then sighed heavily and stood up slowly, signaling the end to the meeting.

"Haven't had a report like this on Adams for six months. I'd call that an improvement. Thank you for bringing this to my attention, Sandy. I can always count on you to keep me apprised of what's going on. Oh, and please convey my personal regards to your mother for a speedy recovery."

*Thank you for bringing this to my attention...Thank you for bringing this to my attention...*words that kept propelling her into yet another nothing-will-ever-really-change Groundhog day.

Just treading water, aren't we, doc? She thought, turning away.

Chapter Eleven

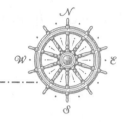

"Honey, I have two days to go before taking over," Will protested as Janice stood with her hands on her hips in front of the couch. "I need to study!"

She took the sheaf of papers he'd been reading and placed them on an end table before guiding him to his feet and propelling him toward their bedroom.

"In there, sailor. Time to head for bed. And, I have a whole bunch of questions to ask you. The inquisition will start in five minutes. I'm still unpacking a few items in the den."

She smiled as he chuckled his way to the bedroom, but the smile faded as she re-entered the small den and stood for a moment looking at the unopened envelope she'd been so deeply startled to find ten minutes before.

There had probably never been one particular moment in the past, Janice realized, when she'd decided Will had seen the formal root cause analysis on the death of his godson, Ronnie Nolan. She'd always just assumed he'd read it, and in Will's typical stoic fashion, dealt with the pain as best he could. But here it was, the original seal undisturbed, the envelope tumbling out of a drawer that neither of them had opened in years. He'd apparently put it aside a long time ago, unwilling to revisit the pain, and then, bless-edly, let it submerge into a dark, painful pool of bad memories.

Intuition told her this was the time. Maybe it had to do with expiation; maybe it was to prepare him for this new battle by gaining closure on the past, or a reminder that he needed to be a different kind of leader. Janice picked up the envelope and walked to the living room, slipping it into his stylish leather briefcase by the sofa. It belonged at his new office, on his desk, to be discovered as if some higher force had left it there.

Composing herself and regaining the mischievous smile she knew he liked so well, she walked into their bedroom and sat on the side of the bed, regarding her husband with a purposefully quizzical expression.

"So, you've been at this undercover boss thing for over three weeks now. We've talked constantly about all the myriad details, the people you've met, the departments you've visited..."

"More like the departments I've haunted. The ER, for instance."

"Right. And we've talked extensively about the needed philosophy. But pull the lens back now, Dr. CEO. You take over the day after tomorrow. What do you know about Las Vegas Memorial that Memorial doesn't know about itself, and what are you planning to do about it without drowning in the esoteria?" she responded. "I don't want you losing your overall focus. So give me a little peace of mind."

He sighed, looking at the ceiling. "These are good folks, better and more dedicated than I'd imagined, but they're all talking past each other on just about every subject, and especially patient safety. They *think* they're communicating, and of course there are those who've given up and are just hunkered down wanting to be left alone and undiscovered. Most go about their daily routines determined to get it right, but the routines they adhere to are not only *not* working for them, those routines, reports, procedures—the way they've always done things—are falsely reassuring. And many of them are at serious variance from evidence-based practice."

"I want to push you into explaining this to me with crystal clarity, okay? What's wrong with Las Vegas Memorial?"

"All right. Overall, Las Vegas Memorial is a traditional farmer's market model hospital operating as just another part of a traditional cottage industry and, thus, run for the doctors of the community, with the patient's benefitting in only a 'trickle-down theory' sort of way. That, of course, can never produce a safe environment. Las Vegas Memorial is also an institution desperately wedded to a fee-for-service model of reimbursement which, by very definition, can never support a hospital whose energy is focused on decreasing the public's need for its services, in other words, a hospital working hard to improve health and prevent illness. And, as a fee-for-service institution, it has a vested interest in increasing the number of things for which it can issue a billing code. In fact, it's human nature meeting economic desperation; We understandably want to do more of whatever makes us money. But that's the very model that has led this country to a rather consistent pattern of medical overtreatment. That's also how we've encouraged good people to make marginal decisions that, in retrospect, at least *feel* unethical: too many back surgeries, Friday-evening C-sections, CAT scans, X-rays, unnecessary tonsillectomies and on and on. Good Lord, we accuse lawyers of being ambulance chasers, but half the time we're the ones driving the ambulances in search of more patients."

"Okay. Understood. So Las Vegas Memorial is like any US hospital; physician-centric. What are its specific faults?"

"In a phrase?"

"Yes."

"It doesn't know itself."

"Now, *that's* interesting!"

"Well, it's true. They don't know who they are, or even *what* they are as an entity. They have little or no unity. The people of Las Vegas Memorial are hiding in silos, like so much of healthcare. While their ID badges all say "Las Vegas Memorial," the reality is that regardless of the happy talk rhetoric, there is little or no *espirt de corps* as a single organization, little or no common purpose or vision other than individual professional survival, and little or no knowledge at the top of what's going on at the front lines. And the people on the front lines don't know what their leaders want, and don't trust them. Worse, there is little, if any, trust running in *any* direction, and fear driving behaviors everywhere. Las Vegas Memorial's internal human-to-human communication quotient, if there were such a measure, would be subterranean. In a sociological sense it's a Tower of Babel populated by insular tribes who all distrust each other. It's 'silo city.' Overlay that with glib and expensive PR campaigns plastered on billboards and TV for the community extolling how great they are—which defies the inherent cynicism of staffers who would never trust a loved one to Las Vegas Memorial—and you have the basic reasons why they can't get out of their own way when it comes to safety, quality, staff satisfaction, patient satisfaction and service to the community."

"And the board and other chiefs don't understand this?"

"They're all trying to run a hospital of the fifties and sixties. They know something's wrong, but the thrust of the board's attitude has been, 'How do we get back to the golden days of yesteryear, where docs were king, the hospital administrator lived or perished based on his ability to serve the physicians, and the public afforded them both blind trust, blind respect and endless devotion: the 'If you build it, they will come' era."

"You do sound a little like a turncoat as a doc, you know."

Will scratched his head in thought for a moment as she waited. "I am a turncoat to the old definition of medicine as a cottage industry. We practice team medicine now or our patients perish. So, yes, I'm at war with the old model. However, I'm anything *but* a turncoat when it comes to what being a doctor is really all about, which is healing. All doctors would be vastly happier if they could go about that process of healing their patients without the enormous, unwieldy infrastructure and liabilities we've loaded on their shoulders. Worse, we know that in the twenty-first century it takes a team, not one person as a lone eagle, to be an effective physician, but you can't create and lead teams if the professional ethos remains 'every man for himself.'"

"Okay, but back up a bit. Las Vegas Memorial doesn't know who it is. I get that. But do they at least know what their mission is?"

Will laughed. "No. Absolutely not. Interesting you bringing it up that way. I was thinking today how different it is in a commercial corporation formed to make money doing something. If the things a commercial corporation makes, or sells, or does, happens to benefit mankind, great! As long as they make money. Public good is a side benefit, not a calling. Their ethos and their goal is being financially successful primarily for the investors, and everyone inside that company has the chance to aid in that success by keeping their eye on the goal. But American hospitals are schizoid! We shouldn't be, but we're really conflicted over whether the goal is to make money or serve patients. With a profit-based hospital, it becomes a little clearer that the two goals are uncomfortably co-existing. But Las Vegas Memorial is a non-profit hospital acting like a for-profit hospital. Take the emphasis on our stalled building campaign, where the angst over its postponement is palpable. What is our true goal in wanting to build more big buildings? Is it so we can use those buildings to bring in more money specifically to improve our ability to serve the patient and the community? Or, has the end purpose morphed into building a larger and larger medical empire, with the process of providing patient services being nothing more than the engine by which we can continue to bring in the money to perpetuate the growth? Across the country I don't think we really know how to differentiate. We've become panicked by the lack of, and fixated on the need for, money—not that we can ignore basic finance. But I promise you, the folks on the front lines believe their leaders are only concerned about, and enamored of, the money. They think that's all we value. Worse, they, themselves, are acutely aware that regardless of whether they consider medicine a calling or a job, basic personal economic survival—their jobs—depend on that same money. Where in that equation do we excite nurses and doctors and pharmacists and everyone else about serving the profession of healing?"

"Honey, so far you've told me two basic things. Las Vegas Memorial is a traditional hospital that is largely confused as to its true mission, and that it's a communication disaster filled with warring silos. Right?"

"Essentially, yes."

"What's *your* mission?"

"Hm-m. You're not asking for another soliloquy, right?"

"Nope. I want to know that you're gimlet-eyed in targeting whatever you're targeting. What's your mission?"

"To get them to change."

"Too easy. Change what?"

"Honey, I'm tired..."

"Humor me, Will. Please. I know you, and you have a tendency to get overwhelmed by the details. Come on. What's your mission?"

"Okay. First, I have to change Las Vegas Memorial and all its decision-making structure from a physician-centric to a patient-centric model. Second, I have to win the hearts and minds and dedication of the physicians to a team-oriented form of medical practice based on science and best practices. Third, I have to create an infrastructure that respects relationships, and permits itself to be re-designed for collegial teamwork and barrier less communication. Furthermore, I have to make sure all those seismic changes positively affect the bottom line, dramatically improve patient satisfaction and experience and get us the maximum reimbursement categories from CMS and everyone else writing checks, as well as to guide everyone toward the day when we'll be paid more for creating an identified patient community that needs us less and less."

"All right, honey. That's a cogent beginning."

"Good. I..."

Janice silenced him with a kiss. At five the next morning Will was sleeping too soundly to notice as she slipped quietly from the bed to engage the computer they'd placed in an adjacent bedroom. The points he'd made hours before were swimming in her head and she felt compelled to write them down. The list was waiting for him at the breakfast table.

"Honey, when did you do this?"

"This morning. Eat. Read. We'll discuss it later. Refine it during the day."

THE BASICS:

PROBLEMS with Las Vegas Memorial

1. Traditional Farmer's Market Model hospital, historically run for the doctors of the community and thus challenged as an entity to control the levels of quality and safety inherently set by the doctors individually. The outcomes of Las Vegas Memorial are hostage to the idea that individual doctors know best in each case, surgically or diagnostically. Leadership, including the board, continue to embrace this 1950s-60s form without understanding its inherent lack of viability for improving safety, quality and reimbursements.

This form sabotages the hospital's ability to provide commonality and best practices, whether in hand washing compliance, universal use of established protocols such as "bundles" for preventing central line infections and ventilator associated pneumonia, or simple adoption of minimized variables and standard orders.

2. Las Vegas Memorial is fueled by the fee-for-service model which cannot support the broader goals of a patient-centric ethic or of improving the overall health of the community.

3. Hospital leadership, including the board, are unsure of their true mission, and confused regarding their overall goals as an organization. The necessary focus on making money to keep the doors open leads to confusion: Is the purpose to exist and serve in order to make money, or make money in order to exist and serve?

4. The staff of Las Vegas Memorial are fragmented and divided into many defensive silos and bound by little, if any, sense of common purpose or common identity. They are a collection of fiefdoms, a form which handicaps any sustained attempt to create a unified organization with a unified ethos and sense of community.

5. The level of effective communication between and among Memorial's people is very poor, and hampered significantly by both the fragmented fiefdoms and a very low level of trust of each other and the leadership. Part of the reason for this low trust is a history of poor communication from leadership at all levels, and an apparent lack of any viable system of feedback beyond the traditional suggestion box.

GOOD POINTS:
1. Without a full understanding of why, the board recognizes that it and the hospital must change in some way to significantly improve safety and quality.

THE MISSION of Dr. Jenkins as CEO:

1. Change Las Vegas Memorial from a traditional physician-centric hospital to a true patient-centric institution. The definition of patient-centric is "an institution in which virtually *everything*, including finance, is subordinate to the best interests of the patient."

2. By a combination of selective retention (not everyone should be 'on the bus'), clear identification of unified purpose, support of early-adopters and board mandate for the most important elements of best practices, create a physician staff (employed and privileged) that is unanimous in their dedication to a team-oriented form of practice based on science and proven methods.

3. By adopting parallel bylaws for the hospital board and the medical staff with identical and crystal clear codes of conduct and professional expectations that treat virtually everyone the same; create and nurture an infrastructure emphasizing the best level of interpersonal relationships, collegial interactive teams, zero-tolerance for disruptive behaviors of any sort, and unquestioned support for anyone using the principles of barrier less communication, even when wrong. Provide courses and simulation-based labs on effective team and interpersonal communication, and exempt no one from such training.

4. Create a proud and cohesive sense of commonality, mutual respect and communication (vertical and horizontal) at Las Vegas Memorial in which enthusiastic ownership (not just involvement or engagement) is the minimum requirement for membership. Paint with absolute clarity what the vision and the purpose of the hospital is, and never vary from infusing that recognition in each employee. This translates to using a "bully pulpit" for the CEO. Openly discuss the need to find ways of serving the public interest of wellness despite the fee-for-service yoke of reimbursement, and solicit everyone's ideas for how to

make and survive the change. Make each employee/ physician an enthusiastic steward of such changes. Eliminate those who can't rise to the challenge, or who refuse to trust Las Vegas Memorial and refuse to participate in changing it. Require physician leadership and even 'professorship' as the price of admission.

5. Re-establish trust as a standard quality at Las Vegas Memorial by going beyond a "just culture" and evaluating human errors and mistakes not as a potential disciplinary occurrence, but as important messages from the underlying system which must be systemically addressed. Build a trustworthy system of response to problems that every participant—doctors included—can rely on to probe and deal with adverse occurrences as disciplinary matters only after all the facts are known. Banish professional 'scapegoating' in which one person is routinely blamed for any adverse occurrence.

Chapter Twelve

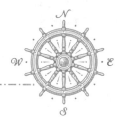

Ivy opened the door to Will's new office with a flourish and waved him in, her excitement showing.

"So, what do you think, Boss? I leaned heavily on Janice for advice, but I figured if you didn't like the things I put on the wall or where they are, I can change it around."

Will entered his newly furnished office and glanced around at the plaques, diplomas and pictures expertly positioned around the room. He'd been dreading the process of unpacking and deciding where to put things.

"I'm speechless, Ivy."

"I just figured you had enough on your plate and all the things I have on your calendar for your first formal day."

"It's perfect. I wouldn't change a thing. Thank you!"

"You're entirely welcome."

"Wait, did you say something about my calendar for today?"

She nodded, pulling a steno notebook into view.

"I've already setup your Outlook calendar and e-mail files, both the personal and professional addresses. It's eleven o'clock now, and at noon you're to meet Angela Siegel for lunch at the Las Vegas Country Club. Tomorrow at eight thirty, as you requested, I scheduled the meeting with our CFO. Ten thirty is the CNO, and the general C-suite lunch meeting is in the board-room at twelve thirty."

"And I'd need to leave how soon for Angela Siegel?"

"No later than eleven forty. They'll valet your car on that end." Ivy pulled several sheets of paper from the file folder she was carrying and handed it to him. "You'll want to get these off your desk and back to me before your meetings. They're dossiers on the folks you're going to see. Nothing really scandalous, but...detailed."

"You're awesome."

"Thank you!"

"By the way, Ivy, I have one small change for the outside corridor. I figured you'd know who to contact in maintenance to get this done." Will opened his leather briefcase and rummaged around for a moment, making a mental note to closet himself with the summary Janice had prepared as he searched for the sheet of paper he'd typed up for facilities management, and finally found it. He handed the paper to Ivy, watching her face transform into a Cheshire-cat grin.

"Got it!" she said.

"Good. And I'd want this to be done after hours tonight. They can be stored somewhere, not destroyed, but just gone by morning."

Will returned to emptying his briefcase, but the sudden look on his face caused Ivy to ask, "Are you okay?"

"Yeah...um...sure," he said, as if the words themselves could catch him from falling. "I just remembered a whole parcel of things I need to think about before that lunch."

"Then I'll leave you alone," she added, moving swiftly out of his office, quietly closing the door behind her.

Will stood in confusion for a few moments before sitting behind his new desk and placing the envelope in front of him. His stomach was tied in knots, but he forced himself to open it and slide the sheaf of papers from within. He took a deep breath, glanced at his watch and began to read the clinically sterile analysis of why Ronnie Nolan had never seen his twelfth birthday.

The short drive from Las Vegas Memorial to the Las Vegas Country Club was a matter of automatically following the voice of the GPS device. Will's mind was elsewhere, dealing with the amazement that the report he'd expected to hit him like a body blow had instead somehow buoyed him in a way he couldn't quite grasp. Maybe it was the opportunity to do it right, or the eight years of distance that gave him a new perspective, or reading the RCA without fighting the pounding waves of guilt that pummeled him to the ground at every error discovered along the way. He'd been kicking himself for years, believing that his interference was a causative factor; that maybe Ronnie's care wouldn't have been so rushed, but that's not what it said in the root cause analysis.

My greatest failure, Will thought to himself, *was believing that I could actually control outcomes in a complex system; that my position and power as CEO, the work that I poured my heart, mind and soul into every day that had seemed so productive, was on the right track to keeping our patients safe.*

Deep inside, Will still questioned his past motivations. Why had he felt so compelled to get involved in every detail of Ronnie's care? Didn't he trust his own system—the very system that he was in charge of? In truth, it was something he never, ever admitted to himself until this very moment.

The reason he had hovered over Ronnie was because he had known his institution was not safe.

No wonder the IHI said that the greatest barrier to patient safety was culture. Clearly, the culture of his Portland hospital had been generically unable to prevent small things, metastasizing into the death of a young boy—but was it actually possible to create a culture that could? Essentially he'd said the right things to Janice last night, but did he really believe they were achievable goals? Wasn't he trying—then and now—to change the course of a fully-loaded supertanker with a wooden oar?

But wait a minute, he concluded. *That's what St. Michael's is all about. The real possibility of massive change.*

He pulled up to the country club more determined than ever that when he was done at Las Vegas Memorial, there would be no more eleven-year-old boys unnecessarily zipped into body bags.

Angela Siegel had elected to meet him at the front entrance of the club, which Will immediately understood to be a gesture of respect and camaraderie offered in advance of really knowing this new CEO. She led him to the dining room with the practiced grace of a woman who had been forever in circles of money and power, but the recitation of her life offered over wine as they waited for lunch was quite different: a litany of challenge, pain and controversy—made all the more acute by the war she'd fought with the board and the senior executives of his company following her husband's death.

"I was the dutiful wife, you see, raising three kids while he built the firm from the ground up, mostly by being gone. From a little air conditioning provider in the backwater of Las Vegas, he had the idea of heating buildings even in the Arctic in the middle of winter, expanding our building season from four months to year round. One brilliant idea that he pushed and shoved into profitability he then expanded to building our own heating equipment, fighting the competitors to their knees all over the planet, and keeping an iron grip on everything. But he liked to hire scheming and greedy people as executives and pit them against each other. He died of a massive heart attack yelling at one of them in a staff meeting. I showed up at the company two weeks after the funeral for a joint meeting of the board and the executives I'd requested. They expected the poor little widow to tell them I was selling my shares. Two of them had a criminal scheme ready to convince me the shares were next to worthless so they could buy me out for a pittance and seize the whole corporation—stealing tens of millions. Instead, I announced that I was taking over as majority stockholder and their new CEO, chairman and boss. If I'd brought in a team of armed terrorists and announced they were all being hung at noon, the expressions in that room wouldn't have been any different. I fired half of them on the spot, won two resulting grudge lawsuits and helped put the ringleader in federal prison."

Lunch arrived and Angela waved away the rest of the story.

"Anyway, I understand business, I understand greed and I think I understand human nature. I joined the Las Vegas Memorial board because one of the members was a local businessman sucking up to me with an invitation, but I accepted because I thought I could give something to the community."

"And have you?" Will asked, immediately shocked at his own question.

Angela smiled slowly. "I knew I liked you, kid," she said. "That's exactly the kind of candor I've been starved for at Las Vegas Memorial. All of them are gentlemen, well, almost all. Everyone smiles at you while inserting knives in your back in the most genteel fashion. Look me in the eye and tell me what you really think and I'll respect you. That is you, Will, am I right?"

"Yes, it is."

"Okay. So, why did I ask you here? We're here because I'm on the board of a hospital that has no idea what the hell it's doing."

Will smiled, but decided not to give voice to the face that he'd said much the same thing to Janice just a few hours ago.

"You mean in terms of patient safety?" he managed.

"Judging from your expression, Will, I have no doubt you know the answer. No, I mean in terms of serving this community. Forget the glitter and the lights and the hookers and the headliners, the real Las Vegans are good, hardworking people who, like all Americans, need a better healthcare system than they have. They need a medical system trying to keep them healthy, not just one that reacts and provides fee-for-service care after something goes very wrong. Of course, we also need to ditch a stupid system that uses 17 percent of our premiums for the profitability of insurance companies who call every dollar they're forced to spend on our care a 'medical loss,' but that's another rant of mine. We have great hospitals in this town, not just ours, but they're all here to react, not prevent. Las Vegas Memorial is licensed by this state and charged by our own stated ethics to provide that preventative care, and yet all we're protecting is the income stream, just like I was saying in the meeting several weeks back...the things none of the other members wanted to hear. If we were institutionally honest, we'd have, for instance, a robust program to minimize the massive number of asthma attacks that fill our ER. We know for a fact that every dollar invested in prevention gives a return on investment of over three dollars, and yet we can't seem to find that dollar! Will, I know about these things because I am a large self-insured employer. Why aren't we making major efforts to control diabetes and attack sugary drinks in our schools and deal with coronary artery disease, depression, asthma and a host of other things we absolutely know how to control? You know that failing to control just five major diseases sucks up over 40 percent of our national healthcare dollars? In other words, if we applied what we know to prevent acute attacks, we'd spend 40 percent less because people wouldn't need the expensive care that follows.[1] Also, we're failing the youth of America horribly! School nurses have been cut all over the nation. We have principals and secretaries administering medications and doing procedures like emptying colostomy bags and we don't find this insane? Where are the nurses we need in each school? That's preventative medicine, and we, as a people, seem completely blind to the lack of a preventative approach. And why, Will, can't Americas' hospitals be the leaders? Why haven't we at Las Vegas Memorial been a leader in the community we're sworn to serve? Primarily because there's no direct profit in it!"

"Angela, clearly you're very passionate about these things, which I respect greatly. But let me ask you a tough question. Other than our meeting several weeks back, have you stated things this clearly to the rest of the board? And if so, what was their reaction?"

She nodded and smiled ruefully. "I have walked the talk, Will. I've harpooned my fellow members with this on at least two major occasions in the past two years. The first time I got polite expressions of appreciation. 'Good points, Angela! And we should be aware of these things and look for opportunities, Angela.' The next time, when I essentially threw down the gauntlet and demanded to know why the hell nothing had been done in a year—not even an attempt to help with the school nursing shortage right here in Las Vegas—the reaction was consternation. But when I suggested that healthcare is the prime public utility in the United States and may need federal prodding to change, you should have seen them come out of their seats. 'Angela, what's the matter with you? You're a businesswoman, you don't want the feds in this! And where are we going to get the dollars? Angela, we can't move that fast. These things take time.' In other words, enough already with the uncomfortable truths. Be a good team player and shut up."

Will sighed. "I rather imagined that was the response."

"Until we learn how to rewire this ridiculous illness-perpetuation system we have, we'll never significantly reduce costs."

"Angela, I couldn't agree more, but let me take the devil's advocate position for a second. We're just one hospital in a sea of thousands running like the traditional medical farmer's market, and there are other hospitals right here in Las Vegas that are essentially competition. I had an earful about that just the other day, about how they're all ready, willing and able to steal any of our physicians who're unhappy with any change we try to make. We can't do all this alone, can we? Change the entire ethos of American hospital practice to a preventative system based on quality of care, and not quantity? I mean, this is a matter of scope as well, the way I see it. I have this massive, largely dysfunctional flotilla of little boats called Las Vegas Memorial and my first task on a philosophical basis is to get them all aboard a single vessel with unity of purpose and unity of method. To do that I have to build something entirely new, while I'm sailing it and keeping it afloat, using top-down as well as bottom-up and core value approaches simultaneously, at least at first. In other words, I have to play Noah and herd everyone aboard this new vessel, then skid onto the bridge and throw the wheel over to dramatically change course, so to speak."

"I noticed you like nautical metaphors," she smiled. "Thank God! I get so tired of the sports analogies."

"But you see what I mean? I don't want to lose sight of the overall societal change either, but what can we do, while I'm trying to get all these other things started, that isn't going to impact us so badly on a financial basis that the board decides to throw me out and return to aiming for the icebergs? Even if the board is with me, if I start a war I can't win with the docs, we'll squander the opportunity or at least get bogged down."

"Will, far be it for me to assume the position of the board's conscience, or yours, for that matter. But if you take over with only intermediate goals in mind and lose sight of what we should become—even if it's practically unattainable in the short term—you will end up failing even your basic mission of zeroing the potential for accidentally harming patients. The little battles and the mid-level battles will obscure any imprecise targets, and you'll drift away, accepting lesser and lesser goals. President Johnson had a term for it, although he was describing a president's life with the press. He said it was like being nibbled to death by ducks! In Middle Eastern cultures they refer to the same principle as 'death by a thousand cuts.' My counsel, Will, is to set the course with iron determination, paint the target with stark clarity and as the leader, let no one diminish that vision. Sure, Las Vegas Memorial is not going to be able to reform all of American healthcare, and we might not even survive long enough to see zero patient safety disasters in our own shop. But we can damn well create a program for keeping nurses in Las Vegas schools, and we can do something to encourage primary care docs to interface with us in ways that prevent major asthma episodes and dozens of other opportunities for pushing preventative care. True, if we're too successful, we'll hurt the business of medicine in terms of the bottom line because people will be less in need of emergency services and hospitalization. I don't pretend to understand how Medicare is going to help us become an accountable care organization, though God knows I've read everything provided so far; But those changes are coming at us like a runaway freight train anyway, forced by an increasingly furious population and a reactive, polarized, unspeakably dysfunctional excuse of a Congress dedicated to party over country. To survive, we have to be ahead of that tsunami and shift our focus now to quality of outcomes and prevention leadership. Lead on the local level now. Explain ourselves clearly to our community now. And I say we can do those things while steering steadfastly for perfect patient safety and remaining solvent. The feds, after all, have essentially issued the death penalty to the fee-for-service model, and it's high time."

Will had been listening carefully, and now he smiled at her. "You're a darn good conscience, Angela! That helps substantially, set an iron-willed course. I just have to be very careful to not let that deteriorate into a top-down myopia."

"You won't."

"In many respects, what's being called the 'Triple-Aim' should become our mantra and our motivation."[ii]

Angela was smiling and nodding. "I just committed that to memory last month. Improve public health, improve the quality of existing healthcare and lower the costs. In a nutshell."

"By the way, there's a new position I want to create immediately, and I'm going to approach every board member about this before the next meeting because I want to act now."

"Tell me."

"Chief research officer, whose primary duty will be to provide, on literally a daily basis the underlying research, conclusions, even legal rulings that we need to know. I know some hospitals have people dedicated to research, but I have yet to encounter one that is senior officer level, and I think it's that vital. For example, everyone was excited about hiring a new neonatologist until we discovered that—as first reported in the book *Overtreated,*—4.3 neonatologists per ten thousand births is best for reducing the chances of death.[iii] Physicians were also lobbying for an additional cath lab—until we realized that there is a perfect correlation between the availability of cath labs and the propensity for excessive angioplasty or bypass surgery. When supply is inducing demand, you have to base decisions on the facts. If we expect our practitioners to adopt EBP (evidence based practice), then it has to be our total organizational mindset, not just a subset. All of our decisions must be data driven.[iv] Also, it's difficult to duel with doctors who, like me, are trained to push-back on a pseudo-scientific basis against any research if you don't have the latest and most precise view of that research, or if the person advocating a change doesn't have sufficient authority to cite. But if we say that we're going to adopt a new procedure to achieve zero catheter-associated urinary tract infections, for instance, I want a stack of papers and a cogent in-house summation coming from a senior member of my team and speaking for me and the board. We need the force and urgency of such changes to be compelling."

Angela Siegel was smiling broadly. "So happens, I was going to discuss something similar, although I didn't have it as well thought out." She reached down to a small folder and pulled out several sheets of paper. "There's a major new book, an uncomfortable work aimed at medicine and the general public, called *Demand Better!* by Drs. David Nash and Sanjaya Kumar, and there's an excerpt I want to read you from their introduction. I've ordered a copy for you, by the way."

"Thanks."

"They say this: *"If somebody were to ask, 'In three words or less,*

explain what's wrong with our healthcare system,' that's easy: **unex-**
plained clinical variation. *Different doctors practice different ways to
treat the same illnesses, with little scientific backing. Care patterns vary
by zip code, even in an individual city. This central problem leads to a
cascade of corollary problems: waste, overuse of dangerous procedures,
and preventable medical errors.*

*Why do doctors diagnose and prescribe treatments for the same illness
differently? We will see that most doctors, especially in the primary care
setting, practice in a completely data-free environment, devoid of feedback on the correctness of their practice. That's a staggering truth that's
incredibly scary, even to doctors, let alone to patients. When there's no
countervailing data to say that you ought to change what you're doing,
the natural human reaction, even among physicians and other highly-
trained professionals, is to continue what they are used to doing."*

"In other words, Will, along with the chief safety officer,
which we need immediately, you couldn't be more correct.
Every hospital in the country needs a chief research officer
reporting directly to the CEO."

"Ditto on the chief safety officer. I've already started the
search. But do you think the board, as a whole, will agree?"

She laughed and rolled her eyes. "They'll be gravely concerned
that you're spending more money, but you have enough support.
Don't worry about that. Instead, worry about your CFO. That
was the other reason for this meeting. To warn you. Richard
Holbrook is a decent fellow, but he's old school bottom line, and
for most everything you'll be doing, he'll be terminally skeptical.
No margin, no mission."

"Isn't that what I want, though, Angela? Healthy pushback
and skepticism?"

She was shaking her head. "No, you don't understand. If you
could win Richard over, then yes, he could be your greatest touch-
stone of financial realism, but the previous CEO wasn't able to do
so, and he became a very practiced saboteur, determined to neu-
tralize any of her efforts he thought were financially dangerous."

"Behind her back?"

"Yes. Not that he didn't dissent to her face, but if she decided
to go ahead with whatever he objected to, he simply went underground and became chronically and very cleverly insubordinate.

He elected himself the guardian of the hospital's best interests."

"Did the board know this?"

"Some did, and they grew to trust him more than they trusted her, which was a function of poor communication on her part with the board, and her refusal to face him down."

"Thanks, Angela. I've spent the previous weeks getting to know the people of Las Vegas Memorial. Now I have to get to know my executive team, and I have to have loyalty."

"May I make a suggestion?"

"By all means."

"Richard's an honest guy. If you make it clear what loyalty means, he'll conform or he'll come and talk to you. Just don't assume compliance where he's involved unless he's promised compliance or agreement to your face. Never assume."

"Funny, that's the one word and practice that frightens me the most about everything and everyone I've met at Las Vegas Memorial. Assume. The propensity for acting on unwarranted assumptions seems to be a universal malady."

"That was actually the song Joan Winston was singing before she gave up prematurely." A smile spread across Angela's face. "You might say the song is over, but the malady lingers on!"

"Oh, no, you *too*?"

"I'm afraid so," Angela said with a wry smile, enjoying his feigned discomfort. "Your assistant, Ivy, and I share a particularly pungent passion for puns."

"Not to mention alliteration, it seems."

Chapter Thirteen

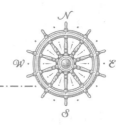

Terri had worked with Dr. Adams for so long she would bet her paycheck on guessing his blood pressure. He hadn't said a single word, but he was angry about something today, and now he was bringing all that anger into her operating room. She decided to wait until he calmed down and the Darth Vader breathing stopped before she approached.

"I can see you're having a bad day. Do you want to postpone the case?"

"Don't be ridiculous! I'm a surgeon for Christ's sake."

"Yes, but you're also a human being like the rest of us. And research shows being upset affects our critical thinking, and you'll be doing a lot of that in the next few hours."

"You and your soft stuff research! As long as *you all* don't mess up, then things will go smoothly. Just get my preference card straight this time."

The intermittent stream of put-downs traveling just underneath the corporate radar frustrated Terri. She didn't even bother writing him up anymore because in her last conversation, Dr. Adams expressed strong feelings that she was acting like a vigilante when he hadn't even said anything—and she couldn't argue with that. As the manager, she'd had numerous conversations with senior leaders which resulted in improvements, for a period of time. But the sourness and lack of respect would inevitably erupt again, and what was worse, everyone knew it, they just couldn't predict when. *Good thing they can't,* she thought to herself, *because my entire staff would've called in sick today.*

He's such a good clinician, she thought to herself. And for that reason alone, everyone tolerated him, well, almost everyone.

She had a very strong suspicion that Adams's temper was the underlying cause for losing her two new OR nurses. Much to her relief, however, they had denied it in the exit interview.

Terri was monitoring the four operating rooms, moving fluidly through the chaos, creating order and a sense of support wherever she went. Fortunately, Dr. Adams's surgery went off without a hitch. *Probably because no one spoke at all,* she thought, looking into the room through the window at the rigid body posturing of her hyper-vigilant staff. Laying low was a tactic that even she had learned as a new nurse. Even the vendor who visited the ORs last month had pointed this out to Terri—as if she couldn't see it herself. He was so naïve. She tried to tell him, "That's just the way it is around here."

"There's just nothing you can do about the fact that some surgeons close staff up as fast and tight as a Venus Fly Trap with their non-verbal cues: no eye contact, not bothering to learn their names, sending off 'I'm too busy' and 'I'm so much more important than you' messages in subwoofer vibes."

"So what do you need for things to change?" He'd asked.

The question had come out of left field from this seemingly innocent bystander who had asked to shadow the circulator. "My name is Will," he'd interjected, "and sorry to interrupt your conversation, but I'm just wondering, what do you need for things to be different?"

What a concept! Things being different! It was hard for her not to laugh, but she was sure he caught the fleeting sarcasm that ran across her face.

"Seriously, what do you need?" He insisted. If the very question hadn't been as entertaining as a far-out fantasy, she wouldn't have bothered answering. But, heck, she needed a fantasy.

"I need the CMO and all physicians to understand that they didn't just learn medicine in med school; they learned archaic behaviors that do not serve the patient. I need them to know that how they feel comes across every time, that those feelings are never subtle; that they are more important than they ever dreamed in creating an atmosphere that acknowledges the vital part that everyone plays on the team; that we desperately need their leadership in creating a new culture where incivility is never tolerated by anyone, for the good of the patient. I need leadership to clearly state the norm—black or white. I'm sick of living in the gray.

And I need to know somebody has my back when I take care of situations using managerial discretion. When I want to send a nurse home for being on Facebook while on duty, or decide a surgeon should not operate because he is upset or exhausted, that decision should be final and supported. That's my fantasy."

"Fantasy?" he had replied.

"Gotta go now. Nice meeting you, Will. Thanks for the lotto moment."

Terri's attention was pulled back to the present by a question about the surgery schedule, and she scanned the daily clipboard. A yellow sticky was pasted onto someone's name. It read: "Mrs. Mildred Keaton in pre-op Bay Four is Sandy Keaton's mother, our risk manager. Just want everyone to have a heads up."

Terri was angry. "I hate this," she said to no one, ripping the sticky note off and throwing it in the trash. "Everyone is *somebody's* mother or son or daughter!" Was administration really so oblivious that they didn't understand how much of an insult such a note really was? Weren't they aware that EVERYONE was treated with all the skill and care they could muster? It was such a slap on the face. She glanced down at the surgeon who would be doing the case. Cooper. Good. No problem there. Now she could move onto the major drama of the day. She opened the report and forced herself to review the cases.

Terri's best friend had made a career of teasing Terri about her job. When they met after work for drinks she'd say, "Quick! Give me the next scene in *As the OR Turns.*" And this one was a particularly good episode: a very married anesthesiologist had seduced the CRNA months ago. It had been obvious to the entire OR that the two had a relationship, and Terri had already spoken to both of them, twice. Now, rumor had it that the relationship was on the rocks and the doctor was furious at being rejected. "Oh no," Terri said out loud, scanning the schedule to confirm her memory. Both of them were scheduled for the OR today, and the dark impetus to do something or purposefully ignore it was gathering force when her pager went off: "Waiting for you—Madge."

Where did the hours go? It seemed like it had been just five minutes since she walked in, and now it was past five! Now she was unprepared for the meeting on absenteeism issues—not mentally unprepared (because she said the same thing every single time), but emotionally.

Terri did a quick mental review of her last meeting with Madge. Why did she feel like this employee just sucked the life out of her? The mandatory meetings triggered by edict from human resources were exhausting. The hospital policy stated that an employee could have no more than four absentee occurrences a year, so for the last five years, Madge would 'stretch' every occurrence out to be a weeklong event. It was quite evident who was using whom here; and what was worse, everyone could see it. Everyone, but HR! Staff had even joked to each other when Madge called in sick last Monday saying, "Just mark her off for the entire week."

It was the same way with the performance improvement plan they had directed her to do for Michael for being on Facebook. He would "improve" for exactly ninety days. Then, like clockwork, on day ninety-one, she would come into work and find an incident report from someone for Michael being on Facebook again! She could deal with Doc Adams, love triangles, preference cards, sterilization issues and through-put problems. But these situations, these situations always left her feeling completely impotent, like an exhausted gerbil on an exercise wheel. She could see the look in the eyes of her staff and read their thoughts; *"What kind of manager are you? Why don't you DO something about this?"*

Terri opened the door to her office just as her pager went off again; OR – STAT.

Chapter Fourteen

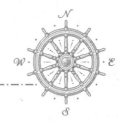

So, day number two!

Will locked his car with the remote as he walked through the parking garage toward the increasingly familiar side entrance to Las Vegas Memorial. He could remember almost nothing of the drive from the condo, so intense had his concentration been on the meeting he'd scheduled with Dr. Kirk Nelson, the grandfatherly cardiac surgeon, who'd been interim chief medical officer for the past six months.

Dr. Nelson was waiting for him in the foyer of the C-suite— a bow to the new alpha wolf and a subtle request to have his position made permanent.

"We apparently had a theft last night," Nelson began, shaking Will's hand, as he inclined his head toward the wall where the heavy wooden doors to the C-suite had been the day before.

"Any idea what happened?" Will asked, tongue clearly in cheek.

"Someone apparently took down our defense perimeter, exposing us to the peasants."

"Yeah, however are we going to manage without a moat to keep the barbarians at bay?" Will replied, following the chief medical officer to his office.

"Frankly, Will, it's about time. Good move!"

"Assuming, of course, I had anything to do with it."

The office they entered was replete with personal mementos and family pictures, including a long-ago three generation shot of a young Kirk Nelson with his father and grandfather, both doctors. It took fifteen minutes of personal reflections and stories before Kirk Nelson was ready to find out what was on their new CEO's mind.

"So, Will, how can I help you get started?" The CMO stood over six foot two, his face broad and craggy. He sat back comfortably in his office chair and gestured toward the rest of the hospital with a huge, weathered hand. "I know you have some ambitious plans for this place in terms of patient safety improvement."

"Ambitious may be a distinct understatement, Kirk, for one thing, I'm going to be asking a lot of you. We have to dramatically change the interface between our physicians and the entity that is Las Vegas Memorial, and I'm going to need your leadership, energy and loyalty, even if it conflicts with what's comfortable."

The smile faded slowly from Kirk Nelson's face as he sat forward, listening intently, yet cautiously as Will launched into a lengthy explanation of his vision for Las Vegas Memorial and the methods he intended to use. The soliloquy ended with a copy of Janice's summary, which Nelson read carefully, keeping his expression neutral until he'd finished.

"So, what do you think?" Will asked, watching Nelson's eyes carefully as he looked up and sighed.

"Day after day, Will, since I took this job," he began, "I've sat here dealing with everything a large collection of physicians can throw at you, from the functional to the dysfunctional. I've tried hard to emulate the best CMOs I ever saw in action, despite a lot of behind-my-back name calling and eye rolling. You know, I counsel, suggest, beg, plead for compliance at times, dispense oil over troubled waters, calm people down, all of it. Father confessor. Defender of physician autonomy. Yet I'm considered a turncoat if I critique anyone with an MD or DO after their name. No one trusts the CMO. I understand that dynamic, of course, having been a doctor for forty-six years. See, I'm one of those dinosaur pre-boomer guys who embraced my MD status like a priest embraces his ordination, twenty-four seven, always on duty. I try to understand these new guys and gals—what I call our time-card punchers—and they have their right to be the type of doc they want to be, including have a home life, but..." he paused, his eyes on the floor, his mind in deep thought before snapping his eyes back to meet Will's and shaking his head. "Will, I know

I'm just a caretaker, an interim CMO, but to tell you the truth, it didn't take long for me to get really weary of the Sisyphus act, doomed to eternally push the boulder uphill only to have it roll back every time. Once that kind of combat fatigue sets in, you just capitulate to the inertia. I'm sorry, I have to apologize and admit that I've been too frustrated by the lack of support from my colleagues and my fellow officers to even try to be effective lately."

"You want out, Kirk?" Will asked as gently as he could, fascinated as the older physician sat in thought for a few moments drumming his fingers quietly before suddenly looking up with a growing smile.

"No. Dammit, no, I don't want out! In fact, Will, I can completely understand if you came in here thinking that, given my rather obvious lack of energy lately, when you described all these earthshaking changes to me, I'd elect to step aside. I mean, you're asking a tired senior guy for a huge effort."

"That I am."

"Well, you know what? I hope this shocks you, it even shocks me—but even at the age of seventy-two, I'm ready to shake things up. You're right that the way we've been doing things doesn't work. I'm the bloody CMO and yet I have no real authority, and often times, even less credibility. Nothing's improving. Brent Roget told me you know about poor old Doc Adams, for instance. Poor and old my posterior! I tell you I'm thoroughly sick of Adams and his arrogance, but I don't have the power to do anything but plead with him to be nice, and he knows it. If I threaten to suspend him, the board will overrule me and make me look like an idiot. If I sanction him, he'll lawyer up and scare our in-house counsel, who'll force me to reverse course. I should be able to suspend his sorry derriere on the spot, but the last time someone in this office did that to a misbehaving doc, the CMO was undermined, attacked, demeaned and almost bankrupted. Whoever sits here needs to be deeply concerned with the humanity of our docs as well as how they practice, as well as be deeply respectful of them, but he or she also needs to be backed up completely in creating a unified medical staff. What's that like, Will? I've never experienced it. So—bottom line? You want a general to shove change up their you know what? I'm your man!"

Will couldn't suppress his smile. He had, indeed, expected a resignation, or worse.

"You're serious, Kirk? Because if you are, you may be helping me eliminate your position."

"I know. I get that. But I'm more than ready! You just make me a promise."

"What's that?"

"That if I'm holding you back or not doing what you need done, you'll let me know and let me resign in good graces."

"That's a promise."

"One more thing. You gotta get these HR and in-house counsel folks under control, Will. The tail is wagging the dog. What should be at times a good talking to—for a nurse or doctor or anyone—ends up a federal case because they got involved and no one can turn them off. Or, it takes us forever to get someone out of here who's dangerous because HR and legal are shaking in their boots that we'll get sued. Try explaining *that* to a family that's just lost their dad to a medical mistake!" Dr. Roget reminded me recently that the medical staff functions used to report to the CMO before the hospital started employing physicians. We may want to review whether that was such a good decision moving the medical affairs duties to HR.

"HR and in-house legal are next on my agenda, Kirk, and in fact, let's go get some coffee. I'd like you to tell me all the verifiable horror stories you know about them."

"How many legal pads do you have?"

FROM: WILL.JENKINS@LVM.com
TO: JACK.SILVERMAN@STM.org

Jack,

Thought you might like an update, since I've just taken the helm. After having dinner a few weeks back with the former CMO, now one of the principal board members (Dr. Brent Roget—I wrote you about the conversation and his old school resistance), I figured I would have to dismiss the current interim CMO, a very senior surgeon, for being ineffective. I was happily shocked today to find out that this current interim CMO (Dr. Kirk Nelson) wants things changed as much as I do and may turn out to be a great asset. It got me to wondering how many others are waiting for the same type of opportunity, but too jaded or burned out or apathetic—or too scared—to have hope, let alone say anything.

On the other hand, I do have a problem-child department I have to address immediately, and I have to ask you, how did you get your human resources department under control? They're essentially "Vigilantes of the status quo." Both Dr. Roget, our former CMO, and now retired and on the board, and Dr. Nelson, our current interim CMO have reminded me in the past couple of days that the medical affairs department used to report to the CMO before the hospital started to employee physicians. At that time the function switched to HR. I am wondering if that was such a good idea. HR holds everyone hostage from the board and the C-suite on down, even though the director is a very professional and personable young woman who seems to know her stuff. I think this is some-thing Las Vegas Memorial's leadership has permitted to happen over time, rather than any misconduct on HR's part, but first on my agenda in the morning is a 'Come to Jesus' (CTJ) meeting with this lady, and after that, a very critical couple of hours with my CFO in which I either have to gain confidence in him or let him hit the road. What's happening in the HR situation—and I've verified this personally for the last month at all levels—is that the rule and procedural structure for dealing with any serious personnel matter has been so set in concrete that lower and middle level managers in particular (as well as directors) have been warned severely that failure to follow HR's dictated procedures will lead to the hospital being sued and *the loss of their jobs.* We have, therefore, effectively removed any real discretion in dealing with human problems. If a complaint, however solveable, gets into the HR pipeline, no one has the backbone to interfere, and whether it's getting rid of some-one dangerous or retaining someone redeemable who crossed a line, HR marches in and takes over with no quarter given. I have a similar problem with our in-house lawyer (title is General Counsel) in that he's issuing dictates more than giving advice. I think we need to take some risks at times, and of course his professional ethos is to protect us at all times from any liability potential whatsoever.

One more tidbit—I'm sending a really useful overview that Janice wrote the other morning after a deep conversation the night before. (I am so blessed to be married to a leadership expert!)Your comments, though, would be very helpful. Am I forgetting anything?

Will

--- ---

FROM: JACK.SILVERMAN@STM.org
TO: WILL.JENKINS@LVM.com

Will,

First, you and Janice have captured the essence of the task ahead in that summary. Well done. I'd suggest you keep it with you at all times as a Flight Plan. The only change I would make is actually an addition: Don't forget—both with your board and with the other members of your C-suite—that they have been so infused with the principles of 'return on investment' (ROI) and linkage between any dollar spent and a guaranteed result, that there will be subtle but powerful internal rejection of any initiative you have not thoroughly grounded in financial realities. In other words, while you do not have to create an ROI for everything that needs to be done, it is important to never present a programmatic or even philosophical change without clearly addressing the question (as crass and objectionable as it is) of 'what's in it financially for us?' Never let any of your team think that you haven't clearly considered the financial aspects of this upheaval, and challenge *them* with proving that the eventual financial gains from culture change are not real (if that's their stance). It amazed me, but at the beginning of our transformation at St. Michael's, much of the eye-rolling pushback which was largely behind my back came from the belief that since I had not articulated how my proposed changes would affect the money, therefore those changes were unrealistic and unworkable. Lay out a clear line of reference for them between the money, the changes and the eventual gains, and that level of pushback (based on the presumption of leader naiveté) will disappear. In doing so, do not hesitate to draw lines that have never been drawn before. In other words, we know disruptive behavior seriously reduces patient safety, which threatens the institution's finances on many levels. Draw all those points together along with items that impact your community reputation. In fact, what Dr. Kissinger taught us so well in diplomacy is also true for us: Linkage. It's all linked, and we ignore that reality at our financial peril.

In addition, our folks tend to think of things in hospital-centric terms, but the larger story is that change in virtually all facets of healthcare—from hospice and nursing home through home care and day surgery centers et al— is not just inevitable, it is virtually unavoidable in a society that spends over 18 percent of its GDP on a healthcare non-system that affects at best only ten percent of the overall health of Americans. 2.8 trillion dollars a year as a nation, Will, for affecting only 10 percent of the wellbeing of our people! Pure insanity! Your team must understand this, because there is no business-as-usual component to resisting major alteration of the model. In nautical terms, the old model can be summed up by a single bow-on picture of that half sunk cruise ship, the Costa Concordia. The ship of state of the average healthcare system that refuses to change fast will look pretty much the same, in metaphorical terms, in very short order.

Another major point, by the way: For patients to receive optimum care, there needs to be a balance between what is good for patients based upon evidence based research, what is good for physicians and nurses in terms of satisfying their fundamental human need to be of service in a personally meaningful way that does not violate their personal code of ethics and morality, and what is good for the hospital itself in order to balance population health and good preventative healthcare with a healthy bottom line. The transition from a physician-centric to patient-centric environment carries a danger of being seen by physicians as a reactive crusade rather than a realistic and sustainable attempt to right the balance among the three key elements of healthcare: a patient seeking better health, healthcare providers seeking patients to support and heal and a healthcare institution (or structure, such as a hospital) willing to balance its ethical and moral based mission with the pragmatic need to achieve financial solvency. Our present system typically has little balance, with the majority of the power vested in the doctors. A Draconian change placing all the power in the hands of the institution devalues the contribution of physician responsibility and engagement. Similarly, placing total power in the patient's hands (rather than a balance focusing on the patient's best interests) becomes a cottage industry in reverse. In other words, shifting to the patient-centric model should not be interpreted as driving the physicians and nurses to journeyman status, rather than full partners in a system that ultimately and always puts the patient's best interests first by using the best their professional expertise can bring to bear.

By the way, I use that phrase 'Great American Non-System of Healthcare' but George C. Halvorson, chairman & CEO of Kaiser Permanente, coined the phrase.[v]

As to human resources, this may seem basic and it may seem like I'm lecturing on a class HR 101 basics, but in my view, too many people who get upset about inordinate HR rules and procedures forget that HR's mission (other than to fill the slots) is very finite and seldom aligned with the goal of great medical care or happy employees. They are there to keep the hospital out of personnel lawsuits and government sanctions. Maybe that serves the purpose of great medical care, and maybe it doesn't, but it's a subset, not THE set of goals. Their job description seldom includes anything about morale, happy, engaged employees, trust, understanding, or consideration for correctable human foibles and inherent human mistakes. What are you missing? Nothing. The problem, as you've discerned, is more than likely not the people in that department (because it sounds like they're doing a great job of what they've been taught to do). The problem is that Las Vegas Memorial has obviously never grappled with the task of aligning the goals of the HR function with the goals of the hospital. Start with that, and if the leader of HR can't make the change, get someone who can— someone who balances rules with human understanding and the goal of great personnel relationships.

Your lawyer is a different challenge. There you absolutely must have someone who understands that his or her role is to provide advice, NOT to control what risks the hospital deems appropriate. Many lawyers become so concerned about their hospital making any mistakes they become increasingly insistent and shrill regarding compliance with legal advice. We can appreciate the dedication that leads to such intensity, but they're not able to see the bigger picture. Ultimately, you and the board must make those decisions, and they must not all be made by default to the safest course of action. That's exponentially true when someone has been hurt or killed in your facility and your lawyer advises everyone to keep quiet and disclose nothing. Of course, we know the safest and the only moral course is to immediately and fully disclose, but a worried lawyer can be very persuasive, so it's up to the CEO to adamantly tell his lawyers to immediately stand down.

Let me know how the first day goes!

Jack

Chapter Fifteen

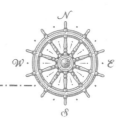

"Where's my next case?" said Dr. Cooper loudly, de-gowning from the bilateral knee that had taken much longer than he had anticipated. He glanced at the time and winced internally.

"Ready and waiting for you to mark the site in pre-op Bay One," Maria responded. But Cooper was already off, walking toward pre-op in long strides. She smirked, wondering why he even bothered to ask. They had worked together for over ten years now and long since had come to an unspoken understanding of each other's roles—he'd ask a question to assert authority when he *already knew* the answer. But she liked Cooper; and he was a great surgeon. She was also alert enough to see how the other surgeons subtly pushed him away. Was it because he was black, or because his infection rates were the lowest? But Maria was equally savvy to keep her suspicions to herself. After all, whenever she slipped into her native Tagalog when talking to her mother on the phone, she felt like an outsider, too. She liked hearing Dr. Cooper's stories of being raised in a dirt poor family with six children and how his mother taught them all to "soar like eagles," instead of pigeons, "pecking on the goodwill of society." Once last month he had even asked her to accompany him to a sister hospital where he was going to teach minimally invasive hip procedures. He explained how important it was that everything goes "just perfectly" and that meant; only *she* could be his circulator.

Pete Cooper yawned unconsciously as he picked up the chart, noticing the red sticker stating the patient's allergy to Penicillin and Cephalosporins, double checking the orders to make sure that he had ordered Vancomycin as the pre-op antibiotic. He hated add-ons when he was already so tired at the end of a long day. But Thursday was his last block time for the week and he wasn't about to hold the old lady off till Monday, or even worse, come in on a Saturday when he wasn't on call this weekend. Cooper smiled to himself in anticipation, thinking of the long awaited anniversary weekend he had planned for his wife at Canyon Ranch. He unconsciously leaned against the counter, letting his thoughts drift for a few seconds. As a surgeon, being "tired" was a pejorative, something beaten out of him in residency as a state unbecoming a surgeon. Only wimps got "tired" and "fatigued," and he was anything but a wimp when it came to shouldering the immense responsibilities that faced him daily.

There was, however, a tendency in him lately to imagine life without a daily surgery schedule. When had it stopped being fun, or at least deeply enjoyable? Even the respect he had taken for granted as a young doctor—the respect that would be afforded him when he achieved the "rank" of senior surgeon—seemed to have evaporated. Everyone was engaged in a campaign to tell him how to practice, how to cut, what to say and do: federal rules, Joint Commission policies, hospital rules, protocols, time-outs and overly-sensitive nurses who would write you up if you sneezed sideways rather than just speaking with you. The OR scheduler controlled his life—what his office manager didn't already control of it, that is. And then there was always the omnipresent threat of some bottom-sucking lawyer filing a suit and trying to prove he was the worst doctor on the planet. What sane individual would choose such a life?

And yet, the pride of knowing what those fingers of his could do with the tools of a surgeon, and how many people had been given a better life by what he'd learned to do—that drove him on.

I AM tired! He thought, trying to adjust his attitude in the old familiar mission-oriented way of mentally shedding reality to focus on the job at hand.

Methodically he took the permanent marker and initialed the patient's right hip after double checking with the patient, checking his personal notes and matching them all to the surgery schedule. It was his routine. And it comforted him.

But as Cooper headed to the OR he walked right into an argument in progress. *Adams again!* He thought, wanting to ignore the whole short-man syndrome. But Adams was already in full swing, yelling loudly right in the middle of the hall at the surgery scheduler for assigning him to the "small" room when he had a "big surgery," and Cooper was going to have to walk right thru the chaos.

"Excuse me," said Cooper turning sideways and making a bee-line for his room before Adams could turn his attention to him. "Running late," he added smoothly, with a broad smile and a mission as his shield.

When everyone was finally gathered in OR Five, Maria began the time-out checklist after a nod from Cooper. She skipped over the introduction to the members of the team, as she assumed Cooper would wish because only one person was new anyway, just a nurse shadowing for some course work. She noted that Melody, the CRNA, was particularly quiet today as she put Mrs. Mildred Keaton under anesthesia—no doubt due to the recent tension with Dr. Matson, the anesthesiologist, who was on the computer just outside the OR and the silence made everyone, but Cooper, uncomfortable. Cooper was living in his own world, totally focused on the incision and prepping the site for the new titanium hip implant the rep had introduced last month. For a brief moment Maria longed for the old days when cream donuts always accompanied the hardware. But the tension escalated even further when an alarm sounded and Matson suddenly entered the room.

"Okay, its shift change, I'll be taking over now."

"What?" said Melody as Matson gestured for her to move over.

"You can step aside now," he added flatly, stepping into her space.

Power play, thought Maria as she noted the time of the exchange on her clipboard.

"What?" Melody echoed again.

"Time to switch," clarified Matson as Melody stared at the clock reorienting herself and assuming she had somehow gotten the schedule wrong. *Must not have been enough action on Facebook,* she thought caustically to herself.

"Can I get another sleeve for Dr. Cooper?" asked the circulator.

"I don't need one," replied Cooper, irritated, "I didn't contaminate myself."

"Kelly clamp," said Cooper loudly, signaling the end of that conversation.

Melody deftly repositioned the tube to silence the alarm, increased the oxygen and left the operating room. But just minutes after the door swung shut, the alarm sounded again. Matson's eyes darted from machine to tube to chart searching for clues.

"What's going on?" said Cooper, eyes riveted to his incision.

"Don't know yet," answered Matson, "give me a minute."

The shadowing nurse started to interrupt, but Matson silenced her sharply. "Quiet! I can't think."

Now everyone in the room was staring at the monitor watching the blood pressure dropping slowly. One hundred over fifty-two, ninety-two over forty-eight, eighty-four over forty-two.

Hell, thought Matson, trying to grasp the situation, meticulously reviewing his actions since entering the room, *all I did was turn up the fluids.*

"Dammit, Matson," said Cooper after a minute had passed and Maria had calmly announced "seventy over thirty-eight."

"Get Melody back in here STAT!"

As Mrs. Keaton's face suddenly began turning an alarming bright red, Maria paged Melody and the manager, while grabbing and hanging another bag of IV fluids.

Chapter Sixteen

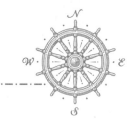

Will pushed out through the front entrance of Las Vegas Memorial intent on occupying one of the benches in the small, tree lined mini-park the hospital had built just outside. He smiled and nodded to a patient with an IV bag slowly leaving the small glade and sat by himself next to the fountain, letting the burbling water have its calming effect as he thought about calling Janice and then decided to wait. Will had harbored no intention of firing Lucy Martin when he'd arrived at seven this morning, even though his first conference with her had left him disturbed at what appeared to be passive-aggressive response. But, this morning, after thirty minutes of feigned compliance by the director of human resources on just about every subject he'd wanted to discuss, there had seemed no viable option. Less than one day into his leadership of the hospital and one of his people had already essentially crossed swords with him in a way he simply couldn't accept.

But, thought Will, *I probably shouldn't have pushed her into an explosion.*

"Are you refusing to work with me," Will had asked. "Lucy, are you in essence saying that you will not vary from the way you've always done things to help soften up the perceived rigidity of the HR function?"

"Will, I'm certainly eager to work with you, but what you're asking me to do is dismantle all of my efforts to get this place running by the rules over the last six years."

"Whose rules, Lucy? Yours or the hospital's?"

"Well, when it comes to proper procedures for handling the people of Las Vegas Memorial, when they've misbehaved, when we need to build a case to dismiss them, when we have a disruptive complaint, when there are allegations of sexual pressure or misconduct, then we have to abide by the rules that will keep this hospital safe from lawsuits, Equal Employment Opportunity Commission (EEOC) complaints and a whole bunch of other legal hellholes our board does not want us to experience. I'm sure you would agree with that. That's what rules are for."

"And you and your staff discern those rules?"

"Well, yes, of course. Who else? We involve our General Counsel if we need help, but, yes, that's one of our functions."

"And the board works with you on this, or receives regular reports?"

"What? No! Of course not. They expect me to do my job and that's exactly what I've been doing."

Lucy Martin had come half out of her chair, abandoning her rather transparent dance of pretended agreement. She was gesturing at Will over the small conference table and obviously a millimeter away from losing it. Will had motioned for her to calm down, which had had the opposite effect. She'd been shaking slightly as she took a deep breath and looked at him. "With all due respect to you, Will, as incoming CEO, we've managed to get the HR department running very smoothly. I know what I'm doing. It would be a huge waste and even dangerous to force me to change it. In fact, I don't even know how to run an HR department without complying with the basics."

Will kept his voice calm and friendly and fought back the irritation he felt at her response, substituting as sincere a smile as he could. "My desire, Lucy, is not to force you to do anything. Rather I need to win you over to a much broader view of your function based on the way you and your team affect the people of this hospital. When it comes to hiring good people and working to keep them here, I think you're right. Obviously you've done a good job. But what you don't know is that I've just spent a month undercover, sitting around this hospital and learning what's really motivating people. Regardless of how pure your intentions are, and how classically in compliance your procedures and rules are, what I'm telling you is that most of the people at Las Vegas Memorial are too frightened of this HR department to interfere even when they know something isn't black and white and needs a more nuanced approach to dealing with our people."

"Frightened? Well, they have no business interfering! I've never tolerated interference."

"Exactly. That message has been received, but instilling fear is counterproductive. Do you know what onerous word keeps coming up whenever HR is referenced in the trenches?"

He waited her out until the silence was unbearable and she had to say something. "What?"

"Nazis. Certainly you folks don't deserve that, but Lucy, from a leader's perspective, you can't jawbone the wind into compliance. The impression they hold is the reality, and you can't wish it or order it away."

"That's insulting and regrettable, but I suppose it's the price we have to pay for being a rule-based organization."

"Is it? The way I look at it, one of your primary duties is to be in lockstep with the philosophies of this hospital, and one of the most important philosophies is that management is here to serve the staff in their front-line efforts to provide the best care. That means that the responsibility to be acutely aware of how HR policies and procedures affect the people is paramount. Solving the so-called great debate on measuring the 'impact' that all of the HR programs have on the organization and its ability to execute the business strategy is not an esoteric exercise, but a prime directive. But the department you've built makes no attempt at it. Worse, our managers, directors, leaders and chiefs have been beaten into submission and simply defer to your rules, even when they need to make intelligent decisions on their own of who to discipline, who to protect and when to act. How can they lead their people if all decisions are taken from them?"

"Will, I'm sorry, but that is grossly unfair and overstated!"

"Perhaps, but let me give you an example. Several months ago, a very dysfunctional senior nurse who had been dragging down the attitudes and performance of the night shift and essentially operating like a little Caesar, made the mistake of cursing out a younger nurse in front of a patient, and in her room. The patient was wide awake, a member of the local clergy, and very upset over the language used and the vitriol and—as he put it—

'inherent hatred in the woman's voice.' The confrontation ended with the senior nurse grabbing and twisting the younger nurse's arm until she cried out, and the younger nurse fled the floor, went home and resigned by phone the next day. The clergyman contacted her later at home and offered to be a witness if she filed a criminal or a civil complaint, but the young nurse was too traumatized. She's still unemployed."

"I know that case. We handled it after the nurse manager screwed it up."

"Screwed it up? Well, that nurse manager was called at two in the morning by a very upset charge nurse. If you remember the facts, you'll recall that the manager came into the hospital in the middle of the night, heard the story and calmly interviewed everyone on the floor including the upset patient, taking copious notes. She then pulled the senior nurse off the floor, demanded she apologize immediately to all concerned, and when that was refused, she took the woman's ID badge, fired her and had security escort her to the front entrance."

"But...but she had no *authority* to do that!"

"Oh, really? She was the Nurse-Manager of that floor. In what way did she not have the authority to make an emergency dismissal?"

"There's a proper way to handle such things."

"Which is?"

"You preserve the record and let *us* know. We start the process. That's the way we've *always* done it!"

"Right, and just as had happened four times in previous years, this sour but savvy veteran knew exactly which buttons to push to get HR to kick her loose—all she had to do was take a behavior course and not attack anyone verbally for six months. That's our rule, right?"

"Yes, it surely is."

"Did you know the last occurrence for her had been seven months before, and she knew she was now free and the letter in her file would have been pulled?"

"But, Will, don't you see? That doesn't matter. The manager had no authority to fire her on the spot. She could've forced the employee to clock out, but that's all."

"Which is why you opened a case on the nurse manager and eventually put a letter of reprimand in *her* file, right?"

"Yes. Of course."

"So, what message did you send to all the other managers by handling it that way, Lucy?"

"To follow the rules or you'll pay a price."

"No. The message you sent to every manager and every director and every charge nurse was that managers have no authority to address egregious behavior in a timely fashion; that they are powerless. Don't you understand how that guts the ability of a manager to be a manager—how the other employees look at her as impotent as a result? In fact, the senior nurse was rehired by you the next week, paid back pay, given a letter of apology and the nurse manager was essentially stripped of her authority, which is why *she* quit a month after that."

The bonds holding Lucy's fury back at being challenged were slipping further, and she leaned forward almost to the point of wagging a finger in Will's face, her eyes little more than angry slits. "Will, please! Surely you should understand how big a lawsuit that nurse could've filed and won against Las Vegas Memorial for wrongful discharge?"

"Lucy, who gave you the impression that determining which risks this hospital takes is your function?"

"Pardon?"

"HR's disciplinary actions and the procedures for handling internal complaints are all very important, but they are all subject to management revision, are they not?"

"No! They are organizational rules. I mean, yes, if you or the board wants to overrule or change things, but we can't have every little manager running around disregarding the rules. We'd have a dozen lawsuits a week! We'd have anarchy!"

"And, again, where did you get the idea that this is always your decision?"

"That's the way it's always been," she said, as internal caution suddenly pulled her back from the brink again. She sat back slightly, her fingers drumming unconsciously on the table. "Will, may I ask what you would've done, if you think I got it wrong?"

"In that case? I would've reported the whole affair around

the hospital with complete transparency within twelve hours, held the nurse manager up as a paradigm of excellence, personally apologized to the young nurse and pleaded with her to come back and told the fired nurse to make my day if she wanted to sue *and* would have filed a criminal information report with the district attorney of this county for assault and battery."

"But, you see, forgive me, but in my experience all that's foolhardy! That's begging for a lawsuit!"

"Lucy, don't you understand what I'm trying to point out, that it's the trust and morale of the workforce that is vastly more important than being occasionally hamstrung by our own rules, or even sued?"

"No. I really don't. I've been an HR professional for a long time and all I can see in that is an invitation to anarchy. Your HR director is here to keep people from doing such dangerous things."

It had gone downhill quickly from there, with dismissal as the only choice. Watching Lucy's disbelieving expression when he'd told her to draft a message on the essence of their disagreement was worse than unpleasant. Obviously she was a good person and a hard worker, but equally apparent was the fact that she had no clue about the existence, or the importance, of trust and morale in a stressed workforce. *Worse,* Will thought, *she regarded the people of Las Vegas Memorial as adversaries of everything she believed she was supposed to accomplish.*

Will let the mental replay evaporate, sighing as he glanced at his watch, aware once again of the peaceful surroundings. Hopefully, the rest of the day wasn't going to be as stressful as that confrontation, but if he had to deal with a steady procession of Lucy's, his hair would be steel gray by sundown. He got to his feet and decided to reward himself with a latte from the Starbucks in the lobby before meeting with his CFO.

And to think I could be fishing in a cold, Idaho stream right now with no worries! When did I become a masochist?

Richard Holbrook, the chief financial oofficer, by contrast, sat down with a confident ease about him that Will hadn't noted in their previous encounters. Thirty minutes of laying out his observations and philosophies were met with an even expression from across the table, and Will let his guard slip just a notch by the time he asked the experienced CFO for his thoughts.

"Well, you're obviously a man of great and noble intentions, Will, and I have great respect for what you just laid out. The emphasis on patient safety—the 'patient-centric' model—the getting our doctors in lock step, all of that is a laudable and even exemplary, and I agree that would put us on a course to emulate St. Michael's."

"But?"

"You know what I'm going to say, surely. You pointed out yourself that the fee-for-service model is under terminal assault, and yet it's all we have. So how to pay for all this and keep the doors open is the beating heart of the challenge."

"No disagreement there, Richard. Don't you think we can figure it out as a team?"

"Okay, let's take some of these head on. First, you said you think we should look into the feasibility of becoming an accountable care organization (ACO), like CMS is asking—even though Congress may dismember the underlying legislation in a year or two. What's the essence of an accountable care organization as of today? They're asking us to give away our money in hopes we'll qualify to get it all back by keeping everyone in our identified group healthy, even though we're not really sure what rules we'd have to follow to get that money back. Nor would we have any assurance that we *would* get it back. And this, when we're teetering on the brink of insolvency, with each percentage point rise in non-payment or reduced reimbursement, let alone refused reimbursement of never events. It's too much to ask."

"You think we can fence sit, Richard?"

"No, no..." he came forward slightly in his chair, gesturing for Will to wait for a clarification. "I know what you said to the board about not fence-sitting, and I agree we have to move smartly in many directions, but entering an ACO form at this stage seems reckless."

"Richard, we both know the idea and the form for ACOs are evolving almost by the hour. Why can't we work on our own approach instead of waiting for the government to mandate how to do it? Why should we declare it dead on arrival? The stated ethos of this place is to serve the population. Can't we find a better way to do it than just respond to illness? Why is that reckless?"

"Will, the essence of an ACO by any definition is to identify a certain group we're responsible for and make them healthier. We become accountable for the care of that defined population segment, either by ourselves or, preferably, with a group of providers in which we're just the hospital. Great idea, but the end game of making people healthy and no longer in need of the very services that pay the bills is bankruptcy. I don't like that conundrum any more than you do, but we're stuck with it if we want to keep the doors open."

"I didn't say I had the answers, Richard, only that I want us to work together on finding them, and that I need your loyalty to me and to the mission."

Richard snickered. "Well, as long as that loyalty doesn't mean I'm supposed to sit back and let you or anyone else bankrupt this institution, no problem."

"Are you the guardian, Richard?"

"Excuse me?"

"Is that the job description of the CFO, that you are the final authority and the appointed guardian of Las Vegas Memorial's financial survival?"

Will could feel caution clashing with confusion as the CFO searched for the right way to respond. For the first time in their conversation, Richard Holbrook sat back and really looked at him.

"My job description, Will, is to provide you and, when asked, the board, with financial reality, as well as to make sure the financial equipment that is under my direction, so to speak, runs perfectly. I get to advise you on policy, and hopefully participate in policymaking discussions, but ultimately I don't *make* the policy."

"And, yet, like a good officer of anything, you shoulder responsibility for speaking up, and very loudly at that, when you think someone like me is making a dangerous mistake."

"Of course."

"And I agree. But let's cut through any shadowboxing, shall we? I know you disagreed with my predecessor's policies, and I know you approached her honorably and head on. I also know that when she overruled you, you went to the board behind her back and essentially tried to protect the hospital. Are my facts correct?"

"Well, I didn't sneak behind her back, if that's what you mean. I warned her I would not stay silent."

"Here's the thing, Richard. When I say to you I need your loyalty, I do NOT mean loyalty to me and some sort of Omerta doctrine with respect to the board. But what would cause us to part ways very rapidly would be a maverick approach to the board, or any board member by you.

"By that you mean..."

"I mean if you think I'm wrong about something and I disagree with you, tell me clearly and we'll convene as a senior executive team and work it out. If we can't agree, and you really feel strongly about whatever it is, we'll come up with either an integrative solution to present to the board, or several alternatives—one of them incorporating your suggestions. Richard, if you were sitting here in the CEO chair, you'd say the same thing, or should, to me. You are not the lone ranger guardian of this hospital. We are, a team, and while I'm in charge, I won't ever muzzle you, but I also won't tolerate working with the lone ranger. It won't work any other way. Can you live with that?"

"As long as you can live with the reality that I *will* object vociferously to you if I think you're about to seriously injure us."

"But to me directly, right? Not an end run to the board?"

"Yes, sir."

"Okay. I know you're an honorable man and I'll hold you to that promise. Now tell me about patient safety."

"You mean, how we're going to pay for safety?"

"Richard, I think that we can make major changes in this culture without significantly increasing short term costs, but in the long term, I'm convinced the programs we'll institute will actually result in significantly lower costs. Happier employees, for instance, means lower turnover. Instead of losing 18 percent of our nurses every year at a cost of up to eighty five thousand per nurse..."

"More like ninety thousand."

"Okay, ninety, but that means if we can save ten nurses from quitting, we've saved just shy of a million dollars."

"And I have to be concerned about the costs of the programs that *you* hope will accomplish such a good goal."

"Fair enough. For one thing, we will have to do some dismissing and transferring of people in the wrong positions, or those who simply can't uphold the standards of ownership and performance we need. For every nurse we lose, that's ninety thousand. So initially there will be a bigger one-time cost. But those actions will lead to much lower operating costs."

"I understand that's the expectation."

"And, Richard, we also must become experts on simulation, both with and without the instrumented dummies and procedural training suites. We also need an entirely new program for training our new hires and our existing people. One day is a mere fraction of what's needed."

"Which means more personnel expense."

"Yes, but let me ask you. What's my return on investment (ROI) time factor?"

"How long to achieve a return on investment, you mean?"

"Let's say I use a few million dollars in the first year for new positions and training courses. How long do you think I have to make those improvements pay off in measureable bottom line results, both to cover the initial boost in cost and perpetually pay for themselves? Two years? Five?"

"Well—that's an amortization question. Maybe five. Preferably only two or three."

"Okay. And how about entirely new C-suite positions?"

"Such as?"

"I want a chief research officer (CRO) position and a chief safety officer (CSO), and I'll need a lot of cash to hire the right people."

"Will, we can cover those, but we have capital expenditures, as well, to complicate things."

"I know, and I want us to reexamine every one of those programs to see if they're really justified. The second PET scanner, for instance, that's about to be ordered."

"By what measure should we reexamine planned and

approved expenditures?"

"By focusing on what it will take to serve our patients better, not what it will take to earn more money, with the idea that a bigger institution is by definition better. Are you familiar with St. Mary's in Grand Junction, Colorado, and how they and the other hospitals in the area have learned to parcel out big equipment and specialty services rather than all compete with each other?"

"Somewhat. Didn't the primary care doctors in the area pretty much direct that by telling one hospital or another they wouldn't send patients if they built a second CT center, or MRI center?"

"Essentially, yes. I know we're in cutthroat competition here, but we can respect the same ideas."

"Our doctors will simply leave. The new orthopedic center, for instance. We ditch that and we might as well shut down our orthopedic services."

"Maybe, Richard. Maybe not. And maybe we should shut down orthopedics. Are you willing to question all those assumptions? No sacred cows, and no blanket conclusion that docs will leave if we don't do A or B?"

"Sure. But it's a really perilous attitude."

"All I'm asking is zero prejudice and a careful reexamination of our financial assumptions. Can you, and will you, provide me with that unwavering support?"

"If I can't, you'll have my resignation on your desk. But only after we've talked it out."

"Excellent."

"Will, one question. I'm—forgive me, but I'm more than curious. Frankly, I need to know."

"Go ahead."

"Look, you're probably aware of what you're taking on here, not just in coming aboard as CEO, but in terms of all these monster changes you want to make. I mean, Lord, man, you're the proverbial ram trying to break a concrete dam open! Regardless of what happens in the rest of the country, do you really think you can pull all this off, creating the perfect level of patient safety and zero preventable impacts, the happy staff, the doctors in lock step for, maybe, the first time in history?"

"At least the second time in history, if you count St. Michael's in Denver," Will corrected with a wry smile.

"Right. But, seriously, while I don't think you're either delusional or naive about the world, or medicine, are you truly convinced we can make such a transformation?"

"Perfect question, and the answer is twofold. We can't accomplish it overnight, but within a few months, we can begin to create the very sturdy and certain framework that will take us there. This culture can be changed, and from that change, everything else will flow."

Chapter Seventeen

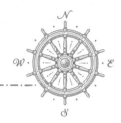

"Report," called Laurinda to Maura over the intercom into room nine forty-two. "Report on the line for nine fifty-four."

Mrs. Finch observed the lines of concern on her nurse's face. It had taken Maura fifteen minutes just to walk her into the bathroom, exercising her new hip for the very first time.

"Go ahead, honey," she said sweetly, waving Maura off "I'll be fine. I'll just wait right here until you come back." Quickly, Maura showed Mrs. Finch the emergency cord and instructed her to pull it if she felt dizzy or needed help.

As the night progressed, the pressure was increasing exponentially. Maura rapidly ran through her mental list: pain pills for nine forty-two, blood sugar for nine forty-three, dressing soaked in nine sixty-four and she still needed to check the last hematocrit.[vi] And now, nine forty-three needed help to the bathroom, again. Her assignment had been split because Ethel, an older nurse with more seniority, had coerced the charge nurse into assigning all *her* rooms together so she wouldn't have to walk so far 'after all these years.' As a result, Maura's rooms were scattered down three halls and she was running all over the place.

Maybe if Ethel lost fifty pounds she wouldn't mind all the walking, thought Maura. And now, report's on hold for my fifth patient!

"I can take your post-op if you can't handle five patients," said Julie, with a conspiratorial glance at Megan. It wasn't the words; it was the tone of voice that insinuated that Maura couldn't pull her full share of the workload if she was already so busy with *only four* patients. It was the look that Julie shot at Megan, lobbying for agreement. But hadn't Diane commented in last month's staff meeting that Julie and Megan were such a great team?

More like a gang, Maura thought. Everyone knew that Megan never came back from lunch on time, and Julie was always arriving to work late. And together, well, the only teamwork Maura ever saw was how they covered for each other.

"No thanks. I'm good," replied Maura, hurrying to the main nurse's station.

"Can you ask Charles to take report," she asked Laurinda, adding, "Puh-lease? I'm just swamped."

"I'll ask him," Laurinda replied, "but he's really busy with the new admit from the SNF."

"SNF or sniff" was slang for Skilled Nursing Facility. These older patients usually consumed a lot of time and resources because they were confused, on numerous medications and couldn't remember their history—or even their symptoms.

"Thank you, Laurinda!" she said sincerely, while looking up the hematocrit level on the computer. "And can you page Dr. Cooper for me?" Maura was concerned about the blood loss in nine sixty-four. That was the second time she had changed the dressing and now the blood pressure was trending lower.

Laurinda liked working evenings because eventually things would calm down—unlike the day shift, which was a two-meal circus with a steady stream of visitors, physical therapists and doctors all writing new orders. Now that the hospital was computerized with a complex physician order entry system, she no longer had to copy the paper orders into the computer. And, after twenty-six years, she felt entitled to a little payback for all she'd done for the hospital: coming in on her days off, picking up extra shifts and working without a break. It was about time; and payback tonight was in the form of a paperback.

Laurinda sent a Metrocall page to Charles and returned to her romance novel until the next call light buzzed. The tall, dark, handsome hero was now seducing the heroine who didn't even know she was being conned! He was really a CIA agent who only wanted her for the information she could provide, and bless her heart—poor Vanessa was unlocking the chain on her hotel room when…

Laurinda jumped slightly when the phone rang again. It was the post-anesthesia care unit (PACU), and the nurse on the other end was adamant that she had to give report *NOW* and go home because she was already on overtime and needed to relieve her babysitter. Laurinda flagged down Charles with a wave of her hand to take report just as Sandy Keaton arrived at the front desk. Charles raised his finger and pointed to the report with a reassuring smile; so Sandy proceeded on down to her mother's room, ruminating about the post-surgery conversation with Dr. Cooper.

There was something about that conversation that bothered her, but she just couldn't put her finger on it. Not yet, at least. Obviously, her mother had reacted badly to the Vancomycin and had developed something called "Red Man's Syndrome." During surgery her blood pressure plummeted and they'd had to give Vasopressors and a lot of Benadryl. She should've asked if this was an unexpected adverse reaction, and whether or not an incident report had been filed, but in that moment the daughter in her overshadowed the risk manager. In a paternal gesture, Dr. Cooper had put his arm around Sandy's shoulder, reassuring her that her mother would probably be very sleepy and "not to worry because the hip surgery turned out just fine." Still, she wished that Cooper would be around for the weekend, and secretly prayed Dr. Henderson wasn't on call for the practice.

Sandy rearranged the flowers and cleaned up the room while making a mental note to say something to Diane about the mess: a wrapper from a syringe on the floor by the trash basket, papers and blankets piled on the side table. It wasn't long before she heard the rattle of the gurney, and anxiously went to the doorway to welcome her mother.

But the transporter was waiting in the hall, refusing to come into the room until the nurse arrived to verify that she had received the patient and that this was indeed the right room. It was Julie who saw him waiting in the hall first. She signed the card so that he could proceed, scribbling "B.S." and winking at the transporter who shook his head and smiled broadly in response. Almost two years had passed since administration had begun the "Passport to Safety" program to reduce errors. In that entire time, no one had noticed there wasn't a single employee with the initials "B.S." The translation, however, was no mystery to anyone.

Concern overshadowed Sandy's face as she tried to wake her mother. "Mom," she said, squeezing her hand and feeling anxious as she waited for the return squeeze.

But Mrs. Keaton was not responding; her face pale, her breathing shallow.

Where was Charles? Who was her nurse? Why wasn't anyone here? Worried, Sandy pressed the call button just as Maura swung around the corner to take the vitals.

"Hello, my name is Maura Manning and I will be your mother's nurse until eleven."

"I'm Mrs. Keaton's daughter, Sandy."

"Nice to meet you, Sandy," replied Maura while setting up the portable blood pressure machine and attaching the cuff as her eyes scanned the room for the portable oxygen monitor.

"What's the matter?" asked Sandy.

"Oh, nothing really. I was just looking for the oxygen monitor that I put in the room earlier, but someone must have borrowed it." Someone named Megan, she thought.

"I'll be right back," she said to Sandy.

Maura looked up and down the hallway, but it was empty, so she went to the back hall where Julie and Megan were chatting and drinking coffee. "Did either of you see the oxygen monitor?" she asked.

"Yes, I borrowed it for my surgery patient. It's in room nine forty-one," Megan replied.

Maura retrieved the monitor and was heading back to nine fifty-four when her pager went off again.

"Nine forty-two needs help back to bed."

Oh, poor Mrs. Finch, Maura thought, trying to juggle priorities. She immediately called Laurinda back and asked her to find someone else since the post-op had just arrived. Laurinda sighed heavily on the phone before uttering a long, drawn out, "All-r-i-g-h-t" in a tone of voice that really said "F-a-t – C-h-a-n-c-e."

"Then please alert Charles," Maura added quickly before Laurinda could hang up.

As soon as Maura returned to Mrs. Keaton's room her eyes went straight to the monitor and she became worried. The blood pressure was only eighty-eight over forty-eight, her respirations were shallow and at only eight per minute; and she needed to turn the oxygen level up to four liters just to get the saturation monitor to register 92 percent.

"Sandy, I'm going to find Charles since he took report for me," Maura said, using her most reassuring tone of voice before turning to leave the room. But "false reassurance" was a skill that Maura had not yet mastered, and Sandy turned all her attention to her mother, immediately picking up on the poorly veiled sense of alarm.

The monitor was programmed to take another set of vitals every few minutes. Sandy waited anxiously for Maura, Charles, or a set of numbers on the machine that would reassure her nurses.

"Mother," she whispered softly, "wake-up. It's me, Sandy. It's time to wake up now. The surgery is over and you're back in the room. Can you squeeze my hand, Mom? Mom?"

But there was no reassuring squeeze in return.

Gently, Sandy removed the blue, gauze surgery cap and brushed a few long, wispy hairs across her mother's forehead. The gesture was a memory trigger. How many times had her mother done the same for her? When she had her tonsils out; when she was upset and didn't want to go to school and crawled out from under her bed on her second day of kindergarten; at her sister's funeral. It felt so strange and yet so natural, all at the same time, for her to be returning that simple wave of the hand that revealed how deeply they cared for one another.

Sandy heard the machine activate again and pulled away. Like bingo balls settling into a pattern, the machine finally revealed a set of numbers; it was not good.

A loud beeping sound filled the room. *The alarm!*

Sandy pushed the call light, but impatience overwhelmed her—the complaints on "call light response" times still fresh in her mind from last month's patient satisfaction scores. She turned and ran out of the room to find Charles giving Maura report at the main station.

"Hurry!" she called out to Charles, "Come quickly, the alarm is going off...something's not right!"

Charles, Maura and Sandy raced back to the room. Charles took one look at Mrs. Keaton and commanded sharply, "Call a Code."

Chapter Eighteen

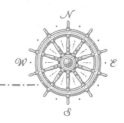

Will replaced the phone and sat in silence for a few seconds, focusing on the newly drawn lines connecting the various projects on the whiteboard covering most of the wall opposite his desk. He needed to make a few notes about the just-completed call, but the sheer number of boxes on that board were all but mocking him and grabbing his attention. Was it too much, this seemingly manic hit-the-deck-running quest to spin up a hospital full of new programs and rally the troops to follow his lead? It certainly wasn't stage fright that created the small knot in his stomach at the thought of the hundreds of employees he'd be addressing in the next few days. No, he thought, it was the question of whether they would consider him terminally naïve—and the nightmarish possibility that they might be right.

The phone rang and he reached somewhat absently for the receiver, startled to find Ivy on the other end.

"Ah, Doctor Jenkins?" she began, her use of last name signaling someone was in her office and listening.

"Yes, Ivy."

"I...ah...there's an unemployed nurse out here who says she knew you in an earlier life."

"I'm sorry, what?"

"She says she hasn't seen you in ages, and she wants to come in right now and say hello."

"Well...who *is* she?" Will asked, truly puzzled and slightly off-guard as his office door swung open and Janice strolled in with an exaggerated gait and a smile.

"Your wife by marriage, remember me? You said we'd always have Las Vegas."

Will shook his head and smiled as he rose to greet her.

"Honey!"

"Had you worried, huh? Ghosts of girlfriends past?" she teased, nudging the door closed behind her.

The expression crossing Will's face was one of concern, she noted, as if he really was worrying that she might feel neglected. Normally, she loved pulling his chain, playing with his tendency to be overly serious. But maybe now wasn't the best timing.

"I'm kidding, Sweetheart," she said leaning over to kiss him, and then settling into the armchair opposite his desk. "I just wanted to come by and provide reinforcements, if you needed any."

"I'm doing fine."

"You seem to be doing 'worried,' if I know that expression."

Will gestured to the wall behind her. "This looks like an impending military campaign, and I'm just trying to make sure I'm doing it right."

They were interrupted by the intercom before Janice could answer.

"Honey, I need to take this," he said. "It's Angela Siegel." She nodded as he punched the lit button on the desk phone. "Angela. How are you?"

Janice could hear Angela's voice through the handset.

"Great, Will. Got a minute?"

"I certainly do. Janice just dropped by to see if I'm hiding under my desk yet. She says hello."

"Well, put her on speakerphone, if you have one."

He punched the requisite buttons and the two women exchanged greetings.

"So, Will," Angela began, "are you having fun yet?"

"I'm pumped and I'm in motion and I know I'm kicking over hornets' nests and chasing sacred cows, but there's a sort of perverse fun in watching eyebrows shoot up."

"Excellent. Oh, first, I really should say again for the record that I'm well aware our board doesn't exist except when it's in session, and we're not in session, so I'm calling ex parte. But I'm curious to know some details of how your first week is going?"

"I'm going to need another board meeting very soon."

"Good. Mason is expecting that I'm sure. Next week?"

"In the next few weeks. I've identified an excellent candidate for chief research officer and I'm going to ask the executive committee for approval, but I think I need a preliminary meeting to report what I'm doing in detail and answer questions. By the way, did you know that it takes an average of seventeen years for valid, conclusive research on best practices to reach the clinical front lines? It's no wonder we can't make any real gains in quality and safety!"

"Where did that statistic come from, Will?"

"Two researchers named Ballas and Boren[vii]. Given what they've documented, we need a qualified, energetic CRO on duty yesterday. Anyway, that's just one of many things on my agenda. This afternoon, I have the first of a series of physician meetings that will undoubtedly trigger a cascade of upset calls to all of you."

"You warned us, and I appreciate the briefing sheet we received yesterday. So you're working on the docs first, but all next week you're holding staff meetings?"

"Not exactly. I'm working on my own team first and we're holding an off-site retreat on Friday where my primary goal is going to be to listen, align and realistically assess the level of trust among my own senior leadership team. I'm keenly aware that firing the director of HR shook everyone. After that retreat, I can concentrate on the physicians, and I've asked for required attendance. As for our employees, it's going to take a lot of repetition on my part, but I want everyone on our payroll to hear the plan directly from me—especially those who met me during my month of undercover work. Then, I plan on assembling virtually all the folks we consider to be middle management and task them with convincing us that they have what it takes to create solid relationships and communication among their people. We need them to understand that their job description is maturing, and they absolutely must have the willingness and ability to lead their folks. That requires relationships, not just hiding in their offices and filling out paperwork. Every manager, director and leader at any level is going to be subjected to a rather extensive employee survey on how effective and responsive they are to their people, and they're all being asked to learn how to do and actually accomplish a real three-sixty evaluation. All responses will be anonymous, but I still have some serious ground work to do to instill enough trust to get serious and probative answers."

"We're not talking about an up or down vote on managers by their people are we?"

"No. But I expect we'll be able to get a preliminary indication of who our ineffective, troublesome or absent managers are, and we can address it from there. We're also administering safety attitude surveys to everyone with our ID cards, with no opt outs, and I'm going to personally send the results with a full narrative explanation to the entire payroll, as well as to all of our privileged docs who practice here—our so-called privileged physicians. As *for* our physicians, 100 percent participation will be required, and medical privileges will be suspended if a doc refuses to complete the survey."

"You'll need a bylaw change for that one, you know."

"Already in progress and I'll ask you guys to vote on it at the next meeting. Believe it or not, our CMO suggested it."

"*Kirk Nelson?* You're kidding!"

"No, he's jumped at the chance to help, and he's prepared a letter that all of our physicians will get tomorrow, entitled: 'What is it about the word 'Privilege' we're having trouble understanding?' His help has been the biggest shock of the last week."

"I'm very glad to hear he's on board, but don't kid yourself. You will have bomb throwers."

"You bet I will! Dr. Adams, for one. If Dr. Nelson doesn't cashier him, I may have to."

Will paused, shaking his head before continuing. "You know, Angela, I have to fight my own internal battle between wanting to change the world by lunchtime, and realizing that, as the principles of the Lean methodology teach, it takes at least eight years. We don't have eight years, but when it comes to the middle managers, for instance, I'm going to have to walk a delicate line. I'm going to tell them up front, nose-to-nose, that their most important duty is to directly facilitate the ability of everyone on the front lines to do their jobs with total safety in a supportive, and even fun environment. We will probably need aggressive retraining, of course, to polish those skills, but there will inevitably be some who can't rise to the challenge. The last thing I want to do is create fear, so we'll concentrate on recruiting them to the overall vision while teaching them what we really need from their leadership, and steadily moving out those folks who can't cut it. But most of all, my plan is that they see how my team and I have changed our behaviors."

"Good. I'm loving this. What else?"

"Richard Holbrook and I had a heart-to-heart, and thanks to your heads up, he assured me he's on board, and in fact he's already sparking some great ideas on the financial front. I mean, ideas that really do go to the heart of service and safety."

"Good."

"Angela, I figure another few months of very intense communicating is going to be necessary before I get the kickoff message clearly to everyone that this is all real, and not another flavor-of-the-month. We've retained two of the top experts in the country on simulation and role playing using video to help us set up a robust simulation program, mostly without instrumented dummies, although we really need to ramp up a robust simulation suite with qualified facilitators for tactical, clinical training. I'm aiming at the OR teams and the surgeons first, then a heavy concentration on the emergency room, followed by the ICUs and then all over. This is transactional simulation for just about everyone clinical. And, I'm announcing to the docs tonight that one of my goals is to have high-definition (HD) quality video cameras in every OR for every procedure within six months."

"How's our in-house lawyer taking that one?"

"Amazingly, he's up to speed and loves the idea. Apparently he's done the research and understands it's probably our most effective defense in a medical malpractice case, provided there have been no infantile outbursts during a procedure, that is."

"Six months. That's ambitious, Will."

"Not really. I can buy six HD cameras with mounting brackets and a multi-channel hard drive recorder for under twenty-five hundred dollars. Ten years ago it would have cost perhaps twenty thousand or more."

"How about my pet project, the school nurse program?"

"In progress. Ivy will call you in a few days. I'm recruiting an interdisciplinary group to work, under your guidance, to get a pilot project started, and then I intend to try to shame our competitors into joining us. My office looks like a war room with a huge whiteboard installed at one end to track the initiatives. Janice is shaking her head at it as we speak. But I have to be very, very careful not to launch something and not keep it running at the same intensity."

"You're dead right about that! Don't bite off too much too soon. By the way, Janice...?"

"Yes, Angela," Janice answered. "I'm still hear."

"You did a great job writing that targeting summary. Order out of chaos—wonderfully succinct! It's comforting to know Will is backed by such solid academic knowledge."

"Thanks, Angela."

Janice sighed softly as Will hung up the phone. It was the hallmark sound that he knew only too well after twenty-four years of marriage—more than she even knew. It was the sound that he both loved and hated—the dynamic tension that kept their relationship alive because as much as he was loathe to admit it, she challenged him.

Will drew in his own deep breath, automatically preparing himself for the comments that were certain to follow.

Chapter Nineteen

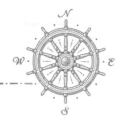

"Well?" Will asked, watching her intently.

Janice stood up to study the whiteboard more closely and then pulled out the clip holding up her shoulder length brown hair, shaking it out. She sat back down in the maroon leather chair in front of his desk, keenly aware that the seating arrangement was perfect for the impending conversation.

"You can storm the Bastille, Will, but you won't win the revolution that way," she said, her eyes glued to the boxes and arrows—his magic formula that, from her view, seemed overly simplistic and authoritarian. For a moment she hesitated, doubting herself. But then again, that whiteboard was, well, so commander-like, and there was no question in her mind that he didn't see it.

"What do you mean?" Will replied, acutely aware of the cat and mouse game; the one word answers that would inevitably open Pandora's Box. Suddenly, he wasn't feeling so pumped.

"How CEO of you," Janice said, giving voice to her thoughts.

"What's that supposed to mean?"

"Well, it's how every dedicated CEO commands his ship. They follow the exact same well-intentioned course you've laid out. Senior leaders meet in private and identify a brilliant solution to a problem, and then go about trying to create some ephemeral energy called 'buy in.' Only the king and his court are allowed to attend these formative meetings which are by invitation only, and always held secretly behind closed doors. The magic *formula* from the king ends up being called an *initiative* when it is announced to the plebeians; and very shortly after its creation, it's re-formatted into something called an *action plan*, which is then translated for teaching the masses into a *PowerPoint*. Months, even decades later, the *PowerPoint* is transformed into a *blue flyer* on the back of the unit's bathroom door. The paper used to be white, but then it became hard to differentiate all the king's many *initiatives*, so the king started using different colors as the marketing advisor suggested. These different color flyers eventually become known as the *flavor-of-the-month*. Of course, the flyer still retains the king's seal, the hospital logo."

"That's not funny," Will said flatly.

"No," Janice responded soberly, "it's not funny. It's not intended to be funny. It's the allegorical truth. It's the corporate hospital culture."

"Honey, I'm taking great pains not to do the top-down dance, but I have to knock out a few walls before I can convince everyone we have to remodel."

"Like ditching the doors to the C-suite, which was good. No, I know you understand it, Will, but you're making the very mistake you yourself have warned against."

"Well, tell me, then. What am I *not* seeing? What's wrong with my strategic plans?"

"They're not just well-intentioned, they're *Will*-intentioned."

"Meaning what, exactly? They're all good, solid ideas—many backed by solid research."

"The problem is, Darling, *they're* your ideas, and they radiate too far beyond the opening rounds of this revolution you're starting. You'll never create the energy and synergy you seek past the initial stages if you impose your ideas on others—no matter how wonderful and noble those ideas may be. Remember what you said about leadership needing to spark the torch-lighters in the first hours of the cultural upheaval?"

"Isn't that what I'm laying out here?"

"Look at this!" she said, standing and tracing the lines between the various stages radiating to carefully drawn boxes with neatly lettered descriptions of what was to be done.

"This is a perfect progression, but since it's all neatly decided beforehand without the majority of ideas coming from the rank and file and from your senior and middle leadership, it really forms the typical, hierarchical model of power. What was your plan, anyway? To *GIVE* them their shared vision?"

"No, to guide them to it," Will replied, sounding slightly offended. He got to his feet and walked around the desk toward the whiteboard, as if needing to make sure he'd read it correctly. "They have to be jolted into reality, Janice. I would love it if there was some form of spontaneous combustion that would instantly ignite their passion and dedication, but it seems to me that change is urgently needed. How else can I get there?"

"Why do you think they need to be guided?" she prompted.

"Because if they didn't, this place would already be St. Michael's and my transformative leadership wouldn't be needed. The idea that I could just *suggest* this organization into zero patient safety disasters and collegial interactive teamwork and a patient-centric ethos is just plain silly."

"I am not suggesting you just use the power of suggestion. Remember the theory course I taught last semester, Will? Remember the quote I gave you in the card I stuffed in your briefcase when you first came down here?"

"Of course." Will knew exactly where he'd put it: inside the inlaid wooden box she had given him for Christmas. He walked over to the bookcase and took out the greeting card. Because it was just the two of them—no family, no pets, no legacy—he treasured every piece of paper she'd ever given him, even though she chided him for being such a pack rat. Will studied the bright blue-green geometric circles on the front of the card before opening it and reading the words she had inscribed inside:

"No person, no matter how wise or powerful
Can control outcomes in a complex adaptive system"
(Lindberg/Nash)

He knew exactly what she'd been trying to do with those words: soothe his tortured soul; offer consolation; hold out a hand or some shimmering ray of redemption to help him get back up when he was doubled over in pain about Ronnie, and so much more.

Suddenly, Will looked as somber as Obama accepting the presidency.

"What's going on, Will?"

"I wasn't even captain of this ship when we hit an iceberg."

"What?" replied Janice, struggling to follow.

"I found out yesterday that we lost another patient the very day I accepted the position—a young mother of two. And the general thinking is just like the Titanic: You're bound to hit an iceberg every once in a while, but it won't sink us; we'll survive. We always survive. No one sees the human damage, or the human drama. By the time the report hits the CEO's desk, the patients we've harmed or killed are just a statistic: three deaths now, instead of two, and the board will see that as an improvement. But I'll bet, Janice, if their jobs depended on it, not one person on the board—and probably most of my team—could ever tell you those patients' names."

"They don't care, then?"

"Oh, I'm sure they *care*, but they disconnect themselves from the humanity involved. For us docs, it's maintaining a protective clinical distance which allows us to keep practicing when things go wrong. For the board and the non-clinical leaders, it's a process of telling themselves that keeping their emotional distance leads to more effective management. But what it really does is make us callous."

"It's called cognitive dissonance, which keeps the very information that organizations need so desperately to succeed at arm's length."

"Absolutely!"

"People need to identify with safety on a personal level. Remember the keynote speaker at last year's Institute for Healthcare Improvement (IHI) meeting? Marshall Ganz? He spoke about how stories are effective learning tools and how they connect us to our values. That's what I'm saying, Will, if your message is not personal, and doesn't resonate with their core values, all your efforts will just become another flavor-of-the-month. And with that, I think you need to stop assessing the stars and start planning your heading. What's the course, Captain?"

Will moved to the whiteboard, picked up an eraser, and began selectively altering "the plan."

"Well, if this is far too top-down, then I have to come down from the bridge, so to speak. I thought I was already doing it, but

I guess if I can flatten the hierarchy some more, I'll improve chances of eliciting that buy-in and ownership and getting everyone moving in a common direction."

"Yes, that is precisely what a shared vision means. Shared, not provided or dictated, although I agree, you weren't trying to be dictatorial."

Will stood in thought for almost a minute, and Janice remained quiet, letting him puzzle it out. "I guess," he said at last, turning to her, "it has to be a combination. I get it, what you said Honey, about being spring-loaded to issue top-down directives. But I'm right, too, about the impossibility of just suggesting our way to cultural change. So how am I going to do it? First, I need all hands on deck. I think I need representatives from virtually every major department in the hospital who can meet with me regularly, carry water in both directions and be swapped out often to prevent empire building. I need these folks to know they have twenty-four seven access to me, and that they can use it, and even more importantly, I need them to truly believe that their input is critical. Because it is. And for that to happen, they will need to see results."

"You're going to let them invade the C-suite at will?"

"At Will, huh? You're beginning to sound like Ivy and her puns."

"Seriously, Will, are you going to listen to every minor complaint? I'm not sure that's the best..."

"They'll be better guardians of my time than Ivy by just knowing they can always reach me. Besides, that's a very telling behavior on my part. I've read more than once that if you want to change a fear-based culture, you focus on behaviors, as well as language. It's going to be vital for me to explain things thoroughly and repeatedly. I've seen plenty of examples of the current fear-based culture from my Undercover Boss project, but I haven't yet had the opportunity to share those insights, and when I do, I have to be very careful not to step on toes or betray their trust. This is a group silenced by fear."

"Fear of litigation?"

"That, along with the prime fear of hurting a patient; being diminished in the eyes of one's fellows; being rejected by your peers; and fear of losing a job in this economy. Of course, here I am preparing to come in and say *Trust me!* when the rank-and-file reputation of the average CEO is more akin to a corporate mafia Don who will threaten their jobs—which are their lives. I know exactly how they're going to regard me at first, as if I'm saying: *Trust me! You don't need your defenses anymore. You don't need those rumors, elevator conversations and important liaisons that have been protecting you for the last forty years. Everything is different because I'm here. Speak up! No one will freeze you out, make your life a living hell if you point out a problem, or clandestinely report you, or eliminate your position; and on and on."*

"When I was undercover, and people were talking to me with no clue I was going to be their new CEO and I said, 'hey, I hear you're getting a new leader,' the universal response was a 'big deal' and an eye roll! It's going to take very honest and sustained effort on my part to overcome that prejudice."

"Eye roll, huh? That's not good, but it's also not unexpected, right?"

"Well, down in sterilization, for instance, the shift manager told me she hadn't even seen a CEO in her twenty years at Las Vegas Memorial. She wondered if they even knew where the sterilization department was. When I asked what a new CEO should do to show that everything's changed, she said it wasn't possible. 'Any CEO,' she said, 'who knows where we are and what we do, would never be appointed a CEO because he'd be too busy steering the ship way up on the bridge to pay any attention to us.' How's that for convoluted logic? But what really saddened me is that they don't perceive their value. They're unaware of their own pivotal role in keeping the patients safe and the hospital afloat."

Janice stood up, glancing pensively at the board before looking Will squarely in the eye. "Remember when I drafted the summary of your mission?"

"Of course. I have a copy right here on the desk." He picked it up and Janice took the sheet, looking for a particular passage.

"When you were defining your mission that night," she began, "this is what I heard you say: *Create a proud and cohesive sense of commonality, mutual respect, and communication (vertical and horizontal) at Las Vegas Memorial in which enthusiastic ownership (not just involvement or engagement) is the minimum requirement for membership."*

"I remember. And I concede the point. I guess I was just falling back into my old familiar ways—to enforce, cajole and motivate from the top like in Portland—and we both know that didn't work. I was applying the same leadership principles you would use for a factory to a complex adaptive system."

"Define 'Complex Adaptive System' for me, Honey?"

"This is going to be on the final, isn't it, professor?"

"Yep. Passing grade or sleep on the couch," she teased.

"Glad you don't actually use those criteria for your real classes!"

"No, they arrest that kind of teacher. Go ahead. Define it, please."

"I'd rather defer to your definition."

"Okay. A complex adaptive system has dominant elements of self-organization, non-linearity, unpredictability and others. The term comes from a work by Mary Chaffee and Margaret McNeill."[viii]

"I remember that work."

"But you do understand the concept?"

"Of course. It's *applying* the concept that's challenging me!" Shades of regret passed across Will's face and he turned back and stared at the whiteboard for several minutes until Janice grew uncomfortable with the silence.

"What was the patient's name, Will?"

He looked around, momentarily confused. "Sorry?"

"The young mother who died as you came aboard."

"Oh. Yes."

There was a white space directly in the middle of the board where Will had reluctantly erased some of his preliminary plan. He picked up the marker and wrote "Kari Markowitz" inside the circle.

"Her children are young—six and eight years old," he added.

Janice said nothing, vowing to remember the name, wanting to throw Will a lifeline. But it was Will who eventually tossed the saving gesture.

"Free for dinner, Sweetheart? I think I may have an idea."

Chapter Twenty

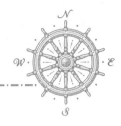

Sylvia's pager beeped loudly, alerting her to the code in room nine fifty-four.

"I'll be right back," she said to the worried wife she'd found pacing nervously just outside her husband's room in the ICU.

"I have to supervise a Code that's been called on one of our floors," Sylvia explained, extracting her hand slowly from the worried wife's clasp. "I've put a call into Hector Padilla, our chaplain. He should be here shortly, and I'll return as soon as I'm finished."

Mrs. Salazar finally nodded and smiled, unable to comprehend anything but the kind energy that emanated from Sylvia's eyes. She was frightened—more frightened than she had ever been in her life.

If only Lilia would come soon. Lilia with her college education could help her understand what happened to her husband of forty years.

Mrs. Salazar felt as if she'd been zapped into the cast of some bizarre TV medical reality show and all she wanted to do was *TURN IT OFF!* Had it only been a few minutes ago that she and her husband were sitting at the dinner table, snacking on left-over lumpia, the dish he loved from their native Philippines, and arguing about whether to give their son another loan?

Is all this my fault? Did my angry words make him sick?

Her eyes searched the tiny room so that she could at least place herself in time: ten thirty-three p.m. No, not minutes at all. It had been four hours now.

Where is Lilia? Where is that girl? She felt so stupid with her broken English; so overwhelmed in this strange environment of machines that hissed and beeped like alien animals. She

151

searched her husband's pale face again looking for hope, but his eyes were still closed. Plastic tubes of various sizes snaked into his veins, his mouth and his nose, while the white coats spoke in words she could not comprehend...*sudden cardiac arrest...code status...elevated cardiac enzymes.*

Sylvia bounded up the two flights of stairs, her mind continuously triaging the various requests from every area of the hospital. There were so many balls to juggle, and her job as hospital nursing supervisor was to keep them all in the air from seven at night until seven the next morning. The ER needed another bed, but the ICU was full. The whole reason she had gone to the ICU to begin with was to speak with the charge nurse about why the patient in room seven thirty-three was still taking up a bed. That's when she'd heard Mrs. Salazar sobbing, and she was diverted into consoling her. Med-Surg was short two nurses due to sick calls for the night shift, but she had the staffing office working on that one. Three West had received a patient from the ER an hour ago but now that patient's lab work indicated that she should have been admitted to the telemetry unit—a reoccurring mess that just never seemed to go away. And now, almost at shift change, a code.

By the time Sylvia arrived on the ninth floor, the code was already in progress. She stood in the doorway talking to Charles who filled her in as best he could; the patient had been on the floor less than ten minutes.

"Sandy!" said Sylvia, suddenly recognizing her colleague, "your mother?"

"Yes," replied Sandy, her eyes darting from one person to the next trying to absorb all the action in the room. Clearly the drugs the physician and resident were giving her mother had restored her vital signs, but she was worried. *What had happened, and will it happen again?*

"Sylvia, can we move my mother to the ICU for closer monitoring?"

"That's the doctor's call, Sandy."

"I know. But you know as well as I do that the hospital puts all the new nurses on the night shift and that her night nurse will have seven patients. Even if my mother is stable, I want someone monitoring her closely so this doesn't happen again."

Sylvia couldn't catch the sigh before it escaped. She was already short one bed in the ICU and there was simply no way she was going to find another. Since it was Sandy, she would just tell it like it was.

"There are no beds, Sandy. I already have a head bleed in the ER waiting and that patient is top priority. But I'll see what I can do. Let me work on it."

Let me work on it? Sylvia thought to herself heading for the stairwell. The words echoed in her head almost mockingly. She wasn't a damn magician. She knew from experience what this would entail: a late night phone call to Dr. Yablonsky whose ICU patient should've been placed in hospice care four days ago. His reputation as an oncology physician stemmed from his extreme dedication and passion to his patients who would wait for three to four hours in his office without complaining because he gave them what no other physician would: Hope.

False hope, thought Sylvia, *but big revenue from keeping the ICU full, so who's going to stop him?* She'd been relieved to hear Dr. Atul Gawande at a conference say, "Our ICUs are warehouses for the dying," because it comforted her that at least it wasn't just Las Vegas Memorial, but every hospital. The fine line between administering or withholding aggressive treatment seemed to be more obscure all the time because no one had the guts to draw it with absolute clarity.

Sylvia's pager beeped again. Staffing had found one nurse for Med-Surg. She picked up the phone and made a quick call to the Med-Surg charge nurse asking her to find someone who could work a double shift. From experience she knew that she couldn't under-staff that floor. Over the last ten years the acuity of the patients had literally doubled, and it was now the unit with the most falls. The hospital had spent a tremendous amount of energy on the fall prevention program, but there had been little improvement. When she had made rounds earlier, 28 of the 32 beds had "Falling Stars" posted on their doors. *Why not just slap the sign on every door?* she'd thought caustically.

Sylvia's mind operated with the same speed and efficiency as an advanced cardiac life support flow chart. She looked down at her notes: Yablonsky. First, she was going to have to get all the facts from the patient's nurse. She sought out Charles and found him inserting an intravenous line in room seven thirty-one.

"I'll be done in just a minute, Sylvia," he said, nodding to the family members in the room. Then he added, "And I think what you're looking for is in the side drawer of the main desk."

"What?" Sylvia replied, confused. But Charles was already re-immersed in his task. Curious, she went to the main station and opened the drawer. These were the moments that warmed her heart. After twenty years as the beacon of light for the night shift, there wasn't a staff member in the hospital who didn't know that Sylvia *loved* chocolate. Bless the family members, she thought, selecting the nut cluster which most resembled dinner with its protein value.

When Charles returned she simply said, "Yablonsky?"

"God knows I've tried. But I'm never here when he arrives in the morning to have a face-to-face. The lady in room seven thirty-three is a frequent flyer, been here four times in the last six months. She's emaciated, exhausted and barely hanging on, but what I got in report was that Yablonsky won't change her code status because he said he was going to try one more round of experimental chemo. Honestly, Sylvia, this situation breaks even my tough heart because all the family expects her to turn the corner any day now, and yet all the nurses know that that's just never going to happen."

"Did you ask social work to help?"

"Sure, over a week ago when she started going downhill again. But after you raise them from the dead three times, the family's expectations just rise even higher and they think you can do it a fourth. When you try to talk to Yablonsky, he gets belligerent; as if you're insinuating that he failed just by asking the question."

"Thanks, Charles," she said, "I'll talk to the family." But Charles rolled his eyes and shook his head in a gesture that said, "*girl, you are tip-toeing through a minefield!*

If only she didn't need the damn bed then she wouldn't be in this mess, Sylvia thought, approaching the daughter who was on vigil at her mother's side. A review of the chart had turned up absolutely no reason why this patient would not be in comfort care. The conversation would be delicate and quick, as Sylvia still had to get down the rest of her to-do list before change of shift: staffing, Sandy, and the ER were now paging her again about the head bleed.

"May I speak to you for a moment, Mrs. Campbell? I need to have a conversation with you before I call Dr. Yablonsky."

"Why, certainly," she said, rising from the bedside chair and tucking a tissue into her sleeve.

I wonder how old she is, Sylvia thought assessing the difficulty the daughter was having standing up and her hunched-over spine. She offered her arm and together they walked into the family quiet room.

"Is something wrong, Darling, that you have to call the doctor? He's such a wonderful man. Done for my mother what no other doctor could—just a saint, that man."

Sylvia offered the daughter a drink and then sat down next to her at the table. "Mrs. Campbell, as a nurse I have seen a lot. And sometimes what I see troubles me, which is why I'm having this conversation with you. I think we could do better by your mother. My problem is this: The way we are treating your mother is not what I would want for my own mother."

"Whatever are you saying, Darling? Did something happen? Why?"

"Mrs. Campbell, my goal here is to be honest because I need your help. The most important thing here is your mother and her wishes. Do you know what she would have us do if she could talk right now?"

Mrs. Campbell pulled out the tissue and started blotting her eyes before the tears even fell. "I know," she began slowly, "that the last thing she said to me was, 'Tired of fighting, Sweetie. Time to say goodbye.'"

"And then what happened? Do you know why her code status is still Full Code?"

"Well, the day nurse and the social worker asked us on the second admission to change the status, but Dr. Yablonsky said no flat out. He said, 'Nonsense, we're not giving up! I have a lot more tricks up my sleeve.'"

Sylvia said nothing. All she could do was picture Yablonsky in his white coat. She reached over and put her hand over Mrs. Campbell's, noting the dark circles under her dark brown eyes. These conversations were unpredictable and never easy. "I'm going to tell you three things that I know for certain. First, Dr. Yablonsky is a great doctor, and like most physicians, he was trained to prevent patients from dying at all costs. To make a patient like your mother a 'No Code' or 'Do Not Resuscitate' patient makes a doctor feel like he's failed. In other words, he professionally does not understand why a patient would not want all heroic measures used to stay alive. Secondly, your mother is suffering. To continue on this path of heroic measures will only lead to more suffering. Her lips are blistered; she's barely conscious and emaciated and this is her fourth hospital-ization in six months. And thirdly, my ethical standard here is that I treat every patient as if they were my own family member. If this was *my* mother, I would transfer her to palliative care knowing the experts there would have the knowledge and skills to manage her very complex, chronic problems, as well as her emotional and psychological needs. I would replace the burning chemo with soothing pain medication, and I would put her in a room with a window and a view to look at the trees and feel the sunshine, because that is what I would want for myself if I was in this situation. Or you may even consider taking her home."

Hector Padilla had appeared at the door in search of coffee after speaking to the Salazar's. After multiple hospitalizations, Mrs. Campbell knew him well and they hugged for a long minute.

"I'll leave you two alone to talk," Sylvia said, "and please call me if there is anything else I can do."

Her beeper went off yet again. It was almost eleven and no one wanted to work a double shift on Med-Surg.

If only I could redirect eighty percent of all the money spent on the last six months of life to pay for more staff, she thought. The hiring freeze had dropped the hospital's staff to a dangerously lean level, and even the retiring nurses had not been replaced. Due to the recession, Las Vegas Memorial was running below census budget by 15 percent. She would have to pull a nursing assistant from orthopedics, but since it was so late, she'd have to run down and talk to the orthopedic charge nurse to break the bad news herself. Then she would strongly suggest to Sandy that she spend the night with her mother.

Sylvia headed down the hall toward the stairwell noting the barely audible sobs coming from another room. She glanced at the whiteboard for updates and reached into the drawer for more chocolates—her all-encompassing weakness and a frequent substitute for dinner. *So far, so good,* she thought. She had handled all the evening's numerous challenges, thankful that none of the balls had dropped. Her right calf cramped up, reminding her of the forty hours she had already put in this week. She sat down for a moment to stretch it out while briefing Charles on the head bleed; happy for any activity that would delay the call to Yablonsky. But no sooner had she begun her report than her pager text screen lit up:

"S.O.S. – Garvin again," it read.

Sylvia winced out loud, recalling the last *Hospitalist vs. ER* game she had refereed as Charles prompted, "Better call Yablonsky now—getting late."

She reached for the phone list and dialed the service, leaving her pager number with the operator before reluctantly heading for the emergency room. *It's not that I mind all the juggling,* she thought as the elevator doors closed, *but when it came to the ER it was more like juggling knives, and someone always ended up getting hurt.*

Chapter Twenty-One

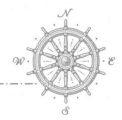

The challenge in planning business lunches in Las Vegas, to hear Ivy tell it, was all about the noise. For those meetings that were more ceremonial or dutiful, not conducive to meaningful exchanges, there were dozens of great restaurants before you even got close to the Strip. But for serious meetings and reasonable silence, there were only a few nearby spots, and Ivy apparently knew them all.

The pro-forma dance of being seated, ordering food and commenting on the eclectic decor was pleasant enough, Will noted, but there was a coiled-spring tension to his chief nursing officer, Claudia Ryan. It crackled in the air around her like an electrical field, and a faint veil over her expression whispered of sadness and concern. The clear depth of her unknown feelings and attitude left him off-balance, examining his words and feeling self-conscious. He was close to just blurting out an admission of befuddlement when she finally spoke.

"I appreciate the lunch invitation, and just getting out of there, Will."

"My pleasure. I dislike having serious conversations in what amounts to the throne room."

"The CEO's office, you mean?"

"Right," he chuckled. "I don't do 'pretentious' well."

"Thank heavens. By the way, congratulations on holding and leading the best officer retreat I've ever attended. You have a way of very clearly painting your vision for us, not to mention really demonstrating how to create a team by starting with the level of trust among our own group."

"I'm hoping it's more than just 'my' vision, Claudia. I'm hoping it's 'our' vision."

"I share that hope, Will." She hesitated for a second. "I share it, but I'm not sure everyone's on board. Oh, they are as far as the philosophy goes, patient safety and high-quality service above all else. But the proof of universality will be when we truly start acting, not just talking, in 'patient-centric' terms, and we're nowhere near that."

The statement took Will aback momentarily. But after all, the goal of this meeting was to get a truly honest appraisal from the chief nurse's point of view. "I really appreciate the candor, Claudia. I have to tell you that one of the reasons I wanted to have some time for us to talk is that I sensed a reserve about you, and frankly, I've been worried that what I was sensing might be resistance to these changes."

"It's not resistance." She smiled rather sadly, he thought, as she looked away for a few seconds before returning her gaze to him, eye-to-eye. "Will, you know as well as I do that our level of mutual trust has not yet matured. You're not sure that you know my mind, and I'm equally unsure that I know yours, despite your great words and stated intent."

Will sat back slightly, unconsciously drumming his fingers on the table before he caught himself and stopped. "Have I done something to raise doubts about my sincerity, Claudia?"

She shook her head energetically. "No, absolutely not. But we've just started working together, and there are a lot of uncertainties when any major additions occur in a senior officer team, so our trust is naturally at arm's length. For instance, what's driving you to make these changes with so much passion?"

"Well, as I was telling the team regarding St. Michael's..."

She raised a finger to interrupt. "I know, and I'm very excited that there is a St. Michael's for us to emulate. No, what's driving *you*, Will? Before my nurses and I climb aboard yet another train to nowhere, I need to know."

It was Will's turn to look away, wondering where the line was between summarizing a tragedy and reliving it. Her voice broke into his thoughts. "At the retreat you made mention of something that had happened to you, something that changed you, but you never told us what it was."

Will sighed deeply. "In effect, Claudia, as CEO of a hospital in

Portland, Oregon, I was in charge when my very own hospital killed my best friend's son, my godson."

"Ronnie Nolan was eleven and already one heck of a kid. Wayne, his dad, and I had grown up as best friends. Ronnie had hurt himself in an after school wrestling match, and I had Wayne bring Ronnie to our ER. He was in severe pain, and Wayne told me he thought Ronnie's shoulder was broken and displaced. They couldn't verify it on examination. The X-ray just didn't show a break. Our docs sent him home with his dad and a lot of pain medication, but when I heard Ronnie's arm had gone numb, I had Wayne bring him back in for an MRI and arranged a referral to the best vascular surgeon we had. So now we had X-rays, and an MRI, orthopedics and vascular and no indication of any physical problem, although Wayne kept pointing out that Ronnie's scapula was a bit lower on the right side. You know us, if it doesn't show on the X-ray, it doesn't exist. Months later, Wayne calls terribly concerned. Ronnie's right arm is blue, numb, and cold. He rushed Ronnie to our ER and I met them there. One of our techs did a doppler, but we didn't discover until later that the tech was incompetent; he failed to scan high enough for a valid study, and therefore found nothing. Ronnie's case was handed off to the incoming resident who failed to read the notes, and came and told us that there was no indication of circulatory problems. Wayne blew up and I wasn't far behind. I jumped in the middle of it, alienating the resident as well as the orthopedic doc on call, ordered a new X-ray, Doppler and MRI all at once, and got the vascular guy to come in. Much to everyone's shock, we discovered that there *was* a break in the clavicle several months earlier and we had completely missed it. Wayne, in other words, had been right from the start. The broken, displaced clavicle had been pressing down on the subclavian vein and his brachial plexus supply for months, and Ronnie, as a result, had developed a potentially lethal ten millimeter long clot half an inch away from his lung. We admitted him immediately, put him on heparin, and the vascular surgeon went home to get some sleep before the procedure the next morning. Here I am, the CEO, whipping everyone to action and it's no secret I am not a happy camper. The warning that under no circumstances should a blood pressure cuff be used on Ronnie's right arm does not get posted at his bedside when he arrives on the floor. Before his dad and I can even get up there, a nursing assistant, who floated from another floor, put on a cuff to take his blood pressure and pumped it up. To her, it's as much a ritual as breathing. But the cuff pressure dislodged the entire clot, which shot through his system like a runaway freight train, fragmenting as it went, shards blocking various veins. In other words, we lost him."

Will was wholly unprepared for his voice to catch as the narration turned to the agonizing moments in Ronnie's room as they tried to get him back.

"Good Lord."

"I simply can't erase the horror of that moment. It plays over and over in my head like a skipping CD, my lifelong best friend standing there in tears yelling, 'Do something! Dammit, DO something Will!' But there was nothing anyone could do." The details of the downward spiral that had resulted in Ronnie Nolan's death seemed to keep her attention riveted, he noted, even though he was slightly disgusted with himself at his clinically disengaged tone.

Claudia sat quietly, taking in the story and holding it until he was ready to speak again.

Will cleared his throat and looked away for a moment, slowly, painfully winning the battle over the flood of emotion that was lapping at the top of his dam. "Sorry. It's all too painful, I guess."

"I understand."

"There is an overwhelming sense of failure at having all the things we struggled to do and tried to change at my hospital be proven ineffective in a horrid flash of mortality. It was just too much. I was a flat out failure. Later, months later, it became a very determined mission for me to find out how we'd screwed it up, and what could've been done differently. I don't mean just the clinical mistakes, I mean how that culture could be so different that there would never have been a blood clot missed, or a warning message disregarded because I had done everything that was recommended by my peers and in the literature—*everything*—and still patients died."

"And that's how you found St. Michael's in Denver, right? Searching for solutions?"

"Absolutely. And, it was a relief to not only find St. Michael's, but to find it was led by a physician."

"So, the loss made you question whether a clinical background was a good thing in a CEO?"

"Wouldn't you, Claudia, after such an experience?"

"It depends. It seems that all the significant and highly influential physician leaders in patient safety have had their 'aha!' moments, too, which enabled them to understand why we hurt and kill so many with preventable mistakes and infections. Those pivotal moments took them from professional to personal. But I have to get parochial here. There is still a major blind spot even among the most enlightened patient safety leaders regarding nursing. Physicians, of course, traditionally have little understanding of what nurses do, or how vital they are, but too many nursing leaders seem to miss the basics as well. Nursing is drowning as a profession, Will, and the current medium of its demise is budgetary myopia. In the viewpoint of the average CFO, a nurse is little more than a cog in a big machine. Most CEOs, whether physicians or otherwise, have even less understanding of nursing, and they tend to adopt a strong CFOs prejudice as their own. Or worse, they just hand over the keys of the hospital to the CFO whenever nursing and budgets collide, as they always do."

"You really think the average CFO is that callous about the value of nurses?"

"No, not callous. Oblivious. I just read last week about a CFO who was considering out-sourcing his entire nursing department! Another hospital, don't worry, it wasn't Richard. Let's just call this kind of thing a serious knowledge deficit, like being so focused on nursing hours per patient day versus ratios that there's no hope of understanding how such measures relate to safety and staff, or patient satisfaction. Another issue is measurement: how do you measure the bad things that don't happen because of good nursing care? There is a serious disconnect between operational habits and outcomes. Most CFOs *don't* get that the business case for nursing is the business case for patient safety and quality!"

They sat in silence for a while, picking at their just delivered food. Finally she gestured as if dismissing her own line of thought, and fixed him eye-to-eye before continuing. "Let me get to the point, Will. I need to know precisely where nursing stands, and for that matter, where I stand. To whom, in other words, do I *really* report? Holbrook or you?"

He started to answer and she waved him off, her lips pursed, her gaze on the table for a second as if gathering the courage necessary to say what she wanted to say. "What I mean is— speaking from experience—I've heard all those words before and it will eventually come down to resources and an arm-wrestling with the CFO who believes 'a nurse is a nurse' and you just move them around the floors and the time clock like widgets."

"Has Richard been abusive to you?"

"No. But he's a traditional CFO devoid of clinical expertise or sensitivity. Richard's not a bad guy, but he's counting beans, not people. Again, based on my experience."

"What experience, exactly?" he said, zeroing in with gamma-knife accuracy on the weight of the feeling behind her words. "I'd like to hear more."

Claudia placed her utensils carefully across the barely eaten pasta, pushing her plate to the edge of the table. Folding her arms, she stared out the window and took a deep breath. She was a strong woman, accustomed to controlling her instincts and emotions as she moved up the corporate ladder. Hadn't she learned the hard way to never demonstrate vulnerability? She studied Will carefully before responding.

"Will, I've been a CNO for ten years now—only a year at Las Vegas Memorial. I moved here from a hospital in the Northwest where everything was going very well the first three years. In March of that last year, we went over our budget. We missed it by less than one percent, mind you, but it was as if someone flicked an invisible switch and turned the CFO into a financial fanatic. Suddenly, the CEO melted into the shadows and permitted the CFO to essentially take over—not by formality, but by fear, effrontery and intimidation, holding financial inquisitions and intimidating my directors and managers."

"Without formal authority? How?"

She smiled ruefully. "There is a decorum and mutual respect expected among senior officers, right?"

"Of course."

"At one of our senior leadership meetings, I began explaining why nursing was ever so slightly over budget and the CFO, an officer of equal rank according to our organizational chart, rudely holds his hand out in a 'Stop' gesture right in my face in front of everyone and says, 'I'm not interested in hearing how you screwed up. We're either doing a lousy job of managing, or some people just don't care.' I looked at the CEO for support but he remained silent. I looked at the COO, and clearly he was as shocked as I was, but he hunkered down in his chair and said nothing. In that moment, the entire leadership of the hospital shifted to this CFO, who ran it with brutality. I won't bore you with everything he did, but eleven days later when I asked him precisely how we were supposed to make budget he says 'Go without!' And so I said, "What does that mean?" Then this man who doesn't care and has virtually no knowledge of the details and challenges of clinical medicine or patient safety or staff satisfaction half comes out of his chair, points his damned finger at me and yells *'You need to stop mollycoddling your people! Okay, Claudia? You and your people just don't get it. Our train's leaving the station so you either get on or get off!'* In the next two weeks I watched what I thought was a great team disintegrate into an illicit dictatorship. The CEO ran and hid. The board refused to get involved, or maybe they never knew. The COO and I left within six months and the level of trust within the hospital was utterly destroyed. Oh, and at the end of the fiscal year, we ended up coming in under budget by one and a half million—which, of course, did not elicit an apology from our self-appointed Caesar."

"And the CEO did nothing to stop that?"

"No. In the aftermath I was really furious and wounded at the same time, and very professionally depressed. Here I was, once again, feeling like I had been naïve to think that anything could change in this idiotic system in which we preach service to the community, but act like the only thing that matters is the bank account. It's the dominant force in my career that wins every time: money. The budget. Patient safety and service quality be damned. Just like that insufferably rude CFO said, he didn't care what the reasons were or the challenges we faced or even whether we were twenty-five cents or twenty-five million over budget, we were just children to be spanked if we placed any other consideration over the bottom line."

"This fellow hadn't shown his colors before?"

"No. I thought we were aligned. In our retreat, the entire team nodded their heads and agreed wholeheartedly when I said, 'patient safety is not a priority. Priorities change. Patient safety is a core value.'"

She sighed and looked away for a few seconds, wondering whether sharing such deep assaults had been useful or useless— or worse. Her eyes finally swung back to Will. "My bottom line, Will? I just don't have the energy to go down that road again. To play the game. To find out that once again you've inadvertently ended up landing on the same place on the board and are going to get sent back to the beginning again, like a game of corporate Chutes and Ladders. Sorry, Will, too much time with the new grandkid."

"Understood," he said, chuckling, before fixing her with a steady gaze. "Claudia, with every ounce of integrity and determination I have, I can promise you here and now that you will not see a repeat in any way here. You report to me, and only to me."

"Understood. I appreciate your attitude."

"Now, I need your help, Claudia. I have an empty legal pad and a pen, and I want to know what nursing needs, and what you need to make this shared vision come true. No punches pulled."

Claudia looked at her watch and smiled wearily. The conversation had been more intense than she had anticipated, and besides, answering this question was going to take considerably longer than twenty minutes.

That's all, just one legal pad? She thought.

"I'll tell you what, Will. Let me sleep on it and I'll get together with my team and we'll craft a critical needs analysis by the end of the week."

"Good," he said, reaching for the check. "I only have one more question."

Claudia shifted in her seat. She didn't realize that she always sighed while composing her thoughts—or that these deep breaths helped buy her more time so that she could maintain her corporate composure. But Will had already picked up on the foreshadowing nuance.

Internally, she geared up for "the question," which would undoubtedly have to do with extracting her pledge of allegiance to a balanced budget, or some assurance that she was a "team player." That's the way these things always went.

"Yes?" she said with as much of a smile as she could manage.

"What's the name of your grandchild?"

Claudia's Wish List

Stop asking me to prove the business case for nursing—there are too many things that can't be quantified; adequate staffing, catching errors and rescuing patients from potential or actual devastating outcomes, psychological support, etc.

A budget designed for the patient, instead of the hospital.

A true partnership between nurses and physicians—both groups think they already have great relationships! MD/nurse rounding program where patients will be seen by a team, including at least the primary nurse and rounding MD.

Plan to have each member of the executive team spend time on a clinical unit, following a nurse and better understanding the "reality" of healthcare delivery.

Monthly off site retreats for nursing leadership and line staff to work on delivery of care, quality and safety and closing the loop on identified problems. There is simply no time at work, and training—which retreats are—are NOT an ancillary expense.

Formation of a joint practice committee composed of nursing leaders, MD leaders and staff to do case review WEEKLY of identified "problem" cases—to strategize ways to communicate more effectively and work as a team—with the authority to change policies and procedures.

Clerical support for the nursing leadership team to streamline our time, and question whether we're wasting time on minutes, setting up meetings, communicating, investigating, etc.

Creation of a patient safety team composed of a representative from every department who will receive training and education on how to create a culture of quality and patient safety (feedback is a gift, patient advocacy, reporting events as they occur, personal accountability).

New onboarding program with emphasis on unit-based, experiential learning by trained preceptors. Monthly hospital wide education day focused on creating a culture of quality and patient safety for all new orientees.

Expansion of the education department with the building of a state-of-the-art simulation lab—start with basic videotaping of teamwork and communication challenges. Use both procedural, tactical, clinical trainers and empty-room training focusing on team interaction and communication.

Mandatory hospital wide education for all staff beginning with managers teaching crucial conversations, accountability and teamwork. Each department will be expected to complete a needs analysis and create four simulations based on the results.

Give charge nurses the training and flexibility to staff the unit —they can be stewards of the hospitals resources as well as the patient's best interest. They are the only ones that can, due to their position on the front line. This may be the most important element of all!

Chapter Twenty-Two

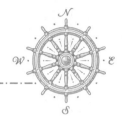

Both Ivy and Las Vegas Memorial's director of education had warned that the hospital cafeteria was too small to comfortably accommodate the entire morning shift without people standing, but the only alternative would have involved nearby hotels, busses and easy excuses to not attend.

In the end, the cafeteria won out.

"I'd like a stool in the middle along one wall, all the chairs circled around, in a semi-circle and a good microphone," Will had requested.

The invitation sent to everyone had stopped short of being a directive, but it was clear from the language of each e-mail and flyer that only those blasé enough to be disinterested in their future at Las Vegas Memorial should consider sitting it out.

"*As your new CEO,*" Will's message read, "*I'm here to make sure that management at virtually all levels serves one primary purpose: To make it easier for you to take care of our patients safely and effectively, with zero avoidable patient injuries, and to make this such a deeply satisfying and enjoyable place to work that you find yourself personally transitioning from someone who works at Las Vegas Memorial to someone who IS Las Vegas Memorial. I am also well aware that I can't achieve this vision unless it's yours too, and I can't hope to excite and engage you without meeting you face-to-face and really listening to you. This is why I need everyone to attend one of the six sessions during next week. Everyone!*"

Janice had disapproved of Will's insistence to send word through the back channels to all the managers and directors that their leadership abilities would be gauged in part by employees' percentage of attendance, but from the number of people pouring into the cafeteria by seven forty-five Monday morning, it was apparent all the various efforts had worked.

Will stood at the entrance shaking hands and greeting each of the staff members as they arrived, grateful for the clearly imprinted names and positions on the ID badges. Dr. Kirk Nelson was standing at a distance, and Will was momentarily distracted by the knowledge of what the noon hour would bring: a disciplinary meeting with Dr. Adams. The impending sanctions about to be imposed on Adams would anger more than a few of his colleagues, but it was an acid test. Adams had lost it again two days ago, leaving his patient open on the table while he screamed again—this time about some perceived failure to follow his preference card. The incident had quickly escalated to an emergency meeting involving Dr. Nelson, Will, and a reluctant general counsel. Dr. Adams was to be given a high-noon ultimatum: Enroll in a no-nonsense six week remedial anger management course for doctors at his own expense, or immediately and permanently lose his privileges at Las Vegas Memorial.

Will had insisted on attending that meeting.

He pulled himself back to the present as a clearly startled senior nurse walked in, looking at him carefully and shaking his hand with reluctance.

"Welcome. Terri, is it? Oh, yes! I remember you."

"Good Lord," she said, "you never mentioned you were the new CEO!" Terri Bradshaw was not smiling.

"And you're probably wondering if I remembered our conversation?"

"Well, I hope I didn't say anything..."

"If I recall correctly," he interjected, "you wanted, among other things, to know that we really did have your back when you needed to send someone home early for being on Facebook, or if you decided a surgery needed to be cancelled even if the surgeon went ballistic. Am I right?"

"I...think so. That sounds like me."

"Well, Terri, that was invaluable to me, and I want you to know the answer is 'Yes,' I personally have your back. And don't feel alone. No one else here knew I was the incoming boss either." He let go of her hand and began fishing in his right coat pocket. "Oh, and I have something for you. I wasn't sure which one of these meetings you'd come to but I was looking for you, here it is."

"What's this?" She said, a tentative smile slowly creeping across her face as he handed her a small piece of paper and placed his left hand on her shoulder.

"You said to me that night, 'Thank you, Will, for the Lotto moment,' remember?"

"Not really."

"Well, you did, and I decided that reference deserved a real Lotto ticket! Hopefully it's a winner."

Will introduced Terri to Janice and watched with amusement as the senior nurse moved on into the cafeteria looking at the lottery ticket, and glancing back at him in mild confusion.

When every chair was filled and many left standing, Will made his way to the stool and sat down. "Okay, how many of you remember meeting this slightly dorky guy named Will in the past month who showed up to ask you questions at odd hours of the day and night?"

A scattering of hands went up.

"And of those who raised your hand, how many of you are sitting here now worried about what you might have said?"

A smaller number of hands went up.

"Stop worrying. What you encountered was my 'Undercover Boss' experiment, which was my way of getting to know what life at Las Vegas Memorial is really like. Every one of those conversations was in strict confidence, and every bit of information you shared has been incredibly valuable to me in being able to take the helm here and help steer us in the right direction. And that 'right' direction, by the way, is, for the most part, something you folks need to give *me*. If anyone wants a private follow-up conversation, just let my assistant Ivy know."

Will let silence fall over the group for a few seconds as he looked around, cognizant of the fact that the sensitivity level of everyone in the room was rising almost exponentially with every second he remained mute. What was coming next? He cleared his throat and raised the microphone again.

"You all saw the fliers, or if you didn't, I want you to grab one on the way out, because there's a phrase and a concept in there that is very, very important. I said that our management team at all levels is going to be tasked with, and evaluated on, how we can support you in making safe and effective care of our patients easier. Let me be blunt. Some of you are trying not to roll your eyes right now, and some of you are thinking, 'Yeah, right, flavor-of-the-month.' And now I know why. After three weeks playing 'Undercover Boss,' I have a glimpse of the chains that prevent you as individuals and as departments from soaring. I heard far too many stories of disrespect—despite the vision and values statement on that wall that claims 'respect' is one of our core values." Will turned and pointed to the plaque at the entryway to the cafeteria as a wave of heads followed his hand. "I encountered managers who could not fire incompetent or hostile employees, friction between and within departments, and the life energy being sucked out of people by a system that held them hostage to 'CYA' rules. But most of all, I listened. And the vast majority of your conversations were not about how to make Las Vegas Memorial the safest hospital in the United States. The last word in every requisition, innovation request or decision, was money. How to conform to the budget imposed from above. How to satisfy what appears to be management's monetary myopia. And because, as an organization, we do not walk the talk of patient safety first, you have lost faith in our leadership—and rightly so."

There was dead silence in the room as well as disengaged and downcast gazes.

"On the day I accepted this job, we lost a patient. Does anyone know her name? Mrs. Kari Markowitz. She and her husband, Doug, and their two young daughters, ages six and eight, put their trust in Las Vegas Memorial...and we betrayed that trust. It is my primary goal that no one ever dies or is harmed accidentally at Las Vegas Memorial again. Ever. Is that your goal? If so, I know how to get us there. If not, you may be on the wrong team. Here's a verifiable truth that's going to sound like a pipe dream: We can get this great institution to the point of never letting a mistake harm a patient, and never giving a single person an infection or condition they didn't arrive with. I know you don't believe that right now, but I'd appreciate it if you would take my word for it in the interim. We can do this, and we must. Now, here's the rest of the story, the truth about aiming for that indispensable goal of zero preventable harm: I can't give you the kind of support you need without your constant, open and frank communication, participation and ownership. That means each of you, regardless of your title or position or longevity. If we're of a single mind on this, if we're determined that no one else will have to bury a loved one unnecessarily, or live with a life-changing disaster suffered at our hands, then we must construct together an organization that doesn't just listen, but one that takes the absolute best information from each person to build a cohesive, trustworthy and effective system. Is one of our budgetary proposals a threat to your ability to care for our patients? We need to know it immediately directly and it becomes the responsibility of whoever first realizes it to make sure that we know. What does that take? Trust. You have to trust us, and we have to earn and sustain your trust over a period of time by our response. First and foremost, virtually everyone has the right and the responsibility to—as the Toyota method dictates—'stop the line' if you perceive anything wrong or especially if you see something dangerous. And every one of you has the responsibility to work together to find your own solutions at the point of need. Now, we are determined that all of you who are our mid-level leaders—our managers directors, charge nurses and supervisors— are going to lead this transformation by responding to any criticisms or problems any of our people report by giving energetic support. But should the mid-level leader's efforts ever fail, and you feel the message is being squelched; you have the right to come directly to me. Not only will my door be open, so to speak, but you'll be leaving here with my phone number. Obviously, I need you to be wise guardians of my time and only pull that emergency cord when needed, but you will *not* be second-guessed if you think it's needed and you use it. This isn't some cute statement that your opinion counts. This is me saying that everyone who carries a Las Vegas Memorial ID must be a leader; a thinking, feeling human being who vows to always speak their truth in the name of patient safety. If you can't embrace that level of accountability, responsibility, engagement and love of this mission, then you need to think hard and fast about whether you belong here. We must expect of each other—regardless of organizational rank—that each and every one of us is responsible for each and every patient all of the time as if they were our own family member. Las Vegas Memorial must become—if we are to survive and fulfill our charter to the community—a patient-centric hospital. That means that virtually everything, including money and budgets and professional considerations must be subordinate to the best interests of the patient. Everything. All the time. No exceptions. But you know what? I can set that vision in front of you, but only you folks can tell me how to really achieve it, and what it will take for us in the carpeted C-suite to help you make it happen. I can't order you to care. I can't order or direct you to put the patient first. What I *can* do is elicit all of your ideas and your participation and your help in figuring out how to do it, and who's with us, and figuring out how we retrain, reassign, or say goodbye to those who don't want to practice patient-centric care. I want to open this up for a very robust discussion in a minute, and I'll want your questions, your comments, your disagreements and most of all, your ideas. There's no attribution. This is a no-fault comment zone. But just to show you I'm dead serious, as you're leaving this cafeteria in an hour, you'll be handed a little laminated card that contains my direct e-mail, my direct office number, and my cell phone. Yes, my personal cell number that's with me twenty-four seven, not some surrogate number poor Ivy has to answer. I'll answer it, even at two a.m. You have no idea how many people have told me I'm nuts to give you my contact information, but I know I'm not."

Once again, Will let an uncomfortable silence envelope the room, noting that far more gazes were now turned directly to him.

"How will we know when we've succeeded? When your friends and family stop calling you to ask for the name of a 'good doctor or surgeon' at Las Vegas Memorial, because through you, they will know all of our folks are good. You'll know it when there are no longer 'heads-up calls' to managers that a board member or physician's spouse is in their unit. You'll know it when any doctor, any nurse, any pharmacist, and any staff member can take care of your loved ones. It will be then that we become a truely, patient-centric team. We're changing a culture, and no culture change is complete until there's no one around who can remember how it used to be. You know, and now I know, that we have a long way to go before that day arrives, but if you'll help me and guide both me and my leadership team, we *will* get there. Oh, and by the way, my definition of a 'leadership team' includes every one of you."

Will slid off the stool and stood, looking around at everyone for a few seconds and nodded to offered smiles. The feeling in the room was tentative, as if they wanted more than anything to believe in what he was saying, but history had always dashed such hopes. In the end, it always seemed just a matter of time before things slipped back to the way they'd always been.

"Let's take a few minutes for coffee, restroom breaks and diet cokes—hopefully diet—and then you can start telling me how to put together ad hoc counsels and advisory groups that involve as many people as possible—groups without titles or any great formality—groups that can give me and our senior team not happy talk or neatly wrapped up evaluations or surveys, but the down and dirty things you tell your spouse at midnight about what we need to change. Ten minutes, and let's get started."

Chapter Twenty-Three

Claudia Ryan smiled genuinely at her nurses as she walked into the hospital. She had no right to call them "hers," but still, she felt an affection and dedication to them after hearing stories of their patient care that went above and beyond the call of duty. Last week, one of the nurses had used her lunch break to run to a nearby Russian restaurant to bring back "borscht" for a distressed Russian patient who was not eating the hospital food. Then, an ICU nurse discovered a potential drug interaction that was not caught during rounds thereby preventing a serious adverse outcome. And after her meeting with Will...well... she was feeling a bit more optimistic, and it showed.

"Good morning, Diane," she greeted the orthopedic manager who was toting two supersized lattes. "Gearing up for a long day?"

"No, one of them is for Sandy Keaton. Her mother is up on our floor and she spent last night in her mother's room."

Diane paused, considering whether or not to say more. This was, after all, the CNO. To say too much was considered complaining or "being negative," especially if you had said it more than once—and boy had she done that. The new CEO had already caused enough of a stir with his pep rally, and what usually followed such introductions was a massive reorganization. Now was not the time to be labeled a complainer. She swallowed the complaint and smiled.

"How is Sandy's mother doing?" Claudia asked, filling the tiny lull.

"She's fine this morning, but she coded last night. I have the incident report on my desk and plan to look into the details this morning."

"Sorry to hear that. Let me know what you find out," Claudia said, parting with Diane at the C-suite hallway.

"Will do," Diane promised.

But before Diane was out of earshot, Claudia changed her mind. *Hadn't Will asked in the senior leadership retreat for making rounds? What were those two questions she was supposed to ask?*

"Diane," she said, turning around. "Would you mind if I made rounds right now on your unit?"

"No, not at all," Diane replied, working to hide her surprise. "Let me just put my things in my office and I'll be right up."

"OK," said Diane, relieved. *That will at least give me the five minutes I need to tell the nurses to hide their breakfast muffins and coffee cups that aren't supposed to be cluttering the nurse's station.* Diane never did have the heart to enforce that policy; it was the least she could do for her nurses since she felt that she had failed them in so many other ways. Guilt panged at her still from admonishing the nurses in the last staff meeting to monitor their over-time when she knew they were already working without meals and breaks on those very same shifts.

Already the unit was a whirlwind of activity that peaked each day about eight a.m. Physicians, physical and occupational therapists, social workers and visitors all arrived about the same time with different agendas. Ever since the electronic charting had been implemented last year, Diane had noticed that the physicians and nurses rarely communicated face-to-face. Most of the physicians made rounds when the nurses were in report. For a moment, she felt a whisk of nostalgia for the old days when the charts were kept at the main nursing station. It was the charts that had brought the physicians and nurses together in conversation as they would talk about the best plan of care, new drugs and even their families. But then, in the name of efficiency, the charts were re-located outside the patient's rooms and flagged for secretaries, *and now,* she thought, *they are in a cloud.* She felt strongly that the resulting lack of face-to-face interactions had impacted patient care because it had drastically reduced their time together; and that had hurt morale in general. They simply didn't know each other anymore. No one had time. These days both physicians and nurses felt like hamsters on an exercise wheel, and the economic forces and never-ending changes seemed to spin the wheel ever faster. Her last two physician complaints were actually a result of an overdependence on electronics as a substitute for conveying important information to nurses themselves. *We may be getting the patients in and out faster, but it certainly isn't better care,* she thought, picking up the census sheet in her mail with the twenty four ADTs (admissions, discharges and transfers). *Seventeen in one day! No wonder complaints from housekeeping were escalating. They had to clean the continuous passive motion (CPM) machines, the patient-controlled analgesia (PCA) machines, the sequential compression devices, and then remove commodes and IV poles before they even started cleaning the rooms.*

Diane briefly scanned the two incident reports from her in mail basket filed by Ethel, an experienced nurse of thirty years. She'd recognized the handwriting immediately; the words block-lettered and angry:

1. Two EKG pads found on the back of a patient who was post-op day three! No bath for three days? No nursing care!
2. Felipe on Facebook again. Third time—not while on his break!

Diane sighed and chugged another gulp of coffee. By the time she opened the door to her office, Claudia was stepping off the elevator. Now, there would be no time to clean up her desk that was covered with papers and topped with a yellow legal pad "To Do" list. They sat down at the tiny corner table. Diane noted the air of power and control Claudia wore like a fine perfume—the corporate scent.

"What did you think of Dr. Jenkins's presentation the other day?" began Claudia.

"Very nice message," Diane slowly responded. Perhaps it was because she was originally from the East Coast where people spoke their mind, but Diane had been corrected more than once for telling it like it was in her evaluations—especially in closed quarters. "Of course, we all want no one to be harmed, but as you and I both know; we've been trying to do that for our entire careers. We work very, very hard at keeping our patients safe."

"What do you need to keep your patients safe?"

"A bottle, a genie and three wishes," Diane replied smiling. But Claudia wasn't smiling. Diane shifted her weight and picked up the cue. "Claudia, I've worked here as a manager for seventeen years and I have to tell you, not once in all that time has anyone asked me what I need to do my job; to keep patients safe. Not once. I'm supposed to ask the patients, physicians and staff if they have what they need every single day, but no one *ever* asks the manager."

"I'm asking now," replied Claudia.

It had been so long since Diane entertained the question that she had to think hard. These days she felt like she was hitting fast balls from an invisible pitching machine: staffing shortage problem, *meeting;* patient complaint, *meeting;* physician upset, *meeting;* adverse event, *meeting.* And there were lots of curve balls too: finally getting permission to post a position and then a hiring freeze; working on the medication reconciliation committee; and then the doctors abdicating their role and responsibilities. Until Claudia asked the question—and she actually did sound sincere—Diane hadn't realized that a big part of her had given up. Days had seamlessly turned into weeks, months and then years as she attacked each of the day's problems with racquetball speed. The only reality she knew now was the game.

"If my staff and I are responsible for the outcomes—quality, safety, patient care—then I think we should also be responsible for the resources to attain those outcomes. So my first wish is to staff the floor as needed on a four-hour basis. After all, we are the knowledge experts in this area, but we can't apply or ever use that knowledge. It's not about the number, it's about the patients. My charge nurses are the only ones who know both the current condition of the patients and the experience level of the in-coming staff."

"Next," she said, thinking of Christmas, "There is never a moment when we are not bailing out the sinking life raft. This bucket brigade mentality isn't working because we never have time to patch the holes. Instead, we just protect the boat from sinking which has become the status quo. I need time with my staff, they need time on the unit to figure out better processes and procedures, and we need time together to create a lean workplace and build a collegial interactive team. And for my last wish, Claudia, honestly, I wish someone would pass an edict that says: 'Effective immediately: no more meetings.' In the future, I want to only attend meetings that I feel are productive, and that means an agenda, action items and time to explore new ideas and brainstorm. Meetings are the biggest waste of my time."

Claudia expected the first two requests but was a little surprised by the latter. She noticed the legal pad "To Do" list on Diane's desk and reached out for it, asking, "May I?"

Claudia skimmed the first three pages as well as Diane's calendar and got an idea.

"Diane, I'm preparing a report for the CEO on nursing's needs this week. I plan on presenting it at our nursing leadership meeting on Friday and eliciting feedback. I hope you can come to *that* meeting. I'll be asking for a pilot study to roll the recommendations out one floor at a time, and I hope you will consider being the first floor. Also in that meeting, I will be asking the nursing leaders what they need and I would like to be able to count on you to start that conversation."

Diane said nothing, nodded and listened intently as Claudia continued.

"I was going to ask you another question, 'What drains you?' But from looking at this list of reoccurring problems—especially the personnel issues—I think I know. I believe the energy that we need for creating a better system, for patching the holes on the life raft, to use your example, is being absorbed into a black hole of bureaucracy and tradition. In order to use that entropy, we need to carefully assess where our energy is going and re-direct it in ways we have never done before. We will have to re-build our own nursing leadership team first on a foundation of trust. If we can't say whatever we're truly thinking in our own group, then we have failed. Are you with me?"

"I don't know, Claudia," Diane responded, more honestly than she'd planned. "It's not that I don't trust you personally, but you represent a system that I've learned from experience is not trustworthy. I've seen it hurt my peers. I've seen senior leaders turn on each other. I learned the rules the hard way: lay low, don't ever disagree unless absolutely necessary, keep your job by keeping within budget and pretending to go along with everything or you will be considered an outlier. And now, you want to change the rules of the game I've played for seventeen years; do I have that right?"

Claudia inhaled deeply. This was not going to be easy, but Diane's honesty was a refreshing start. "Yes."

Their meeting was interrupted by a phone call from the front desk. Sandy Keaton was asking to see Diane.

"OK," Diane said, standing and shaking Claudia's hand. "I'll see you on Friday."

"Great," replied Claudia. Then sensing Diane's skepticism and reluctance she added, "You know, Diane, if they can do it at St. Michael's, then we should be able to accomplish the same goals here at Las Vegas Memorial."

Saint Michael's, thought Diane, smiling and reaching into her parochial school past and picturing the twelve foot high stained glass portrait at her church. *Saint Michael, the Defender of Justice, the Healer of the Sick with super-sized wings, triple pedigreed in three Abrahamic traditions, that smacked down the son of darkness and stomped on his head. Now, if it had been St. Jude, the patron saint of lost causes, she would have to abandon this quest…but maybe, just maybe that fighting archangel energy would give them a chance.*

Chapter Twenty-Four

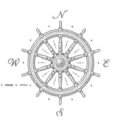

Will checked his watch as the forty-five minute video continued to play in the boardroom, the last item he wanted his senior team to see and absorb. His eyes fell on Kirk Nelson, seated halfway down the table, now watching the screen with rapt intensity.

Will chuckled to himself remember their conversation a day before when he'd leaned into the CMO's office with what seemed like a bright idea, and Kirk had responded immediately.

"If you feed them, they will come," Kirk had responded to the idea of hijacking the annual medical staff meeting for the pivotal summit with the rank and file physicians.

"In other words, that's an excellent idea," Nelson had said, "but I would *not* consider it a hijacking, Will, when the CEO is presenting seismic changes. Normally, as you know, we use the get-together to talk about bylaw changes, challenges and the things that are worrying us as a group. Of course, we also throw in the dinner, make it a social occasion by inviting the spouses and significant others and book the best speaker we can find to resonate with the theme of the evening. But, for heaven's sake, this year everything's changing, so of course our featured speaker should be our new skipper. Especially since you're a fellow physician."

"What percentage do you think will attend?"

The chief medical officer chuckled. "Thirty to forty percent. Of course, if we hire the cast of Scrubs, or maybe some cute actress, maybe seventy."

"Seriously, only forty? Even with all the changes we're launching? What can we do to increase attendance? What if I send a letter by certified mail to each of them?"

Nelson had sat in thought for a few moments before answering.

"Tell you what, Will. Let me draft it. Let me draft it as, in essence, a clarion notification that very serious and permanent changes to the bylaws, the hospital staffing, and the very operation of Las Vegas Memorial will be decided at this, and only this, meeting, and we need every doc who can possibly attend. No attendance, no voice, no vote...and no whining allowed post-meeting. My phone will explode when the letter is delivered, but I'll just use the new methods my grandson is teaching me about twittering the details on what it's all about. If we get our guys and gals stirred up enough, we'll get the attendance up."

The letter—a study in eloquence—had appeared on Will's desk within an hour, and had reached the majority of the medical staff within two days.

Will brought himself back to the moment and reached for the keyboard of a small laptop computer to toggle off the video. He motioned for Ivy to bring up the lights as he surveyed the reactions of his senior team, taking note of who was looking comfortable and who might be showing signs of running.

Richard Holbrook, the CFO, was leaning back in his chair and smiling—whether from amusement or incredulity—Will couldn't tell. Clearly Claudia Ryan was energized, as was Dr. Nelson, the CMO, but Randall Williamson, the chief information officer (CIO), seemed caught somewhere between puzzled and concerned. Jon Anderson, the general counsel, was taking notes.

"So," Will began, "that's the distillation of six repetitions of my staff presentation in the cafeteria. I know lengthy meetings are the bane of your existence, mine too. We talked a lot about that two weeks ago at our retreat. But we're going to be breeding and leading a revolution, and I thought you needed to know what I'm saying to our people, and what they're saying back."

"Those were the only ones who spoke up?" Randall asked. "I'm sorry I didn't get back in town in time to attend any of them."

"No, I cherry picked a representative number of the ones who really engaged me during the discussion part. And those truly *are* representative. Did you see how reluctant they were even when a few brave souls had broken the ice and had the temerity to speak up? Even when the questions and comments were coming hot and heavy at the end of each session, they were still very guarded and exploratory."

Claudia was nodding. "I am having precisely the same experience, even in one-on-one conversations, with my nurse managers. They don't think that real change is possible, and even then, they seem puzzled. Clearly no one has ever given them the time and opportunity to consider and evaluate what they need to do their jobs."

"You were with me on three sessions, right?" Will asked.

"Yes. Not so much that I can parrot what you said each time, Will, but enough to see how tough it was to crack through that top layer of ice."

Richard was chuckling. "I only came by during one session, Will, but what I heard was exactly what I would expect when you encourage the troops to peek out from behind the budget structure with the question of what they'd do if they won the lottery." His words, Richard noticed, were not triggering the reaction he'd expected from the others in the room. In fact, it was painfully obvious no one was chuckling along with him. Richard let his smile fade as he leaned forward in a well-practiced gesture of serious trumping frivolity. "Here's what I mean. Most folks on the front lines, as you refer to them, Will, have little or no understanding of what it takes to keep the money balanced and keep a huge institution like this in business. If you'll recall, I was making the same point at the retreat. The rank and file think budgets are mere discretionary decrees handed down by heartless despots, so when you tantalize them with the thought that maybe the budgets are not law, asking them what they need as if we can do anything they want, it's almost cruel. To paraphrase that *Top Gun* movie, you're writing checks your budget can't cash."

Whether it was a chill in the boardroom or just a contemplative silence, Richard couldn't tell, but he had seldom felt this uncomfortable.

"Richard, what are you saying," Will asked evenly, "that I shouldn't ask them what they need? Are you implying we should just *tell* them what they need, and how they should feel, because otherwise they might actually challenge our budgetary prowess?"

"Well, that's a very pejorative way of stating it, Will, but I'm trying to say that if you raise the staff expectations to unrealistic levels and then can't even come close to delivering, you'll smother your own revolution in its cradle."

Will nodded slowly, his body English clearly giving the CFO's words respectful consideration as he turned to the CIO.

"Randall? Your thoughts? Any chief information officer lives and dies by the budget, but you're usually on the staff side begging for funds, right?"

"Well, I wouldn't say I was begging..."

"What would you say? Aren't you more often than not the one that has to come convince the rest of us to peel the money away for information technology products we don't know we need?"

"Yes. But I'd use lobbying, not begging."

"Okay, then help me evaluate Richard's point. And I know that no personal criticism was meant by Richard of my efforts, and none is implied in my examining this. But, who's on the wrong track here? Am *I* wrong for raising the hopes of the staff that things might change even if it involves the budget? Am I— as Richard puts it by citing a film I love—writing checks he thinks we can't or shouldn't cash?"

Clearly, Will thought, Randall was still not used to an intense, officer-level, sleeves-up discussion devoid of rancor or personal animus. He had continually held back at the retreat, and Will could read his well-concealed apprehension beneath his smile. The jury was still out, Will thought, on whether he was the right person for the job, and he couldn't help but wonder why exchanges like this were not comfortable and common in Las Vegas Memorial's C-suite. *Had someone in their past dictatorially suppressed open discussion, or were they venturing through uncharted territory?*

"Randall?" he prompted again.

There was a resigned sigh, as if the interrogator had finally cracked the suspect's resistance, and a real answer was coming.

"Yes, Will, as the CIO, I'm not only supposed to manage and recommend our information systems, I'm supposed to come beg for the money before the high court of finance. No aspersions,

Richard, but you do tend to hold court on such things, and yes, Will, Richard has a point. If he dances past my door one morning and asks what would I buy and install if budget wasn't a barrier, I would have my hopes substantially raised, and be positively difficult to deal with for weeks if he later tells me he was only kidding. My cat would probably get kicked."

Will nodded and scribbled a note before looking up.

"Okay. Good. We've joined and defined a very real, very important question here, and if we're to be a cohesive team, which is what I dearly want, this is precisely the kind of discussion we have to wrestle into clarity. Let me hear more."

The discussion began, with Dr. Kirk Nelson and Jon Anderson, the general counsel, joining in, all of them debating the propriety of how far staff hopes could be raised without them later challenging the budget. Will shepherded the discussion until it began to get repetitious, and then stepped in.

"Okay, have you been listening carefully to the thrust of everything that's been said? This whole debate is about one thing, and one thing only. Control. And why wouldn't it be? We're the chiefs, and we're all about standing on the bridge and commanding the ship. But to continue that metaphor, we can issue a thousand commands to the crew to throw the wheel to starboard or increase or decrease speed or batten down hatches or whatever they do on a big ship, but if the crew can't or won't tell us that we're hard aground on a sandbar and going nowhere, we're wasting time and essentially looking silly. So here we are debating how to control the crew to get *some* information from them and get *some* involvement from them but not run the risk of a mutiny by letting them even glimpse the budget or the priesthood that controls it."

Will could see Richard leaning forward with a finger in the air looking none too happy.

"No, wait, Richard. I'm going to command the floor here for a few more seconds," Will said rising from his chair. "We're discussing command and control, not leadership. We're discussing defending the budget, and we set the budget. Unfortunately, once we set the budget, we then elevate it to an altar and essentially start worshipping it. Okay, okay, you could slip into aviation references and call it a flight plan, but guess what? Flight plans get modified all the time, especially when the crew or air traffic control finds out modification is needed because there are storms blowing up along the route, or high winds, or other traffic in conflict. Plans are just that: plans. Not laws. Budgets are just that as well: plans, not laws. But here's the essence of my argument. Are we here to serve the budget, or is the budget here to serve us in our quest for serving the best interests of the patient? I want you all to think very hard about this, please. To my mind, everything we've been discussing—starting with Richard's very cogent observation—is about our serving and worshipping the budget, not about the budget being a tool for serving our mission. Our mission is the patient, not the budget. But there's more in this point. This exalted strata we occupy has tactical responsibilities, of course. We have to control the inflow and outflow of revenue as if it were the gasoline to keep the engine running, just like an aircrew keeps tight control over the fuel and whether there's enough for the journey. But our most important task is being leaders and speaking with a common voice, just as my most important responsibility to you is achieving unity of purpose and vision. To the rest of the institution, the middle managers and the front line folks, we either set the vision or there is no vision. In order for Las Vegas Memorial to change, we must change. We must be fully aligned and set a clear and attainable vision; paint a picture with our words and actions until they can literally feel what it would be like to work in a hospital that harmed no one. And right now, the challenge before us is clear: We do not have consensus, and we must have it. What is the most important value of this organization? And how much hope and power should we give to the masses? Healthcare is a complex adaptive system with an unfathomable number of things that could go wrong at any time because of the multiple providers and services. Because of this, we must lead differently; never take our eyes off the vision and hold each other accountable to the new course. A Naval commander may set the destination, but he leaves it to his captains and chiefs to make it happen, to figure out how much fuel, how many ships, and all the other tactical details needed. Leaders control the vision, not the people. The people, if appropriately chosen and led through vision and engagement, will do most of the hard tactical work, provided we train them, we trust them and we listen to them. And yes, that means running the risk that many of the ideas they bring to us aren't fiscally achievable. But in my view, that risk is not a legitimate reason to shy away from raising hopes, and you know why I say that? Because we should never have so much arrogance as to think we have all the financial answers. Why has St. Michael's in Denver succeeded so brilliantly? In part because they weren't afraid of their people and their ideas. Yes, I said afraid. We think of it rather arrogantly as control, but we're really institutionally afraid of having the inmates run the asylum. At St. Michael's, the people on the sharp end of care know the problems and the solutions. Administration isn't afraid of letting their people get frustrated when they suggest solutions but don't have the funds. That's because those engaged, frustrated people at the sharp end learned to get together with management's vision guiding them and find ways to achieve the financially impossible. They consistently found funds where no one, including the CFO, knew where they were hiding. Not in the budget, but in what they could change and improve. The wisdom of crowds. There's a book by that name, and it's a valid concept with us. That's the nub of it. So who's in control, and what are we in control of? We're in control of the vision, and we have to live it by trusting and engaging."

"Will," Richard interjected, his voice even and thoughtful, "I think I'm following you, but we have a lot of practical conflicts to resolve. I mean, if we ask people what they want to change but we can't afford it, you're saying we should go back to them and say, 'YOU find the money?'"

"I'm saying, Richard, that we must change this institution to effortlessly embrace a process by which the folks on the floors and in the ER and central processing and pharmacy are sufficiently exposed to the financial realities, and that most of the time they'll automatically be searching for the dollars. I'm saying that the front lines can find the 50 percent waste in our hospital faster than you ever could, that in addition to holding the vision, you have to insist on *Evidence Based Practice* while engaging front line experts. I'm saying that we have to stop departmentalizing the budget because each department then seeks to maximize the performance of its own silo, thus sub maximizing the whole."[ix]

"How are we going to do that for heaven's sake?"

"By using a different philosophy. By creating a new financial structure internally, budgeting the throughput of service lines, not departments. That's just one structural flaw impeding a true unified effort."

"I don't know how to do that, Will."

"We can both learn though, right? Our job is to give them the time and resources to make Las Vegas Memorial safe and we are going to have to leap over that quality chasm without a safety net and do the right thing. Like Geisinger's *Proven Care* model where the same forty steps are taken for 100 percent of coronary bypass surgery. Only afterwards did they see that the margin was driven up 100 percent while reducing readmissions by 45 percent. Geisinger didn't have a financial guarantee before they invested in the project. They did the right thing. And, for example, you know as well as I do that the 15 percent of beds occupied by readmissions consume 60 percent of hospital resources. And take another suggestion Claudia is working with already, the idea of increasing efficiency in nurse scheduling by handing the nurse managers and charge nurses control over staffing, a method that has been highly successful at St. Michael's. She suggested it because her nurses desperately need more flexibility to provide safe care, but the nurse manager already had a well-thought-out argument for why it would not be just revenue neutral, but would save us up to 20 percent when the program matures."

Richard was leaning forward but still looking uncomfortable. "You want to educate everyone on the *budget?*"

"Can't we do that? I don't mean make miniature Richards out of them, but give virtually everyone in this institution the *chance and the responsibility* to understand what we and the board grapple with financially every day, especially as CMS alters the landscape and fee-for-service crumbles and reimbursement for more and more 'never events' is denied. The budget isn't just our burden, it belongs to all of us who carry a Las Vegas Memorial ID. To frame practicality with vision I'm saying that every suggestion or decision in this organization must be framed with an eye on how the results will ultimately serve patient care. How will it serve the patients? How will it make them safer?"

"I guess we can do that."

"I'm not saying, by the way, that every proposal has to have a grass roots funding solution. There's a lot we must spend right now way in advance of grass roots salvation."

Now the CFO looked alarmed. "What, for instance? You have to remember the guiding phrase, Will, 'No margin, no mission.'"

"Let's turn it around. No mission, no margin. And the mission is patient-centric care, for which the only legitimate target is the outcome for each individual. So let's redraft that phrase: "No outcome, no income."* We will have a lot of delicate and sometimes gutsy funding decisions to make in the next year, things that may not have an established return on investment (ROI) timeline. Some we can't do, many we will do even if it pushes borrowing or strains our ability to balance the budget. Sometimes, Richard, I'm going to need you to support a spending decision on faith alone. For instance, we're going to fund a very substantial number of staff retreats, we're going to hire top-flight facilitators to teach our managers how to conduct those retreats, and we need a big place with dormitory-like accommodations, probably on Lake Mead, and we need to ask our board if anyone has a place they can donate or at least rent to us at discounted rates."

"How much is *that* going to cost?" Richard asked evenly.

"You're focused on the dollars again, Richard, and you miss my point. The correct question is what value will this provide? How will it benefit the patient? I'm not saying you don't need to ask how much it costs, but that's your *secondary* concern to the prime directive, not your first. Correct me if I'm wrong, but how much did that wrong-site surgery cost this hospital in dollars and reputation a few years ago? How did it impact our capacity to borrow? How much did we pay out to the family for the three wrongful death suits last year?" Will asked, looking at general counsel Jon Anderson, who just shook his head.

Richard sighed and tried to affect a smile, but it wasn't working, and Will waved it away. "We'll get the numbers on the retreat thing figured out for you shortly, Richard." He turned to the rest of the team.

"Okay, two things. First, are we all of the same mind that a state of zero preventable patient injuries is our mutual, heartfelt goal?"

Everyone around the table responded affirmatively, Richard Holbrook included.

"Second, what we've just had here is the type of respectful, collegial, no-holds-barred discussion that leads to unity. That's not unity based on my command authority, but unity of vision based on our mutual agreement of what we're going to accomplish. Only when these conversations are held off-line will they be detrimental to our team. Zero avoidable patient safety disasters, an energized and highly engaged staff, and an advanced state of what's called 'Servant Leadership' means a C-suite that is here for one purpose: Facilitate the ability of the people of Las Vegas Memorial to carry out our mutually-held vision. In other words, we are here to create a psychologically safe culture where it is easy for people to do the right thing."

Claudia made it a point to never look at her BlackBerry® in an important meeting, but this was the third time the little thing had vibrated in as many minutes, she pulled it out as stealthily as possible and read the screen before looking up, her forehead wrinkled as she tried to place the author of the text she just received. *Bernie was it? The interim nurse manager from Med-Surg?* The text read:

> **If safety is our top priority, I need an additional nurse for next shift. Staffing says NO.**

The cat was clearly out of the bag, she thought, and it would mature into a tiger in very short order.

Claudia shoved a disturbingly familiar thought out of her mind, but it was as persistent as a defensive lineman hell-bent on sacking the quarterback. She composed herself outwardly by organizing her leather notebook as the words from her previous hospital echoed in her memory, taking her down again: *"You need to stop mollycoddling your people! Okay, Claudia? Our train's leaving the station so you either get on or get off!"*

Inhaling deeply, she packed up her things, made her excuses to her fellow officers, and headed straight to staffing to approve the 'extra' nurse.

Chapter Twenty-Five

As soon as Sylvia swung open the back doors to the ER she overheard a comment from the nurses' station, "Bay Four is just a psych patient." The words annoyed her, and she immediately made a mental note to deal with the offending nurse after finding Dr. Garvin, the physician in charge of the emergency room tonight.

Full moon so soon, she wondered, gazing through the small window at the packed waiting room. Research didn't validate the 'full moon equals total chaos' theory, but she didn't need the research—she had over thirty years of experience to draw on and tonight was yet another validation. *Maybe I should start coordinating my work schedule more closely with the moon's phases,* she thought.

Garvin was sitting in his usual spot at the computer in the middle hall. He stared at Sylvia for a moment before raising his eyebrows, feigning surprise. But his bushy, dark eyebrows and full head of hair made the gesture slightly comical. After more than ten years working together, they knew each other well, especially each other's hot buttons. And Garvin knew what Sylvia hated the most. *Just the mere mention of the word should do it,* he thought, frustrated.

"We're going to have to go on *divert* if you don't place some of these patients fast, Sylvia." Garvin said the words *on divert* slowly for emphasis.

"I'm waiting for Yablonsky to call back. Should have an ICU bed for you shortly for the head bleed patient. Who's next?"

"Well, if you can get the damn hospitalist on call to answer his page, it would be the COPD patient for Med-Surg. What's the definition of 'on-call' anyway? The thoracic guy hasn't called back yet and it's been an hour. Are there any rules for that?"

"Not so fast," replied Sylvia. "I haven't seen the hospitalist since rounds on orthopedic and he's really swamped."

"He can look at him on the patient floor. I wrote holding orders and I've already got two in the hall."

Sylvia was growing tired of the banter between the two groups. The outside hospitalists saw almost thirty patients a day and they worked their butts off to get the diagnosis right and the length of stay down. They were an overworked, impersonal but conscientious lot who got dinged for wrong admits and usually ordered more tests than she personally thought was needed for "CYA" reasons.

As for Garvin and the rest of the ER, they were so busy that she realized she would just have to gather the information herself. Report was always a rapid firing of information that usually lasted less than two to three minutes and the only time appropriate to give it was now. Never knowing what was coming in the doors next, having to be prepared and skilled to handle anything and everything along with never being able to say "no" compounded the stress. *Welcome to the ER, she thought, where everything is important all the time—except for the psych patients who aren't "real" patients.*

Carefully Sylvia studied her census notes. Med-Surg was already understaffed as it was and she was concerned about their ability to take on another patient, especially at change of shift. The float pool had been cut down and they couldn't replace the nurse who called in sick for night shift, despite numerous calls. No extra help. The rules made it clear that you had to go through a complicated bureaucratic process to get permission for an outside agency that didn't always result in an approval. So it wasn't an option, she just didn't have the time.

"Who is your next priority?" Sylvia asked looking up from her clipboard.

"Broken tibia in Bay Seven needs surgery, but he's 66 years-old and he's been on Coumadin."

"Orthopedics is full."

"Then put him on another floor! Christ, it's not my problem where you put him."

Garvin's tone of voice told her all she needed to know: *they were in the get-'em-in, get-'em-out fast mode again.* And the last time Garvin was this frustrated, someone almost died. It was a simple knee patient they had hurried to place in a bed, but no one had seen the dangerously high potassium level, and within two hours of being admitted to orthopedics, he was rushed to ICU with hyperkalemia.

"Let me work on it. I'm going to talk to the charge nurse and I'll catch you after your next patient," Sylvia replied with caution. She needed a few moments to access the situation and think.

"Nothing to talk about, Sylvia. Just act! Just start getting these patients out of here!"

Garvin was already halfway down the hall yelling to Esther, the unit secretary, "Where the hell are the results from the CT for the patient in Bay Six? I should've had them thirty minutes ago."

"I'll check again," replied Esther, now accustomed to his occasional flare ups. All she had to do was remind herself that Garvin's voice always got louder when he was worried. And everyone knew he was apprehensive about the patient in Bay Six. She paged CT again.

Sylvia studied the whiteboard. Bill was the charge nurse tonight—but she had just passed him starting an IV in Bay Five. She liked Bill. He was military; always calm and composed no matter what the situation. The maladies of the patients in the ER couldn't hold a candle to the blazing explosions of reality he'd seen with his own eyes overseas. People respected him, and his steady nature was like a rocky pillar in a sea of turmoil.

Sylvia needed to get a better idea of the volume and acuity of the patients in the waiting room. As she approached triage, she could hear Bianca saying to the patient, "So let me get this straight. You've had these symptoms for five days, right? And tell me again why you decided to come to the ER tonight when you've had the same symptoms for five days now and we just saw you two weeks ago?" The tone in her voice was condescending and it made Sylvia cringe.

"Excuse me," she said, acknowledging the patient and peeking through the curtain. "Bianca, may I speak with you for a moment when you are done here?"

Bianca, surprised, just nodded.

Typically the ER ran smoothly and staff did a great job. The new manager was awesome and really focused on teamwork; the retention numbers were up and waiting times were down. But lately, Sylvia noticed, people seemed more agitated. Maybe this was just one of those nights, or the cumulative effects of the recession, or the full moon. Usually Bianca was so professional and kind that Sylvia couldn't help but wonder what had gotten into her.

There were only two empty seats remaining in the reception area. Sylvia walked through greeting patients, asking how long they had been waiting. Because of HIPAA (The Health Insurance Portability and Accountability Act of 1996: Privacy and Security Rules) regulations, she couldn't ask much more in a public area. Two toddlers on fire with fevers from the looks on their flushed faces, a deep finger cut on a workman that would need stitches, an entire family of Vietnamese huddled around an elderly gentleman that looked to be at least a hundred years old, and a sprained ankle with an ice pack. Although the workman had the most minor injury of the bunch, there was something about him that Sylvia just didn't like, something that pinged her internal radar. *Why is he sweating? It isn't hot in here.*

Nothing too acute here, though. She could take a few minutes.

Bianca approached Sylvia defensively, explaining, "I only have a minute. I haven't had dinner or a break and as you can see, I won't be getting either." *Maybe now wasn't the best time.*

Sylvia looked Bianca in the eye. "First," she said emphatically, "it's unacceptable that you haven't had a break or meal. I will triage the next patient, take twenty minutes for yourself."

"No, that's okay, there are patients waiting." Bianca responded, feeling guilty.

"No, it's not okay," Sylvia replied emphatically. "Go on now, please. We need you fed and hydrated."

Bianca's reply was reluctant. "OK. I'll tell Bill. But I'm also the one trying to get hold of the thoracic on-call. I've paged twice over the last hour. Dr. Garvin needs to speak to him ASAP about Bay Six; he's uncertain about something and wants him to come in and take a look himself."

Sylvia glanced at her watch and called the next patient into the tiny space. "Alex?" She propped the door open with one foot for the large construction worker. But no sooner had he taken a seat next to the desk when an annoyed family member approached her speaking loudly.

"Are you in charge here, Ma'am? My wife has been on a stretcher for over two hours in the hall and she's thirsty and needs her insulin. When are they going to get her a real bed so she can get some food and medicine? She's a diabetic you know, and we haven't seen a doctor or a nurse the whole time she's been in the hall."

Sylvia turned again to the injured workman as he said, "it's OK, go on, the bleeding has stopped now." But the pressure dressing was saturated. Briefly the man lifted it up so Sylvia's doubtful eyes could assess the situation for herself. The large cut would definitely need at least forty stitches, and it would be difficult because of the ragged edges. She donned a pair of gloves, replaced the wet pack with clean gauze adding quickly, "I'll be right back."

Sylvia knew she needed to de-escalate the angry husband and immediately put out her hand. "My name is Sylvia and I'm the nursing supervisor, and you?"

"My name's is Bill Myers and my wife's name is Myrtle Myers and we are none too happy," he all but shouted.

"I understand. And I apologize. Let me talk to your wife right now and then I will call for more help," explained Sylvia.

At the same moment a young, heavily-tattooed man came out of nowhere and charged Sylvia like a bull. She had been blocking the exit and before she could react, she was splayed on the floor as he lunged for the door screaming, "I told you I needed a cigarette!" Dr. Garvin ran to help Sylvia up as the security guard sprinted after the patient.

"Are you alright?" Garvin asked offering Sylvia an arm as she limped to a chair struggling to reorient herself.

"Who? what?" Sylvia sputtered, trying desperately to regain her balance and make sense of the chaos as the hospital loud speakers blared, "Dr. North to the ER, Dr. North to the ER" and two security guards raced down the hall. But it only took two words from Garvin for Sylvia to reassemble her thoughts again.

"Psych patient!" explained Garvin.

Chapter Twenty-Six

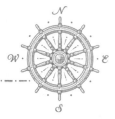

The sun was sinking over the La Madre wilderness to the west of Las Vegas as Will slipped outside the beautifully prepared Sunrise Room at the Spanish Trail Country Club. The first wave of doctors and their spouses could be heard coming down the corridor, but his attention was focused on the spectacular display above—shafts of sunlight through the otherwise crystal clear sky, one of which was catching the contrail of a high-flying jetliner miles above. He could hear the rhythmic swish of a sprinkler on the nearest golf green, along with the buzz of insects and the distant roar of traffic, all of it rather soothing as he focused on nothing for a few moments.

The day had been long, the preparation for his pivotal evening somewhat laborious, and yet he felt buoyed, happy, almost, in a way he couldn't explain. Certainly the surprisingly high number of attendees for the annual medical staff meeting helped, but it was the overall feel of the last few days that had raised his spirits. A few casual conversations in the corridors, a hasty and enthusiastic report from the CFO—who had literally leaned into his office before rushing on—and a rising tide of suggestions, ideas and notes from the front lines and the middle level managers, all responding to his request to help design the structure they would need for constant feedback and reinvention.

People were testing, too. The nursing directors had suggested a four day work week for themselves while HR, still leaderless, was in a panic that they were losing control.

Even Ivy had given voice to it, noting a certain something in the air.

"Enthusiasm?" he'd asked.

"Hope," she'd replied. "Tentative...but hope."

Will turned back toward the open doors leading to the dining room where he'd already tested the microphone and computer holding his brief PowerPoint. The appointed time of six p.m. had arrived, and true to form "doctor time" kicked in as a sudden surge of invitees flowed into the room at the last minute.

Will had elected not to set up a formal reception line, so he moved now into the dining room shaking hands and greeting the crowd at random, thankful for the name tags they were issuing at the door. He was immensely pleased with the turnout—though slightly puzzled at how it had been achieved and said as much to Kirk Nelson, who just winked and whispered, "I'm on my way out, Will. I can afford to take chances. Let's just say that I'm going to go out in a blaze of story." Will couldn't help but smile broadly as he punched the older man lightly on the shoulder. He'd liked Kirk Nelson from the very first scotch.

A superb dinner behind them, Kirk Nelson rose to give the introduction, reprising their first conversation at how impressed he was that at last someone had taken the helm with real sustained determination to change things, coupled with a deep understanding of medicine, and the nuances of leadership.

And then their new CEO took the microphone and let the perfunctory applause die down as he sat down on a stool, taking a minute to survey the faces around the room. One hundred eighty of the two hundred fifty privileged docs at Las Vegas Memorial had shown up, and he was acutely aware that the key to success of everything he had signed on to accomplish at Las Vegas Memorial would hang on the words to be spoken in the next hour.

"Somewhere around the year sixteen hundred in England," Will began, "when William Shakespeare, or Sir Edward DeVere, or someone using the pen name of Will Shakespeare, was writing perhaps the most brilliant prose in the English language, a courtier named John Donne wrote the words: 'No man is an island' as the opening of a brief poem. Unfortunately, the vast majority of professors in America's medical schools do not subscribe to that sentiment, or even recognize the principle involved. According to the ethos of formal medical training, every physician—every one of us—is supposed to be an island—an 'autonomous scientist.' That perfectly descriptive phrase, by the way, was coined by Dr. David Nash, formerly of Jefferson Medical College, now dean of his own The Jefferson School of Population Health at Thomas Jefferson University in Philadelphia. David is one of the rare exceptions as a medical school professor and dean who uncharacteristically understands that we doctors were trained to practice in a cottage industry—a data-free environment, devoid of meaningful feedback, unburdened by reliable evidence of what really works, and insulated from the need to conform to best practices by over two centuries of assurance that only *we* know best. We were taught that this was the best way to ensure professional commitment and accountability, but our autonomous philosophy only serves to isolate us from the larger healthcare community. Worse, it deprives us of the training and ability to orchestrate the talents of the vast array of fellow medical professionals who stand ready to be our teammates in providing the best care. What we were never taught was how effective a collegial team can enhance and validate the quality of work we perform.

In short, we've been set up to create precisely what Dr. John Wennberg of Hanover, New Hampshire, has authoritatively documented as an unacceptable American pandemic of inexplicable and non-value added clinical variation.[xi] In other words, your treatment as a patient in America depends on geography, socio-economic status and third party coverage, because we all do things differently in different settings, with different populations and at different times. Podunk Junction has ten times the rate of hysterectomies than Main Street, USA. Dallas and Denver may differ in tonsillectomy frequency by one order of magnitude. Why? Because most of us have been acculturated to believe that the only correct diagnosis, the only correct interpretation, procedure, or course of treatment, is that which we alone as individual doctors decide is right. But that concept is an illusion—as much as the idea that any of us, *any* of us—can achieve absolute perfection 100 percent of the time without the benefit of collective expertise, and the myriad benefits of a well-functioning, high-reliability system. I'm talking about a human system of collegial teammates across professional disciplines who, when well-led, can paradoxically achieve successful outcomes far more consistently than we can achieve on our own autonomously. Once you see this truth, David Nash's phrase, 'autonomous scientist,' begins to resemble an oxymoron. In fact, while patients and families and the nation depend on us to utilize the best that medical science has to offer, the illusion of autonomy as an unassailable value, and the tradition of decisional isolation, significantly contributes to our inadvertently killing between twenty-two to thirty American patients per hour on average in hospitals across this land."

Will stopped for a few seconds and met eyes across the room, most of their owners looking uncomfortable.

"Yeah, I know," he continued. "Not *your* patients. Not at *your* hospital, right? Those numbers are about the rest of the country. We've only accidentally killed and harmed a few people at Las Vegas Memorial this past year, and you personally had nothing to do with it, therefore—as we are all led to believe—you have no reason to alter the way you do things. But that's the crux of the problem, you see: the traditional assumption that *you* don't need to change, as well as the idea that there is no 'we' in your practice. As my friend Dr. Joe Bujak says, "There is no such thing as the word physicians, plural, only physician, singular."

Will could see the furtive, questioning glances between various physicians in the room, slightly veiled looks of: *What the hell is this all about?* shooting back and forth. He gave them a few more seconds to process what had to feel like an assault on their most sacrosanct values.

"In the previous two weeks, I have utilized just about every technique the younger generations have pioneered to communicate with you about a very special place near Denver called St. Michael's Memorial. I've sent you a short video, tweeted details, sent you faxes, Facebook notices, e-mails, and old fashion papers through snail mail, and despite your busy schedules, I'm hoping most of you did, in fact, take a few moments to read about St. Michael's. Why is it so important? Because it's a model of the type of hospital I'll bet every one of you would love to work in. We need a new model because the old model—the status quo, grade "C" level institution that has been the American standard—does not keep our patients, our practice, or our livelihood safe. In fact, radically transforming the old model is precisely what we're here to discuss tonight.

Let me ask a few questions before telling you a very personal story. How many of you in here—please be brutally honest—have had a person that you cared deeply about either injured, killed, or impacted negatively by an inadvertent medical error?"

Approximately 40 percent of the hands in the room went up, many of them held barely high enough to see; a few raised a mere finger.

"How many of you have had people you care about imperiled but not hurt, a near miss, something terrible that was about to happen because of a mistake, but didn't?"

Another scattering of hands went up.

"This is the big one: how many of you have accidentally killed, or inadvertently harmed a patient?"

The energy shifted and all was still. The question, an obvious breach of etiquette; the audience sat shocked. Slowly, Will raised his own hand and held it steady, watching as a few fingers left their wine glasses and pointed upward in reluctant honesty.

"It's not easy to discuss, or even admit, is it? It wasn't for me, the morning I killed a young woman through the arrogance of the false certainty that I'd been trained to toss about."

Will begin relating the details with the scene playing like a high definition nightmare.

"I'd completed my residency. I was a full-fledged doctor, an internist, fully formed and licensed to heal for over ten years. And one morning I found my conclusions being questioned by a mere resident who thought a twenty-nine-year-old woman was septic. I looked at the charts, the tests, the patient, and told him no, he had it wrong. He insisted, and worse, he said the nurses agreed, which really torqued me off. I asked him how the heck he had the audacity to think he and a bunch of nurses who'd never been to medical school knew best, and this idiot looks me in the eye with incredible chutzpah and says, 'I don't know, Doctor Jenkins, but I've just got a very strong feeling it's sepsis, regardless of the tests.' I insulted him, dismissed him, and released the patient to go home, where over the next forty-eight hours, unsupervised by anyone because she lived alone; she slipped into what must have been at least a hundred and six degree fever and died. The body wasn't discovered for a week, but the autopsy said it all. The young doctor I'd called an idiot had been right, and I—had been so wrapped up in my cloak of infallibility that I had no capacity to listen—I hadn't just been wrong, I'd been the instrument of her death. I was the reason she would never marry, never carry a child, never get a college degree. And her formal cause of death?" He sighed involuntarily, fighting a surge of emotion that threatened to dampen his eyes and choke off his throat. "It...it was everything I could do not to write the truth on that death certificate. Hubris. Excessive pride, instead of sepsis. I can argue that I was trained that way, and I was. I can argue that I was, by no means, the first to learn physician autonomy *'uber alles'* is wrong. I can argue till the cows come home and it doesn't give that young woman her life back. Her name was Brenda Diane Collins, and just speaking her name out loud is always a permanent reminder of my own humanity."

As Will took a sip of water, he heard a clock ticking loudly on one of the walls.

"Hopefully, none of you have or will experience quite as devastating a form of the same lesson, but we all have stories, and many of us do go through a form of post-traumatic stress denying the impact and hiding from the consequences of not being that perfect doctor we were told we had to be. And the reason that I am so certain that everyone in this room has a story? Because we are all human. No exceptions."

Another pause, this one to compose himself and dissolve the lump in his throat.

"My original matriculation to the C-suite was a direct result of that very humbling experience, and even years later—after years of running a hospital in Portland, Oregon—I still carried enough hubris to think that I *now* had the way and the light! I reorganized the heck out of my hospital as CEO, and still one night, by intervening and substituting my judgment for that of my practitioners, I ended up participating in the totally avoidable loss of my godson." Will stopped and reached for the water bottle again, taking a long swig before continuing. The questioning glances and raised eyebrows were no longer in evidence. Everyone in the room was riveted.

"It took me several more years and one very self-reflective, scotch-soaked night to realize the truth: I wouldn't have intervened that critical night if I'd truly believed my hospital was safe. Oh, I *said* it was safe! That was the story I told myself. After all, I reasoned, look at our metrics! Look how hard we work! I didn't realize that as a human being I was subconsciously selecting the information I wanted to hear to validate the time and energy that I was pouring into that hospital every day. But, actions eventually speak louder than words and betray a deeper truth. You see, as physicians at that hospital, we were still asking each other questions like, 'Who would you recommend for a total knee?' and 'Who's the best general surgeon we have?' And, while we and our families were privy to that very top secret information, the general public was not. So on a deeper level I knew about my Portland hospital exactly what you know about Las Vegas Memorial: That we're not truly safe until any doctor and any nurse can take care of your loved ones. And if someone isn't worthy of that trust—doctor, nurse, manager, CEO—what the devil is that person doing here? Worse, if we aren't willing to work tirelessly as a team to use the very best methods and techniques and evidence-based treatments in order to improve the health of everyone, not just our own family, where is the morality of our calling?"

The audience of doctors and spouses stirred quietly, and Will glanced to one side where Ivy stood with a microphone at the ready.

"Before I continue, I want to open this up to any questions or comments. No problem with interrupting me as it won't be an interruption."

A younger physician Will did not recognize raised his hand and Ivy hurried the microphone to him. He introduced himself and stood. "Doctor Jenkins..."

"Will, please."

"All right. Will. Yes, I have my own stories—we all do, as you said—but we're all working our tails off for diminishing revenue and barely keeping up. We're all trying to keep our patients safe, and I doubt there's anyone here tonight who doesn't want to do the right thing, but medicine is inherently dangerous and we're all human, and I think there are a lot us here tonight who believe like I do that we're whipping the horse as hard as we can. I frankly don't think a few mistakes here and there—especially if we try to learn from each of them—makes us an unsafe hospital. In other words, I think you're overstating the case."

"Fair enough," Will replied. "Let me ask you to take a moment and honestly answer that same question. Would you allow any doctor here, and any nurse in our institution, to take care of your mother or daughter or wife if they were very ill?"

The physician smiled and looked around for support before looking back at Will. "Well, there are always a few you trust more than others in any medical center."

"Really? But does that make it ethical to let those guys or gals you don't trust as much work on someone else's loved ones, but not yours?"

"We don't all agree on who's okay and who isn't. I mean, these are value judgments."

"Right. Value judgments made not as a team, but individually, which is why they vary so much just as with our individual decisions on what constitutes best practices."

"But, Will, that's the nature of medical practice."

Will's index finger flew up in an exclamation point. "Yes! It is! Which is precisely the reason that I need physician support for change—to lead that change—and to understand why we can't continue to function as autonomous professional islands. Thank you for that!"

The physician surrendered the microphone and sat down, obviously puzzled, as Will continued.

"See, we are NOT safe at Las Vegas Memorial as long as we are a fragmented collection of independent practitioners inherently suspicious of each other's best practice, despite the evidence, suspicious of minimizing variables, suspicious of new techniques such as checklists, and suspicious of each other. We are *not* safe, and we can never approach safety or quality or even professional survival, unless we can accept evidence-based best practices where warranted, and build and nurture teams in which each and every member can and will pass any information deemed critical to any other team member, without condemnation or chastisement or fear, and whether right or wrong. We are also not safe until there are no rank barriers stifling communication, no nurses afraid to speak to you or call you at two a.m. We are *not* safe until Las Vegas Memorial is full of mutually respectful people who take the time to know each other, and speak to and complement each other, and make it a fun place to practice. And please mark this, we are *not* safe as long as there is a single doctor who will look the other way and stay silent when a colleague is violating the rules, the standards, or the basics of safe practice and by doing so putting our patients and by association all of us in danger. Virtually all of you want to do the right thing and achieve zero preventable harm, great outcomes and a happy practice. The problem is—practically speaking—as a profession, we have not done the right thing. Perhaps we have never really known *how* to do the right thing—create unity and standardize our procedures and our care—until now. And here I come, with great respect for each of you as the physicians of Las Vegas Memorial, but asking you to accept the reality that we have to drastically abandon the old ways of practicing medicine, and we have to do so now."

A loud rattle of dishes to one side and Will caught the eye of the offending busboy.

"Let's hold the cleanup for a little while," he said, earning an apologetic nod.

Will turned back to the audience. "As physicians, we pride ourselves on our vast knowledge, skill and experience base. After all, we spent an entire decade of our lives accumulating this body of knowledge. Yet, what I eventually realized was that as a profession, we are virtually ignorant, I was ignorant, that the most fundamental knowledge deficit of all is that 'You don't know what you don't know.' And that, ladies and gentlemen, is where medicine is today, and the focus of my brief PowerPoint for tonight. Fasten your seat belts, because the following statistics and realities are hurtful, embarrassing and completely true."

Will clicked the forward button as the title appeared on the screen and Ivy dimmed the lights slightly, followed by a dizzying array of facts and figures that painted a dismal and depressing picture of American healthcare: 6,000 drugs, 4,000 plus procedures, 9,000 billing codes, with none of them covering health; 5 percent of the population spending 60 percent of the dollars, and 1 percent using 35 percent of the money (5 percent of the Medicare pool), while an annual national expenditure of 2.8 trillion or 18 percent of GNP—affected no more than 10 percent of the health of Americans.

The slides rolled on and on: 48th in infant mortality, killing 22-30 people per hour from mistakes and avoidable infections, fifty million uninsured in a country with universal healthcare expressed through emergency rooms, and an impending shortage of eighty-five thousand physicians, and perhaps as many as two hundred thousand by 2020.

Will paused on the last slide and waited for the urgent conversations to die down.

"Dr. Paul Batalden of Dartmouth and IHI is widely quoted as saying that 'Every system is perfectly designed to achieve the results it consistently achieves.' If that's correct—and it obviously is—then our cottage industry system, where we are all compensated on a return on investment basis and not a return on optimal outcomes, is, itself, the culprit because it's perfectly and inadvertently designed to kill those hapless 22 to 30 people per hour who trusted us. But what, exactly, IS this traditional 'system' I keep referring to? It's us, a cottage industry of individual physicians in which each professional is an autonomous island and each hospital is built to serve as a farmer's market dedicated to maintaining physician satisfaction. Keep us happy as docs and good things will trickle down to the patients. Physician-centric, not patient-centric. It's an environment in which we have access to the tools and the teams that could enable us to achieve superior outcomes and zero preventable harm, but our autonomous; lone-eagle culture falsely blocks our proper utilization of such people and assets. Here's a staggering truth: There is virtually no way to create a unified, coordinated, effective and safe medical center with that model. Independent silos, uncoordinated care and overtreatment propelled by a fee-for-service business model are failing us nationwide, not just because of Medicare policies, but because we can't deliver evidence-based, consistent care this way. The patients become merely grist for our mill, not the purpose of our production. We're squandering money and lives perpetuating a failed model, and squandering the overall health of America in the process. Want particulars? Well, we *know* how to control diabetes, but do we do it? We *know* how to prevent asthma attack patients from ending up in the ER, but do we employ that knowledge society-wide? We *know* how to minimize the effects of congestive heart failure, depression, widespread obesity, but is that our focus? Of course not. We have enough trouble pulling our own barge day after day and keeping the doors of the hospital open. We do less, we get paid less. Las Vegas Memorial is no exception. That's the most hurtful reality. Las Vegas Memorial is no exception, and yet, we have to break away from the crowd and make it a major exception."

Another hand in the air and a surgeon in his sixties took the microphone to force the issue Will knew many of them were burning to ask.

"So, what do you want us to do, Will? Where is this going with respect to changing Las Vegas Memorial?"

"First," Will replied, slipping off the stool and walking slightly toward the surgeon. "First, I want to acknowledge that many of you are already struggling to make changes that are profoundly at odds with the ways we were all taught. You're asking about best practices, you're adopting 'foreign' new procedures like time-outs, you're investigating things like crew resource management (CRM) philosophies, and TeamSTEPPS®, and you're working hard to change the way you relate to nurses and each other. Don't think I don't recognize and appreciate you early adopters, you early leaders. And there are many more of you watching those changes and are willing to adopt and change and lead when you're certain it's the right thing to do. There may be a few in here who're totally resistant, due to fear that surrendering any part of our precious right to autonomy and self-determination will somehow hurt our patients and ourselves as professionals. We don't mean it this way; of course, but that fear is the equivalent of saying we want to insulate our patients against all outside opinions, procedures and practices not invented by us. But autonomy is not a protection for our patients if it screens them from the science of evidence-based realities. I'm not here to force you to do anything. I'm here to show you the power you already have, and cheer you on in learning to use your immense power for good, as a team, like never before. We can change things immediately if you decide to!"

Will paused and pulled a small leather case up from alongside the stool, searching for and extracting a piece of paper.

"You know what the principal element of our mission statement is? Let me read it to you: *We exist to serve and improve the health of the community of Las Vegas.* Do we do that?" He shook his head. "Only by accident. After all, traditionally that's not our focus—an individual patient with a problem is the focal point. We provide excellent reactive healthcare based on treating illness and injury rather than improving health. We don't prevent, for the most part, we treat. So why has this been so difficult to see? Because of something called myopic embedding. When humans live and work totally enmeshed in a culture, they can't see the essence of that culture. How many of you saw that movie, *The Matrix?"*

More than half the hands in the room went up.

"Bear with me if you haven't, but it involved a metaphorical choice between the status quo, and evolving the ability to know reality, however harsh. In those terms, I appear to be holding out a red pill and a green pill and asking you to choose. Take the green one, continue believing that everything is okay and your life will seem as good as it always was, at least for a little while longer, until the tidal wave hits. Take the red pill and swallow the reality that we are not fulfilling our mission, that we must pull together and change drastically and there will be short term pain, leading to long term solutions. Perhaps even salvation is the right word."

Will punched the advance button until a single red pill appeared on the screen.

"Here's one of the most hurtful realities that comes with the red pill: If someone waved a magic wand over the country and reduced the need for doctors and nurses and hospitals by 50 percent from tonight forward, we'd bankrupt every hospital in the nation within six months, with the exception of the VA and military installations. What does that tell us? It tells us that we're dependent on a steady supply of sick people to keep the doors open, and making them too well—protecting them from overtreatment and mistreatment and suppressing the need for emergency visits with appropriately applied preventative care—can be hazardous to the health of our healthcare institutions, as well as our wallets. What a conundrum! If we do the very thing we're dedicated to doing, we eliminate our economic viability. See, nationally, we've become addicts to a fee-for-service focus that thoroughly corrupts the noble reasons for being in healthcare, or for spending those ten years to become a doctor in the first place. And while we in this room can't unilaterally fix it for all of America, we *can* fix *this* operation, *this* ethic, *this* team and become a vital example for everyone else. That's why I asked you to be here tonight, because all of this depends on you. Lord, how it depends on you!"

Another pause and another sip of water, but he could feel the intense questions in the room building as he continued, describing how chaotic and frightening the airline industry would be if it were run like healthcare.

"Every captain, every copilot and every flight attendant would bill separately, and they would all set their own fees and make their own operating standards, and bundling agencies would pay those professionals and sell you a travel policy at a standard monthly fee that would cover your occasional trip and, for the same price, those who flew every week. You can imagine how exorbitant the costs would be. In addition, if the airlines lost the same number of passengers as we lose patients, they'd crash at least three seven-forty-sevens a week. Tickets anyone? We'd all be walking! But, even with this simile we don't see the absurdity of our own so-called industry."[xii]

The next few slides were going to be much more difficult, he knew. As if picking up on a nonverbal cue, the group shifted uncomfortably in their seats. But no one had left, Will noted, and so he continued, laying out the evidence of the seductive nature of fee-for-service, energizing overtreatment and unnecessary testing, questionable surgery and the unsettling study that claimed physicians made the right diagnosis only 55 percent of the time.

He triggered a slide of a family of four: a Christmas photo complete with the family dog wearing a Santa hat.

"This is Doug and Kari. In this picture, Kari is twenty-eight years old and the happy, loving mother of those two small girls. Kari is now dead. "He flashed two other happy faces on the screen, giving each a name and a short synopsis of who they were.

"Until today, you knew these people only as a number, and that number is three. These are the people that we at Las Vegas Memorial accidentally killed in the last thirteen months. My goal is to never have to show you pictures like these ever again. And yes, that is possible, but not without your unwavering dedication. Are these people any less important than your own family? If you think so, you do not belong here, or in healthcare. Remember our primary Hippocratic admonition? Let me tell you, 'First, do no harm,' is not a suggestion. It's a moral imperative."

He paused, letting the words sink in. "So what do I want you to do? My challenge is to recruit and excite you to an entirely new way to practice, as a team, as physicians dedicated to finding the best ways to do things and embracing best practices with a vengeance. I'm here to ask your leadership in setting a new course for ourselves and therefore, our profession. This is exponentially more difficult for us physicians than any other group because our core value is autonomy, and when core values are threatened, so is our very identity. But in this new medical model we are being handed the *keys to the kingdom* because we are in the most optimal position to affect change, momentous change. I'm here, at the behest of the board, to change this hospital into one as successful as the one we've told you about, St. Michael's in Denver, a hospital that eight of you have already taken the time to visit. It doesn't matter how great we are as individuals, only how great we are as a team because only a team can keep our patients safe. I am asking each and every one of you to lead this Cultural Revolution. And yes, there are other hospitals you can run to in Las Vegas, good hospitals. But they'll end up changing, too. It's inevitable. Want to be in the forefront of a better medical world?

Want to shed those midnight worries about the cynicism we all feel and recreate medicine as a calling serving humanity? Then stay with us. Guide us. Lead us."

Will glanced at Ivy, who was smiling broadly standing off to one side and pointing to her watch.

"Please don't forget John Donne's admonition, '*No man is an island...*' Even if you're the best surgeon in the world, and perform a difficult surgical procedure flawlessly, what difference does it make if, afterwards, we place your patients in a MRSA infected room? You may think you have the best nurses in the world, but what if materials management runs out of sequential compression devices (SCDs) and your order can't be carried out because there is a shortage of equipment and your patient develops a clot, or the nurse misunderstands your order because he or she is working a double shift, or dietary doesn't see the severe allergic reaction to eggs on your anterior cervical patient?"

Will paused and took a deep breath, looking intently for a moment at the pictures on the screen.

"And even if you think you're the best CEO in the world, how good can you *really* be if people still continue to die or are harmed in your care when it was possible to keep them safe? As your leader, I am not willing to take a chance that the next accident will be *your* daughter, *my* wife—*anyone's* child or spouse. We can do better, all of us, and we must!"

Chapter Twenty-Seven

Kirk Nelson had never given much thought to the exclusive nature of Las Vegas Memorial's physician lounge. With a top quality breakfast, lunch and dinner provided daily without charge for the hard-working surgeons and doctors, it also served as a kind of locker room and boys club—although the conversations shifted subtly when the female physicians entered the room. But when one of the most senior OR nurses emerged from a meeting with Will Jenkins and suggested that perhaps all members of the OR teams should be allowed to use the physician's lounge, even Kirk had been momentarily offended.

It made sense, of course, if you were going to build true collegial teams across professional lines and not perpetuate the concept Jenkins had described with an amusing term: "Medical Apartheid—docs over here, everybody else over there." This morning, however, Kirk was thankful the transition hadn't already occurred. He'd slid into a comfy chair in a far corner with a cup of coffee and a newspaper he was pretending to read, but his ears were tuned to the reaction from the annual medical staff meeting the night before—a reaction that probably wouldn't be openly shared anywhere else. He and Will were both eager for real feedback, since the respectful questions asked of their new CEO at the country club last night had ranged from restrained caution to supportive. Both men knew there would be a strong current of upset running somewhere beneath the calm surface. There would also undoubtedly be generational clashes between the early adopters—who were excited things might really change—and the walking institutions, who would be outraged at Las Vegas Memorial being anything but their personal fiefdom. In fact, as Will spoke, Kirk had carefully watched two of the most vociferous bomb-throwers, somewhat amazed that both of them had uncharacteristically kept their mouths shut during the *back and forth exchange*. Kirk, in particular, knew all too well their silence was not an indication of agreement, and one of them was now in the lounge and eager to be heard.

Dr. Bill Radke had blown through the doors of the physician's lounge like an angry general ready to enlist troops for a counter-attack. The fact that several of his fellows did not seem equally infuriated by their new CEO's words the previous evening was incomprehensible to the very senior cardiac surgeon. Radke cornered two colleagues—one of them, a slightly younger doc, who had slipped into Kirk's office barely a month ago worrying out loud about the cardiovascular surgeon's vicious refusals to follow surgical time-out procedures. Kirk could hear Bill Radke's sharp-edged voice clearly across the room.

"What I'm saying, gentlemen, is that the gloves are off, okay? I've been here thirty years, and I've seen this kind of attempted takeover before, and you have to stop an attack like that in its tracks. I'm taking this to the board!"

"Ah, Bill," one of the other two docs responded, "the board is in full agreement with Jenkins and all those changes he was talking about last night. They gave him a blank check. Didn't you read their letter?"

"And," the other surgeon added, "I would hardly call last night an attack. A 'Come to Jesus' meeting perhaps, but not an attack."

Radke whirled on him. "Let me tell you two overly-trusting guys something you obviously need to understand. That touch-y, feel-y diatribe last night was nothing in the world but a declaration of war by an armchair doctor who couldn't make it on the front lines. You heard him, failure after personal failure, and he has the temerity to show up here to tell real doctors how to practice! Here's how it goes in the slimy world of the C-suite with their false sincerity and their obscene six figure salaries. First they seek your cooperation and your—your *leadership*," he mocked the word in a higher register, "but it's really just a linguistic code for cookbook medicine and controlling even how you run your own office, forcing you to use their computer programs and crap like that. If we let them think we're buying this B.S., in just a few months they'll start working toward a clandestine orchiectomy—professional castration—slicing off your free will as doctors and handing us checklists covering every incision, every stitch, everything we can and can't say in our ORs, eliminating our preference cards and turning the nurses into Nazis. You might as well put surgical masks on monkeys."

"Bill, I know you hate the checklists, but Jenkins has a solid point, man. None of us do things the same and our procedures could use some standardization. I like his idea for a chief research officer to help us with best practices and feedback."

"A good surgeon doesn't need any third party feedback. You know in your gut how well you're doing."

"So, evidence-based medicine is what, an interference with our art?"

"You don't see that?" Radke laughed. "I guess they've already compromised you, Jeffers."

"Bill, neither I nor John here are compromised. We just accept the reality that, as Will Jenkins said last night, we can't continue to do things the same way and especially surgically, without a firm grasp of best practices and standardized procedures and good feedback on the outcomes others are getting with the same surgeries. Did you read Atul Gwande's recent *New Yorker* article on the value of personal coaches even for world class musicians and surgeons? There's nothing wrong with that, or with learning new tricks."

"Yeah, right."

"Look, Bill, John's right. We killed people last year at Las Vegas Memorial. We don't communicate with each other worth a damn! When's the last time you called a team of colleagues together to coordinate your approach to a difficult case, someone with multiple co-morbidities: the hospitalist, the family doc who referred him, the pulmonologist who's been involved."

"Surgeons don't do that."

"But, maybe we need to. We don't have all the answers."

Radke was shaking his head. "Good Lord, listening to you two, pretty soon, only the weak sisters will be surgeons and they'll be cutting by the numbers."

"You calling me a weak sister, Bill? Me and John? We're weak sisters?"

Bill Radke tried to shake it off and turn to the steam table with a plate for some breakfast, but the other surgeon was still in his face.

"Hey, man, if you're going to insult the two of us, you don't turn away."

Radke turned back. "I didn't say you two were weak sisters. I said that's what we'll be breeding if we let clowns like Jenkins come in here and make us cogs in a machine. We're surgeons, dammit. If he thinks he's going get by with all that standardized crap, he'll end up with half of us taking our cases across town."

Across the lounge, Kirk Nelson scribbled a note to himself and decided to stay out of it. For a moment—as Radke's well-known temper was slipping and his face reddening—Kirk thought that he might have to step in and cancel Radke's first surgery; it had made him almost nauseous. The fallout from such a move would consume days of angry protests and threats from Radke. But how could he, in good conscience, let the man operate on a patient while he was in the thrall of an eye-popping fury? Fortunately, Radke now seemed to have shifted from outraged fury to cynical pity for his two weak colleagues, and the need to intervene had correspondingly declined.

There was, Kirk thought, *a frightening lesson in his own reaction.* He had been measuring the need to intervene against the force of the anticipated outraged response, rather than assessing the welfare of a patient about to go under Bill Radke's self-assessed omnipotent and infallible knife.

People like Radke wore you down, Kirk thought. They were always righteous and the sole protector of what was truth, railing and raging until even the most confident CMO would lose confidence in his own judgment.

But the bottom line I already know, Kirk thought, *I wouldn't let that bastard within a country mile of my wife or daughter if either were on the table. So what's Radke even doing here?*

Disturbed at the implications of his thoughts, Kirk got to his feet and moved through the small group of docs, greeting most of them by name before passing the steam table. The breakfast looked enticing, and his stomach was grumbling loudly, but for once food was taking a back seat in his list of priorities. He passed the donuts, pretending the bear claw that had been calling his name since entering the lounge didn't exist, and grabbed a cup of coffee before heading to his office. *This is going to be a long day,* he thought, glancing at the list of e-mails as his Droid® vibrated yet again.

Kirk retrieved the latest root cause analysis (RCA) out of his briefcase and laid it on top of his desk. How many times had he reviewed RCAs in his fairly brief tenure as chief medical officer? At least a dozen. It had shaken him that every time he'd felt the average performance of his doctors was excellent, a new disaster or near disaster—seemed to rudely puncture that balloon.

No, he mused, *Will Jenkins was so right, and just about every MD on staff had been either living a lie or collectively hallucinating to think the cottage industry approach could keep the patients safe.*

His thoughts ran to what would surely be a lawsuit from Adams, who'd been listened to carefully a few weeks back and then dismissed from privileges at the same meeting. Adams had lawyered up within two days and started a campaign to get the support of the local medical society, but if it worried Will Jenkins, he wasn't showing it. Kirk, as CMO, had been ready to pull the trigger on Adams himself, but Will had made a convincing argument that it was the CEO's role and the board's role to boot a repeat-offender non-conformist as a clear and present danger to their patients. What was the phrase Will had used to describe the chief medical officer? *Oh, yeah, an ambassador without a country. Damn if that didn't nail the way he'd felt as soon as he moved into the position.*

There were eight pink phone message slips waiting for him, including three from other angry surgeons no doubt calling to scream about Adams's dismissal, and one from an old medical school buddy now retired and living in Vermont. He shouldn't take the time, Kirk thought, but he and his old friend had always played father confessor for each other and today, there was a lot on his mind. He punched in the number, volleyed an opening discussion of family and fun things for a few minutes to catch up, and then found himself launching into a major retrospective of the past few months.

"Where is this place in Denver, Kirk?" Dr. Dave Rollins asked after an impassioned description.

"Just north of Denver. Basically a suburb."

"And you've been there?"

"Two weeks ago, Dave. Our new guy, Will Jenkins, insisted I make the trip, and I'm glad he did. I spent two days there because I really thought the idyllic descriptions had been effusive—you know, deliriously happy staff, no communication problems. But he was right. What gives me hope for us are the stories they told about the major pushback at first, the docs who left, the initial fear when incompetent managers or staff were fired, and how incredibly cooperative and basically content the ones are who stayed. We're actually testing that now. We booted one of our sanctimonious bad boys and he's declared war already."

"What, exactly, is so different about this St. Michael's?"

Kirk launched into a detailed description of the dramatic differences in philosophy and strategy, and how their training and constant involvement of the entire staff kept their vision, of never harming a patient, so alive.

"We did a lot of those things at my place, Kirk."

"Really?"

"Yeah, but I guess we never coordinated much of it. We just kept instituting programs to improve doctor and nurse communication, for instance, and launched another program for simulation, and then another one to improve cooperation in the OR."

"Not a major cultural overhaul, though, right?"

"No. Pretty piecemeal, but it alleviated our conscience, and our board was never involved."

"I'm convinced that's the difference, Dave. Everyone and every department and every entity, especially the board, has to be in a kind of continuous convulsion before the starting message even gets out there that this is a true seismic alteration of the medical landscape. It's just too damn easy to slip back to business as usual. I've been thinking the last few days that it's going to take years, but if we keep rattling the cages hard every day to shake out the old ways, maybe we can do it, too. I don't think we doctors are naturally given to professional suicide, but when there's no blow torch to our posteriors, we go back to sleep far too easily."

"You have the stamina for all this, Kirk? What you're describing is an epic battle."

"Hey, I can retire any minute that I want. In the meantime, I think this may even be fun!"

They ended the call and Kirk looked at his widening expanse of notes arrayed on his desk. One note in particular caught his attention and he picked it up underlining the date twice.

We're approaching our docs in isolation...gotta get our nurses on board too. Maybe train with them? Couldn't we use simulation with surgical and ER teams? I know they'll hate it, but how about videotaping all our OR procedures and requiring the team to review the tapes every so often, or if something wasn't quite right? Do we speak a common language with agreed upon terminology? How about launching physician-nurse teams to identify the problems in dealing with each other and identify the solutions, all for the patients' sake, not ours?

Slowly his eyes returned to the RCA report. A wide array of things had gone wrong in the uncoordinated care of the late Mrs. Markowitz, and even a cursory read uncovered at least a dozen things they, as a system, could have been done far better. He'd never truly grasped the objection some safety leaders had been articulating about the incorrect terminology of a root "cause" analysis versus a root "causes" analysis, but now, just reviewing the hierarchical staff clashes that had contributed to the woman's death, it was painfully obvious the process itself needed dramatic change for any real increase in the safety of their patients.

For one thing, Kirk Nelson thought, *an RCA should involve an interdisciplinary team ready to follow the problems we turn up wherever they lead. I should really speak with Claudia.*

At precisely the same moment, Claudia Ryan opened his office door.

"Have a minute, Kirk?" Claudia asked, walking into the CMO's office.

"Sure thing," Kirk responded, standing up and waiting until she was seated. It was only the second time she had been in his office—the first time being when she accepted the position of CNO a year ago.

"I wanted to speak to you about the RCA for Mrs. Markowitz. Have you read it?"

"Yes. Read it twice, matter of fact and was planning another review this morning. What's on your mind?"

"I've been rounding up on the floors and ran into a new nurse named Maura Manning. Her name rang a bell and then I realized as I was talking to her that she was working the evening Mrs. Markowitz died. So I took the opportunity to pull her aside and ask a few questions about that evening and the process of the root cause analysis. There is so much more to the story than that report reveals."

"Like what?" asked Kirk, still holding his cards close to his chest. It wasn't even a conscious gesture, just the way he typically responded to the unknown.

"Well, for one thing, I learned that the very same conditions that existed that evening have occurred again. Not quite to that extreme and not all at the same time, but independently. The staff was overworked, the doctor not as responsive as he could've been and—well—a sense of helplessness that resulted in nursing not advocating for the patient. The new people have a different view than the experienced staff. Have you experienced that too?"

Kirk put down his pen and sat back in his chair. He preferred being prepared, but welcomed the collegial dialogue with his peer. They had always worked well together.

"Yes, I have a new hospitalist, who in his ninety day review gave me similar feedback. He was worried about the coordination of care between the emergency room and the floor. But when he expressed his concerns to his mentor, she just stared and then explained that 'Everyone was doing the best they could' and that 'Las Vegas Memorial is a really great place to work.' So, what's on your mind, Claudia?"

"This culture thing is going to be harder than I thought. I'm used to implementing initiatives and projects that get measureable results, but when it comes to culture, I'm beginning to see that we are pretty naïve. What we see, day-to-day, is not what we get. But right now, I want to focus on the RCA, specifically doctor-nurse relationships."

"I was just thinking about the problems with the traditional RCA before you dropped by. But you're talking about the physician-nurse relationships?"

"I am."

"I recall you telling us in a meeting recently that you had surveyed the nurses about their relationships with the doctors and you were very pleased with the high scores. And as you know, I get very few complaints. In general, the physicians think very highly of the nurses here at Las Vegas Memorial."

"That's the problem Kirk. Both the physicians and nurses believe they have great relationships and ignore the few outliers in both groups. People are seeing what they want to see. The only thing that is great around here is the status quo. We have a long way to go, and I'm going to need your help. Currently, 'great' is working together with few hassles and people knowing their places. We need to redefine 'great.' G-r-e-a-t means that you look at me as a peer, an equal. That means that if you're a doctor, you look me in the eye when you speak to me or we may share a coffee or a meal or discuss a case or you ask me for my opinion. None of those things are happening."

"Any ideas?"

"Yes, I want to use simulation to crack open the realities of the way it is. I want to use the small high definition (HD) camera my husband gave me for Christmas and start with collecting the stories that I've heard while rounding. I thought we could focus on communication; videotape some difficult situations; showcase the staff who take the leap. And I'd like to start by asking doctors and nurses to shadow each other, at least one from each floor every month for a year; then introduce them to intentional rounding every day on every floor. What do you think?"

"I think I should've retired," he joked, laughing heartily.

"No, no. I need you to lead this push! We have a long way to go, Kirk. By the way, can I get you to round with a nurse on orthopedics for an entire shift?"

"Well Claudia, I've been a doctor for over thirty years, and I'm here in this halfway house of a position. I'm not sure it would do me any good."

"That's precisely why you need to. That halfway house is going to be of immense importance in guiding and leading our doctors. Look, here's the deal. I'll round with a surgeon for a day as well, if you'll spend at least half a shift rounding with a nurse.

Eat when she eats, or not, go where she goes—the restroom being the exception."

Kirk sighed.

"Let's do it before the next board meeting. I guarantee you it will be an eye opener for both of us. Plus, it sends a message. We need to be role models for the relationship that we want our staff to have; we can each share what we learned from rounding. It's an excellent way to affect the power structure from a hierarchy to a tribe. What do you say?"

Kirk rubbed his hands together wishing for just a moment that Claudia would disappear. He made a mental note to say "no" next time she stuck her head through that door. Too much work. His eyes scanned the desk and were drawn to the pink phone message slip from a Mrs. Madeline Peters. The conversation with her earlier that morning had been downright painful, and her story of helplessness had struck a deep nerve. Usually Jose took care of all the complaints, and the only reason this one even reached him was because Sandy was taking the day off to be with her mother.

"Well?" prompted Claudia.

"Okay. Half a shift," Kirk responded, now curious about the part where Mrs. Peters was left in pain and ignored. "I can commit to four hours, Claudia, without my arthritis kicking up."

"Good, but this is only a start. By the way, we had considered that Markowitz RCA complete because we thought we'd discovered the causes of the event. Yet, as a system, we really failed to address those systemic causes and have allowed many to exist by our passivity. I'd like to introduce a 'pending status' to the RCA, and not consider it complete until the system issues are resolved."[xiii]

"And, now that you mention it, I don't think the right people were at that table," Kirk added. "Let's require the C-suite to be present at an RCA meeting along with a physician or nurse who were not involved in the case, and other department representatives. Also maybe change the name to something like *root causes analysis and response*. Perhaps if the CFO could be helped to see more clearly the impact of his staffing cuts on patient safety, our discussions and decisions would be based in reality. Our budget meetings don't ever include the question, *What's best for the patient?*"

Claudia shifted in her seat, gathering her things. "I have to be honest with you Kirk. Until recently...until I visited Denver...I didn't think it was possible to ever not harm or injure someone. I had lived in that world for so long that I didn't realize that there was another way or see how we reinforced that false reality. I even thought our relationships with the physicians were great, because of the last survey, when in fact it was one way. No one ever even asked the nurses for their opinion of the doctors. That lack of feedback really veils the truth. One of the things Jack Silverman posed to me was, 'Pretend you are offered the job of your dreams in a nearby hospital. Will you take all your VPs and directors with you?' Honestly, Kirk, the answer was 'no.' So, he looked me squarely in the eye and said emphatically, 'So why are you tolerating them now Claudia? Accountability starts at the top.' He might as well have slugged me."

"Lunch?" asked Kirk, after his rumbling stomach broke the silence.

"Where?"

"Doctor's lounge, of course. You don't expect an old doc like me to start paying now, do you?"

Claudia smiled, and accepted saying, "Great, we're already redefining the word!"

As they walked down the C-suite hall, Claudia commented on the grip-and-grin photos of the past executives and medical staff leaders. "Even these pictures reinforce our belief in greatness, because in a subtle way they're saying: *Look at all the money, time and prestige that important people have poured into Las Vegas Memorial.* In other words, with all that investment, this place must be good. But this place is only people, not things."

Kirk looked up for a second to follow her comments. "Claudia, what do you suppose would happen if we replaced them for even a month with all the photos of the patient's we've harmed or killed?"

Chapter Twenty-Eight

There was nothing notable about Richard Simonson's arrival in the parking lot of Las Vegas Memorial just before nine in the morning. His specially-equipped silver van slid into one of the handicapped spaces the same way every other driver nosed their car into a parking spot. The side door slid open automatically and deployed a ramp down which the former Air Force officer could maneuver his wheelchair. Yet, the procedure somehow caught Sal Bertelli's eye as he stood with a cup of coffee watching through the windows of the hospital's fifth floor boardroom.

There but for the grace of God, Sal thought, recalling the head-on collision he'd survived a decade ago. If the oncoming car had been a mere six inches to the right, the experts told him, he'd have lost both legs just below the waist, if he'd even lived. He thought of the intervening ten years of health and happiness, his wife, and the freedom to run and climb without restriction.

All of which led to a brief, momentary pang of sympathy for the handsome, anonymous man in the wheelchair below.

A voice over his shoulder pulled Sal back to the room as three of the other members of the board walked in, hailing him by name.

Las Vegas Memorial's boardroom accommodated comfortably up to fifteen seats around the highly-polished, twenty-foot long table. But with the addition of six members of the C-suite and several invited staff members, the room was becoming a bit crowded.

Will finished shaking hands around the room and returned to the front as Gary Mason called the special meeting to order and turned it over to the CEO.

"It is time," Will began, "that I give you a detailed view of the initial portion of this massive journey of cultural change. That means a combination of chalk talk and briefing. The folders before you contain a much more detailed version, showing each thrust of change and giving you a living, breathing glimpse, of a constantly-evolving effort by virtually everyone in this hospital. By the way, there's a major point I want to make. I'll speak a lot about the things we're doing and it may sound as if those efforts are 'programs,' but from the get-go I need you to understand that we are not launching or creating cut and dried programs because, traditionally, cultural changes end up imprisoned and eventually asphyxiated by the structural rigidity of those very same programs. You've heard of the fog of war? To a certain extent, I'm going to be introducing you to the fog of a cultural revolution; an ever-changing, ever-evolving human effort to completely redefine our hospital."

One more board member opened the door and slipped in, wincing at the fact that he was late, and Will welcomed him and pointed out an empty chair.

"We just started, Bill," he said. "Okay, so I told you when we first met that my number one goal was leadership, and that to be successful we needed to quite literally make true leaders out of everyone in this institution, and to do that, we had to alter the basic programming of the human minds and souls who are this hospital."

He paused as the noise of a passing jet overhead reached an uncharacteristically high crescendo.

"Leaders must possess an unshakable vision, and the team and means to implement it, not programs to execute, measure and metric it to death. Vision, as opposed to programs, is the prime element of what I will be briefing this morning, a myriad of efforts pushing many facets of that shared vision, shared, by the way, because I only rolled out the prototype. Our people further defined Las Vegas Memorial's vision, and it's nothing less than the creation of a truly superlative, patient-centric hospital where no patient is ever unnecessarily harmed again. Eventually, this vision will grow to embrace the whole community, but we have to start with ourselves."

Will paused for a moment to gauge the apparently supportive response.

"You know we're not there yet, right? Everyone here fully understands that!" He let his eyes range around the room, noting the nodding heads and lack of demurrer.

"Okay, I make a big point of this because the primary reason why we can't realize the vision in six months, or maybe even six years, is that we're fighting to reinvent a deeply ingrained, calcified and resistant healthcare culture that is myopically mesmerized by the status quo. The status quo—the way we've always been and the way we've always done it—is, in fact, the beating heart of the problem. The belief creates a monstrous, cynical inertia that resists change with great force and eye-rolling. Like most American hospitals, Las Vegas Memorial is filled with great people who are paralyzed by the erroneous belief that zero preventable patient harm is unattainable, and essentially, a naive goal. Oh, yes, our folks will smile and say they understand the changes we need. They'll tell you and me that collegial interactive teams would be wonderful, and standardizing procedures and best practices will improve things, but they don't even realize in most cases that those statements are disingenuous because in their medical heart of hearts lurks the ingrained preprogramming of a Candide-level philosophy—for those of you who remember Voltaire and his book *Candide*—that this is the best of all possible medical worlds. One of our very bright nurses called it a *Lotto Moment,* the mere thought that anything could actually change. Listen to some of the quotes from our work force gathered in just the last few months."

Will picked up a paper from the boardroom table and adjusted his reading glasses.

> *"Hey, this is a human institution and humans will always make mistakes, so we're going to kill or hurt someone every now and then, we can't be perfect all the time."*

> *This as a great hospital and a great place to work and we're doing a great job. All this talk of perfect safety is insulting because it ignores all the good we do.*

Hospitals are full of sick people, and medicine is very complex, and of course some aren't going to make it.

What's the overall translation of those quotes? That the status quo is as good as it's going to get no matter what we do. In other words, the belief that no amount of effort directed at improving patient safety, service quality, efficiency, cost-effectiveness, common goal recognition, teamwork, or best practices is *ever* going to reduce the number of medical mistakes, or improve the bottom line, or decrease the infection rate. And as long as we hold that cynical belief as the bedrock basic philosophy, we won't. Sounds pretty depressing, right? You have to wonder about my political prowess that I'd call this board meeting just to relay such negatives to you. But I need everyone in this room to keenly understand the magnitude of the problem. Before we can get anything else to improve, we must change our own belief system. Everyone in this institution needs to truly believe that the status quo *can* be stabbed to death and buried, and that zero preventable harm to patients *is* truly possible, and that doctors and nurses and pharmacists and housekeepers and valets and receptionists and C-suite officers *can* look at each other as equal colleagues when it comes to starting the journey. That, in a nutshell, is why throwing tactical programs at things never work, and why most hospitals fail at significant improvement because they don't address that underlying, limiting belief that the status quo is unchangeable by definition. Before I continue, anyone have any questions about what I just said? Questions, challenges, or objections?"

"Just one, Will," Jason Baldridge replied. "You'll recall I was a tough convert to the idea that we were *not* a great, quality institution, But since we started board rounding—which is a brilliant concept, by the way—I've had my nose rubbed in the realities you were talking about. And since we were always metric driven, I just want to underscore what you said about programs that get measured to death. Probably most of us are beginning to understand this," he looked around to be inclusive of the entire board, "but here's how I'd put it, and I hope it startles everyone. You know what our goal has really been up until your arrival?

Measurement, not outcomes. Measurement, and in too many cases, how to either game the system or fill squares to improve those numbers and then run away without asking the wicked questions. Hell, I know better than that from my construction experience, and yet I've been just as complicit. Measurement is merely a means, not an end, and we've traditionally been treating it like the goal. Furthermore, in retrospect, it was our panacea. Got a green on the dashboard? Mission accomplished! When we stare at the numbers, we're staring at our feet, and I completely endorse what you said about not letting this initiative degenerate into compartmentalized programs measured by colors on a chart. I shouldn't even call it an initiative. What did you call it?"

"A cultural revolution, Jason."

"Right."

"Thanks for that! I couldn't agree more. Anyone else?"

The room was silent and Will nodded and picked up a black marker.

"Okay, I sincerely request that you study the far more detailed chart and accompanying descriptions in your folders, but I want to briefly take you through what we've accomplished these past six months."

He turned to a large easel with a blank sheet of paper and wrote: *Undercover Boss.*

"I could spend a week telling you how incredibly effective that spin-up month was for this effort. Primarily, I discovered that neither you, nor I, nor our senior team, really had any idea what was going on in terms of the front line attitudes, perceptions and as I said, the belief systems of what could and couldn't change. Number one, I found that this hospital was a Tower of Babel, a collection of silos with occupants who had little or no understanding of anyone else's role, and no belief that anything could change. The worst part of that, however, was that the people themselves did not see it at all. I found both great people who'd lost heart—they were the vast majority—and I found some who frankly should not be here. I found a hospital run for the doctors, while the doctors had no idea, and no training how to communicate, or a clue they needed to. On and on, a virtual horror story if you compare it with our threshold beliefs, but knowing that—and meeting the front lines, gave me an invaluable start."

He turned back to the easel, writing: *Introduce Myself and the Vision, and Obtain Commitment to Co-operate and Lead.*

"The key components of this early out-of-the-gate phase included our first board meeting together, individual C-suite and staff leadership meetings, and establishing our senior team and our mutual respect and promises. If I were to teach this to another incoming CEO, I'd teach exactly the same sequence. And two more milestones: my series of mandatory staff presentations, and most critically an evening with our physicians in which I walked in with both carrots and sticks, so to speak, and challenged them regarding the creation of a common vision and a unified approach to medicine—the end of our physician-centric version of Las Vegas Memorial and the end of the cottage industry as practiced here traditionally. Many of you know of the difficult few weeks after that with many brave early adopters going toe-to-toe with some of our walking institutions until they themselves led the group, not to consensus, but to critical mass. And, as you know, we've terminated the privileges of a few people who either wouldn't or couldn't change. The wonderful part is, those decisions were made by our docs themselves as newly empowered leaders—decisions based on the concept that those who flatly refused to accept or even entertain this new vision of unanimity and patient-centric practice, simply can't be members of this team."

Will wrote a few more words on the chart.

"And then we—not just me, but we—as a senior team, with all our intermediate managers, directors, charge nurses and anyone else with a smidgen of direct management authority, began a whirling, continuous series of conferences, retreats and some-times ad hoc get-togethers in which we asked each other what we needed to do to support the front lines, because by doing so we were asking what we needed to do for the patient. You can't imagine how few of our folks had ever been asked this simple and vital question: 'Do you have what you need to do your job?' Our managers laughed, but most just stared in confusion the first time they heard the words. When they realized we were sincerely begging for their thoughts and their answers, the dam broke and the level of participation has, and continues to be, fantastic. The changes we need will come, and are coming from the folks providing the care, which means that they are automatically owners of the process. The importance of that distinction cannot be overstated."

Will continued writing new lines on the chart, flipping the pages, and explaining each one, until he turned to them with a quick summary.

"Okay, so setting up the initial structures for cultural and clinical change required, and continues to require, deep-thought from the front lines, interdisciplinary involvement in all major structural questions; such as best practices and checklists and starting a regular program of what I call empty-room simulation with video cameras. More than anything else, these initial questions let us set up the paradigm of the interdisciplinary ad hoc group with no barriers to membership, and no empire-building chairmanships. These are living and breathing advisory groups and have already empowered our middle level managers into a dimension of leadership they've never experienced, and they would have never gotten off the ground without trust, feedback and accountability. We asked every one of our leaders to immediately commission a three-sixty performance review of themselves, inclusive of their own personal review, and that review, in two cases, led to voluntary resignations by folks who were honest enough to realize they were mismatched for the job of nurturing people. Some of those folks realized that as managers, they needed—sometimes desperately—much more education and specific help on how to lead *people,* not paper. It was almost eye-watering how many bonds were created between those managers, and the people they thought they were leading, just because they bared their necks and sincerely asked the questions, 'How am I doing?' They were educated to ask the questions, 'What do I do well?' and 'What would you like to see more of?' Incredibly powerful questions. Also, we deployed newly-formed, hospital-wide multi-disciplinary groups on an emergent basis to ask and answer the following key questions: First, where will our next patient safety disaster, or near-disaster, come from? And second, what steps should we take to immediately address and improve communication and establish strong relationships across silos and hierarchies? This process got us essentially doing a home-grown version of a *failure mode and effects analysis,* a so-called FMEA. The results of just those two focused questions staggered many of us because they nailed the communications incapacities as the ranking engine of patient safety disasters, and led us to understand the degree of departmental distrust and ignorance of each other that has been the status quo. Based on what we found, we realized that there was a major knowledge deficit because our staff avoids confrontation. Some of the effort to uncover these traits and highlight them has resulted in people stating forcefully that they need new funds to establish simulation as the norm, or to conduct off-site retreats to form and nurture true collegial relationships. In addition, we have a major study underway to either establish a type of command post center to track twenty-four seven the continuity of care for each patient and keep the effected docs in touch with their situation at all times, or expand the traditional role of the charge nurse with truly collegial relationships to the docs, so that we never again have five physicians taking care of someone and not talking and coordinating with each other. Will some of these things cost more? Of course. Richard and all our senior officers will have an opportunity to add their viewpoints in a minute, but suffice it to say, we are all true stewards of this hospital's precious resources and focused on the same goal, but we're agreed that we express our management philosophy this way: The only reason for our existence as leaders is to make it easier for our people on the front lines to provide the best care possible. We're here to support them. Oh, we still have intense collegial debates, but not defensive or passive-aggressive conversations across silos. We all know who will win every time because every decision is framed by answering the most important question of all: *What is best for our patients?"*

Will stopped to take a drink, aware of the many small conversations and comments being exchanged among the board, most of them seemingly enthusiastic.

"Okay, there was one area that tore me up. Since I came aboard, I made it a practice to ask our people at random just how many people we've killed or hurt in the past year, and the majority of the time, they didn't have a clue. Worse, as for the most serious disasters where patients were harmed or died unnecessarily, very, very few knew the names involved. Accidental patient harm was completely invisible and impersonal. Worse than that, the docs themselves only heard rumors about what had happened to their peers. There was no formal method for sharing our knowledge of harm. I heard far too many references to *airing our dirty laundry* and *unnecessarily scaring the public*. Well, we've changed that totally, and I will openly admit to you that this one was a top down initiative that, I believe, is now generally understood, if not thoroughly appreciated. For one thing, taking our lead from Cincinnati Children's Hospital, when you turn on any of our computers, a non-cancellable box appears in the upper right hand corner which says, 'How many days since we've injured or killed a patient who was in our care?' If you click on that box, you can view the clinical details. The families have waived the name restriction from the previous three disasters, and their loved ones are listed there for all to see and remember. How dare we do anything less? There is more, of course, much more, much of it detailed in the papers you have. But as fast as I can describe it in writing, these living, breathing initiatives will be modified, added to, recreated, or subjected to more creative debate. Sometimes the word 'creative' will actually mean 'angry and contentious,' but as we work toward a complete commonality in our vision and our goals, those debates will become less contentious."

"Will, I hate to ask it this way," Sal Bertelli interjected, "but you said we've ditched a couple of docs. How much revenue did we lose with their departure?"

Will smiled and nodded. "I actually thought that particular question was going to come from Jason," he chuckled, noting the laughter in response. "Not to be flippant, Sal, but I don't care. I can't care. Now, in the aftermath, Richard has run a quick projection and found out that the loss from those docs' departures, if realized fully, would probably hit two percent of revenue. But you know why I say 'if realized?' Because one of those doctors has already come back, hat in hand, and asked what it would take to stay. Several others we do not want back, and one in particular, Dr. Adams, has lawyered up, and I took a Clint Eastwood stance and told him myself to *make my day* and sue us. This man's expulsion is a crystal clear message to everyone that belittling our people will not be tolerated regardless of the number of admissions, regardless of length of time here, regardless of anything. Yes, Adams has created a tiring distraction, trying to recruit other doctors to come to his aid, stirring up the peer review committee and using language about me and Las Vegas Memorial unbecoming to a doctor; but the battering is worth taking and we won't flinch. That message will be in granite, by the way, on my watch: Everyone who is Las Vegas Memorial is held to precisely the same standards regardless of professional background. In Adams's case, the man had a long and tawdry history of hurting our patients and our employees with his withering arrogance. And, Bill?" Will looked at William Randolph, one of the longest serving board members and a retired surgeon. "I know Adams is a friend of yours, and I'll be more than happy to discuss this one at length if you'd like."

Bill Randolph was shaking his head, his hand out in a stop gesture. Bill liked to keep the peace and rarely spoke at meetings, but from the shifting in his chair, it was clear that today was different. His words surprised everyone.

"Will, it is tough because I recruited Adams, and because— well—I too used to exhibit some of that kind of arrogance. That's the way we were trained, as you well know. You would've expelled me, for that matter, if I were still here today as a surgeon believing that I had to be absolutely perfect and that if anything went wrong, it simply could not be my fault. But I can't sit on this board as a responsible and honest member and raise some sort of impassioned defense of Adams when the world has changed so profoundly. Oh, yeah, he's exhausted me with his phone calls, too. So, no, you don't have to justify it to me. I'm sorry it came to his expulsion, but I get it. And, after all, as you asked in our first board meeting, 'Is it working for you?' It hit me that day that the answer was so clearly 'no,' and that the age of the autonomous, iconoclastic physician was done, because acting as cowboys no longer works. Hell, I recall Atul Gwande saying that even cowboys use checklists and best practices today!"

"Thank you, Bill. I truly appreciate the candor."

Will waited for a moment before taking his eyes from Dr. Randolph and glancing around the room. "Okay, everyone. I asked my senior team to attend today because I want to ask them to speak their minds in regard to all this seismic change. But first, I'd like to introduce our newest member of the C-suite, Sanjay Ghalia, who has come aboard as our first chief research officer (CRO). I also want to specifically thank Sanjay for jumping right in and recommending that we *not* hire another neonatologist— something we were poised to do—because the research is clear that more than 4.3 neonatologists per 10,000 increases mortality. Also Sanjay, your presentation on our perception of bed capacity— especially the perceived need for more ICU beds—was a real eye opener."

Sanjay Ghalia, Claudia Ryan, Kirk Nelson, Randall Williamson and Jon Anderson, the general council, spoke briefly in turn, each highlighting the way the whirlwind of cultural change had personally reoriented their thinking and the leadership of their respective areas. Richard Holbrook was the last to get to his feet.

"Wow. What a ride this is, and we're just at the start. We all know each other and you know I'm a rather traditional finance guy. When Will and I first met, when he came through those doors, what, six months ago, let me charitably say I had serious doubts that he knew what he was doing, let alone had any confidence that he could create the sort of environment he and Jack Silverman in Denver were describing. Frankly, I was not impressed, Gary, when you guys chose a doctor without a business degree as our new leader. But I want to tell you, I was not only wrong to doubt Will, I was catastrophically wrong to think I even understood the broader implications of my own job. No way in heck would I have voluntarily participated in rounding, for instance, if Will hadn't more or less forced me into it, nor would I ever have spent time sitting through an RCA, or sitting with a bunch of lower-level employees in what I would've originally regarded as a bitch session about petty things. After all, I was the all-seeing CFO trying to keep the damn ship from sinking while it seemed like everyone else was sitting around staring at the stars. What I've learned in these last few months has frightened the heck out of me. I had no concept of how profoundly a CFO's monetary and budgetary decisions affected the patient: clinical problems, safety levels, the infection control rates and the overall dysfunctionality of this institution. I'm still learning, of course, but that's what I think you folks need to hear as our board, because we're looking to you for a whale of a lot more than the level of participation boards usually provide, and I know Will has outlined this. Frankly, I know some—many of you—were not planning on really going to Boston as a board for education, but I want to urge you to change your minds. We need you at a level of participation *and oversight* that few hospital boards have ever achieved, and I, as the finance guy, am going to need your thinking on a new level. Everything is changing, and we need you with us every inch of the way. Am I having the usual battle keeping us in the black with the reimbursements falling like a boulder? You bet. But the front lines are doing amazing things in reducing our costs already, and we'll figure it out."

Richard paused, glancing at Will before continuing.

"A major example of how much my thinking has changed are 'hospital consumer assessment of healthcare providers and systems' (HCAHPS). You know how much we've discussed and fretted over them, and I had signed off on bringing in a group that guaranteed to raise our scores to the eighties and nineties and keep them there. In fact, I was of the opinion that even safety needed to take a second seat behind HCAHPS, since poor scores were being advertised and would hurt our reimbursement in short order. But what I didn't get—*really* didn't understand—was that the very things that are the heart of patient safety and clinical quality are the permanent fix for sagging HCAHPS. I mean drastically improved doctor-nurse communication, collegial teams, minimized variables and best practices. I wouldn't have believed that mere communication and coordination and collegiality between doctors and staff would be an almost perfect predictor of HCAHPS, but that's true, and you can count me as a surprised convert. So, far from pushing everything else back to concentrate on raising HCAHPS—as an awful lot of hospitals are doing—we're going to be pulling them up by concentrating on the causative factors, not gaming the system."

Richard sat down, aware of the thoughtful expressions on the faces of the various board members. Will started to respond when Angela Siegel rose to her feet.

"I must say, gentlemen, this board meeting is a galaxy beyond refreshing. But I have to let a skunk loose in here, and to some of our much appreciated officers, this is going to sound like an assault. Please understand I don't mean it to be. But I'd like to ask all my fellow members, and our C-suite, something that every board and every C-suite in the nation needs to be asked. We have evolved a system for rewarding effective officer performance on something other than a whim or the fiat of a small committee, and, of course, it's called the balanced score card. No surprise there. But, how can we—how can *any* of us—allow a bonus to be paid after someone has died unnecessarily in our care, or been terribly harmed in our care? How can we morally square that with our responsibilities? Yes, I know this question falls on the backs and the bank accounts of our officers—and if boards are ever paid, as I believe they must be eventually—it will fall on us as well. But, how can we look someone like Doug Markowitz in the eye after letting his wife bleed to death because of our failure and justify writing bonus checks at the end of that year? Morally? Ethically? How? Isn't that what performance-based bonuses are all about? Performance?"

She paused, searching the uncomfortable looks on the faces of her fellow board members before continuing. "I know, I know. Leave it to Angela to ask embarrassing questions. But as my friend Dr. Bruce Avolio says, I am one of the 'No People' for I will forever say what I see; and I will not back away from this. Gary? Mr. Chairman? I have a motion here in writing to prohibit the payment of any bonus anywhere in this hospital, or the payment of any other monetary benefit above basic pay, in a year in which we have permanently harmed or accidentally killed someone."

Angela sat down to silence at the same moment Claudia Ryan stood. "I am directly affected, Angela, and of course I can't vote, not being a board member. But I want you to know I completely accept that challenge, and agree with you entirely. I'll admit I had never thought of it that way before, but clearly, it would be an obscenity to accept a bonus in such a year, because we are all responsible."

One by one, the rest of the officers rose to their feet to endorse the idea as well, the very deliberative gestures capped by Will.

"I never discussed this with you, Angela, and I'm embarrassed that I didn't think of this myself. It was, after all, my responsibility. I consider my contract amended immediately to include that precise provision, and will sign the appropriate paper memorializing that modification, and I am very proud of my fellow officers for everything they just said."

Will stood for a few moments looking down at his notes on the table, but actually his eyes were staring through them, and for the first time, he was fighting a wave of deep emotion that threatened to produce tears. He regained control and looked up, smiling, locking glances with Janice who had just slid inconspicuously into the back of the crowded room, well aware of the agenda, and that the next twenty minutes of his presentation would change them all.

Chapter Twenty-Nine

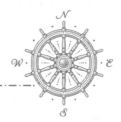

Janice Jenkins studied her husband's face intently as he thanked Angela, searching for the familiar expressions she recognized. His brow was slightly furrowed in deep concentration, yet his blue eyes were shining with an enthusiasm and energy too long absent. Despite the long days and late night hours, Will looked like his old self again, and as she'd watched him conducting the board meeting with such passion and professional case, the veil of worry she'd borne silently for the past several years slowly began to lift.

Not that the past half year hadn't featured moments of exhilaration along with a few moments of near-despair. She thought back to the conversation last month that had erupted just before midnight from a single question.

"Do I suck at listening?" Will had asked, almost as an aside.

She'd put down her textbook and studied him in the subdued light. "Why would you ask that, Honey?"

"Well," he chuckled, "one of the hazards of asking people what they think of your performance is that after a while they'll really tell you. And today, I got some feedback that I didn't want to hear. Am I a bad listener?"

"Usually not. Occasionally, we all are. What was the context?"

Will had sighed and sat forward on the bed. "Well, I think I really did screw up."

"Tell me? What happened?"

"You'll say I got dictatorial, but all I was trying to do was end one of those perpetual, tiresome debates that go on forever after you've already made a decision."

"Details, please!"

"Okay, one of our working groups—two nurses, a doctor and a pharmacist—had been working on a new idea: the concept of a hospital-wide command post to keep moment-to-moment track of each patient, their meds, their doctors, for smooth transitions, handoffs and to prevent other forms of patient abandonment. Good work! They've been dropping by my office about once a week, and a month ago they wanted to know if they could get enough cash and at least one room to set up a demonstration project."

"And you said yes?"

"I said in my judgment it would be better to keep pushing the design until we could just deploy it. They said OK, yet every week they keep dropping by to reopen that decision, and frankly, I was getting just a bit irritated. Last week, however, I asked what was up, and they opened the same damned subject once more. I had someone else due in the office in a few moments, a conference coming up on that damnable Dr. Adams and his lawsuit and I was desperate for coffee when the very same entourage returns with the exact same request as the week before and the week before that."

"You lost it?"

"No! Nothing that bad. I know I'm always 'on camera,' so to speak. But I was too harsh. All four of them looked kind of funny, thanked me in a cursory fashion and filed out. And then Ivy filed right in with an even stranger look."

"Ivy?"

"We'd left the door half open and her situational awareness is spooky. She got kind of military on me and asked, 'Permission to speak frankly?' and of course I said yes. And she said, 'I think your new ship just took a hit, Captain.' I asked her why, and she tells me—gently but firmly—that I blew them off and hurt their feelings, and that if they went away feeling like that, their experience would leak and contaminate all our efforts at open communication. I mean, I respect this lady, but..."

"Don't tell me you snapped at Ivy?"

"Of course not! I knuckled under and thanked her and then chased them down. They were all pretty cold at first—Ivy had been right—but I apologized."

"Then what happened?"

"I got a dose of the new culture we're creating. The pharmacist asked for a ten minute de-brief on the process to ascertain what we could learn from it and to offer each other feedback. We re-opened the discussion and I was really horrified to discover that they'd mentioned an important point each time we'd met that changed the whole equation and I had been so intent on wanting the issue closed—well—it was difficult to hear that I could've listened better."

Irritated with himself, Will jumped off the bed and did what he always did when something had to change inside. He paced outwardly. Like a guard protecting the bedroom door, back and forth, and back and forth he stewed and fretted for more than an hour over being human. Janice knew better than to say much at these times. She reopened her book saying, "That's a real mark of success, Will."

This would take some time.

Janice kept her cool as Will paced, but inside misgivings welled. Certainly she had the academic chops and the medical as well as business experience to guide him, but the uncertain little girl in the confident young woman would come stumbling out of her long-forgotten hiding place every now and then. Those momentary encounters were enough to shake her confidence for hours, and would call into question every assumption, every conclusion and every bold move she'd ever had the chutzpah to make. Or, Janice wondered, studying her husband intently was that momentary flutter merely an echo from the past?

She shook herself as if shivering from a cold breeze, and sent the little girl back to bed as her husband continued to pace and perseverate.

That had been a low point; along with Will assuming he had more alignment and support than he actually had, failing to address some undermining comments by a few physicians who he had thought were on board, and grossly underestimating the pace of change. He had forgotten that a new culture needs a new language; thinking he could change their expectations, and create a higher purpose with the same words they had always used, but Terri Morales, the manager of the OR had coined a phrase one day that was rapidly adopted after she shared it in one of their hospital huddles. She had told a disgruntled circulator that he was "going off course" when he was pushing hard on decreasing turnover time. So whenever a decision or behavior deterred from what was best for the patient, staff all over the hospital started saying, "we're going off course here."

Janice had slid into the board room with only one purpose: to support Will. *"Bringing the future into the present is no easy task,"* she had whispered numerous times over the last few months during their ritual morning hug, coffee and goodbyes. There was nothing she loved more than being Will's armchair leader in this journey, listening night after night to his stories. And nothing was more profound than the trip he was taking today.

Chapter Thirty

"I've invited some folks here this morning for whom the status quo is, and will forever be, totally unacceptable," Will said. "The people I'm about to introduce have graciously accepted my invitation to help us. They, and many more with a history at Las Vegas Memorial, are being formed into a team that we intend will communicate, work with, teach and touch everyone who is Las Vegas Memorial. They will become an integral part of this hospital and our cultural change, and an unforgettable reminder of our vision and true mission. It is my firm intention that over time virtually every member of the Las Vegas Memorial team will come to know these folks personally."

Will turned toward Ivy and nodded and she opened the double doors, ushering in two women and a middle-aged man in a wheelchair. Will greeted each of them warmly before turning back to the board members as the doors silently closed behind them.

"First, I'd like to introduce Mrs. Mildred Keaton, the mother of our risk manager, Sandy Keaton. Mrs. Keaton was in our hospital as a patient a few months back. To her left we have Mr. Richard Simonson, also a former patient of ours, and to his left," Will turned to the stunning woman, "another former patient, Mrs. Susan Wilson. Thank you all for coming." Will turned back, picking up his notes.

"First, Mrs. Keaton came to us for a hip replacement operation, but during the procedure she had a severe and dangerous reaction to Vancomycin called 'red man's syndrome.' In truth, we almost killed her because of a massive failure of communication in the OR. Not only did we almost kill her in the operating room, but because of a lack of ownership and skewed priorities—an employee wanting to get home being the top priority—she later suffered a code and we almost lost her on the unit. The reasons why all this happened are both simple and complex, complex because there were many mistakes made during her care, and simple because most of them involved impeded human communication. Understanding what happened and why at every single, solitary juncture will be vital in making sure no one ever gets handled this way again. Mrs. Keaton?"

But Mrs. Keaton just sat frozen in her chair and said nothing for one very, long minute. Despite numerous prepping conversations with her daughter, she still could not comprehend that she had been in such grave danger when her own daughter worked in safety! Eventually she glanced over at Sandy, and as their gazes locked, Sandy hesitantly rose to address the group.

"On the afternoon my mother went to surgery, Terri Morales jumped into the elevator with me—just to have a discussion. Terri is the manager for our operating room. For months she had been asking for 100 percent support for time outs and for some authority to insist on decreasing the number of preference cards. As it turned out, those items were just the tip of her iceberg of issues and I failed to listen, to advocate or to act. What Terri wanted more than anything was for me to, how did she say it, was for someone to 'have her back.' On first impulse, after my mother's incident, I was furious with the staff, and with Terri for her failure to deal with personnel problems that had escalated, and with the physician who I trusted to be in charge—and with Las Vegas Memorial for allowing this to happen." Sandy took a deep breath and looked around the room before continuing.

"But it wasn't too long before I realized, I am Las Vegas Memorial; I am responsible. And this concept, I'm afraid,"… Sandy paused, wiping away a few tears and looking back lovingly at her mother, "this concept is something my mother simply cannot grasp."

The room was as motionless as a glassy pond as everyone watched the concentric rings expand from the pebble Sandy had thrown into the still waters. Will slowly rose to his feet again, cleared his throat and moved behind Richard Simonson's wheelchair.

"Richard Simonson is the gentleman I told you about in our first meeting. He's a former Air Force civil engineer who settled here after a stint at Nellis Air Force Base. He's married with two young sons with whom he used to mountain bike and play tennis —two abilities we forever destroyed for him and his boys when we committed a string of errors that put him in this wheelchair. These were totally avoidable mistakes, committed not by bad people, but by a deeply flawed system we're working hard to change—a system that traditionally maintained that the status quo was as good as it's going to get. Richard is here today to help us stamp out that prejudice, and make sure we never again make a paraplegic out of someone who walked in on two good legs looking for the quality of care we promised in those bill-board ads around town; billboards I have now had removed. Richard?"

Richard Simonson pushed a button on his wheelchair that elevated the seat almost a foot. When the motor stopped purring, he began.

"I'm glad that I am not speaking to you any time right after the accident—it's been just over three years now—because, for the first year, I was so depressed that all I wanted to do was sleep twenty-four hours a day. I felt I'd been mugged and robbed, everyone knew the culprit and that an unholy, Mafia style med-ical-legal protection system was positioned and ready to take care of the cover-up. Slip the poor guy some money, seal the record, and slink silently into the night with no one the wiser. You might think that the injury was the worst part, but I assure you...*I assure you*...it was not! The worst part was everyone in this hospital nullifying, ignoring, abdicating and running away from any responsibility. The worst part was the code of silence and the fraternal handshake with the passing of that blood money that felt...*that felt*...illegal, immoral and just flat out wrong. I wanted my legs; I got some money, but the worst part was this sinking feeling late at night that I had just participated in an ambush on the next patient, maybe a small child, a new mother, my own sons? Who could know what had happened and how to prevent it in the future if everything was covered up? I couldn't sleep and I couldn't stay awake. I was caught in a purgatory with vengeance aflame, so all-encompassing that my own wife nearly left me and my children didn't recognize me. Hell...I didn't recognize myself."

Everyone could see that Mr. Simonson was struggling, searching for the words ...exasperated. Their eyes averted and darted around the room as they recapped their pens, shuffled their papers, and furtively hid from his gaze until finally Sandy let him 'see' her. She, as both victim and perpetrator, was safe. And in her glance, he found the courage he was seeking.

"Until today, you have only known me as the number three victim in the year 2009. Let me re-introduce myself properly. I am Richard Simonson," he said, his voice now choking with emotion. "I am a paraplegic because you transferred me to the ICU and a relatively new nurse was afraid—no, intimidated—by her senior peers. She did not want them to think she was stupid or incompetent and so she didn't ask, 'Is there anything I may have forgotten on this patient?' She did a great job addressing my heart condition, but had no idea that she should've checked the nerves in my feet every hour or two after back surgery. Nor did the transferring nurse say anything to the ICU nurse. NO! Who was she to remind an ICU nurse what to do? So, number three of 2009 was permanently paralyzed by your culture of fear—and I am at the very least grateful for this opportunity to speak with you, and work with you, the leaders of a place where people worry more about their own psychological and social safety than the safety of a vulnerable and trusting patient placed in their care. I, who can no longer walk, will walk with you on your journey to ensure that no one has to ever go through what I went through."

Two people suddenly stood up and left the room as Ivy placed a box of tissues on the table.

Will took the floor again, his voice steady, but Claudia perceived the strain. "Mr. Markowitz and his..."

Suddenly, Claudia interrupted. "Will, may I?" Will was both touched and relieved by the gesture and sank back into his chair as Claudia stood up to address the group.

"Mr. Markowitz and his wife, Kari, trusted us to do a rather simple and straightforward tonsillectomy. But we let Mrs. Markowitz bleed to death internally. For over a decade, our weak leadership, by their passiveness, allowed a surgeon to intimidate the nurses endless times and responded to calls from the floor only when he deemed fit. So when something really worrisome was afoot, the culture prevailed and the nurse did not escalate the concern, or follow the chain of command, or call the rapid response team. Poor staffing, poor communication, poor relationships among physicians and nurses, and a host of other systemic, cultural failures killed this man's wife, the mother of two young girls. Any one of those errors and omissions and incapacities could become a link in the causal chain of another disaster next week if we don't find each such link, understand it, and forever prevent it from recurring. So today, no *root causes analysis* is filed as complete until we are 100 percent certain that all of the conditions that led to the event have been addressed, and we are 100 percent certain they can never happen again. Furthermore," added Claudia, as her gaze circled the room, "I want you to know about the second victim, or victims, I should say. The nurses who cared for Mrs. Markowitz were deeply impacted by this loss—one has taken an extended leave of absence. It was devastating—as it is for many healthcare professionals. In the Northwest, my peers told me of a nurse who recently took her own life after making a medication error that killed a child in her care." Claudia sat down slowly, but she was still talking, "Not only have we failed our patients who blindly trust that we will keep them safe, but we have failed to protect those we claim to lead and serve."

After a nod from Claudia, Will stood up again to address the group.

"There is no doubt that healthcare is a high risk organization, an intrinsically hazardous human enterprise. But unlike nuclear power plants, high rise buildings and aviation, healthcare has not succeeded in becoming a high *reliability* organization—an amazingly safe institution that has instilled processes to reduce potential and actual harm. Why? Primarily because its leadership has failed to change the culture and cultural change is a long, hard road. So today, over a decade after the infamous Institute of Medicine (IOM) reports, our baggage is still safer on any airline than our patients are in our hospitals."

Mrs. Keaton slowly raised her hand, finally grasping the realities before her.

"So, Will, are you saying that all of these tragedies were... were *preventable?*"

"Yes, Ma'am," Will answered flatly. "Yes, they were, but we have been so mesmerized by decades of tradition that all our energy went into managing the staff instead of taking care of the prevention of human error. *Leaders* are responsible for culture. Cultural change starts in this room, with leaders who have the courage to challenge their own perceptions of reality and change their own behavior, as you have just witnessed. Thank you, Claudia, Sandy and Mr. Simonson."

Will stood for a moment referring briefly to the papers laid out on the table before looking up.

"Let's talk about what we're going to do if we ever, *ever* hurt someone unnecessarily again. Our general counsel over there, Jon Anderson—who, by the way, correctly advised everyone to fully and completely disclose in the cases of Mrs. Markowitz and Mrs. Keaton—will not be the first one or even the second one contacted. We know what's ethical, what is humane and what also happens to be the best path to economic salvation: full and immediate honest disclosure, apologies, hand-holding and a blood oath that we will ferret out every facet of what happened and change all applicable areas of our practice and our system to make sure it never happens to anyone else again. How many of us have admonished our kids about the shameful nature of having to learn the same lesson twice? That also applies to us. What you've witnessed in the last ten minutes is a staggering, humbling show of deep compassion; that even people who have lost so much are willing to join us and lead us, provided we unhesitatingly dedicate ourselves to fixing this system so no one else suffers the same fate. I don't care how tough and high-minded and unemotional we're supposed to be as leaders, as board members with hardened experience, look deep in your own soul and answer this: Can we look Richard, Mrs. Keaton, or Doug Markowitz in the eye and have anything left to say in defense of the status quo? Any of us still want to explain why we're such a great or quality institution, and that their experiences really don't change things because a few lives lost and damaged per year is just inevitable? Good Lord, who among us would dare? These are the people we serve, and when they're right in front of us, full of compassion for *us* and willing to put aside the hurt and the rage and still work with us in the future to make sure we don't ever wreck someone's life again, *how could any of us not be moved?* And, I can see by your expressions, that that was, indeed, a rhetorical question."

Will turned thoughtfully toward the last guest—a middle aged woman sitting stoically against the wall—and nodded in her direction. She was elegantly dressed in a cream cashmere sweater and a short, stylish haircut that showed her neckline. But her posture was as stiff as a mannequin.

"Until now, we have been speaking about harm and injury in cases where surgery was necessary. I would like to introduce you to Mrs. Susan Wilson who, like every consumer, trusted her physician and the hospital in which he was allowed to practice...ours...to do the right thing. Mrs. Wilson?"

"Call me Suzie, please," she interrupted.

"Thank you, Suzie. Perhaps I should explain how we met?" said Will as she simultaneously nodded her consent.

"Suzie spoke at a round table meeting for healthcare hosted by the casinos in this city, a town hall meeting that was held in the hope of bringing together consumers who wanted a stronger voice in how healthcare was delivered. We are, by the way, a major sponsor of such meetings. This new system will be built around primary care centers. Hospitals won't be the center of the healthcare universe anymore. And we need more voices like Suzie's to tell the truth. Let me give you an example from a large Midwestern city, where the gang warfare has escalated the need for more trauma beds. One hospital was just about to build a new tower last year to accommodate the increased need for beds when suddenly, at a town hall meeting, a consumer asked, *'How much will it cost to build that new tower?'* And the hospital representative answered, *'About ninety-seven million dollars.'* It was like David and Goliath, the hospital momentum was rolling, they had posters, a model in the lobby and a huge media campaign poised to break when the consumer made one slingshot comment that challenged everyone. He said, *'Well, if the need for the hospital is based on the crime rate, why don't we take one tenth of that money—nine million dollars—as a community and increase our police force and give them the resources to reduce that crime rate? Then we won't need to build a new tower on the hospital.'"* See? Our whole focus <u>must</u> change from the *business* of healthcare to prevention and wellness of the community, which brings me to Suzie, who is another consumer who certainly has opened my eyes. Suzie?"

Susan Wilson stood up and faced the board members, notes in hand. "I am not a naïve person. Friends would even describe me as worldly wise in business investments and foreign affairs. That's why talking about this subject is all the more difficult; because I was a naïve patient in your hospital blindly trusting that you would never do surgery unless the benefits out-weighed the risks. I trusted that you would never do an invasive procedure not thoroughly backed by hard science. But the public interest is clearly not paramount in this society because Medicare and private insurers still continue to pay for treatments that do not work, and in many cases are not needed. Recently one young family in Arkansas was shattered by the news that their seemingly healthy husband suddenly needed a heart transplant. The company he worked for refused to accept a single cardiovascular surgeon's demands to schedule the surgery immediately, and they sent him to the Mayo Clinic for a second opinion against the surgeon's angry objections. Mayo's physicians did the tests and came out flabbergasted: 'You don't need a heart transplant!' they reported. 'You need a single prescription and a stent.' The surgeon down south was going to literally cut this young man's heart out, perhaps just to make a buck, perhaps because he couldn't appreciate that he might be wrong. True story." Suzie paused, locking eyes progressively around the room and diverting from her notes. "The patients that roll into your operating rooms have surrendered everything: their clothes, their consciousness and their bodies. There is no more vulnerable place in the world than an operating table. We are like fetuses depending on you for life itself; you breathe for us, you literally hold our beating hearts in your hands, put us into a deep sleep from which *only you* have the power to awaken us. It is an absolutely terrifying vulnerability requiring tremendous trust."

For a moment, Suzie Wilson looked lost. Quickly, she re-shuffled her index cards and continued. "According to one Harvard study, one-third of the patients in this country who had bypass surgery did not need it, neither are stents warranted the majority of the time. Mt. Sinai Medical Center reviewed the records of hundreds of children and discovered that three quarters of them did not have a severe enough condition—*as defined by the Academy of Pediatrics itself*—to ever have tubes placed in their ears. Nearly 300,000 women a year that have had hysterectomies also have had their ovaries removed—just because—without any medical evidence to support such removal. Because dogma, not data, dictates who shall or shall not go under the knife, and 'when all you have is a hammer, everything starts looking like a nail'"

Will noted the surprised looks around the room. Clearly over-use and overtreatment were problems that had never blipped on the radar screen of the group. He noticed Jason Baldridge leaning forward onto the table as Suzie continued.

"I was one of those patients. I trusted you. I now have a higher risk of dying from coronary artery disease and an increased risk of hip fracture because the ovaries that prevent heart disease and bone health even after menopause have been stolen from my body. So it was no surprise that I suffered a fracture skiing last year which forced me into a lower position at my company due to a lack of mobility. I have now connected with others in our community, like Mr. Matheson who had unnecessary bladder surgery for a cancer that never existed, because the surgeon decided to operate before the results of the biopsy had been returned from the lab and Mr. Gonzalez, who you never told there was no research to support putting in his stents."

"At least ten percent of all surgeries—and many say up to thirty percent when scientific evidence of the benefits and risks are available—is patently unnecessary or just wrong, totally unsupported by medical evidence. Do you know where that ten percent is in your hospital? Do you trust your doctor like I trusted mine? Don't. They are good people with a genuine interest in healing who routinely do harm because of an archaic system, and I will never trust one of them again."

Suzie Wilson sat down, face flushed with an indignant anger.

Will let a few moments pass as he looked down, composing the final words he had considered for days. He looked up again and took a deep breath.

"There are protocols for how a CEO should approach his or her board, and the parts that require mutually respectful interaction and gentlemanly demeanor are sacrosanct to me. But the traditions out there that tend to say that truth should be delivered delicately, if at all, do not comport with our ethical obligations. So, assaultive or not, I need to be brutally direct. I could ask for your unwavering support for the many years in the future necessary to make these changes permanent and reach and stay at zero preventable patient harm. But that would give a lie to the urgency of the task, the emergency of the mission. Folks, forgive me, but I'm not asking, I'm demanding your support and your participation and your full attention and your willingness to go as a full board to Boston if that's what we mutually determine is necessary. I demand you reach out from board heaven and draw the appropriate lines in the sand, which you've already been doing, when some big admitter has to be blown out of the door backwards for a level of arrogance or non-conformance that endangers our patients. I demand you look first at what's good and right and safe for the patient from the patient's perspective, not the doctor's, and I demand you consider what's going to improve the overall health of this community, rather than maintaining the bottom line as the primary focus. And one more vital thing. If there is anyone in this room—director, officer, employee—who believes that zero preventable harm is not really possible, or who believes that we should not adhere 100 percent to the vision I've just presented, then I want to ask for one of two things: Either submit your resignation, or accept mine."

Chapter Thirty-One

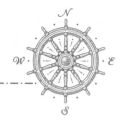

Four Years Later

Will swung his gray suit jacket over the back of his chair as his eyes scanned the office. Ivy, it seemed, had been on a seasonally induced cleaning spree. The weather for the last few days had been so balmy and warm that even Janice had filled several boxes to take to Goodwill, obviously while Will was at work. "Just what are you planning on doing with a cassette player and a VCR?" Janice had pleaded as Will rescued the items from the give-a-way pile just in the nick of time.

On top of a small box labeled "Take Home" was a stack of photos that immediately caught Will's eye. He picked up the first picture, surprised by the wave of nostalgia—his first speech to the employees over four years ago in the hospital cafeteria the surroundings now barely recognizable. All the square tables for two and four people had been replaced by round tables of six. The staff had turned one corner of the room into their 'Doodle Corner,' patterned after the space "Google" provides for their employees. The walls themselves were whiteboards, and it was this tiny corner of the hospital that generated so many ideas because employees from all levels met there to brainstorm and share solutions, and everyone knew Will could always be found there on Thursdays.

Two years ago the facilities manager had provided a presentation on the impact of physical space on innovation, replete with stories telling of how other companies rearranged their workplace to foster creativity. Who would've thought that even the plant manager would be able and willing to engage staff on that level? They had become exactly what Will envisioned: all of them a group of leaders—and enthusiastic ones at that.

Will smiled as he placed the picture into the inlaid half-moon box on the shelf.

At the bottom of the stack was the envelope containing the RCA summary on the death of Ronnie Nolan. Will put the summary back into the "take home" box. He didn't need it anymore. The picture of Ronnie from his 11th birthday had sat squarely on his desk for the last four years, right next to Mrs. Markowitz, the last patient who unnecessarily died from mistakes at Las Vegas Memorial. Oh, there had been numerous near misses and adverse events those first few years, but after the board and leadership had made the harm unblinkingly visible and intensely personal, their organizations commitment went viral: the information they needed to keep patients safe rose to the surface through their incident reporting system as well as the constant stop-the-line safety alerts from the front lines. The fear of negative feedback that had kept accountability in the closet was gone; as well as just more than 15 percent of the employees and managers that probably never should have worked at a hospital in the first place.

Will never did erase the half of the whiteboard that held his original plan. It had had to be altered, of course. And he hadn't counted on the immense amount of perseverance and energy necessary to sustain the plan. After the first two years, managers all over the hospital kept asking when they could stop finding new ways to measure their gains, to which he had consistently replied, "You can stop measuring when you want to stop learning or growing." Initially, he'd failed to invest enough in organizational development. But when the employee benefits function was shifted to a team instead of HR, the extra money was found.

With Will and Angela Siegel and several other board members leading the way in a pivotal series of city-wide conferences, Las Vegas, as a community, began to drop the internecine resistance to multi-hospital cooperation and pull together. They had worked with the Las Vegas School District to ensure the school nurse-student ratio would be 1:750 in the schools, and started the tortuous process of facing the need to drastically improve the health of the population, not just respond to illness. With homegrown solutions beginning to guide the country on a national level, Will was very hopeful that such maladies as asthma and depression, coronary artery disease and diabetes could be brought under widespread management as they were already seeing those rates dropping. The working groups formed in Las Vegas were coming together now regularly to address healthcare issues in quarterly forums that produced practical action plans for banks, schools, restaurants and businesses, and they were just now beginning to reap the rewards of that synergy. Three years ago the area grocery stores began removing one product a week from their shelves that contained no nutritional value, but because the change was slow and incremental, the general public hardly noticed. It was a rough beginning and a hard fought one, but it was a significant start.

The toughest battle, however, had been for financial survival, and at times it wasn't just Richard Holbrook who thought Las Vegas Memorial might hit bottom. But the C-suite Will had empowered had proven a strong team, and they made it through the swing time when there was no safety net, mostly because of the physicians.

Will smiled as he recalled joining a conversation a week before, a discussion in which if he'd closed his eyes, he would have been totally unable to discern which participants were doctors and which were nurses and pharmacists. They had talked to each other with such casual and professional regard that previously defined subtleties were gone. Indeed, it was beginning to feel like St. Michael's, and even Jack Silverman himself had flown out to bestow high praise on them in a special board meeting a few months back—a meeting in which they lamented the fact that so few in the country had come so far.

Like Christopher Columbus's crew, there had been numerous naysayers who'd shouted long and hard that professionally they were all going to die—fall into the healthcare abyss—especially after their surgery volume cascaded downward almost 20 percent followed closely by a severe drop in revenue from imaging. The culprit had been their concerted effort to eliminate recommendations for unnecessary surgery and treatment as well as imaging, and it had been a hard pill to swallow for many of the physicians. But CMS supported and accelerated their efforts by flatly refusing to fund unnecessary and excessive care with their Recovery Audit Prepayment Review. For example, in Florida, 100 percent of stents, ICD and pacemakers begun undergoing review before payment the same year Will arrived. The result had been the beginnings of a new paradigm in which ethics actively required caution and real penalties attached. *For the first time,* Will thought, *not everything the hammer looked at appeared to be a nail.*

Like Columbus, Will had had only a few old maps and the guiding principles from Denver that had felt, at times, as distant as the stars. With ACOs they never knew if the light ahead was a safe harbor, or a lighthouse warning of impending disaster. So they clung to what they *did* know: that it was an ethical obligation to eliminate harm and chase zero, reduce unnecessary medications and surgery and create an accountable care community. Even ahead of the CMS mandates, they found that the cost-effective path that practically no one had believed was possible, was.

They had, in fact, done the right thing.

Las Vegas Memorial still wasn't "there" yet, of course, and he knew the board was weary of that admonition. Two of the board members had retired within a year, supportive but personally unable to meet the dramatically expanded workload. He'd asked a third of the board members to leave, and the request was honored graciously, and the three spots had been filled by energetic community leaders.

And when would they get "there?" Claudia Ryan, for one, was fond of telling people who asked that question to recall the sign on the back of Will's door, the saying from St. Michael's: "You know a cultural change is complete when there is no one left who can remember how it used to be."

Will realized he was leaning on the corner of his desk again, a familiar stance when people were in his office. He shook off the retrospective and looked at his Droid® as his alarm corked off, reminding him that it was time for his scheduled rounding. He picked up a notebook and slipped on his coat before heading for the door.

Several floors away, Dr. Gary Campbell was finishing his morning rounds. For an orthopedic surgeon who'd come to Las Vegas

Memorial twenty years ago, the past few years had been a kaleidoscope of change and challenge—not the least of which was the struggle he'd had conquering the computer.

"Gary?"

The voice was half a corridor distant, but he recognized it instantly as Helen Morales, one of the nurses. They'd just spent the last ten minute together with two of the other nurses discussing the post-surgical patients and their progress.

He turned, smiling, and waited for her to catch up. "Yeah, Helen."

"Hey. I forgot to tell you something that's worrying me about Mrs. Zilinski."

"What's that?"

"It's...a feeling, okay? But I'm worried about her heart rhythms I've been seeing when I've been in the room. No alarms, but something's just not right."

Gary Campbell looked at her and smiled, recalling how he and so many other surgeons would have responded just a few years back to the perceived effrontery of a nurse daring to comment on medical matters without documentation or clinical proof—or a medical degree! But he'd been humbled by the realities and the simulation training in the intervening time, and realized that this could easily be an early warning.

Gary put his hand on Helen's shoulder and turned them both back toward the nurse's station. "Tell me what you're seeing, and then let's consider calling the team and pulling a cardiologist into the discussion."

Helen smiled as Gary followed her down the hall. The team was now a standard approach when there was any doubt and there had been enough "saves" from raised concerns that any resistance had ended. All the physicians associated with that patient's care were obligated to get together—immediately if necessary— to trouble-shoot problems or coordinate care and anyone could ask for that patient safety huddle. Gary, for one, couldn't imagine how they had ever approached it any other way.

Maura Manning finished making out the assignment for the next shift before checking her e-mails. Dr. Cooper confirmed lunch for Friday with the day charge nurses and Dr. Franklin sent a head's up that he was rounding at eight tomorrow morning instead of seven-thirty, due to an early morning dentist appointment, and he was hoping his in-service could be taped.

Shouldn't be a problem, she thought, because she was scheduled off the floor today anyway to evaluate the rapid improvement processes she and the other nurses were continuously implementing on the floor. Last year's goal was to double the time nurses spent at the bedside from the low 40 percent rating of four years ago and everyone in the organization was thrilled with their creativity, determination and progress. She shuddered to think how all this work would have been possible under the old 'regime' as they jokingly called it when nurses had so very little non-productive time and no say whatever in staffing. *We were like hamsters on an exercise wheel and never even tried to get off,* she thought to herself as she reached to answer the ringing phone.

"Hi Maura, it's Diane, calling from beautiful downtown Chicago. How are things on the floor today?"

"Just fine, Diane. You didn't need to call, although I appreciate it. How's the windy city conference going?"

"Great!" replied Diane. "And I know I didn't need to call, just wanted to touch base. Dr. Ramirez and I just finished presenting our program on Intentional Rounding, and we're heading out for a fine Italian dinner. What's up there?"

"I'm working on the rapid process improvement (RPI) for Lean, the volunteer is finishing the schedule for our nursing community outreach program on preventing back injuries, Franklin is doing an in-service because he was concerned we didn't notify him in sufficient time of the swelling yesterday when the patient had a potential for compartment syndrome... oh, by the way, I staffed up a nurse, due to the high acuity level and having two new nurses on the floor, until seven tonight and I'll reassess the needs then. All is well. Gotta run though, or I'll miss afternoon rounds."

"Did you have your crucial conversation with Julie?"

"Oh, yes, and I've scheduled us off for a dinner break together as well. Thanks again for role playing that conversation with me before your trip."

"No problem, have a great day!"

"I will!"

Maura grabbed her clipboard and headed to afternoon rounds with the morning charge. They greeted each other first, then knocked and entered the patient's room as Charles introduced the team to the patient. "Maura is our evening charge nurse. Maura, this is Mrs. Madeline Peters. She was with us four years ago for her left hip replacement, and today she is post-op day one from her right hip replacement."

For a moment Maura froze, flooded by the memories of the worst evening of her life: Karen yelling 'Call a Code,' asking a devastated husband for organs, Doug's clenched hand with Mrs. Markowitz's broken glasses, Hector with one arm supporting Doug and the other holding tissues, the sound of the zipper on the body bag, Mrs. Peters...

"Mrs. Peters, do you remember me? I was just finishing my orientation that night when things went so badly for you." *And another patient,* she thought.

"Yes, I remember, Dearie. Sandy Keaton shared with me the events of the evening and what Las Vegas Memorial has done to ensure that nothing like that will ever happen again." Mrs. Peters reached out and squeezed Maura's hand. "I've been a part of your *Patient's First Program* so I've seen the videos on how to escalate concerns, the staffing resources for nurses, the peer review process that ensures that every physician in this hospital can operate on any of their own family, and I'm even in some of your simulation videos!"

"I didn't know that, Mrs. Peters. But I do know that you are going to have a wonderful stay here, and that you will be safe." Maura pulled a chair up to the bed and sat down before continuing. "That wasn't always the case. When I started here I noticed that people worked really, really hard but bad stuff happened once in a while and...well...I guess we all shared a collective belief that bad was inevitable—*primarily because we were working so hard*—and were already doing so many of the recommended things."

"What happened?"

"Our perception changed Our expectations of what was acceptable *or not* acceptable changed and we saw things differently. Leadership, I guess, if I had to narrow it down to just one word.

It's as if all of us were plodding along a trail and every day we just put one step in front of another. We knew we were on the right path because there were foot markers measuring our progress. Let me give you an example. One of the markers said we were in the green because we had 85 percent hand washing, and everyone was happy. Then our senior leadership team tore out all the mediocrity markers, demanding that we look up and see a place where no patients were ever hurt because we had formed collegial interactive teams that could catch errors before they ever happened. Now, unless hand washing is 100 percent all of the time, we are failing our patients.

For me personally, it was a revelation that there were real, tangible ways that we could ensure nothing bad happened and that was by understanding how human beings fail. Now, when we see the places we could stumble, we prepare, depend on our team and communicate our concerns immediately."

"Why did it take so long?"

"Oh we're not there yet. Cultural change takes a lot of time and consistent leadership at the helm with constant reminders of the course. You have to make sure everyone can see that North Star no matter where they work on the ship, and everyone has to know how vital their role is in keeping the ship on course. It's like turning an ocean liner that is three football fields long and thank you, Mrs. Peters, for helping us turn course."

Maura stood up slowly noticing that the call light was out of sight. She pulled it out from under the covers, placing it by Mrs. Peters' hand and filled up her water glass casually walking over to the opposite side of the bed to check the urine output in the foley catheter that she had been monitoring hourly. *Not even thirty cc per hour,* she thought logging onto the computer to send a page to Dr. Cooper; alerting him to the decreasing trend, while encouraging fluids.

"What is the North Star, Dearie?" Mrs. Peters asked looking puzzled and reaching for her water. Maura turned around slowly and looked Mrs. Peters directly in the eye.

"You, Mrs. Peters. It's you."

APPENDIX A

FROM: JANICE.JENKINS@Northnet.com
TO: JACK.SILVERMAN@STM.ORG
SUBJ: The Prime Template

Jack,

I'm more enthusiastic about this new organizational roadmap every
time I dive back into it. I promised to coalesce my thoughts on a
plan for exactly how a hospital should proceed out of the starting
gate toward aiming at St. Michael's-Class status, and here it is.
Every institution would, of course, need to construct a latticework
of specifics around this plan interfacing with their institution and
where it is on, for instance, electronic medical records, bundles,
etc., but I think it's a valid basic template, and it will be the basic
lesson plan for my new class.

The PRIME TEMPLATE for Beginning the Voyage—
Taking Your Hospital to St. Michael's-Class status.

1. **First, Coalesce the Vision**

   Take a long look at your statement of mission, vision and values. Is it specific enough with respect to your promises to the community and each patient each and every time? Have you ever tested it against the concern that it might be too broad and easily complied-with as a general statement of vague principles? In other words, does your mission, vision and values statement express both what you truly believe as a board, senior leadership and the medical leaders of your hospital (or medical system), as well as express it as a blood-oath promise to your community? Secondly, is your hospital *at every level* living the "statement," and do you really have the means and the will to fulfill those promises in full?

   This is a vital point, since a mission statement should be a well-understood credo known and lived by all. Consider seeking the input of everyone at your facility if you redraft it— don't just make it a top-down exercise. How do the folks in housekeeping, or central sterile processing, or on the Med-Surg floors feel it should be written? What promises are the people of your hospital not willing or able to fulfill? Consider rewriting it to express precisely what you should be promising, and then make sure it's not only hanging in the foyer, but constantly available to everyone who IS your hospital. Make hiring, membership and retention directly contingent on living up to those principles and promises, with one standard for all.

2. **Eliminate the Illusions**

   A. Through multiple episodes of long-visit rounding, test the "image" you have of what your hospital is accomplishing with the realities you find on the front lines. Do so in part by seeking honest answers to these key questions:
   - Is patient safety really a core value as lived hour-to-hour by staff, physicians included?
   - Is there really a full appreciation of what the highest quality of medical care consists of, and do you see that

inculcated in everyone's actions even when they're under serious pressure?

- How do the doctors, nurses and other staff members answer the question: Do you have the resources and support you need to do your job?
- How do the folks on the front lines respond when you ask: "Can anyone here take care of a loved one suddenly admitted in serious condition?"
- If asked the question, "What do the leaders of this hospital value the most?" Would the answer be "money," or something higher?
- Do you see carefully thought-out systems, best practices, and standard approaches being used at all levels of clinical care systems that assure your patients the best outcomes possible? Do you see such systems adopted, but not consistently used?
- When you're on the clinical front lines—regardless of the department or service line involved—is it clear and irrefutable by the actions and attitudes you see and witness that your hospital is living the full spirit and intent of providing the safest and highest quality of care attainable?
- (And, one of the most important questions:) Is your hospital truly a patient-centric hospital, or is it—like the majority of American hospitals—in practical terms being run for the physicians? In other words, are the physicians the *clients,* or the *prime team leaders*?

B. Convene a widely-cast interdisciplinary group to openly and deeply examine whether the metrics the board and the C-suite have been relying on provide accurate and true reflections of your hospital on the clinical front lines.

3. **Establish trust through accountability:** Trust = same rules for all roles. Progress depends on leadership.
   - Ask every leader to perform a 360 degree examination of their own leadership, communication effectiveness, ability to nurture relationships and support their people

and their stewardship of safety. We have provided a checklist to follow, but they are free to add additional questions and asked to share results with their people; to freely and openly discuss results.

4. **Establish <u>the foundation</u> of a just culture:** one single, unified code of conduct for everyone who walks through the doors of your hospital, with board-ordered unanimity of application.
   - Train and sustain the primary lesson that any accident, incident, or shortcoming isessentially a "message from the underlying system," and that discovering and addressing virtually every supporting link in such a chain of causation (versus looking for someone to blame) is the only acceptable philosophy and methodology.

5. **Use the "Bully Pulpit"**
   The vital role of the CEO, the board chair and the CMO as the master communicators of the vision, values and mission of your hospital cannot be overstated. Through all available means—but especially personal presence and communication—the message that you *will* be a single, collegial team striving for a finite goal that is patient-centric in fact as well as theory must be established, repeated and sustained on a constant basis. It will take many months of sustained effort before a significant majority of the personnel—physicians included—realize and accept the fact that something profound is changing, and that this is not a new "flavor of the month." While managers, directors, charge nurses and supervisors at all levels must echo and sustain this direct and powerful message, the steady communication push by the leadership is the factor that will initially propel your hospital into true and sustainable change.

6. **Make Harm Completely Visible and Personal**
   - Always include a picture and the name of the patient with every review of serious adverse events.
   - Every sentinel event or significant "near-miss" over the

past two years should be thoroughly described in clinically-useful terms as well as humane terms (effect on the patient and family involved) and communicated in written form to everyone with a hospital badge, with the cover explanation that while you as a family will celebrate the wins and the good things, it will also not hide from its mistakes—especially since each mistake, fatal or otherwise, must be understood and never repeated. Two things are important here: One, there is NEVER just one cause to any such event; and, Two, regardless of subsequent compensation to a patient or survivors, your hospital should clearly, steadily and publically dedicate itself to making sure that the injury or death did not occur in vain. This is done in perpetuity by making sure no one else suffers the same or similar error/mistake/occurrence, and that, in turn, is done by making sure no one forgets the basic lessons.

- Establish a means (such as with Cincinnati Children's Hospital) of keeping the entire staff informed of any incidents or near-misses.
- Approach as many people who have suffered past harm at your hospital as possible and ask them to join a team of such folks to assist in teaching the people of your facility about the profound impact of an incident and the ways such occurrences should be handled. Ask them to participate in any planning activity involving improving patient communication, patient understanding (such as discharge instructions) and patient cooperation.

7. **Setup the initial structures for cultural and clinical change:**
   A. Mandatory weekly rounding by all leaders and managers, and full-shift periodic rounding by board members.
   - Education on <u>meaningful</u> rounding, philosophy, relationships
   Monitor the culture to ensure the same rules apply to everyone
   - Flatten the hierarchy by following front line staff

- Ask the right questions: *Can anyone do surgery on your mom? Care for her?*

B. Harmonize medical staff bylaws with the corporate bylaws and include identical behavioral standards in annual evaluations.
- Adopt 'team covenant' as a condition of employment (MD recommendation).
- Never abandon a team or member in the case of an adverse occurrence and support each other through full and open discussion of truth. Privileges terminated for those who abandon a team or leader by lack of disclosure or refusing to share all available information or attempts to illicit shame

C. Repetitive education on **Team Training** from different sources both internal and external to organization: Invite folks from other industries and share success stories
   1. Use videoed empty-room simulation for team training, and as soon as possible begin training the facilitators needed for such guidance.
   2. Provide on-line educational tools and resources

D. Elicit deep-thought ideas from the front lines—all departments—on how to proceed setting up informal membership (no empire building) advisory groups, continuous engagement, and rolling discussion; and shepherd our mid-level managers and directors into a facilitator role after coaching education

E. Physician-nurse role. Minimum of 6–8 physicians and nurses to meet monthly in every department. No time together = no improvement.
   1. Provide education to group on history and culture of MD/RN relationships
   2. Ask all participants to share last medical error as opener—evens playing field
   3. Describe the current MD/RN norms—create a new set of norms together

F. Hardwire safety huddles per department and inter-department to answer the following:
   1. Where will our next patient safety disaster or near-disaster come from?
   2. What steps should we take to immediately address and improve person-to-person communication and establish relationships across silos?
   3. Make harm visible

G. Design and launch a continuous effort to support on-going education on communications and relationships: **culture change focus is on language and behavior**
   1. Increase non-productive budget and educational budget for on-going staff and leadership development.
   2. Results must be visible and gains shared to maintain the momentum.
   3. Hardwire support for relationships issues which are sure to arise when you change a culture...Employee Education?

II. Establish and invite widespread participation in monthly facilitated "think tanks"—indicator of success will be multi-level participation and hard-wired into culture
   e.g. Re-designing nursing to increase time at the bedside vs. non nursing tasks
   e.g. Provide time and space for all departments to address issues

APPENDIX B

Will's PowerPoint presentation during his presentation to the physicians in chapter 26, and an additional portion of the address (in summary) not included in the text (The actual PowerPoint presentation can be found at the website for this book, www.WhyHospitalsShouldFly.com

SLIDES:

1. **Complexity-** The Great American Non-System of Healthcare: 9000 billing codes, 6600 drugs, over 4000 procedures

2. **Cost-** Five percent of the population spends 60 percent of the dollars, the majority of which involve unnecessary complications we know how to avoid. One percent of the population uses 35 percent of all dollars. Currently, healthcare takes 2.8 Trillion of our GNP, about 18 percent to be19.3 percent by 2019.
"We cannot economically prosper when 7 percent of the economy wastes 30–50 percent of what it spends."

3. **Quality-** In 2011, we spent 2.7 Trillion, (1/3) of which failed to improve health and often led to harm. We rank 48th in infant mortality; 134th in overall mortality worldwide.
We spend twice as much per person for half the quality of the rest of the industrialized world.

4. **Access-**   Our dollars go to: diabetes, CHF, CAD, asthma and depression, each of which we know how to control and minimize.

The looming shortage of primary care physicians will top 85,000.

Nearly 50 million Americans are uninsured.

5. **Safety-**   "First Do No Harm"—We kill or injure 22–30 patients AN HOUR on average, which is the equivalent of crashing ten 747's each week, killing 100,000 to 250,000 people per year.

(Additional Portion of Will's Address not included in the text)
What do we know about ourselves? What is known about American physicians? Bear with me while we look at

1. **Physician practice styles are culturally transmitted—**
   depends on the number of specialists in your residency program and availability of different kinds of doctors.
   "When your only tool is a hammer, everything looks like a nail."
   "Regions that have fewer specialists and more primary care physicians have better overall health."
   The number of specialists affects mortality: e.g. > than 4.3 neonatologists/10,000 patients.

2. **We routinely order unnecessary tests.**
   A survey of over 800 physicians found that 59 percent ordered unnecessary tests. Most common reasons: patient demand and worry about malpractice.

3. **We perform unnecessary surgery.**
   a. Supply of number of physicians determines how much surgery is performed.
   b. (SPORT trial 2006 which found no difference between surgery vs. conservative treatment for backs).
   c. No change in rate of heart attacks over the past 15 years despite angioplasty and stents. "a half million stents of questionable value."

d. According to cardiologists, of the 1.2 million elective cardiac procedures.

4. The use of CT scanning has not improved diagnosis.
   a. JAMA '98 Imaging tests have not improved accuracy of diagnosis.
   b. David Flum study of appendicitis '87-'98 examined 63,790 records.
   c. No change in rate of mistakes over 11 years: still 15.5 percent.

5. Type of specialist determines testing—"Who you see is what you get"
Dr. Richard Deyo, Univ. of Washington.
   * Rheumatologists will give back pain patient's blood tests to look for rare disorders.
   * Neurologists perform nerve conduction tests.
   * Surgeons order MRI's and scans despite the fact that 27 percent of patients over 40 have a herniated disk with no back pain.

6. Roemer's Law: Medical demand expands to consume resources.
Study of ICU beds showed that physicians were astonishingly unaware that the supply of hospital beds affected their clinical decision to admit.

7. We prescribe the wrong drugs and/or fail to monitor side effects
Over 700,000/yr. are treated for adverse drug events.

8. We deliver recommended care only 55 percent of the time.
   a. End of life care—3.3 vs. 11 days depending on bed availability.
   b. 80 percent of healthcare dollars spent on first 6 months and last 6 months of life.
   c. "Chronic diseases sap more than 70 percent of the nation's healthcare costs, and of those chronic conditions,

five form the vast majority: Diabetes, Congestive Health
Failure, Coronary Artery Disease, Depression, and Asthma."

9. **We pre-judge—and don't listen**
   The average time it takes a physician to make a diagnosis and
   plan a course of treatment is 18 seconds after the patient
   begins talking.

10. **And here is the clincher—we physicians firmly
    believe as individuals and as a profession that we are
    doing the right thing.** Nothing could be further from the
    truth. If you still want the green pill, please…find another
    place to work.

Source: *Overtreated* by Shannon Brownlee

STUDY GUIDE

The following pages are presented with the intent of providing an introductory means of discussing, dissecting and learning from the ideas, recommendations and principals in this book. To do so, we've carefully selected chapters that should spark further discussion and included questions and additional resources.

While the task of changing a major healthcare delivery system (such as the fictional Las Vegas Memorial) is clearly complex, the components of that challenge *can* be identified, broken down to their essential elements, and clearly understood. That, in fact, has been our quest in writing Dr. Will Jenkins throughout this story: To reflect the *average* American hospital and deal with the *typical* problems of reaching the paradigm of quality and safety that virtually everyone wants to achieve.

We highly encourage you to use these Study Guide pages in a way that fosters deep thought as well as deep honesty in comparing what is, to what can (and should) be for your particular institution. We've written these primarily as discussion guidelines because head-on, honest grappling with the necessary elements of change is the prime element of what Jack Silverman's St. Michael's Hospital was all about *as a model and paradigm.*

Changing Cultural Norms: (A 'norm' is defined as a pattern or trait typical in the behavior of a social group: a widespread or usual practice, procedure, or custom (Webster). Norms are the behaviors that are silently accepted by a group. *To create a new culture, you need to focus on language and behavior and change the norms (*Tribal Leadership, *by David Logan).*

CHAPTER 1

What principal mistakes did Will—by his own admission—make in his prior position as CEO?

1. **He failed to instill a common vision and create a single-minded focus on achieving it.**

   (Suggested Exercise: Randomly walk through your hospital or facility asking your staff "What is your *boss's* top priority?" Then ask, "What is *your* top priority?" When everyone's answers are the same, you have aligned passion and purpose and created a shared vision. The question then becomes: Is that shared vision the right one?)

2. **He believed that instilling higher levels of patient safety was a top-down initiative, rather than a core value.** The immense energy invested in pushing a new and unfamiliar concept or requirement down from a C-suite is typically overwhelmed and neutralized by the far greater force of resistance from people who neither understand nor embrace the new concept as a strategy. Furthermore, research shows that such initiatives only make it two levels down from the top.

   > Example: A major hospital in the western U.S. spent many tens of thousands of dollars and time bringing in consultants to reorganize a surgical unit's approach to patient safety by instilling rigid new rules top-down, some of which were assaultive to the professional comfort and even physical wellbeing of the staff. The result was precisely the opposite of the original intent as the physicians and staff came to regard the phrase "culture of safety" as Draconian and insulting.

   > The lesson is quite simple but powerful: If major cultural changes are not thoroughly embraced by those on the front lines and nurtured by leadership, instead of dictated, they will ultimately fail. Even where staff conform to tactical procedures and changes, the effect of those not-invented-here procedures (such as surgical time-outs) will be compromised if not neutralized by inherent resistance.

3. **Will did not realize that human organizations cannot achieve HRO (High Reliability Organization) performance without minimizing variables, embracing evidence-based best practices, standardizing processes and procedures where clinically possible, and being ready and willing to change when new knowledge becomes available.** The need for doing these things is usually masked by the methods we have of hiding harm, and

the culture of shame and secrecy in which mistakes are generally hidden—especially from physicians.

(Suggested Exercise: Ask your physicians, nurses and others on the clinical front lines [or in any department] to share with the group, with complete honesty, their last mistake. Be prepared for initial silence, but with steady nudging, the majority will respond). *Resource: Article, Begin by reading a story from "Doctors Confess their Fatal Mistakes,"* Reader's Digest, *October, 2010, at Pg. 86.*

4. **Will did not understand the immense power of an established culture to resist change.**

A practical definition of "culture": Everyone knows it, but no one ever talks about it and it isn't written down anywhere. These are the behaviors everyone accepts without thinking or talking about them—for example, a clinically competent ICU nurse whose poor negative attitude is tolerated because she is "a good nurse.'

Suggested Exercises:

A. Think of three or more specific examples that fit this definition of culture in your workplace, and facilitate a discussion.

B. Identify at least one cultural norm of American hospitals. For example:
   - A board of directors' traditional, primary focus is on finances.
   - American healthcare has a boilerplate history of tolerating disruptive behavior from physicians: The classic profile is a physician who is clinically competent and has been with the organization for a long period of time and is a "big admitter," but cannot control his/her temper. The outbursts are consistently minimized and effectively tolerated while such conduct on the part of any other staff member would result in suspension, sanction or termination.
   - A classic unrealistic expectation: The new leader will solve all the organization's problems. This, in effect, is what was worrying Will in the first chapter, that the board was looking to their next CEO to be an organizational messiah.

Reflection on your cultural expectations: Do you believe it is possible to achieve zero harm in your workplace? If not, why not? Would you fly on a commercial airline if the airline industry still embraced the long-abandoned concept that a crash every now and then was unavoidable?

Quick Discussion: From the loss of American Airlines Flight 587 in Queens, New York just after 9/11 in 2001, there were zero deaths among major United States airlines for a full five years, a heretofore never-achieved feat that had been considered impossible. Despite 32-thousand commercial flights every day over the U.S. alone involving a minimum of two human pilots per flight (and thus a total opportunity for fatal error of 32,000 times 2 times 365 times 5 = 10,950,000), the abandonment in 1989 by the airlines of the concept that zero accidents was not a reachable goal led to actually achieving it. In fact, at the time of publication of this book, over 11 years have passed with only two regional airline accidents and zero accidents among the major carriers. During this same time period, and using the Institute of Medicine's most conservative figures on annual preventable deaths from medical mistake and infections, we have unnecessarily relieved 3,083,520 Americans of their lives. And this is the startling fact: The primary method of achieving this incredible record was not new equipment or procedures, but simply accepting the fact that even the best humans make mistakes, and that while preventing all human mistakes will never succeed as a goal, minimizing human mistakes and then creating a systemic ability to identify and stop the mistakes that still occur using collegial interactive teamwork can get us to zero. The nuclear power generation industry as well as the U.S. Navy's nuclear navy and the industry that builds major buildings safely and on time all use the same successful method. Among the most vital "industries" in the U.S., only healthcare has heretofore resisted adoption of the same principals.

CHAPTER 2
Discussion Questions:

1. What are the unmet emotional needs of the following people in this chapter?

   Mrs. Peters • Karen • Doug Markowitz • Maura

2. What <u>system processes</u> made it difficult, if not impossible, for these needs to be met?

3. What is the primary dysfunctional thread running through this

chapter? Flawed communication, lack of a common goal, or a rather startling absence of teamwork and team orientation?

4. What is the principal focus or goal of the people in this chapter?

CHAPTER 3
Discussion Questions:
1. Define QUALITY as traditionally practiced in American healthcare.

2. Consider and explain the quotation Will uses to the board: "The illusion of knowledge has prompted the delusion of excellence."

3. Why is patient safety clearly not a core value at Las Vegas Memorial given the information in Chapter Three?

4. Why is "leadership" Will's top priority, and why did this startle the board members?

5. Find two examples of hospital cultural norms in this chapter. For example:
   • CEO's typically bring in their own team because they are familiar with them and need to produce results quickly to validate the institution's investment.
   • The architecture of a building sends an important message. Trust is undermined when the top of the hierarchy is invisible or inaccessible and consistently meets in private (secret)
   • The normal deferential way for a CEO to approach a board would be politically correct, solicitous and understated in order to protect his position.
   • Is it normal to have a tragedy like Mr. Simonson's every once in a while? Is this the 'cost of doing business?'

Reflection: Is healthcare a business or industry? Should it be? Is there a rational way to maintain the American methodology of delivering health services and yet change the entire focus to major improvement in the wellness of the population (which inevitably will mean less need for the specific 'services' of doctors, nurses and all healthcare professionals).

Commentary:

Will's question to the board chairman at the very end of the chapter is very telling, and very representative of the dichotomy between the perception of hospital boards and what will be required of them now and in the future. The tendency to believe that alarms are overstated is a ticket to oblivion, yet many boards and board members find it very difficult to accept the fact that the old paradigms will no longer keep the doors open in an age where CMS reimbursement approaches 50 percent of a hospital's revenue, and requires inescapable quality compliance, no 'Never Events,' and no liaise faire approaches to perfect patient safety and standardized use of evidence-based best practices. The old-style community hospital board simply brought good members of the community (many of them experienced businessmen and women) together as a civic duty, people who struggled primarily to keep the money flowing and new buildings on the way and for whom clinical matters were simply relegated to the hospital's medical executive team or CMO. For a hospital to survive, that model must end immediately. Today's challenge of guiding a hospital and supporting the C-suite in what absolutely has to occur in reforming a physician-centric system to a patient-centric model will require a far higher level of board involvement and understanding and participation, along with accelerated board education. The pioneering work of the Institute for Healthcare Improvement and their "Boards on Board" educational seminars (mentioned in this chapter) is an important starting point.

CHAPTER 4

Identify the norms in this chapter:

- Orientation is still three months long because, traditionally, 'that's the way we've always done it!' The three month tradition exists despite the fact that the workload, complexity and comorbidities of the patients—and number of required tasks to care for them—have increased exponentially. *(Please see the article on Complexity Compression in our Bibliography.)*
  - The charge nurse is constantly dealing with multiple tasks, and his/her position has been ill-defined and stripped over time of the clear authority (as well as training) to provide positive vigilance over each patient's progress and welfare.
  - Non-verbal innuendos are not called out despite the fact that 93 percent of all communication is non-verbal

- Missed meals and missed breaks are standard and accepted even though they are essentially normalized deviancy from a logical and safe paradigm.
- The staff nurse's comment about not being able to recognize the previous CEO even in a police lineup is representative of the typically sparse contact between the senior leader and those led. This is not a tenable situation, nor one that should ever be acceptable to a CEO who understands his or her responsibility to truly lead by inspiration, example and personal communication. In truth, many CEO's already believe that they fulfill this obligation by rounding, but drive-by rounding (versus creating meaningful relationships) are entirely different things, and merely popping in to show the leader's face will never—repeat, never—suffice to build the bridges that empower true ownership in the rank and file.
- This unit reflects an every-man-for-himself, life-jacket mentality where everyone's focus is on their own survival with little or no room in their psyche for protection of the patients from either error or low-quality engagement.

(Also recall the old but still accurate rubric that "When you're up to your posterior in alligators, it's devilishly difficult to recall that your initial objective was to drain the swamp." This is precisely why one of the most profoundly important duties of the C-suite and the CEO is to create safe environments in which the staff can concentrate their full attention on the patients, not their own survival).

CHAPTER 5

Suggested Discussion Questions:

1. How would you describe the effect of the 'battle' on the previous CEO (Joan Winston) given her statements to Will by phone? Was this lady negligent, clueless, burned out or simply worn down? Understanding how she came to the point of resignation (which does require some reading between the lines in the story) is the pathway to grasping what has to change, and why Will's zeal and determination as major components of his worth as a leader are so important.

2. What is the difference between patient-centric and physician-centric? Give an example from your own experience of both.

Reflection: How could physicians and nurses calling each other by their first name in your facility change the social dynamics? An interesting question is: What should doctors and nurses call each other in front of patients. Some patients feel more comfortable with the humane and familiar (first names) and some would rather prefer a more hierarchical environment to add faith and conviction to the healing relationship (last names and titles). In any event, what you do should be uniform throughout your facility and the result of specific discussion and agreement among the larger team.

CHAPTER 6

Identify two hospital norms from this chapter.

For example:
- The on-call physician is unfamiliar with the patients he or she is covering.
  - What is the potential effect on patient safety and quality of care of such unfamiliarity?

- Bad things happen once and a while, and adverse patient outcomes and impacts are just the unavoidable 'cost of doing business.'
  - Is an acceptable level of patient safety (let alone 100 percent) *ever* possible with this attitude?

- Disruptive behavior is excused from 'good' physicians.
  - What is the effect on the rest of the staff of knowing that there are two standards of behavior: One for the rank and file, and one for big-admitting physicians labeled as "good" doctors despite their behavior?
  - Should we redefine what a "good" doctor (or, for that matter, a "good" nurse) is? Shouldn't we exclude from the "good" category someone whose behavior or demeanor or even lack of basic social skills creates upset, distraction and compromised patient safety?

- Managers are rarely on the floor because their workload has shifted to meetings and administrative duties.
  - To what extent should managers, directors and other intermediate leaders/managers be required to first create and nurture relationships with those they lead and supervise, excluding from

"acceptable performance" those who either prefer to, or cannot change their habit of, remaining primarily in their offices?

- To what extent is it the duty of higher management to relieve managers/directors/supervisors of excessive paperwork and meeting requirements to allow their primary efforts to be focused on direct contact and nurturing of their people?
- To what extent is it the duty of intermediate level leaders (managers/directors/supervisors) to consider their primary duty that of supporting the ability of their people to serve the patients' best interests? How does that comport with what happens in your facility now?

- Managers work long hours and are often too fatigued and/or distracted to deal with small, individual problems, complaints or concerns.
  - Do your managers/directors/supervisors energetically support their people, even when they're wrong? What effect does a failure to do so have on patient safety and service quality?
  - Do people in your unit feel free to bring up any concern to their manager without fear of reprisal or embarrassment?

- Nurses would rather write up a report than address a person with whom they have a problem.
  - Do you have a requirement that no complaint or report will be accepted or investigated until and unless the reporting individual has made a good faith attempt to address the matter directly with the person about whom they are complaining? If not, why not?

- Nurses who are intimidated by physicians once, think twice before trying again.
  - What is the prime prophylaxis for this syndrome?
  - Standardized terms and approaches such as the use of situation-background-a assessment-recommendation (SBAR-communications) are often ineffective because only the nurses have been taught the protocol, and the physicians have no idea what the nurses are talking about when they use the SBAR discipline to describe a problem. In fact, SBAR should be the norm for physician-to-physician as well as physician-to-nurse communication.

- What level of support would be required to introduce, adjust and teach as a standard procedure anything clinically important to ALL participants, physicians included?

CHAPTER 7

Suggested Discussion Questions:

1. How does "drive-by" rounding differ from "management by sitting around?"

2. What constitutes "trust" in a hospital environment, and to what extent does your institution have it at all levels?
   - Trust" can be measured in large degree by the willingness (or not) of front line staff to speak up without hesitation when they see or believe something is wrong *(Ref: The Silent Treatment)*.

3. To what extent can front line staff—physicians included—spot a "phony" when it comes to demonstration of engagement and concern by a senior leader?

Leadership Exercise: If you're a C-suite member or a senior leader, follow a nurse, pharmacist or hospitalist for an entire eight hour shift. While you are so engaged, use it as an opportunity to encourage staff to talk openly with each other and with you. Pay careful attention to the elements of resistance, and what it will take to create the safe environment for transparent communication.

- *If you are a nurse, tech, or social worker etc., follow a physician for an entire day.*
- *If you're a physician and truly want to understand what your nurses are facing, spend an eight hour shift with them and write a description of your experiences for your colleagues.*

Share what you have learned publicly.

CHAPTER 8

Suggested Discussion Questions: (Please see also the Discussion Notes for chapters thirteen and fifteen).

1. Regarding Dr. Adams' conduct in the RCA meeting, please ask and answer in depth whether such conduct is *ever* acceptable or

justified from a senior physician, a nurse, a tech, or anyone else in the hospital environment. (NOTE: The way for you to know if it is organizationally acceptable or not [for someone to engage in such conduct] is whether or not such disruptive behavior in fact exists in your institution. If it exists, it is *de facto* acceptable behavior).

2. If you knew for an absolute fact that there is overwhelming research available showing that disruptive, disrespectful and/or dismissive behavior directly impacts safety by creating upset and distraction that pulls vigilance away from the patient, would your answer be any different? (Rosenstein, A.)

3. Is it possible to create trust when such conduct is tolerated even once by the culture and the leadership?

4. How did the other participants in the RCA scene endorse or otherwise perpetuate Dr. Adams' behavior by their reaction or lack of reaction?

5. What is your reaction to Sandy Keaton's assessment that the meeting had gone "so very well?"

6. Is Dr. Adams a "good" doctor?

Commentary and Study Material:
The so-called root cause analysis (RCA) is thoroughly established in hospital routine, but it needs to be redefined and reoriented. First, an RCA should never consist of a singular meeting because the facts and circumstances needed to evolve a systemic understanding and multiple fixes will neither be served by, nor concluded by, a single "report-oriented" meeting. Second, there is NEVER just one cause to an accident or incident in clinical practice, any more than there is ever one cause to a major airline accident or rail disaster, etc. An RCA should be acknowledged as a root causal or root causes analysis at threshold, and never allowed to give the impression that the participants are searching for a single "cause."

One of the nation's leading children's hospitals, Cincinnati Children's, has evolved a highly refined procedural approach to dealing with any serious incident or accident. While they still use the overall term "RCA," their approach is multifaceted and comprehensive. Hospital leaders nationally and internationally have come to Cincinnati Children's to study this protocol, which has been described as perhaps the best in use anywhere in the world.

When an "event" has been identified:

1. A senior executive (CMO, CFO, CNO or other top level officer) is immediately named as executive of the event.

2. The three-meeting model is used, and the three meetings are immediately scheduled.

3. Immediate actions are taken to support care giver and patient (and patient's family). We recognize that harm impacts the entire team.

4. Legal services does the investigation and identifies the "facts of the case." In many organizations clinicians are assigned to do this work, but the model of using legal services (a lawyer and a nurse/or physician partner) is very powerful and a better practice. Lawyers are specifically trained to get to the essence of the facts of a situation and the clinicians are present to keep the facts clinically precise and the chain of events clearly understood in medical terms as well as human terms.

5. A vision diagram of events is produced, inappropriate acts are identified.

6. The first meeting—The team, which consists of two team leaders where the event occurred, the executive sponsor, frontline staff, safety, legal and others as indicated are given the "rules": The RCA is NOT about people error—it is about system error. Names of individuals involved are not even mentioned.

7. The second meeting reviews the inappropriate acts or omissions and begins to identify the root and contributory causes.

8. The third meeting begins to identify the next steps.

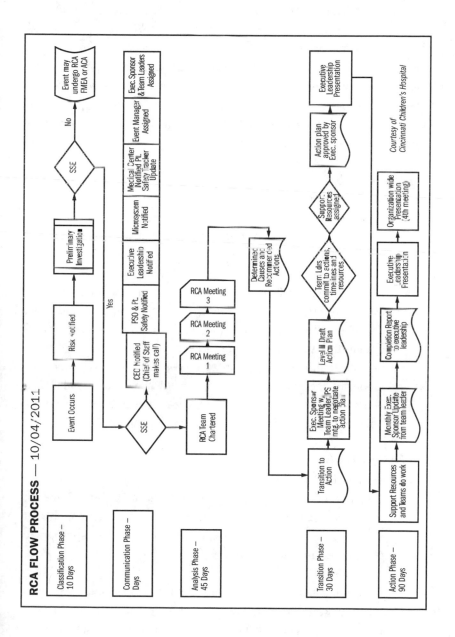

RCA FLOW PROCESS — 10/04/2011

Classification Phase — 10 Days

Event Occurs → Risk Notified → Preliminary Investigation → SSE

SSE — No → Event may undergo RCA FMEA or ACA

Yes

Communication Phase — Days

CEC Notified (Chief of Staff makes call) | PSO & Pt. Safety Notified | Executive Leadership Notified | Microsystem Notified | Medical Center Notified Pt. Safety Tracker Update | Event Manager Assigned | Exec. Sponsor & Team Leaders Assigned

Analysis Phase — 45 Days

SSE → RCA Team Chartered → RCA Meeting 1 → RCA Meeting 2 → RCA Meeting 3 → Determined Causes and Recommended Actions

Transition Phase — 30 Days

Transition to Action → Exec. Sponsor Meeting w/ Team Leader, PS mtg. to negotiate action plan → Level III Draft Action Plan → Team Ldrs commit to actions, timelines and resources → Support Resources assigned → Action plan approved by Exec. sponsor → Executive Leadership Presentation

Action Phase — 90 Days

Support Resources and Teams do work → Monthly Exec. Sponsor Update from team leader → Completion Report to executive leadership → Executive Leadership Presentation → Organization wide Presentation (4th meeting)

Courtesy of Cincinnati Children's Hospital

287

Additional Point: The intellectual investigatory rigor that has led to an almost perfect airline safety record in the last decade originated with the National Transportation Safety Board (NTSB) and their methodology of NEVER considering blame or liability. NTSB investigations seek to find out every contributing element in the causal chain of an accident or incident, and make specific recommendations for immediate systemic change to prevent any one of those contributing causes from helping to create a future accident. Specific study of this NTSB philosophy would be time well spent for any hospital professional, and the principals apply equally to small glitches in daily practice.

CHAPTER 9

Suggested discussion Questions:

1. To what degree are Dr. Roget's attitudes regarding strict physician autonomy also the prevailing attitude of doctors in the second decade of the 21st century?

2. Is the concept and the practice of strict physician autonomy— especially the long-taught concept that each physician must be an "autonomous scientist"—compatible with an evidence-based system that seeks to emulate the successful transitions of other human, high-risk enterprises to high-reliability? How does the model of the autonomous scientist clash with the model of a patient-centric hospital that embraces evidence-based best practices and standardized procedures where available?

CHAPTER 10

Suggested Discussion Questions:

1. When was the last time you received a "heads up" that someone on staff (or in the C-suite or board) had a loved one inbound for your section of the hospital? Did you feel it was an appropriate communication, and if so, why?

2. Regarding hand-washing, many institutions believe they have made great progress by reaching the eightieth or even ninetieth percentile of compliance, but whatever percentage "points" remain unwashed hands expose patients to serious and potentially fatal nosocomial infections. Is it ever "okay" to accept less

than 100 percent hand washing compliance? Would you tolerate that with your loved one at stake?

3. How would you, as a leader or teammate, handle Megan's irritated response to a request for hand hygiene? Specifically, what would you say? And what would you do if your words were met with arrogance or resistance?

CHAPTER 11
(Please see Janice's discussion of "The Basics" at the end of Chapter Eleven.)

Suggested Discussion Questions:
1. Why are change agents typically rejected by their constituent group?
   * Those who would/could make changes often cannot muster the courage to challenge the existing paradigm because they are keenly aware that change agents are typically rejected by their constituent group. For example, people who "rock the boat" make everyone feel unsafe and insecure.
   * Physicians who would foster change and yet who are dependent on referrals to maintain their income, put everything on the line if they speak up. Economic credentialing—being economically blackballed in retaliation for raising an issue others want left alone—is a real and potential consequence. The few physicians who are known to other doctors to be dangerously incompetent or unethical are typically protected by silence arising from such fears.

Paradox: Physicians respect their colleagues primarily based on perceived clinical competence. But those most competent are best served by continuing the current paradigm (of see-no-evil), and therefore are the least likely to be willing to change it. Those least vested in the current paradigm practice outside the "mainstream," and therefore lack the respect of their colleagues to initiate change, and when they try, they are typically dismissed as blind. Plato's allegory of the cave is a perfect reflection of this dynamic and why only heretics create change.

Exercise: How many direct reports can you depend on to speak up when they don't agree with you or a change you are proposing? *(Resource: "The No People" by Dr. Bruce Avolio)*

An anonymous 'comment box' is an indication that "you are closer to the edge of the cliff than you think" (Avolio). Remember the last time someone disagreed with you—thank them again.

For Nurses: In the current culture the "No People" are often viewed as 'troublemakers.' People will say they are 'not a team player' if they present an idea that is at variance with the group. This is one of the reasons that change has been slow in the profession—because there is so little deviance—even positive deviance. *(Reference: "Leadership on the Line," by Heifetz and Linsky)*

CHAPTERS 13 & 15
Professionalism vs. Disruptive Behaviors

Note to Physician administrators:
There is no excuse for disruptive behavior no matter what happened. You can never have a team without trust—and you can't have trust without the 'same rules for all roles.' Disruptive physicians often deflect. Always separate the behavior from the event. When there is a behavioral problem or issue, acknowledge the problem, and say you want to talk about both the behavior AND the clinical or personnel issue. These physicians do not see the EFFECT of their behavior on the team or patient care unless you point it out. They typically have two things in common: they are good clinicians and the behavior has been tolerated for a long time.

A committee should be responsible for reviewing repetitive, disruptive behavior and not the CMO. Possible suggestions would be a BERC (Behavioral Events Review Committee) and a Medical Staff Health Committee are better venues. The BERC is staffed by behavioral experts (who are often NOT on the peer review committee) and the health committee is staffed by vocational experts, skilled in 'fitness for work' evaluations.

Possible Scripting:
"Can we talk? I understand there was a situation yesterday with the team"

"Let me paraphrase the problem to make sure I have it right—This is what we can do to address this situation and ensure it doesn't reoccur. Now, can we talk about the (specific behavior...yelling, condescending voice, anger, etc.)

"Do you have a minute? We really value all you bring to our hospital. (Give specific examples of positive contributions). I'd like to also share some feedback from the team to build on those successes.
   Be specific. Focus on details and the facts as you know them.
   Doesn't matter if they are true or not—perceptions are just as critical.
   State the desired behavior or response. For example, "As physician leaders, we must create an environment where everyone feels comfortable speaking up at any time. I know we're not there yet from the feedback. How can I help you get there?"

Communication Model: DESC

Describe	*Lead with the facts*
Explain	*Explain the impact this has had on you or your team (Pause)*
State	*Clearly state the desired outcome*
Consequences	*What will happen if nothing changes?*

       Or
End with a question. "Can you do that?"

References:
Bartholomew, K. *Speak Your Truth and Stressed Out About Communication*
Bujak, J., *Inside the Physician Mind*
Felps, W. et al, *"How, When and Why Bad Apples Spoil the Barrel: Negative Group Members and Dysfunctional Groups"*
Hickson, *"A Complementary Approach to Professionalism"*

Physician Leadership Exercise: Soliciting Feedback

Physicians on one unit wrote their names down one column and then asked nurses to score them on a Scale from 1–5 on the following: Professionalism, approachability and patient complaints. By doing so they role modeled new physician leadership behaviors critical to changing a culture and created a new norm where feedback is sought by all members of the team.

How do physician leaders typically seek feedback from nurses?

How do nurses receive feedback from physicians?

Do your operating room teams routinely debrief?

Effective Physician-Patient Communication Skills

1. **Data-gathering: Did the physician**
   - ✓ Allow me to finish my "opening" statement without interruption
   - ✓ Establish a chronology or narrative thread for *my* reason in visiting
   - ✓ Keep asking for more information until I displayed "closure" on telling (or revealing) my symptoms
   - ✓ Restate some segment of what I had said (at least once)
   - ✓ Avoid multiple questions at the same time
   - ✓ Elicit *my* reasons (concerns) for being there?

2. **Inter-personal skills: Did the physician**
   - ✓ Name the emotion I experienced or showed (Example: "You seem upset")
   - ✓ Offer understanding of the emotion shown (non-judgmentally) (Example: "living with that unknown is distressing")
   - ✓ Offer reassurance, partnership, support or praise?

3. **Information-giving skills: Did the physician**
   - ✓ Explain the reasons for treatment recommendations—in understandable language

- ✓ Check my understanding, at least once during the visit
- ✓ Solicit my questions
- ✓ Ask whether I am willing to follow the recommended plan or able to follow the plan (do they need the plan in writing?)
- ✓ Address my concerns (Were my primary concerns heard and addressed?)

Reference: Adapted from 1997. Novack, Cohen, O'Brien. "Using a Core Checklist to Assess Clinical Skills." Encounter 13(1):20.

Effective Physician-Nurse Communication Skills

- Does the physician call the nurse by name?
- Is the physician easily approachable? If she/he thinks they are, have they asked for feedback to check out the perception?
- Can a nurse bring up disagreements or ask for clarifications without rebuke?
- Does the physician make good eye contact and engage with nurses?
- Does the physician invite the nurses to round with her/him?
- Are non-verbal behaviors respectful?
- Are after-hours calls received in a professional tone of voice?
- When the physician is upset with performance, can he/she have the skills to go directly to the individual concerned in a supportive fashion?
- Does the physician participate in educational and celebratory events

Henry Pfifferling, PhD

Effective Nurse-Physician Communication Skills

1. Does the nurse always have the pertinent data needed when calling a physician?
2. Use the SBAR tool as a standard of communication—especially telephone conversations.
3. Never begin telephone conversations with "I'm sorry to bother you..."

4. Prepare for rounds. Anticipate late night problems ahead of time.
5. Use the progress notes to briefly communicate your key concerns/interventions.
6. Confront physicians whose behaviors are degrading by speaking to them in private. State the behavior and its effect. Ask manager for support if needed.
7. Take the time to thank and acknowledge those physicians with whom he/she has a good working relationship.
8. Never complain about a doctor to other staff. Always takes problems directly to the physician involved.
9. Demonstrates the ability to deal with confrontation and conflict.
10. Demonstrate professionalism in words, behaviors and appearance?

Kathleen Bartholomew, RN, MN

CHAPTER 16

One primary question should be discussed here: Why is it vital for a CFO and anyone charged with oversight decisions regarding the organization's budget, to not just ask what's going on at the front lines, but to spend time there? Why should we not accept the standard demurrer that CFO's only need to control the flow of money and therefore need no clinical interaction or knowledge of the actual operation?

CHAPTER 20 Palliative Care

Exercise: After reviewing definitions below, attend an ICU staff meeting. Ask staff how many times in the last month they have cared for patients who they believed should not have been in the ICU. Acknowledge the moral distress. Create a palliative care specialist position so that they have someone to call next time they feel the care delivered is not optimal.

Definitions
- Hospice care provides palliative care for those in the last weeks or months of life under a federal Medicare benefit.
- Non-hospice palliative care is appropriate at any point in a serious illness. It can be provided at the same time as life-prolonging treatment.

Resources:

- For patients and providers: www.nhpco.org. A great place to start for getting info on hospice and palliative care; they also have a decent search tool to find local hospice programs.
- Many of their links connect to another site, www.caringinfo.org, which can also be accessed directly—they have lots of good info especially on advance care planning, including living will documents for each state.
- For healthcare professionals, www.eperc.mcw.edu is a great resource. We especially recommend the "Fast Facts" section— these are very brief articles on nearly every aspect of palliative medicine, from running family meetings and breaking bad news to advanced symptom management.
- For people who are interested in policy, advocacy or starting a palliative care or hospice program, We'd recommend www.capc.org

PALLIATIVE CARE SCREENING TOOL
ADMITTING NURSE:
please complete this assessment for all patients.

1. Please check off any criteria on the checklist that apply to the patient.
2. In the right hand column, write a score for each section as follows:
   - Section 1, **Life-limiting disease process:** score 2 points for every diagnosis checked
   - Section 2, **Comorbidities:** score 1 point for every diagnosis checked
   - Section 3, **Performance status:** score 3 points if you checked off ANY of the boxes (not 3 points for each)
   - Section 4, **Other criteria:** score 1 point for each.
3. Add together the scores and place the total in the **"total score" box** at the bottom of the right-hand column.
4. The screening forms will be used to recommend the following actions:
   - **Total score 2 or less:** no action needed
   - **Total score 3:** observe; consider rescreening and consult request if condition worsens
   - **Total score 4 or greater:** triggers a palliative medicine consult request from the attending MD/NP/PA.

PALLIATIVE CARE TRIGGERS Conditions that might indicate need for palliative medicine consultation:	SCORING
1. Life-limiting disease process: ❑ Cancer (progressive, metastatic, or recurrent) ❑ Advanced COPD or other pulmonary disease ❑ Advanced CHF or other cardiac disease ❑ End-stage renal disease ❑ End-stage liver disease ❑ Stroke (with decreased function of at least 50 percent) ❑ Advanced neurologic disease (e.g. ALS) ❑ Advanced dementia ❑ Catastrophic illness or injury (e.g. massive CVA, anoxic or traumatic brain injury) ❑ Other life-limiting illness *(specify:)* _____	**SCORE 2 points for EACH** _____
2. Comorbidities: ❑ Moderate COPD or other pulmonary disease ❑ Moderate CHF or other cardiac disease ❑ Moderate renal or liver disease ❑ Moderate dementia or other neurologic illness ❑ Severe diabetes ❑ Other condition complicating care *(specify:)* _____	**SCORE 1 point for EACH** _____
3. Performance status: ❑ Severely compromised baseline cognitive or functional status, including any of the following: non-ambulatory, chronic bedsores, minimally verbal (<6 intelligible words), dependent in all ADL's ❑ Marked decrease in cognitive or functional status/ ADL's in past 1–2 months ❑ Significant weight loss, decreased PO intake, recurrent aspiration, or dysphagia ❑ Would you be surprised if the patient were to die within the next 6 months? (check box if "no")	**SCORE 1 point for ANY (not each)** _____

PALLIATIVE CARE TRIGGERS **Conditions that might indicate need for palliative medicine consultation:**	SCORING
4. **Other criteria to consider:** ❏ Uncontrolled pain related to life-limiting illness ❏ Uncontrolled non-pain symptoms related to life-limiting illness, including dyspnea, dysphagia, nausea/vomiting, constipation, delirium, anxiety, agitation ❏ Patient, family, or team need help with complex decision-making and determining goals of care ❏ Unmet psychosocial, cultural or spiritual concerns ❏ Multiple ER visits and/or hospital admissions for same diagnosis in past 1-2 months ❏ Patient is in ICU with documented poor prognosi	SCORE **1 point for EACH** _____
Comments: **This section completed by:** _____ **Date:**_____	TOTAL SCORE _____

Please place in the purple
"COMPLETED PALLIATIVE CARE SCREENING FORMS"
folder at the nursing station. Thank you!

PATIENT LABEL

CHRISTINE COFER, MD, MS
Franciscan Hospice and Palliative Care
MS 42-09
2901 Bridgeport Way West
University Place, WA 98466
E-mail: ChristineCofer@FHShealth.org

CHAPTER 21

CEO Exercise:

1. Ask your CNO, "Do you have what you need to do your job?"
2. Ask for a 360 degree evaluation from your senior leadership team.

References:
"The Role of the Chief Nurse Officer in Ensuring Patient Safety and Quality" by Disch, J., Dreher, M., Davidson, P. JONA, Vol. 41, No. 4, April 2011.
"Establishing a Sense of Urgency for Leading Transformational Change", Shirey, M. JONA Vol. 41. No. 4, April 2011.

CHAPTER 25 ER—Hospitalist Patient Handoff

Objectives:
- Assure that patients receive the best care by admitting them to the most appropriate level of care.
- Expedite the ER admission decision process to optimize patient flow through the ER.

Process:
- Improve communications between the ER physicians and the hospitalists.
- Establish an institutional experience curve to support continuous improvement of the patient handoff between the ER and the hospitalists.

Methods:
- Insure that the patient handoff information is complete.
- Promote two-way communications during the handoff to insure a mutual understanding of the patient's needs and the reasons for the decision that was made.
- Standardize the information and process to facilitate communications and minimize omissions and misunderstandings.
- Leadership/peer review process to qualify and verify opportunities identified for learning and patient handoff improvement.

- Leaders review/discussion of qualified opportunities for improvement.

Tools:

- Patient handoff checklist—to serve as a "prompt" to facilitate standardization and to insure all information is covered for a complete handoff.
- Information trail to easily identify and document opportunities for improvement.
- Scheduled meetings (every two weeks) with the ER and hospitalists leaders to identify and validate handoffs for their staff discussion and learning.
- Establish a recurring agenda item on the staff meetings of the ER and hospitalist leaders to "discuss patient handoff opportunities."
- Metrics to assess process results.
  - Patients visited in the ER by hospitalists.
  - Changes in level of care.
  - ER time for admitted patients.
- Regular meetings and surveys to assess improved process adoption progress.

(Courtesy of Spence Byrum
Convergent HRS www.convergenthrs.com)

Support:

There is a fundamental distrust between these two groups of physicians when it comes to the patient information they will "trust." For ER physicians and hospitalists, it is imperative that they regularly meet, face-to-face, to resolve outstanding issues before they further exacerbate the situation. Physician groups that do not develop such a dialog are destined to have communication breakdowns that WILL compromise patient care, quality and efficiency.

CHAPTER 26

To hear this speech live, go to the link:
http://healthreformwa.org/?p=935
Steve Hill, board chair, Puget Sound Health Alliance

CHAPTER 30

- Are the harm or injuries in your institution invisible?
- During rounding, ask staff to tell you about the last adverse or

sentinel event that happened. Do they know?
- What is the name of the patient/s that have been harmed? What is their story? Harm needs to be not only visible, but personal. How does the patient's story travel throughout your organization?

Patient-centric tip: Begin every meeting with a patient story—both positive and negative outcomes, to keep staff patient centric.

In summary: Cultural change takes time. It starts with every level identifying current norms and understanding that these ARE NOT acceptable—only then can you create the new set of norms necessary for true cultural change.

In the old culture, it was *normal:*
- For a hospital board not to have a clue about the current clinical reality.
- For senior management to receive bonuses even though patients have died on their watch.
- For patients to be harmed or die and for the hospital to hide the event from the public and from their own staff due to grossly misguided fear of litigation.
- For 80 percent or more of all communication to staff to be about the bottom line—money—leading to the nearly universal staff conclusion that the only thing senior leadership cares about is money.
- For the senior leadership team (SLT) to say one thing and do the other.
- For management to be virtually inaccessible due to meetings or the lack of training in how to engage and lead humans.
- To ask for a referral for a good surgeon when you worked in that hospital, because it was standard knowledge that not all were good enough for your family.
- For senior leadership to give you a head's up that someone important was coming to your floor.
- For all initiatives to start at the top.
- For hand washing to be below 100 percent.
- For all hospital staff to be unable to answer this question: What was the name of the last person who died or who was harmed in your hospital? We keep it impersonal and invisible.
- For a CMO to be responsible for keeping physicians in line—

which amounted to periodic chats. (Keep in mind that a CMO is, in truth, an "ambassador without a country.")

- For a CEO to believe he could control outcomes in a complex adaptive system.
- For managers to let staff get away with not doing their fair share of the workload.
- For managers not to have a meaningful and caring relationship with their directors—or staff.
- For nurses to be responsible for outcomes, but have no responsibility for resources to attain those outcomes.
- For ideas that cost money to only have leadership support if they came from the top
- For a nurse to think that she is 'better than' her assistant or the housekeeper or sterile processing.
- For a doctor to think he/she is more important than the nurse or the team.
- For a doctor to be vulnerable or talk in public about his/her mistakes.
- For surgeons to use detailed preference cards even for standard surgical procedures in the mistaken belief that 'their way is better,' the battle cry of the autonomous scientist.
- For patients to receive unnecessary tests or medications.
- To fail to take near-misses seriously.
- For many nurses to disagree with a physician over a plan of care, but be afraid to speak to him/her.
- For ICU's to be filled with palliative care patients   for the revenue, not the patients' best interests.
- For the front line voices to be silenced by fear and/or intimidation.
- For personnel issues to be considered an HR problem or 'soft stuff.'
- For senior leadership to believe they were doing a great job—while people still died of errors.
- For the CNO to have to go into battle every day for what he/she needed to do their job.
- To tolerate disruptive behavior if the nurse or doctor was a "great" or "good" clinician.
- To be loyal to your department and work in silos without loyalty to the entire hospital as an entity.

- To use a cell phone on the floor or in the operating room for personal calls.
- To let an incompetent nurse or physician care for a patient.
- To stay silent even when witnessing incorrect, non-standard or incompetent care.
- For doctors and nurses to, in effect, "live" in different countries because they rarely meet, and because the hierarchical culture keeps them both in their respective places.

Ask yourselves:

In our culture at our clinic or hospital, it is normal to:

_____

The new norms we want to create today in my hospital or department are:

_____

STUDY GUIDE NOTES

STUDY GUIDE NOTES

BIBLIOGRAPHY

Abrashoff, D. Michael. *It's Your Ship: Management Techniques from the Best Damn Ship in the Navy.* New York, NY: Warner, 2002. Print

Ackoff, Russell Lincoln, Jason Magidson, and Herbert J. Addison. *Idealized Design: Creating an Organization's Future.* Upper Saddle River, N.J: Wharton, 2006. Print.

Avolio, Bruce J., and Fred Luthans. *The High Impact Leader: Moments Matter in Accelerating Authentic Leadership Development.* New York: McGraw Hill, 2006. Print.

Avolio, Bruce J. *Full Range Leadership Development.* London: SAGE, 2010. Print.

Avolio, Bruce J. *The No People: Tribal Tales of Organizational Cliff Dwellers.* Charlotte, NC: Information Age Pub., 2011. Print.

Balas, E.A. and S.A. Boren, "Managing Clinical Knowledge for Health Care Improvement." *Health Affairs* April 2011 (2011): 567. Print.

Bard, Marc, and Michael Nugent. *Accountable Care Organizations: Your Guide to Strategy, Design, and Implementation.* Chicago, IL: Health Administration, 2011. Print.

Brafman, Ori, and Rom Brafman. *Click: The Forces behind How We Fully Engage with People, Work, and Everything We Do.* New York: Crown Business, 2010. Print.

Brafman, Ori, and Rod A. Beckstrom. *The Starfish and the Spider: the Unstoppable Power of Leaderless Organizations.* New York: Portfolio, 2006. Print.

Brooks, David. *The Social Animal: the Hidden Sources of Love, Character, and Achievement.* New York: Random House, 2011. Print.

Brownlee, Shannon. *Overtreated: Why Too Much Medicine Is Making Us Sicker and Poorer.* New York, NY: Bloomsbury, 2007. Print.

Chaffee, Mary; McNeill, Margaret. 2007, "A Model of Nursing As A Complex Adaptive System", *Nursing Outlook*, vol. 55, no 5, pp. 232 - 241

Charney, William. *Epidemic of Medical Errors and Hospital-acquired Infections: Systemic and Social Causes.* Boca Raton: CRC, 2012. Print.

Conant, Douglas R., and Mette Norgaard. *Touchpoints: Creating Powerful Leadership Connections in the Smallest of Moments.* San Francisco, CA: Jossey-Bass, 2011. Print.

Diamond, Jared M. *The Third Chimpanzee: The Evolution and Future of the Human Animal.* New York, NY: HarperCollins, 1992. Print.

Disch, PhD, RN, FAAN, Joanne, Melanie Dreher, PhD, RN, FAAN, Pamela Davidson, PhD, Marie Sinioris, MPH, and Joyce Anne Wainio, MHA. "The Role of the Chief Nurse Officer in Ensuring Patient Safety and Quality." *JONA* 41.4 (2011): 179-85. Print.

Ebright, Patricia R., Emily S. Patterson, Barbara A. Chalko, and Marta L. Render. "Understanding the Complexity of Registered Nurse Work in Acute Care Settings." *JONA: The Journal of Nursing Administration* 33.12 (2003): 630-38. Print.

Felps, W., T. Mitchell, and E. Byington. "How, When, and Why Bad Apples Spoil the Barrel: Negative Group Members and Dysfunctional Groups." *Research in Organizational Behavior 27* (2006): 175-222. Print.

Fisher, Len. *The Perfect Swarm: The Science of Complexity in Everyday Life.* New York: Basic, 2009. Print.

Gawande, Atul. *The Checklist Manifesto: How to Get Things Right.* New York, NY: Metropolitan, 2009. Print.

Gibson, Rosemary, and Janardan Prasad Singh. *The Treatment Trap: How the Overuse of Medical Care Is Wrecking Your Health and What You Can Do to Prevent It.* Chicago: Ivan R. Dee, 2010. Print.

Halvorson, George. *Health Care Reform Now!: a Prescription for Change.* San Francisco, CA: Jossey-Bass, 2007. Print.

Heifetz, Ronald A., and Martin Linsky. *Leadership on the Line: Staying Alive through the Dangers of Leading.* Boston, MA: Harvard Business School, 2002. Print.

Hickson, Gerald B., James W. Pichert, Lynn E. Webb, and Steven G. Gabbe. "A Complementary Approach to Promoting Professionalism: Identifying, Measuring, and Addressing Unprofessional Behaviors." *Academic Medicine* 82.11 (2007): 1040-048. Print.

Johnson, Steven. *Where Good Ideas Come From: the Natural History of Innovation.* New York: Riverhead, 2010. Print.

Kenney, Charles. *Transforming Health Care: Virginia Mason Medical Center's Pursuit of the Perfect Patient Experience.* Boca Raton: CRC, 2011. Print.

Krichbaum, Kathleen, Carol Diemert, Lynn Jacox, Ann Jones, Patty Koenig, Christine Mueller, and Joanne Disch. "Complexity Compression: Nurses Under Fire." *Nursing Forum* 42.2 (2007): 86-94. Print.

Kumar, Sanjaya, and David B. Nash. *Demand Better!: Revive Our Broken Healthcare System.* Bozeman, MT: Second River Healthcare, 2011. Print.

Lindberg, Claire, Sue Nash, and Curt Lindberg. *On the Edge: Nursing in the Age of Complexity.* Bordentown, NJ: Plexus Press, 2008. Print.

Loehr, James E. *The Power of Story: Change Your Story, Change Your Destiny in Business and in Life.* New York: Free, 2008. Print.

Logan, David, John King, and Halee Fischer-Wright. *Tribal Leadership: Leveraging Natural Groups to Build a Thriving Organization.* New York: HarperCollins, 2008. Print.

Marx, David, and Amanda Bray. *Whack-a-mole: the Price We Pay for Expecting Perfection*. Plano, TX: By Your Side Studios, 2009. Print.

Mayer, Thom, and Kirk Jensen. *Hardwiring Flow: Systems and Processes for Seamless Patient Care*. Gulf Breeze, FL: Fire Starter Pub., 2009. Print.

Michelli, Joseph A. *Prescription for Excellence: Leadership Lessons for Creating a World-class Customer Experience from UCLA Health System*. New York: McGraw-Hill, 2011. Print.

Morath, Julianne M., and Joanne E. Turnbull. *To Do No Harm: Ensuring Patient Safety in Health Care Organizations*. San Francisco, CA: Jossey-Bass, 2005. Print.

Moynihan, Ray, and Alan Cassels. *Selling Sickness: How the World's Biggest Pharmaceutical Companies Are Turning Us All into Patients*. New York, NY: Nation, 2005. Print.

Nance, John J. *Why Hospitals Should Fly: the Ultimate Flight Plan to Patient Safety and Quality Care*. Bozeman, Mt.: Second River Healthcare, 2008. Print.

Ohrn, Annica, Hans Rutberg, and Per Nilsen. "Patient Safety Dialogue." *Journal of Patient Safety* (2011): 1. Print.

Pearson, Christine M., and Christine Lynne. Porath. *The Cost of Bad Behavior: How Incivility Is Damaging Your Business and What to Do about It*. New York: Portfolio, 2009. Print.

Porter-O'Grady, Timothy, and Kathy Malloch. *Quantum Leadership: A Resource for Health Care Innovation*. Sudbury, MA: Jones and Bartlett, 2007. Print.

Quinn, Daniel. *Beyond Civilization: Humanity's next Great Adventure*. New York: Harmony, 1999. Print.

Reid, T. R. *The Healing of America: A Global Quest for Better, Cheaper, and Fairer Health Care*. New York: Penguin, 2009. Print.

Rosenstein, MD, MBA, Alan H., and Michelle O'Daniel, MHA, MSG. "Original Research: Disruptive Behavior and Clinical Outcomes: Perceptions of Nurses and Physicians: Nurses, Physicians, and Administrators Say That Clinicians' Disruptive Behavior Has Negative Effects on

Clinical Outcomes." *AJN* 105.1 (2005): 54-64. Print.

Rubin, Irwin M., and Thomas J. Campbell. *The ABCs of Effective Feedback: A Guide for Caring Professionals.* San Francisco, CA: Jossey-Bass, 1998. Print.

Shirey, PhD, MBA, RN, NEA-BC, FACHE, FAAN, Maria R. "Establishing a Sense of Urgency for Leading Transformation Change." *JONA* 41.4 (2011): 145-48. Print.

Singhal, Arvind, Prucia Buscell, and Curt Lindberg. *Inviting Everyone: Healing Healthcare through Positive Deviance.* Bordentown, N. J.: PlexusPress, 2010. Print.

Surowiecki, James. *The Wisdom of Crowds: Why the Many Are Smarter than the Few and How Collective Wisdom Shapes Business, Economies, Societies, and Nations.* New York: Doubleday, 2004. Print.

Wheatley, Margaret J. *Leadership and the New Science: Discovering Order in a Chaotic World.* San Francisco: Berrett-Koehler, 1999. Print.

Zaffron, Steve, and David Logan. *The Three Laws of Performance: Rewriting the Future of Your Organization and Your Life.* San Francisco, CA: Jossey-Bass, 2009. Print.

"Transcript: Dr. Atul Gawande's Address — HSPH Commencement 2009 — Harvard School of Public Health." *Harvard School of Public Health* - HSPH. Web. 24 Jan. 2012. <http://www.hsph.harvard.edu/news/commencement-2009/transcript-dr-atul-gawandes-address/>.

ENDNOTES

i   HEALTHCARE REFORM NOW! Halvorson, George; (2007, Jossey-Bass, San Francisco), Page 3.

ii   *Health Affairs* May 2008 vol. 27 no. 3 759-769 , Berwick, D; Nolan, T; Whittington, J: Introducing and describing the need for a nationwide push toward the three goals identified by the Institute of Healthcare Improvement. The Abstract of this article is:

"Improving the U.S. healthcare system requires simultaneous pursuit of three aims: improving the experience of care, improving the health of populations and reducing per capita costs of healthcare. Preconditions for this include the enrollment of an identified population, a commitment to universality for its members and the existence of an organization (an "integrator") that accepts responsibility for all three aims for that population. The integrator's role includes at least five components: partnership with individuals and families, redesign of primary care, population health management, financial management.

iii OVERTREATED, Brownlee, Shannon; (2007, Bloomsbury USA, New York)

iv Ibid, Page 106.

v   Halverson.

vi See article on Compression Complexity by Kathleen Krichbaum, et al: COMPLEXITY COMPRESSION: NURSES UNDER FIRE; Nursing Forum, Vol. 42, No. 2, April-June 2007.

vii *Health Affairs* April 2011Vol 30 No. 4 559-568, Chassin, Mark R; Loeb, Jerod M., "The Ongoing Quality Improvement Journey: Next Stop, High Reliability" — Managing Clinical Knowledge for Healthcare Improvement.

viii Chaffee, Mary; McNeill, Margaret. 2007, "A Model of Nursing As A Complex Adaptive System", *Nursing Outlook*, vol. 55, no 5, pp. 232–241

NOTE: **Description:**

From the abstract: The science and theory of complex adaptive systems, also know as complexity science, has emerged as an alternative to existing paradigms. Complex adaptive systems demonstrate identifiable characteristics: embeddedness, self-organization, non-linearity, unpredictability and others. These systems exhibit emergent behavior that arises from simple rules and interconnections among diverse elements with porous boundaries, as they interact with and respond to the environment. The health system and the profession of nursing can be viewed as complex adaptive systems, and when done so, new insight can be gained. While several authors have stated they believe nursing is indeed a complex adaptive system, a visual model has not been advanced. This article offers a model of nursing viewed as a complex adaptive system, a discussion of key properties of a complex adaptive system and potential implications of the use of complexity science in nursing and healthcare.

ix Personal communication to the authors, November 2011.

x Quote attributed to Dr. Charles Denham, chairman of the Texas Medical Institute of Technology and editor of the *Journal of Patient Safety*.

xi The Dartmouth Atlas was the definitive work that pulled the cover off this embarrassing reality, and today you can go to www.dartmouthatlas.org for the latest information.

xii Analogy courtesy of Steve Hill, chair of the board and director, Washington State Department of Retirement Systems

xiii The basic concept of a root cause analysis is deeply flawed insofar as it seeks to find a single cause to any major negative event. In brief, single-cause disasters do not exist in medicine, transportation or any complex adaptive human system; therefore, any systemic evaluation that by its very name indicates otherwise (a single cause) is at best misleading, and at worse a highly dangerous generator of false security when only one problem is addressed.

The traditional RCA methodology actually presupposes a root cause or causes versus a complex chain of intersecting failures, missed opportunities and ancillary supporting factors. The somewhat myopic process tends to eliminate the need to dig far deeper and ask tough questions such as: If this was the wrong person for the job, how did we end up hiring him/her? Why did we not catch the fact that this was the wrong person? What systems could we have had in place to identify this threat in time? How did our policies and procedures support this occurrence, or make it more likely that the initial chain of errors would not be stopped before reaching the patient?

Worse, the inclusion of any question of individual culpability (fault) in an RCA's fact-finding process typically skews the focus of the analysis to the easier method of just pinning the accident on someone and essentially being satisfied with asking "Who's wrong?" versus "What's wrong?" The tough work of ferreting out and pursuing virtually all causal factors whether primary, proximate or contributory requires setting aside questions of professional culpability until the work is completely done and all facts known.

ACKNOWLEDGMENTS

As you can imagine, the task of moving from the coalescing of a paradigm *(Why Hospitals Should Fly)* to creating a highly-useful guide on how to create such an institution in real time *(Charting the Course)* is a major challenge requiring a constant stream of communication, research and most importantly requests for the assistance and guidance from many professionals. Our first task was to keep the bibliographic citations to a reasonable number, providing a highly current and useful list without going overboard. But beyond the citations and endnotes, the true test of currency and applicability comes from those who were more than gracious with their time and their intellect in countless conversations, e-mails, evaluations short and long of submitted passages and those who took their valuable time to review the entire manuscript and provide very valuable suggestions and changes—all with the collegial view to making this an immediately useful work for virtually everyone engaged in the profession of healthcare. Specifically, then, we extend our heartfelt thanks to:

Paul A. Abson, MD
Billie Lynn Allard, RN, MS
June Altaras, RN, MN
Genevieve Bartol, RN, EdD, AHN-BC
Donald M. Berwick, MD, MPP
Joseph S. Bujak, MD, FACP
Jonathan Burroughs, MD, MBA, FACPE
Spence Byrum
Christine Cofer, MD, MS
Per E. Danielsson, MD
Jan Jacob, RN, MBA, CPPS

Diana Abson Kraemer, MD
Gale E. Latimer, MSN, RN, FACHE, FAAN
Jann Marks, RN, MBA, CNAA, NEA-BC
Diane Mass, BSN
Linda R. Mueller, BS, M Ed
David B. Nash, MD, MBA
John-Henry Pfifferling, PhD
Sandon "Sandy" Saffier, MD, MBA
David Vanderwal, BS, BA
Cathy Whitaker, RN, MSN, MS, CNAA-BC

Our publisher, Jerry Pogue (a veteran hospital CEO) and his staff at Second River Healthcare Press in Bozeman, Montana—Sheila Keizer, Sierra Weese, and Tiffany Young—have once again exceeded themselves in providing a level of professionalism, responsiveness, honesty and support that has become all but a lost-art in publishing. Our heartfelt thanks to them and to our own staff members: Lori Carr, Lindsay Bailey, and Emily Yashinsky.

AUTHORS' BIOS

John J. Nance, JD, brings a rich and varied professional background to American Healthcare. A lawyer, Air Force and airline pilot, prolific internationally-published author, national broadcaster, and professional speaker, he was one of the founding board members of the National Patient Safety Foundation in 1997, and has become one of the major thought leaders in reforming the culture of medicine.

John is a native Texan who grew up in Dallas, holds a bachelor's degree from SMU and a juris doctor from SMU's Dedman School of Law, and is a licensed Texas attorney. A recipient of the Distinguished Alumni Award of SMU for 2002, and named Distinguished Alumni for Public Service of the SMU Dedman School of Law in 2010, he is also a decorated Air Force pilot veteran of Vietnam and Operations Desert Storm/Desert Shield and a Lt. Colonel in the USAF Reserve, well known for his pioneering development of Air Force human factors flight safety education, and one of the civilian pioneers of Crew Resource Management (CRM). John has piloted a wide variety of jet aircraft, including most of Boeing's line and the Air Force C-141, and has logged over 13,700 hours of flight time since earning his first pilot license in 1965, and is still a pilot currently. He was a pilot for Braniff International Airlines and a Boeing 737 Captain for Alaska Airlines, and is an internationally recognized air safety advocate, best known to North American television audiences as Aviation Analyst for ABC World News and Aviation Editor for Good Morning America. He is also the nationally-known author of 19 major books, including the highly-acclaimed 2009 book for

American Healthcare *Why Hospitals Should Fly*, which won the prestigious "Book of the Year" award in 2009 from the American College of Healthcare Executives. He lives on San Juan Island, Washington, with his wife and co-author, Kathleen Bartholomew.

Kathleen Bartholomew, RN, MN, is an internationally known speaker and consultant who uses the power of story and her strong background in sociology to study the healthcare culture. The author of *Speak Your Truth: Proven Strategies for Effective Nurse-Physician Communication and Ending Nurse-to-Nurse Hostility*, she utilized her clinical experience as nurse manager of a 57 bed surgical unit to raise awareness of, and provide ground breaking research on, horizontal violence and physician-nurse communication.

As one of the nation's most effective speakers on clinical matters affecting relationships, communication, teamwork, and patient safety, she has become a thought leader in changing the way front-line staff relate to each other and leadership to transform the focus of American Healthcare to a truly patient-centric model. She works with boards of directors, CEOs, senior hospital leadership teams, the military and private industry across North America.

Kathleen lives with her husband, co-author John J. Nance, on San Juan Island in Washington State—thanks to match.com.